DREAMS DIVINE

SHORT STORIES

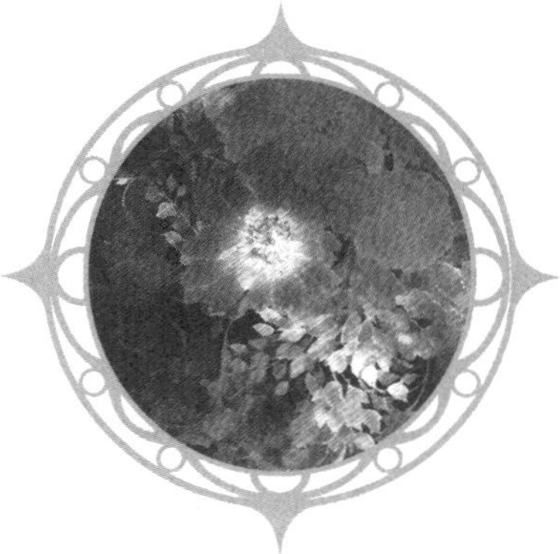

This is a FLAME TREE Book

Publisher & Creative Director: Nick Wells
Editorial Director: Catherine Taylor
Editorial Board: Catherine Taylor, Gillian Whitaker, Josie Karani,
Jemma North, Jocelyn Pontes and Simran Aulakh.
Special thanks to Tim Leng.

FLAME TREE PUBLISHING
6 Melbray Mews, Fulham,
London SW6 3NS, United Kingdom
www.flametreepublishing.com

First published 2026

26 28 30 29 27
1 3 5 7 9 10 8 6 4 2

ISBN: 978-1-83562-795-2
Special ISBN: 978-1-80694-251-0
Ebook ISBN: 978-1-83562-797-6

A copy of the CIP data for this book is available from the British Library.

Printed and bound in China

Represented in the EU for product safety and compliance by Authorised Rep Compliance Ltd, Ground Floor, 71 Lower Baggot Street, Dublin, D02 P593, Ireland. Contact at www.arccompliance.com

DREAMS DIVINE

SHORT STORIES

Romantic Fantasy

Foreword by Alexandra Beaumont

FLAME TREE
PUBLISHING

Contents

Foreword

Alexandra Beaumont

Spoiler alert! I have a confession to make: I'm always a bit too embarrassed to tell people the truth when they ask me where I get my book ideas from. People expect profound answers and an interesting insight into the mind of an author in the wild. The truth for me is a little bit more boring, and not the most literary or profound statement. There would be nothing poetically Byron-like if I confessed the truth: I think about esoterica, then fall asleep or daydream. Often the mashup of many different ideas bouncing off each other in the liminal space of the sleep-wake divide leads to some wonderful story ideas.

So yes, that's the truth finally out there in the world. You heard it here first: my ideas sometimes come from dreams, or the space close to dreams. It does mean one thing, though. I always have a notebook or sketch book by my bed, ready to draw something or write something down that I've stumbled upon in my sleep. Then I just have to hope that my half-asleep scribbling of ideas is vaguely coherent in the judgemental light of dawn. Reading my esoteric sleepy ramblings also gives my husband great joy, which is reason enough to continue this practice in any case!

Mirroring the Dreamscape

So why do dreams provide such a powerful space for ideas? As you may have guessed from my slightly eccentric midnight doodling, I've always been drawn to the sense of doubting what is real in fantasy. I enjoy dream-infused tales like John Connolly's *The Book of Lost Things* where it is unclear which elements of the fairy tale retelling are in the character's imagination and what is real. This has tugged me inexorably to some of the illusionary qualities found in fantasy.

Romantic fantasy is not far away from the dreamlike itself, as fairy tales and the fae realms are often woven into the genre. They are frequently described as escapist, but dreams and romance have been bedfellows for a long time in literature going back to well-known tales such as Shakespeare's *Midsummer Night's Dream*.

Less well-known is another interesting take on the relationship of people with dreams. In *The Faerie Queen*, another Elizabethan-era play, dreams are used as trials and the actions of the characters in their dreams display clearly the virtues or intentions of the characters. In this story, the characters' true emotions and whether they are honourable to the ones they love are put to the test in trials visited upon them in their slumber.

The dreams show the true qualities of the characters. As in *The Faerie Queen*, they often mirror our versions of the world, whether that is the representation of our fears or the outline of our hopes and aspirations. Nothing can be hidden in our dreams, and that creates a vulnerability that makes them more relatable, or sometimes more terrible.

Monstrous Love and Monstrous Dreams

Whether they be the mercurial stories from our sleep, the aspirations that drive us or powerful prophecies as in the fifteenth century *Morte d'Arthur* where they are used as warnings, there are different ways dreams can enthral us. My debut fantasy, *Testament of the Stars*, drew heavily on my background in gothic literature. The dream in the Gothic represents the bleeding between fiction and reality that often infuses its way into the mind of the character. It also serves to provide the typically gothic heightened emotions which has also seeded itself within romantic fantasy. In my writing, prophecy, fate and visions of the future hold power in the same way as in many gothic texts. Once again, this is the liminal space between realities.

A lot of the tropes from the Victorian gothic now find themselves in romantic fantasy, or romantasy, as we now call it. While it doesn't wholly tie us to the romantic, it does provide a setting for the powerful emotions tethered firmly in romantic fiction. We can't control our dreams, or who we dream about, and that reveals a quivering core to a person that cannot be ignored.

Frankenstein is a good example of this. Despite his previous callousness, Victor dreams about the fate of Elizabeth and in doing so reveals his internalized guilt. In that moment we see the truth he cannot hide from as he does in the waking world. His love for Elizabeth, and the fear of what will happen to her, makes a powerful catalyst for the actions Frankenstein will take.

The allure of vampires, who also warp the dreams of their victims, has transposed itself and expanded into the affection for monsters (either physical or metaphorical) that now is a mainstay in Romantasy as well. At the heart of a lot of this is power, and fate, as we see in the 'fated lovers' trope that has become so popular.

Bring Us Sumptuous Fae, but also Gift Us Raw and Ugly Emotion

I want to leave you with this thought: Romantasy has gained a reputation as fluffy and full of happily-ever-after stories, but I want to refute that this is all the genre has to offer. There's a place for the fluffy stories where lovers end up blissfully together in romance, of course there is, but I think so much of the *power* of romance is in looking at what it will drive people to do.

In *Dissonance of Bird Song*, my folklore fantasy somewhat influenced by the Cornish tragedy *Tristan and Isolde*, the characters find themselves torn between cursed love and impossible choices. Fate has broken apart a fierce romance, and turned one of the lovers into a monster who has lost his way. It is a story of broken lives and new beginnings.

I would say if you are writing or reading fantasy romance, don't just look for the stories of happily ever after with a dark (but often delightfully polite and reasonable) fae lord. Leave some room for stories of loss, jealousy and recovery. I try to explore the depths people will go to in order to keep hold of those they love, including the more tragic aspects of that. Could you describe it as Romantasy? Yes, but it is not remotely fluffy and I do not guarantee happy endings.

Love is a powerful catalyst for the most devastating of emotion-driven stories. Even the happiest romance can easily tip from the sublime into the doomed with one wrong step. That's what makes these stories gripping. That's what makes them linger.

Carry the Dreamscape with You

The last thing I'll say is that dreams prevail even in the light of day, drifting through your thoughts long after you've lived through them. The tales within this collection will do the same. Whether it be doomed merfolk, lavish fae balls or fascinating dream lore from multiple cultures, there is something here for everyone. I invite you now to sink into the dreamworld with these wonderful stories that bring the romantic, whimsical and haunting slumbered imaginings to the fore.

Put a pinch of salt in your pocket, a band of iron round your wrist and get ready to dream.

The Dreaming of Dwynwen

Benjamin Adams

Before the first frost of her nineteenth winter, Dwynwen of Maen Gwyrdd had already grown more accustomed to shadows than to sunlight. The wizard Cynfran would come down from his tower on Yr Wyddfa to market, his long yew staff tapping patiently on the ground as he walked, and she could feel his eyes upon her, weighing her for something though she knew not what.

Even with her parents both passed, and no husband, Dwynwen preferred her own company, and she certainly did not want anyone's attention, let alone the ancient Cynfran, powerful though he may be.

She was not alone, not truly. Her companions dwelled in dreams.

On the night of her nineteenth birthday, Dwynwen drifted into her Dreaming as one might slip beneath the skin of another life. The first sensation was cold, like plunging into a lake in autumn. Then the world upended itself and she stood on a bluff overlooking a city built of bones and bellflowers.

She walked, barefoot, and the ground responded by unfurling new paths at her feet. Sometimes the streets were crowded with faceless folk, heads bowed in silent congress; sometimes she wandered alone. She found a market square where vendors sold clouds bottled in glass jars. She passed through each tableau with a gentle awe, never lingering, always searching for what waited beyond the next impossible turn.

On this night the air was charged with a feeling she could not name, like the stillness before heavy rain. And so, when she stepped into the plaza, she was not surprised to find a stranger waiting for her on the rim of the stone fountain.

He sat hunched, his head in his hands, oblivious to the ghostly stags that wept tears of silver all around him. He wore strange garments – dull blue, close-fitted to the body, unlike any tunic or jerkin she had seen – and shoes so flimsy they seemed made for slippers or sorcery.

Dwynwen hesitated. She had met others in her Dreaming before – pale fragments of memory, visitors who never noticed her – but this man radiated a stubborn solidity. He belonged here, and yet, like her, did not. She circled the fountain, slow and deliberate, then perched on the lip beside him, careful to keep a hand's span between their bodies.

"Lost, are you?" she asked.

The man looked up, blinking behind round spectacles that magnified his eyes until they seemed almost amphibian. He took her in with a single, shuddering breath.

"I...don't think so. Or maybe. I'm not sure."

His accent was strange – none of the burrs or sing-song of the valleys – but the words made sense. Dwynwen smiled.

"You're not from here," she said.

The man shook his head. "No. I'm...dreaming. Or at least, I think I am. You seem...real, though."

"Dreams are real," said Dwynwen. "More real than the world, sometimes."

He laughed, a brief, embarrassed sound. "I know that feeling."

"Tell me your name," she demanded, with more force than she intended.

He considered. "Tom."

It was an absurd name but somehow fitting. She extended her right hand, palm up, as if offering him a token. "I am Dwynwen."

He took the hand. His skin was warm, softer than she expected. There was a brief exchange of energy – a shudder, like the crack of summer lightning – and Dwynwen knew, with the certainty available only to dreamers and the very young, that her Dreaming had brought this man to her.

"Is this...your dream?" he asked, scanning the strange city.

"In part," she replied. "But it changes. I think somehow I share it."

Tom wiped his eyes with a thumb, then gave her a searching look. "I lucid dream a lot. But I've never – never met someone like you here."

"You're awake in your sleep," Dwynwen said, delighted. "That's rare."

"I used to practice," said Tom, growing animated. "At first it was just a way to escape—" He faltered. "To escape life, I guess."

Dwynwen nodded. "Life is a muddy business. Dreams are cleaner."

"Cleaner?" Tom scoffed, gesturing at the bone towers. "This is the inside of your mind?"

"Perhaps." She looked at him sidelong. "You seem less afraid than most visitors."

He shrugged. "It's better than where I come from."

"Where is that?"

The question hung in the air. Tom's eyes darted. "It's – complicated. Not important."

"Everything is important in dreams," Dwynwen said softly.

He studied her. "And you? Where do you come from?"

"The foot of the mountain," she replied. "Yr Wyddfa. Perhaps you call it…Snowdon?" The name appeared in her mind, and she said it with pride, as if speaking it could anchor him in her world.

"That's in Wales," Tom said, surprised. "I went there, once. In university. But that was years ago."

Dwynwen's heart stuttered. "Is it still there?" she asked, voice suddenly small.

"Of course," Tom said, puzzled. "It's beautiful. Wild, and lonely."

She exhaled, as if releasing a burden. "Then the world has not changed too much."

They sat in silence. Dwynwen felt the dreamscape tightening around them, the city leaning in to listen. She wanted to ask him everything at once – about his world, his life, the languages he spoke and the gods he worshipped – but she did not want to frighten him away.

Instead, she stood and offered him her hand again, this time in invitation. "Walk with me?"

At length, they reached the edge of the city, to a moorland striped with veins of silvery water. Dwynwen knelt by a stream, cupping the cool liquid in her hands. She offered it to Tom, who took it without hesitation. The water tasted of memory: salt, tears, the sharp tang of desire.

"Will you come back?" she asked, after a time.

"I don't know if I can," he admitted. "Sometimes I lose control. Wake up by accident."

Dwynwen shook her head, fiercely. "I can find you," she promised. "If you come here, I will always find you."

He believed her. She saw it in the way his face relaxed, the furrow between his brows dissolving. He reached out, brushed a stray lock of hair from her brow.

"Are you real?" he asked, voice trembling.

"In dreams, we are all real," Dwynwen said. But she did not say that she loved him already, or that she had waited nineteen years for someone to touch her so gently, even in the shadow world.

* * *

In the waking world, Dwynwen grew quiet and distant to her neighbors in Maen Gwyrdd. Each night, she sought Tom in her Dreaming. Sometimes she had to walk for hours, through forests that bled ink and lakes of feathered ice, but always, at the end of her search, he appeared: on the fountain, in the bellflower market, or at the edge of some newly minted cliff.

With Tom, she learned new magic: how to conjure music from stones, how to weave the rain into nets that caught falling stars. They built a house together out of glass and smoke, and inside it, for a while, there was no loneliness at all.

But as the weeks passed, Dwynwen sensed her Dreaming straining under the weight of their union. The world flickered, sometimes stuttering as if a hand were shaking the globe from the outside. Tom grew gaunt and haunted; he confessed that, in waking, he sometimes glimpsed her in the corners of reflective surfaces or heard her voice singing from the radiator pipes. Dwynwen, too, began to see visions of Tom in the flames of the hearth, or in the way the wind caught the cry of a peregrine.

They were bleeding into each other's worlds. And her Dreaming had never been meant to hold two hearts for long.

She knew then: if she wanted Tom, truly wanted him, she would have to bring him over. Into her world, into the waking.

But for that, she would need help. And there was only one person on the mountain who could breach the boundary between dream and flesh.

The wizard Cynfran.

* * *

Dwynwen walked alone, cutting across fields ploughed black for winter, through forests that bared their limbs in supplication, and finally up the barren switchbacks of the mountain's skirt. Yr Wyddfa loomed above her, immense and iron, but it was the lesser ridge – the one locals called the old serpent's tail – that drew her steps.

The tower revealed itself at the last, breaking from the mist like a snapped tooth. Its stones were quarried from Yr Wyddfa, slick with lichen and veined in green. No door. No windows below the second storey, only thin arrow slits and a band of inscrutable runes circling the base like a curse. Dwynwen hesitated just long enough to let her fear become anger, then pressed her palm against the stones.

The wall shivered. A seam opened, barely wide enough to admit her, and closed behind her with a sound like the tolling of a bell.

The spiral staircase that greeted her was cramped, each tread worn to the curve of a thousand anxious feet. As she ascended, she felt herself grow lighter, almost insubstantial, as if the air itself were subtracting the least necessary pieces of her.

She emerged at last into a chamber alive with the scent of old vellum, melted beeswax and thunderstorms. The room was round and, in a subtle way, endless. Books lined the walls, spines pressed together in a language older than language. The only furniture was a stone lectern and, behind it, a figure in an unadorned robe the color of valley river silt.

Cynfran was neither young nor old but saturated with that agelessness peculiar to those who have forgotten to die. He did not greet her, not at first. He read, or appeared to read, a passage from the open codex before him, lips moving silently. Then, as if she were an item on a list, he acknowledged her presence with a single, deliberate blink.

"Dwynwen of Maen Gwyrdd," he said. "You have come."

She tried to decide if it was a statement or a challenge. "You know what I need, then?"

His gaze swept over her, a weighing rather than an appraisal. "I know only what is spoken to me," he said, and let the silence ferment.

Dwynwen forced her breath to slow. "There is a man. Not of my world. He visits me in dreams—"

"You wish to make him flesh," Cynfran said, with the disappointment of one who expected a harder riddle.

Dwynwen bristled but pressed on. "He is real," she said. "As real as you or I. More, perhaps."

Cynfran closed the codex. "Dream-walking is not uncommon among those of your bloodline. But to pull a soul from your Dreaming is—" He let the sentence bleed out, replaced it with a thin smile. "Dangerous."

She stepped forward, unconsciously. "What would you have of me?"

He looked through her, into her. Dwynwen felt his regard the way one feels a fever: hot, invasive, searching for the softest part. "Tell me about your dreams," he said, voice velveted with command.

Dwynwen recounted Tom as best she could – his gentleness and his stranger's tongue. Cynfran listened, hands steepled, eyes gone blank as moonstone. When she finished, she could not tell whether he was moved, amused, or simply marking time.

"You are sure," he said, "that you love him?"

The question was childish in its directness, but Dwynwen answered without shame. "I am."

Cynfran's lips twitched. "Love is the engine of all great magic. Also, its undoing." He drew himself upright, a gesture that made the room instantly smaller. "Very well. I will help you. But you must trust me absolutely. There can be no second-guessing, no retreat."

Dwynwen nodded, though her throat had gone dry. "What must I do?"

Cynfran moved to a cabinet carved from what appeared to be a single piece of obsidian, its surface so dark it seemed to devour light. From within, he withdrew a vial no larger than a child's thumb, filled with liquid that shifted between silver and deep amber as he held it to the candlelight.

"A sleeping draught," he explained, though his tone suggested the words were inadequate. "It will take you quickly into your Dreaming and deepen it so the ancient magic will work properly. While you sleep, I will observe – and when the moment is ripe, I will anchor your Tom to this realm."

He gestured toward a corner of the chamber where a simple straw cot waited, as if it had materialized from her need. The sight of it filled Dwynwen with a peculiar dread, though she could not say why.

"Will it hurt?" she asked, accepting the vial from his long fingers.

"All birth involves pain," Cynfran replied, though his eyes held secrets he did not voice. "Drink and lie down. I will do the rest."

Dwynwen uncorked the vial and tilted it to her lips without ceremony. The draught tasted of valerian, and something darker, more pungent. It burned as it slid down her throat, then spread through her limbs like liquid warmth. Within moments, her limbs grew heavy, though her mind remained sharp.

She moved to the cot with steps that felt borrowed from someone else's body. The straw rustled beneath her as she settled, pulling the blanket to her chin. From this angle, she could see Cynfran retrieving his staff from where it stood against the wall, a magnificent, terrible thing of yew wood carved with symbols that hurt to look at directly.

"Sleep now," the wizard commanded, though his voice seemed to come from very far away. "Find your Tom. Bring him close."

Dwynwen's eyelids grew heavy as lead shutters. The last thing she saw before darkness claimed her was Cynfran positioning himself beside the cot, staff planted firmly on the stone floor, his grey eyes reflecting the candlelight like a wolf's.

* * *

She found Tom on a bluff overlooking an impossible ocean, his body more substantial than it had ever been in her dreams. He ran to her, and in that instant, she thought the ritual a triumph – two souls, fusing across centuries.

But Cynfran was there as well, a shadow at the edge of the frame, eyes narrowed and calculating.

Tom looked from Dwynwen to Cynfran, confusion and a growing terror mixing on his face. "Who is that?"

"He's here to help," Dwynwen said. "To make you real."

Tom shook his head. "I don't – Dwyn, what is happening?"

Cynfran advanced, staff in hand. The air trembled. "You are not welcome here, boy," he said, voice calm and lip curled in disdain.

Dwynwen recoiled as if struck, stumbling backward on the ethereal bluff. The ocean below them roared with sudden violence, waves crashing against cliffs that had not existed moments before.

"Cynfran, what are you doing?" she gasped, her voice carrying the sharp edge of betrayal. "You said you would help us!"

The wizard's staff pulsed with silver light, its carved runes writhing like living things. His grey eyes, which had seemed merely calculating before, now burned with a hunger that made the air itself recoil.

"Help you?" Cynfran's laugh was winter wind through bare branches. "Child, you understand nothing of what you possess. Your gift, your ability to walk between worlds – it is wasted on this pitiful nothing. This less than nothing." He gestured dismissively at Tom, who had gone pale as parchment. "You must belong to me, my child. Together, our magic can make us powerful as the gods themselves. We could reshape not just dreams, but reality itself."

Tom stepped protectively in front of Dwynwen, though now his form flickered like a candle flame in a draft. "You're mad. She doesn't belong to anyone."

Cynfran's expression darkened, the very landscape around them responding to his anger. The sky deepened from twilight blue to the color of old blood, and the ground beneath their feet began to crack and splinter.

"You are nothing but a distraction," the wizard snarled, raising his staff high. The yew wood blazed with eldritch fire, casting shadows that moved independently of their sources. "A temptation that draws her from her true purpose. I will seal you back in your own time, little man. Back to your grey little world where you can trouble her no more."

The staff's light intensified, and Tom cried out as bands of silver energy began to coil around his limbs like serpents. Dwynwen felt the dream-realm itself bending to Cynfran's will, reality becoming malleable as warm wax in his hands.

"No!" Dwynwen threw herself forward, but the wizard's power held her fast. She watched in horror as Tom's form began to fade, his desperate eyes meeting hers across an ever-widening gulf.

"This is how it must be," Cynfran said, his voice now gentle, almost paternal. "You will thank me, in time. When you see what we can accomplish together, you will understand that love is merely the first step toward true power."

But even as the words left his lips, Cynfran felt a tremor of uncertainty. The look she turned upon him was one of pure, incandescent rage – and something else. Something that made the ancient stones of his tower shudder in their foundations in the waking world.

"You speak of love," she spat. "You know nothing of love and how it makes my heart feel like sunrise in summer. You know nothing of love and how it has broken the web of time to bring Tom to me. Betrayer, liar, spawn of Arawn…we are in *my* Dreaming, and I hold the power here!"

The power in her words struck Cynfran like a physical blow, and for the first time in decades, doubt flickered across his ancient features. He turned the staff away from Tom, the silver bands of energy dissolving into mist, and the young man collapsed to his knees, gasping as substance flooded back into his form.

"Foolish girl!" Cynfran snarled, wheeling the staff toward Dwynwen, its carved surface blazing with renewed fury. "You would squander godhood for this mewling—"

Dwynwen raised her hand, and the gesture held all the authority of storm winds and mountain stone. The air itself seemed to bow to her will. Cynfran lifted from the ground as if caught in a great wind, his robes billowing around him. His grip on the staff loosened, and the ancient yew wood clattered to the stone surface of the bluff, its silver light immediately dimming.

For a moment he lay stunned, the breath knocked from his lungs, his grey eyes wide with shock and something that might have been fear. Then survival instinct overcame pride, and he scrambled toward his fallen staff, fingers outstretched.

Dwynwen's second gesture was smaller, almost negligent – a mere flick of her wrist as if brushing away a troublesome insect. But the power behind it was immense. Cynfran's body lifted again, this time with inexorable force, carrying him backward toward the edge of the bluff where the dream-ocean roared far below.

"You would have stolen everything from me," she said, her voice carrying across the howling wind. "My love, my choice, my very soul. But this is my domain, wizard. Here, love is stronger than your base desires."

Cynfran's mouth opened as if to speak some final curse or plea, but his words were lost in the howling wind that had risen from nowhere, and with a final, desperate scream, the wizard vanished over the precipice. The sound of his body striking the jagged stones below was swallowed by the thunder of impossible waves.

"Dwyn," Tom said softly, approaching her as one might a wild creature poised to bolt. "It's over. He's gone."

She turned to him then, and Tom saw tears cutting silver tracks down her cheeks. "I killed him," she whispered, her voice like the dying wind itself. "I killed the only one who could have brought you to my world."

"But you will see me here," he offered. It was all he had.

"Only in dreams," she said, and clung to him as tightly as possible.

* * *

The draught's hold on Dwynwen loosened like fingers releasing their grip on stone. Consciousness returned in fragments – the scent of beeswax and thunderstorms, the cold press of stone beneath her cheek, the taste of valerian still bitter on her tongue. She opened her eyes to candlelight dancing across curved walls, and for a heartbeat believed herself still dreaming.

Then she saw Cynfran's body sprawled upon the chamber floor.

The wizard lay twisted at an impossible angle, his grey robes dark with blood that had pooled beneath his skull. His limbs were bent as if he had fallen from a great height, striking stone with terrible force. The same wounds that had claimed him in her Dreaming marked his flesh here in the waking world – the deep gashes where jagged rocks had torn through skin and bone, the crushed ribs that spoke of his final, fatal meeting with the dream-ocean's shore.

She knelt beside him, her hand hovering over his chest where no breath stirred the fabric of his robes. "What have I done?" she whispered, though the chamber offered no absolution.

It was then that she noticed the staff's absence. The magnificent yew wood that had blazed with such terrible power in her Dreaming was nowhere to be seen. She cast her gaze about the chamber, searching among the towering bookcases and shadowed alcoves, but found only the wizard's other implements – his obsidian cabinet, his ancient codices, his vials of starlight and distilled moonbeams.

As she turned back to Cynfran's body, it began to emit a faint luminescence. At first, she thought it merely a trick of the dying candlelight, but the glow intensified with each passing heartbeat. Silver radiance poured from the wizard's skin like liquid mercury, the same ethereal light that had coursed through his staff in the realm of dreams.

Dwynwen scrambled backward, shielding her eyes as the brilliance grew unbearable. The air itself grew thick as honey, charged with possibilities.

The radiance collapsed inward, folding upon itself like a star dying in reverse, and silence rushed back into the chamber like water filling a broken dam.

When Dwynwen's vision cleared, a figure stood where Cynfran's corpse had lain – tall and lean, with messy brown hair falling across wire-rimmed spectacles that reflected the guttering candlelight. Tom clutched the wizard's staff in white-knuckled hands, the yew wood still pulsing with residual silver, and stared at her with eyes wide as a startled deer's.

"I picked it up," he said, his voice hoarse with wonder and terror. His strange clothes – the dull blue garments and flimsy shoes she had grown to love in dreams – were solid now, casting real shadows on the stone floor. "In the dream, after you left me. I picked up his staff, and then—" He gestured helplessly at the chamber around them, at his own corporeal form. "And then I was here."

Dwynwen stepped closer, her hands framing his face as if to convince herself he would not dissolve at her touch. "The staff brought you through," she said, understanding dawning in her voice. "It allowed Cynfran to enter my Dreaming. And now it's brought you to me."

Tom leaned into her touch, his eyes closing briefly. When he opened them again, they held a mixture of wonder and trepidation. "But I don't belong in your time, Dwyn. I have a life back there, responsibilities—"

"Do you want to return?" she asked, though the question clearly cost her.

He was silent for a long moment, the staff's weight heavy in his hands. Through its ancient wood, he could sense the threads that connected all things – past and future, dream and waking, love and loss. His old life seemed suddenly thin as parchment, while here, with Dwynwen in this impossible tower, he felt more real than he had ever been.

"No," he said. "I've come home."

The Sky Bride

Aishatu Ado

They say Ayneen Jangaré was born with her hands already clasped, as though she guarded a vow no one else could hear.

The midwife pried the fingers apart to wash her, and when she did, the girl's palms released the scent of rain striking stone, an omen, the elders murmured, of roads that cross water.

In Bintaare, the high plateau town where Fulani herders drove cattle to the wide brown river, people told stories to account for what defied reason. Ayneen was a story that had slipped its teller and learned to walk. She never stumbled on loose rock. Her voice was whole where others fractured, a gift that gathered listeners the way rivers gather villages. The market women said she was born with her breath already pledged to the road.

When the chieftain promised her in marriage to his eldest son, the women shook their heads: she was made for departure.

The son's smile showed every tooth. His gaze measured rooms, tallied people, weighed prices. When his hand closed on Ayneen's elbow in the market, heat climbed up her throat and stayed, heavy. His grip bound like a knot pulled too tight, one that would not slip free. He came to her father's house with cloth and dried meat, placed them in her mother's hands, then turned to Ayneen as though she too were part of the bargain.

Her father's voice rang with pride when he spoke of the match; her mother braided Ayneen's hair, tugging at the roots. Each braid a binding.

The betrothal gifts stacked against the hut wall: gourds of milk, skins of honey, a string of cowries. The wedding mats drank red and gold dye. Neighbors rehearsed the ceremonial songs.

One morning, Ayneen rinsed bowls at the river and let the water name each part of her – wrist, pulse, lifeline. The current pressed cold into the bones of her ankles. Mud needled between her toes. Her ribs locked, refusing the next breath, holding against the swell in her throat with nowhere to go. She bent low to scour millet husks from a bowl and thought of laying it on the water, letting it drift until it vanished downstream, thought of her body following it, thought of how the heaviness in her chest would ease if the river claimed it.

Her hands did not falter – lift, rinse, turn, set aside – while her mind went ahead into the deep channel where the river bent, where the banks rose sheer and the light thinned. She imagined feet leaving the mud, shoulders surrendering, the current closing around her whole, and she wondered whether anyone would search or whether the river would hold her as its own.

Still, she remained on the stones, the bowls clean in a row beside her, the water licking her ankles, the ache in her chest unspooling and knotting again with each pull of the current.

She met Laka three days later, between the first herds arriving for water and the market bells. He was not from Bintaare, sea wind clung to his hair, and his tunic carried a blue that drank light. He stood barefoot in the shallows, rolling a cord between his fingers.

"Do you know how to make a ladder from breath?" he asked, lifting the cord.

She shook her head, wary, yet her feet moved closer.

He took her wrist gently, turned it palm-up. "A breath rung is made by holding air in your chest while you twist the cord three times. The knot remembers it. Stack enough, and you can climb to the place you love most."

Laughter rose sharp and clean, startling sparrows from the reeds. She had not heard that sound from her throat in weeks, and the release loosened a knot inside her.

He returned the next day. And the next. They spoke while tying knots, the cord tugging between them like a quiet tether. Laka asked questions that opened hidden rooms:

What do you fear at night? Whose voice halts your steps?

He waited for her answers; and each bound them closer.

Ports, masts, gulls' cries, his stories smelled of brine. Laka had a thin scar on his cheek he would not explain. He could be harsh when weary, tender when listening. When their fingers brushed on the cord, her ribs loosened.

Rumor said the old witch upriver could weave ladders that reached beyond sight. Ayneen walked there one dawn to know if such ladders could be made.

The hut breathed smoke and wet stone. Jars leaned against the walls, stoppered with rags. Feathers pushed through a crack in the roof, quivering in the draft.

The witch sat by the hearth, her body a reed dried to its husk, her hair white as bone.

"The sky keeps its own," she said, as though finishing a tale already begun. "It will not measure time as the ground does. Lovers, mothers, merchants – below they count their seasons. Above, they vanish."

A thread lay coiled in her lap, black and soft, sparks glimmering inside it like live embers. She lifted it toward Ayneen.

"You will need hair," she said, "to remember the body you came from. And the breaths of one who loves you – to remember the body you leave behind."

The thread dropped into Ayneen's hands.

* * *

The wedding pressed closer. The chieftain's son walked beside her in public, as if her shadow already belonged to him. One evening he stopped her at the riverbank, seized her chin, and said, "Soon you will not walk here alone."

His touch was not cruel, but it was possessive. That night she dreamt of ropes binding her ankles. When she woke, a single cord lay on her mat – Laka's cord – and she clutched it to her chest.

She told Laka about the spelled thread, that making a ladder out of it was for a place beyond Bintaare, where the chieftain's hand could not reach.

They worked in the shallows, her hair braided into the cord, his breaths knotted in the rungs. Each rung a door she might open and close forever.

On the third night, a shadow moved at the river's bend. The witch stepped into the shallows, her ankles dark with silt, her copper-wire hair catching the moon. She did not look at Laka, only at Ayneen.

"It is ready," she said. "But it is not yet bound to the sky." She pressed a bowl into Ayneen's hands. "Fill it with your breath and your tears. Only then will the ladder rise."

Ayneen bent her face to the bowl. She tried to steady her chest, but an image forced itself in: the chieftain's son's hand clamping her chin, his voice declaring, *Soon you will not walk here alone*. Her ribs ached. Then her mother's hands returned, braiding her scalp raw, weaving her into a life she did not choose. She saw her feet stepping into red-and-gold mats, never stepping out.

Tears fell before she could stop them. Breath came ragged, salted. The witch poured both onto the cord. The knots shuddered, tightened.

"When the moon bends like a hook," the witch said, "the ladder will appear. And once you set your foot on it, the choice cannot be untied." She walked back into reeds without waiting for thanks, her body thinning to mist.

The night before the wedding, the moon bent like a hook. The ladder swayed outside her hut.

She began to climb. First rung: the smell of his hair after rain. Second: his voice falling to a whisper when he asked about her fears. Third: the heat of his palm steadying hers on the cord.

Below, his voice rose, raw and unsure: "If I follow…the ladder may not hold. It may be only for you."

The words struck like a shift in wind – no warning, only a sudden, cold change. Her hands gripped until rope cut her skin. She wanted him beside her. She wanted the road carried in his eyes. She wanted to keep every breath they had tied together. She wanted to keep herself whole.

A thread snapped with a sharp crack, curling into the dark. She leaned down, far enough to see his face: moonlight across his cheekbones, eyes wide, hands gripping the bottom rung as if holding the ladder steady to anchor what he would not climb.

She wanted him, his body against hers, wanted his hands climbing, climbing, climbing. She hated him for his caution, his stillness, and the fear that nailed him to the ground. And in the same heartbeat, she loved him, because even from below he kept the ladder taut, even as it frayed.

Another strand snapped, lashing her cheek. The ladder quivered under her feet.

She could let go, fall into his arms, and face the red-and-gold mats; the bracelets locked on her wrists. Or she could climb, though the rungs tore at her palms, though the sky would never hold him.

Her ribs clamped around her heart. Freedom had soured into solitude, but solitude was lighter than chains.

She closed her eyes. Climbed.

It was said ladders made of breath never held. They frayed in the middle, where longing thinned, or at the top, where the sky exacted a toll.

The rope sighed under her weight, every knot a gasp. She climbed, ribs aching. Each rung remembered a fragment: his voice under reeds, the tang of salt, her mother's braids biting her scalp. Memories trembled, broke. A strand snapped; another curled into the dark.

The proverb whispered: *The river keeps what it carries.* Would the sky keep her too?

The rungs thinned to threads. Her breath tore inside her chest. Time staggered: the climb was endless, the climb was brief.

She dragged herself onto the ladder, knees bruising, breath scattering in the high air.

The sky opened. She fell forward into a plain woven of light. Behind her, the ladder unraveled.

The sky was not empty. It opened like a memory the Earth had forgotten. A second ground stretched taut, stitched with radiance. Stars nested there like seeds pressed in a calabash, waiting to sprout. Clouds drifted heavy-bellied, their fire pale and watchful. Winds moved in braids, forever plaiting and unplaiting themselves. Each gust pressed flavor to her tongue: cold iron, wet dust, sweetness of fruit she would never taste below.

She was not dead. Her ribs still rose, her mouth still chewed. She ate clouds that thickened into pulp and waters gathered in hollows of light to cool her tongue. The sky fed her, but it did not hold her hand.

She built her home there – walls woven from cloud, a floor of moonlight that shifted nightly. When she lay down, the moonlight received her like water, and she dreamed of drowning in its silver cold. Other nights it thinned to a thousand threads she had to knot herself, so that survival became her dwelling. The roof changed too: some nights stars hung close enough to scorch her fingertips; other nights a river-black void swallowed every spark.

She listened for the click of a breath rung latching to the edge of the sky. Most belonged to strangers, traders, wanderers, those who had heard her name and paid the price of the climb, falling back to Earth. But sometimes, one carried Laka's salt-smoke scent. She pressed it to her face, felt the ghost of his fingers, the memory of his breath still knotted into the fiber. Rage rose: if he could give her all these breaths, why not the last, the one that would have broken him from the earth? Love without risk was not love; it was a tether disguised as a gift. The echo mocked her: he lived below, still breathing, while she survived on rags of memory.

From the sky, she watched the river move, carrying her name, carrying his, threading them into a current neither could enter. Time warped in that watching: the moment of choice returned, the rungs unraveling, his voice calling, the rope trembling. Each replay left her raw, newly betrayed.

She thought of the bowls she had lined on the stones, of how near she had come to letting the river keep her. If she had chosen that certainty, she would not ache, but she would not know him either. Pain and love had braided; she could not untie one from the other.

At night she tied small knots into the wind, each a remembrance. Some carried rain's scent, some the heat of his palm, some only silence. She told herself these knots would keep him alive within her. But each knot was also a wall. Each loop bound him more securely to the ground she had fled and bound her more securely to the sky he had refused. She cursed him as she knotted and loved him as she cursed.

She wondered if the ladder would have held for him, if she had reached down, pulled him rung by rung. Perhaps they would have fallen together, bodies broken in dust by dawn. Perhaps it would have held, and he would be here, his laughter loosening the air, his questions filling the silence.

But he was not here. No other humans walked the sky. The stars bore witness, the winds braided her rage, the moonlight remembered her body, but no voice ever answered her own. She was free, but freedom cut sharp with loneliness.

The Veil Between

Dee Alberts

Part One

The first time I saw him, I thought I was dreaming.

That would have made sense. His silver eyes shimmered like moonlight on a restless sea, and the way he watched me – as though he had always known my name – felt impossible, unreal. But when I woke, my lips still tingled as if they had brushed against his in a moment I could not recall.

The second time, I knew I was dreaming.

Because the sky above was not one I had ever seen, a velvet dome shot through with rivers of fire and stars that curved too close. The ground beneath my bare feet glimmered with a sheen like crushed glass. He stood at the edge of a dark forest, cloaked in shadow, and his voice – low, rough, strangely tender – said, *You should not be here.*

And then, just as quickly, I woke again.

For weeks the dreams continued. Sometimes he would appear only for a heartbeat, a blur of steel and shadow.

Other times, he spoke fragments that lingered on my tongue all day: *Do not trust the crown...*or *The veil grows thin.* I tried to push them away, to bury them under my chores, my studies, the endless noise of the waking world. But each night when I closed my eyes, I knew I would find him waiting.

* * *

My name is Lyra Vale, though in my village most call me the dreamer. Not because of these visions – for those I have never spoken aloud – but because I have always been caught with my head in the clouds, forever sketching maps of places no one has seen or writing poems about things that do not exist.

Dreamers are tolerated in Calverdine, but not respected. Ours is a small border village, pressed against the forests and hills that mark the edge of the kingdom. We are practical folk – hunters, farmers, stonecutters. We prize strong backs and steady hands. My constant distraction made me the subject of muttered disapproval, especially from my uncle, who raised me after my parents' deaths.

"You'll never eat ink or starlight," he often said, shoving firewood into my arms. "Put away those fancies and do something useful."

So I did. By day, I carried buckets, scrubbed floors, baked bread. By night, I drifted into a world not my own, drawn again and again to the man with silver eyes.

* * *

One evening, when the village gathered at the tavern to celebrate the midsummer festival, I lingered at the edge of the crowd. Music played, firelight flickered, children chased each other with wreaths of wildflowers. My friends tried to coax me into dancing, but my heart wasn't in it.

I had barely slept the night before. The dream had been darker than usual.

Blood on snow. A crown broken in two. His hand reaching for mine, trembling. "You must choose, Lyra," he said. "Choose, or all will fall."

I had woken with the taste of ashes in my mouth.

"Still staring at shadows?" a voice drawled behind me.

I turned to find Marek, my childhood friend, leaning against the fence. Broad-shouldered, sun-browned, with the easy confidence of a boy who had never doubted his place in the world. Marek was kind enough, though he had little patience for my oddities.

"You look like you've seen a ghost," he said, offering me a mug of cider.

"Maybe I have," I muttered.

He laughed, not unkindly. "Dreams again? Lyra, one day you'll tell me what it is you see. Unless you'd rather keep it all locked away."

I smiled weakly and sipped the cider, but my thoughts were far away. For though Marek was real and warm and present, my heart beat faster when I thought of the stranger in my dreams.

* * *

That night, when I lay down, the veil parted more swiftly than ever.

The silver-eyed man stood in a ruined hall, shattered glass glittering like frost around his boots. His cloak was torn, his hair dark and matted with sweat. When he looked at me, something inside me fractured.

"You came," he whispered.

"I always come," I said, though I had never chosen to.

He took a step toward me. The world trembled. "You don't understand yet. But you will. Soon."

"Who are you?" I demanded.

His lips curved into the faintest smile. "A question with too many answers. Call me Kael."

"And why do you haunt my dreams, Kael?"

His smile faded. He reached into the folds of his cloak and drew out a fragment of glass, sharp-edged, glowing faintly from within. He pressed it into my hand. Though I knew none of this was real, the weight of it was solid, the cold searing against my palm.

"Because, Lyra Vale," he said, silver eyes piercing mine, "you are the only one who can mend the veil. And if you fail, both our worlds will break."

The dream shattered. I woke gasping, the imprint of the shard still burning my skin.

And when I pulled back the blanket, I screamed – because the shard was lying on my bed.

* * *

The next days blurred into confusion. I hid the shard beneath a loose floorboard, terrified someone might see it. It pulsed faintly, as though alive. I tried to convince myself I was imagining it, but the evidence lay undeniable at my feet.

Was I losing my mind? Or was Kael real?

Each night the dreams grew sharper, more insistent. He showed me glimpses of his world – towers carved from obsidian, rivers of molten light, forests that whispered with voices of the dead. He spoke of a veil between realms, a barrier weakening. Shadows seeped through, twisting beasts into monsters, corrupting men into demons.

"You were born with the sight," Kael said one night, his hand brushing mine. "The dreams are not illusions. They are doors. And you…you are the key."

"I don't want to be a key," I whispered.

His touch lingered, heat flooding my skin. "None of us choose our fates. But we can choose how we bear them."

* * *

One evening, while gathering herbs at the forest's edge, I saw movement among the trees. I thought it was Marek, come to tease me again, but when the figure stepped into the clearing, my heart stilled.

Silver eyes.

It was Kael.

Not a dream. Not an illusion. Standing before me, cloak swirling, as real as the earth beneath my feet.

"Lyra," he said, his voice low and urgent. "The veil is collapsing faster than I feared. I shouldn't be here, but I had no choice."

I staggered back, clutching the basket to my chest. "This – this isn't possible."

He reached out as if to steady me, then stopped, fists clenching. "I don't have time to explain. The shard – do you still have it?"

Fear spiked through me. "How do you—?"

"Because I gave it to you. And others will come for it. You must keep it safe." His gaze softened. "And when the time comes, you must trust me."

"I don't even know you!"

"You know enough," he said, and there was such raw pain in his eyes that my breath caught.

Behind him, the shadows deepened, swirling into forms with too many limbs, too many teeth. Kael drew his blade, steel flashing. "Stay behind me."

The monsters lunged.

And my world of dreams and waking life collided in a storm of blood and fire.

Part Two

The clearing erupted in chaos.

The creatures that spilled from the dark shimmered like shadows given flesh – spindly limbs, slick jaws dripping with tar, eyes that burned with a sickly green fire. Their screeches curdled the air. My body froze, every instinct screaming to run, but Kael's voice cut through the noise.

"Behind me, Lyra!"

He moved with terrifying grace, blade flashing silver in the gloom. One monster lunged, and in a single arc his sword split it apart. Black smoke poured from the wound, dissipating into the air. But three more took its place, claws raking the earth.

My knees threatened to buckle. This wasn't a dream. The smell of rot burned my throat, the heat of the creatures' breath scalded my skin.

Kael struck again and again, each movement precise but strained. He wasn't invincible. He was bleeding, crimson soaking the sleeve of his cloak.

Something inside me snapped. I couldn't just watch.

I fumbled in my basket for the shard, its glow pulsing stronger than ever. As soon as I touched it, a surge of energy roared through me, so fierce it almost tore me apart. My vision blurred, light searing across the clearing.

The creatures shrieked, staggering back. For an instant the air rippled, like a veil fluttering in the wind.

Kael spun toward me, eyes wide. "What did you—? No, not here, it's too strong—"

The ground split beneath us. A rift tore open, spilling shadows and light. I screamed as the world collapsed, and then—

Silence.

* * *

When I woke, the forest was gone.

I lay on smooth stone, a vaulted ceiling of black crystal arching above me. Strange firelight danced across the walls. Kael knelt at my side, wiping blood from his brow.

"You should not have touched the shard," he said, voice harsh with fear.

"I – I didn't know what else to do." My chest still hummed with power, every heartbeat echoing the shard's glow. "Where are we?"

His gaze swept the hall, wary. "The Veil has carried us into my realm. Too soon. Too dangerous."

I sat up, shivering. His world was vast and terrible – castles carved into mountains of obsidian, rivers of molten light visible through windows that overlooked an endless abyss. Creatures stalked the shadows, watching. But what frightened me most wasn't the landscape. It was the weight of his words.

His realm.

"You're not…human," I whispered.

Something flickered in his eyes – regret, perhaps. "Not as you know it. My people guard the Veil. We were born to keep balance between the realms. But the crown that bound our power has been broken. Without it, the shadows spill through."

"And I'm supposed to fix this?"

His hand brushed mine, tentative, almost reverent. "You were chosen, Lyra. The Sight has always been rare, but in you it burns like a beacon. You can restore the crown, mend the Veil."

I shook my head. "I'm just…me. I don't know how to mend anything."

Kael's voice softened. "I'll teach you. If you'll trust me."

* * *

Days bled into nights in his realm. Kael guided me through winding halls, teaching me how to wield the shard's power. When I concentrated, I could call light to my fingertips, enough to drive back shadows. Each time, I felt the bond between us grow stronger, his steady presence anchoring me against fear.

Yet there was always a distance in his gaze, as though he were holding back. I caught him watching me when he thought I wasn't looking, a storm of longing and sorrow in his eyes.

One night, unable to bear the silence, I whispered, "Why me, Kael? Why not someone stronger, braver?"

He hesitated. Then, with a quiet intensity that stole my breath, he said, "Because when the Veil first showed me your face, I forgot the weight of centuries. I remembered what it was to hope. To want."

My heart pounded. The firelight painted silver across his cheekbones, his lips inches from mine. For a moment, the world shrank to just the two of us, suspended between desire and fear.

But he pulled away, fists clenched. “I cannot. To love you would be to damn you. And I have damned too many already.”

* * *

We were not alone in his realm.

Whispers spread through the obsidian halls – Kael had brought a mortal girl, the one said to hold the shard. Some looked at me with awe, others with suspicion. And one, a woman named Selith, looked at me with venom.

Selith was beautiful in the way blades are beautiful – sharp, dangerous, gleaming. She claimed to be Kael’s second, a commander of their forces. More than once I caught her hand lingering on his arm, her smile laced with poison.

“You don’t belong here,” she hissed to me one evening. “You think he cares for you? You’re nothing but a tool. When your power burns out, he’ll discard you, as he’s discarded others.”

Her words cut deep, but I told myself not to believe them. Kael was different. He had to be.

Yet doubt festered.

* * *

The truth came in shards.

While exploring a hidden chamber, I found fragments of an ancient mural. It depicted a mortal woman standing beside a guardian with silver eyes – Kael. She held a shard like mine, glowing in her hands. The next panel showed her lying broken, the crown restored, Kael kneeling over her body.

The inscription was clear: *Only through sacrifice may the Veil be mended.*

My blood turned to ice.

When I confronted Kael, his face twisted with anguish. "I meant to tell you. But not yet."

"So it's true?" My voice cracked. "For the Veil to heal, I must die?"

He reached for me, desperate. "I swore I would find another way. I won't let history repeat itself."

Tears blurred my vision. "You should have told me."

"I was afraid," he whispered, his forehead resting against mine. "Afraid that if you knew the cost, you'd turn away. And I cannot bear to lose you – not when I have just found you."

* * *

War came swiftly.

The shadows surged across both realms, tearing open rifts, consuming villages. Marek appeared in my dreams, calling my name, his voice drowned by darkness. My worlds were collapsing.

In the final hour, Kael and I stood before the shattered crown, shards scattered like stars across the floor. The shadows closed in, a tidal wave of teeth and claws.

"This is the choice," Kael said, anguish breaking his voice. "If you pour your power into the crown, the Veil will mend – but it will consume you."

"And if I don't?"

"Both realms will fall."

The shard in my hand pulsed, waiting.

I looked at him – the man who haunted my dreams, who had shown me strength within myself I had never known. A man bound by duty, scarred by loss, yet capable of love so fierce it terrified him.

"I don't want to die," I whispered.

His hands cupped my face, trembling. "Then live. Please. We'll find another way."

But in his eyes, I saw the truth. There was no other way.

I kissed him, pouring every fragment of my soul into that single moment – the longing, the fear, the love. When I drew back, tears streaked his cheeks.

"Dream of me," I said softly.

And then I let the shard fall into the crown.

* * *

Light exploded, blinding, searing, endless. The Veil roared as it mended, shadows burning away into nothingness. My body burned with it, my last breath a whisper carried into the void.

When the light faded, the crown gleamed whole once more. Kael knelt beside it, clutching the empty space where I had been. His silver eyes dimmed with grief.

But in the mortal realm, Marek woke from a nightmare to hear my laughter in the wind. And in Kael's dreams, night after night, I stood beside him still – untouched, eternal.

For though the Veil demanded sacrifice, love does not end. It endures, between worlds, between dreams.

The Witch of Ravendell

Danielle Marie Cahill

A steady drip-drip of water was falling from one of the stalactites on the roof of the cave, dampening the end of my sleeping bag. Wherever I moved my feet, another drip started.

I sat up, pushing my hair out of my eyes. Was there anywhere in the whole of Ravendell Cave that was actually dry?

The fire I had been so proud of building had burnt down to its last embers, casting little light around the shadowy corners of the cavern.

I flicked on my torch, shining it around the space. The slim beam of brightness caught on the serrated edges of the rocks, the stalactites and stalagmites, and then the wide pool a few feet away. The water was deep and inky blue. A rickety wooden boat had been left for me to get across. If I wanted to leave the cave – to stretch my legs, buy a flat white from the *Ravendell Food Truck* outside, or trek the mile to a corner shop for a packet of chocolate digestives – I needed to cross the pool.

Geoff Landry hadn't mentioned the boat, or the drips for that matter, in my interview for Witch of Ravendell Cave, nor that he expected me to live and sleep next to a freezing rock face. Perhaps some of the five thousand applicants might not have cackled as enthusiastically, had they realised the truth: being Witch of Ravendell Cave was not just a job, it was a lifestyle.

I picked up my sleeping bag, my bag of clothes, and the pointed black hat that my boss, and landlord – I suppose, as Geoff owned the patch of farmland and the cave at the top of the sea cliffs – had pressed into my hand on day one. He had begged me to wear it, as the children visiting the cave would expect me to be dressed up. Reluctantly, I had agreed, smothering my protestations that I was a born witch, and I did not need a black hat to prove it.

I needed this job.

The hat was damp now, caught by yet another cascade of water from a nearby stalactite. Geoff would probably have said that mould added to the authenticity of my costume.

I stomped up to higher ground, muttering to myself, "Five thousand people would kill for this job…apparently."

The air in the cave was getting colder, I was sure of it.

In the corner, the ground was dry, and the rock was covered with a powdery soil. This would have to do. A faint feeling of regret flitted through my mind. But I banished it. A damp cavern was better than the alternative.

A chill ran up my spine.

I fought to keep myself from thinking about Oscar, who would be snug in his houseboat close to Broadway Market, and sleeping soundly, no doubt, with my black cat curled up by his side. It had broken my heart to leave Persephone behind. I tasted guilt like iron in my mouth. One day, I would go back for her, I promised myself. When I felt stronger.

Grimly, I wrapped my sleeping bag around me, and draped my black cloak over my shoulders. I leant against the stone wall of the cave. It was rough. And so cold. Sleep felt very far away, but gradually my eyelids drooped, and my mind drifted away into darkness.

* * *

The first thing I felt was warmth spreading through my fingers and toes, then a loud purr in my right ear. It was a purr that I knew.

"Persephone?" I murmured.

My cat nuzzled into my neck, the vibration in her chest growing louder.

Hold on. If Persephone was here, that meant I was on *The Queen of Pentacles*.

My eyes flicked open.

I looked up at the wooden ceiling of the narrowboat, which was painted sky blue with fluffy clouds scattered around, and a murmuration of starlings. Oscar's handiwork.

"Oh, you're awake," Oscar said. "That's good news."

My stomach twisted at the sound of his voice.

I sat up, and wrapped my hands around my knees. I was still wearing my long black gown and cloak, although my hat and sleeping bag were missing.

"What am I doing here?" I asked, the words nearly choking me.

Oscar was standing at the end of the bed, wearing his usual dark jeans and Black Sabbath T-Shirt, with a ratty cardigan over the top. His protuberant green eyes were ringed with dark shadows, and his face was even more gaunt than usual. And he was holding a coffee cup in one hand.

"I don't think you're asking the right question," he replied, pushing back his dark hair with a skeletal hand. "The real point is: why on earth did you leave in the first place?"

His words drew me inexorably back into remembering the night I left him. The argument. Oscar's shouting. And the moment I had been trying so hard to forget: when he smashed his fist into the little table in the middle of the narrowboat, and the fish-shaped vase, that had been my grandmother's, burst into a million fragments at my feet.

I could still remember the metallic taste of fear in my mouth, as I ran down the towpath. Away from the narrowboat. With Oscar's cries for me to stop echoing down the canal.

I had escaped a month ago today. And I could do it again. It was just a question of when.

Under my lashes, I flashed a look at Oscar. He was gripping his coffee mug so hard I could see each sinew on his right hand.

"Zelda," he said, moving closer to the bed. "I really missed you. I needed you. You can't imagine how much."

I did not reply.

He took another step forward, with his eyes fixed on my face. And, with deliberate slowness, he sat down on the edge of the bed.

All my senses were screaming. I had to run.

But Oscar was between me and the door of the narrowboat. It was going to be almost impossible for me to make my escape.

My pulse was racing, but I stayed perfectly still.

"And Persephone missed you too. Look at her." He reached out and tickled the cat between her ears. She shrank closer to me. "See? She won't leave your side."

As my cat pressed against me, I could feel her heart pounding. That did it. I could not sit there and let him terrorise Persephone.

Gathering the cat into my arms, I made a sudden spring up from the bed, and I raced towards the stern of the narrowboat. I knew the swinging jump from the door to the back deck, and I hopped up easily, then took the next leap onto the towpath at the same frantic pace. As I landed, and paused for a second to curl Persephone into a better position, I heard Oscar's wild laughter.

His jeering face appeared at the porthole window by my shoulder, then he swung out onto the deck. He stood with legs spread in a wide stance. And he just kept laughing, his face twisting into a mirthless mask. Then he pointed a long finger straight at me.

I flinched.

"Go on then," he shouted. "Why don't you run?"

He jolted forward, as if he was about to leap onto the towpath.

I took off, pelting along the canal as quickly as I could, hurrying past the old gas works, and ducking under several bridges, hoping there would be no cyclists coming the other way, until I reached the edge of Victoria Park. Every few paces, I glanced behind me, as the echo of Oscar's laughter still rang in my ears.

* * *

There were hands gripping my shoulders. Shaking me. And a man's voice calling my name. But the swirling darkness filled my eyes, and ears, choking me.

A roaring sound pulsed through my head. It sounded like the ebb and flow of the ocean.

"Zelda!" the voice came again.

The man would not let me rest.

I opened my eyes.

We were on the edge of the cliff, where the tufted grass fell away down a sheer rockface towards the sea far below. And Geoff was holding me firmly – one hand on my shoulder, the other around my waist.

"Geoff?" I mumbled.

"I'm here," he replied. "Sorry for waking you." He pointed to the sheer drop. "But I had to."

"What am I doing here?"

"You were sleepwalking." A small smile curled the left-hand side of his mouth. "Well, sleep running to be more precise. Do you do that a lot?"

"Run in my sleep? No." I tried not to look down at the stomach-churning descent to the water. If Geoff had not been there, I might have fallen to my death in the darkness without anyone knowing. My legs wobbled at the thought. "Do you mind if I sit down?"

"Of course not." He drew my arm into his, and helped me over to a fallen tree. When I collapsed onto it, he draped his jacket over my shoulders. It smelled strongly of wax and charcoal, and it was blissfully warm. "Have you seen a little black cat?"

"No, I'm sorry," he said. "You were alone when I found you."

No matter what, I was going to have to go back for Persephone. But right now my mind was swirling, and I could not think straight. I leant back against one of the branches of the tree, and took a few slow breaths with my eyes closed.

I could still hear the agitating of the waves far beneath us. The water that had so nearly claimed me for its own. My skin prickled with goosebumps, and I drew Geoff's Barbour jacket closer around me.

"Do you mind if I ask what possessed you to spend the night at Ravendell?"

I opened my eyes to find Geoff's navy eyes were fixed on me.

"In the cave?" I was too shaken to be anything other than completely honest. "I thought you wanted me to live and breathe being the Witch of Ravendell. Isn't sleeping in the cave what you expected?"

He shifted from foot to foot. "Well, no, not really. I thought you'd found a place to stay in the village. If you'd told me that you needed accommodation, I'd have offered you one of the cottages…I can't believe you thought you had to live in a cave."

"Wait, what? I thought this was supposed to be a lifestyle choice."

"It's a job, Zelda," he said very gently. "Not a prison."

I put my head in my hands, and – overwhelmed by the past few minutes – I gave way to laughter that felt a lot like it might bubble up into hysterical sobs.

Geoff put his hands on mine.

"Please, Zelda, I'm so sorry," he said, clearly thinking I was crying. "I never meant for any of this to happen to you." He dropped to the grass beside me. "Look at me, please."

Slowly, I lifted my fingers, and found his face level with mine.

The silvery moonlight illuminated the strong lines of his face – the long straight nose, the chiselled jawline, and sensuous mouth that curled up in the left-hand corner whenever he smiled.

As he was doing now.

"What is it?" I said, when he continued to stare at me.

"You look your best by moonlight," he said. "Perhaps that's a witch thing."

"Definitely part of the lifestyle," I replied.

He winced. "I feel awful. I'll take you to one of the cottages now. There's heating. And most of them have more than one bedroom, as they're holiday lets. You can take your pick."

I touched my forefinger to his lip to silence him, then traced up to where it lifted when he grinned.

The air crackled. Heat curled in my stomach. I needed to know whether he felt the connection too.

For a few nerve-racking seconds all I could hear was the rhythm of the waves, then the small rasp of Geoff swallowing broke the quiet. That nervous and vulnerable sound gave me the hope I needed.

I slipped my hand to the back of his neck, tangling my fingers in his pale hair.

A gasp escaped him.

And it made my heart sing. For I knew then that he wanted this as much as I did.

With deliberate slowness, I leaned forward until our mouths were almost touching. I could feel his breath sharpen, and I stopped. Waiting. Teasing. Letting the tension build.

Electricity jumped between us: sparks that shook me to the core.

I brushed my lips against his, and he answered with fierce and intoxicating kisses that surprised and delighted me. Everything around us blurred, as I focused only on his hands tracing along my jawline and up into my hair, as he slid his tongue deep into my mouth, sending shudders of pleasure trembling to the centre of me. I craved more of him.

He must have sensed this, as he lifted his jacket from my shoulders, draping it over the grass, then he brought me down to lie beside him.

A bright shaft of moonlight glanced over his face, and he looked down at me and smiled.

"You're beautiful," he said, trailing his fingers over my collarbone, then circling around my shoulder, until I was shivering with desire. I ached for him to slide his hand lower. I was groaning with pure lust.

But the grass and the moonlight began to pixelate, disappearing into a sickening whirl of darkness.

"No!" I cried out. But it was no good.

The last thing I saw was Geoff's bereft face, and his hands reaching out to clasp me, but finding only air.

* * *

"No!" I was still shouting, as an echo answered me from the depths of the cave. Around me, the stalactites were dripping, and my sleeping bag was soaked through.

I was in Ravendell once more. The cave was as gloomy as I remembered.

I caught the faint trace of Oscar's laugh in the air. All of this – the nightmare, and the fantasy – were they all my ex's handiwork?

I had to get out of the cave. To touch the grass. To feel the wind on my face. And try my best to work out what was real and what was not.

Going down to the little boat, I hopped in, and rowed inexpertly across the lake. From there I could run towards the entrance. Towards sunshine. Freedom.

I burst out into the daylight, pitching face first into the tufted grass. I lay there with poppies and cornflowers tickling my chin, able to feel at peace with the universe.

I must have been lying there a long time when I caught the sound of footsteps. There, in front of me, were some battered walking boots. Geoff. It had to be.

I rolled onto my side, gazing up at the sternly handsome face above me.

A smile glimmered in Geoff's eyes, and I felt an answering burning in mine. I took my time getting to my feet, and pulling the blue cornflowers out of my hair.

I held out one of the cornflowers for him to take, and I leaned forward to whisper in his ear, "The Witch of Ravendell welcomes you." My lips were so close to his neck that I could feel his pulse racing. He swallowed, his throat jumping. That nervous movement told me everything I needed to know.

Victory danced in my veins.

Last night may have been a fantasy, very likely sent by Oscar in a moment of mean-spirited mischief. But, in the cool of the morning, Geoff's blood was laced with desire for me. If I wanted, he could be mine.

"Now, you may think you know everything there is to know about Ravendell," I said, a seductive tone creeping into my voice. "But there is so much more to explore. Come, let me show you the cavern's undiscovered wonders."

Slipping my hand under Geoff's arm, I drew him after me into the dimness of Ravendell Cave: my kingdom, my sanctuary, and my home.

The Last Night Market

Bella Chacha

The curtains were trembling again.

Adeola lay still, her cheek pressed against the warm hollow of her pillow, listening for the sound of wind. There was none. No rustle of leaves outside, no rattle from the rusted balcony rail. The night air was thick, holding its breath.

Yet the curtains swayed, as though someone stood just beyond them, exhaling softly into the fabric.

She rose. The floorboards gave their usual reluctant sigh under her bare feet. She parted the curtains with a small flick of her wrist, prepared to find nothing.

And then she saw it.

The moon hung low over the city, swollen and silver, but with a perfect crescent missing from its side – a bite, clean and sharp-edged, as if some cosmic mouth had claimed it mid-meal.

Her breath caught.

She had seen that moon before. Once. Fourteen years ago, when she was just a girl in a borrowed nightdress too long for her legs. That night, the moon had looked exactly like this, not a shadow's eclipse, but a devouring. That night was the first time she had dreamed of the market. And the last.

Until now.

The memory rose in her like a tide: lanterns adrift in the dark, the scent of river mud and oranges, a voice speaking her name in a tongue both strange and achingly familiar.

She pressed her fingers to the cold glass.

The bite-marked moon seemed to pulse, a slow beat, like the thud of a drum deep underwater. For a moment, she thought she heard it, the hum of wooden planks beneath her feet, the creak of mooring ropes strained against unseen currents.

She backed away, heart hammering, and returned to bed as if the blankets might anchor her in the waking world. But even as she lay down, even as she told herself *I am still here*, her vision blurred at the edges, and the ceiling dissolved into a vast black sky.

No door. No drifting into dream. Just the sudden tilt of a wooden platform swaying beneath her.

The slap of dark water below.

And light – a thousand lanterns strung not on ropes, but floating untethered in the air, each glowing with its own color: rose, saffron, the green of leaves seen through rain.

Their reflections quivered in the water, making the world double itself in beauty and threat.

Adeola knew where she was. Her breath came fast, sharp with wonder and dread.

The market had returned.

Voices curled around her, speaking in languages she half-understood, bartering for things that made her skin prickle – a bundle of shadows tied with twine, a glass jar of laughter that fizzed against its lid, a length of cloth woven from light.

She moved between the stalls, dizzy from the scents: cinnamon smoke, rain on iron, the faint sweetness of fruit she could not name. Every step made the platform shudder, the tide lifting and lowering her like the palm of a breathing giant.

And then she saw him.

The Tomorrow Merchant.

He stood behind a narrow table lined with objects that seemed impossible: a coin that changed its face when she blinked, a folded note that whispered her name, a compass with no needle.

But she only truly saw *him*.

A young man, no older than herself, with eyes the color of ink poured into water, spreading and swallowing light. His clothes were simple, but his smile – that knowing, waiting smile – was heavy with recognition.

"As if you've been gone a long time," he said, though she hadn't spoken.

"As if you've been expecting me," she whispered, the words tasting strange on her tongue.

The lanterns swayed above them, their colors shifting. Somewhere far off, a bell tolled once, and the market seemed to lean in, listening.

Wonder swelled in her chest, threaded through with something sharper – a foreboding she couldn't name. Because she knew, without knowing how, that every step she took here would cost her something in the world she had left behind.

And she wasn't sure she would ever want to go back.

* * *

The Merchant's stall was smaller than she remembered. A single wooden counter balanced on ropes that dipped and rose with the swell of the black water beneath. On it lay rows of glass vials, each no larger than a child's thumb, their contents glowing faintly – golds like trapped sunlight, silvers like frozen breath, and colors she had no name for.

"This is what I sell," he said, his voice warm as midnight. "Memories of tomorrow."

Adeola blinked. "Memories can only belong to the past."

He shook his head, the lamplight spilling ink shadows across his face. "Not here. Not in the Night Market. You can drink one, and when the day comes, it will be exactly as you've tasted – every joy, every sorrow, every drop of rain against your skin. But…" His smile thinned into something dangerous. "Nothing is free here."

She glanced at the labels. *Tomorrow's Laughter. A Storm at Sea. The Moment Before a Kiss. Regret by Candlelight.*

"What do you take in return?" she asked.

"Something from your waking life," he said. "A memory, a possession, a truth you have lived. The greater the tomorrow, the dearer the price."

Her gaze lingered on a vial glowing a soft, impossible yellow. Its label read: *Tomorrow's Laughter.* She thought of the dull rhythm of her days, the heaviness that had been settling in her bones. To laugh until she couldn't breathe, she would pay for that.

"What will it cost?"

He studied her as though she were a puzzle carved into the tide. "The sound of your mother's voice singing your name."

Adeola hesitated. The voice she had known since birth, warm and lilting, weaving her name into lullabies and morning calls. To give it away would be to lose a part of herself. Yet her hands reached for the vial before she could stop them.

"Done," she whispered.

The moment the vial touched her palm, the memory unraveled. The thread of her mother's song slipped from her mind, leaving only an empty frame. She remembered that her mother had sung to her, yes…but not the sound, not the rise and fall, not the way it curled around her name like a promise.

She drank. The liquid was cold and sharp, like the first bite of ripe fruit, and then warm, fizzing at the edges of her mind.

When she woke the next morning, the world seemed clearer, the air lighter. And when a colleague at work told a clumsy, ridiculous joke about the moon, she laughed... really laughed...until tears blurred her vision and her ribs ached. And in that dizzy moment, she thought of the vial.

That night, when she closed her eyes, the tide rose beneath her feet again, and the lanterns drifted in the air without strings. The Merchant was waiting. His ink-dark eyes glinted.

"You've come back," he said.

She didn't answer. She had already known she would return.

The Merchant told her the market did not belong to clocks.

"It comes," he said, "only when the moon swallows its own light."

Sometimes that meant years between eclipses. Sometimes only months. Time was as fickle here as the tide, and the tide only obeyed desire.

She began to measure her life by these rare nights. Between them, the world felt...faded. Even when she walked through the crush of the morning bus, or sat beneath the hiss of her shower, or spoke mid-conversation with a friend, her mind slid back to him – to the slow, deliberate way he corked a vial, to the weight of his gaze like a tide pulling her under.

When the market returned, it was always without warning – a dream that began mid-step, lanterns floating above a dark canal, the scent of rain and ripe fruit in the air.

Her trades grew bolder. One night she surrendered the memory of her first kiss – clumsy, in the back of a half-lit classroom, the taste of stolen guava between their teeth, in exchange for *Tomorrow's Rain*. The next day, clouds rolled at exactly four o'clock, and she stood in the middle of the street, letting the downpour soak her hair, her clothes, her bones. It was not ordinary rain. It felt orchestrated, a note-perfect performance of water.

Another night she gave up her favorite book, the one she had read so often she could recite its first chapter from memory. The Merchant took it without touching her – simply, the words vanished from her mind, and placed in her palm a vial labeled *Tomorrow's Song*. The next day, walking past a street musician, she heard a melody she'd never known but somehow remembered. It twined around her heart until she wept.

And then there was her grandmother's face. She had hesitated longer over that one. Her grandmother had been the keeper of family stories, her laughter the anchor of Adeola's childhood. But *Tomorrow's Embrace* sat on the counter like a promise too sweet to resist. She drank it, and the next morning woke in the arms of someone she loved but could not name, wrapped in a warmth that made her ache with longing.

Each waking day began to feel *curated*. The right song at the right corner. The exact words she'd wished someone would say falling into her ears. The world was no longer a series of accidents – it was a stage set, lit for her alone.

But the stage had its shadows.

Friends began to glance at her strangely. "You forgot my birthday," one said, hurt thick in their voice. Another laughed awkwardly when she failed to recall the punchline of a joke they'd told just last week. Faces at work blurred at the edges; conversations unraveled halfway through. She started writing notes to herself – reminders, fragments of who she'd been, but the slips of paper lay unread in the pockets of coats she no longer remembered owning.

And yet, each time the moon hid its face, she returned.

Because in the floating market, he remembered her. Every detail. The tilt of her head, the cadence of her breath. He asked about her days as though they were treasures he had kept safe. And when his hand brushed hers as he passed a vial across the counter, the sensation followed her into waking, like the faint taste of something she had once loved.

Love and magic had a weight, she thought. She just didn't know yet how much of herself she could carry before the tide took the rest.

* * *

The market returned on a night when the air in her room felt heavier than the dark. She found herself again before his stall, its shelves lined with glass vials that glimmered like trapped stars.

This time, she did not browse.

"I want *Tomorrow's Goodbye*," she said.

The words startled even her – they sounded like betrayal, though her heart beat in defense of them. She wanted to know the shape of loss before it arrived. She wanted to taste the end so she could brace for it.

The Merchant's hands stilled over a row of bottles. His eyes, usually so steady, wavered. "Goodbyes," he said slowly, "belong to the waking."

"That's just another way of saying you won't sell it."

"I *can't* sell it."

His voice had an edge she had never heard before, not refusal, but something more raw. When he turned to face her fully, there was something unguarded in his gaze, a flicker of...fear? The thought unnerved her. Until now, she had imagined him as part of the market itself, untouchable, beyond the laws she lived by.

"You're afraid," she said.

He looked away. "You think you're the only one who trades here?"

The silence between them deepened, pressing against her ribs. She stepped closer, close enough to see the fine lines at the corners of his mouth, close enough to feel the faint warmth radiating from him.

"What did you trade?" she asked.

He shook his head, but the answer lived in the hollowness of his expression.

Without thinking, she reached for his hand. His skin was warm, but beneath it...beneath the pulse, there was an absence she could feel as clearly as bone. Not emptiness, but an outline where something used to be.

A memory. Gone.

Her breath caught. "Do you even remember your own name?"

The corner of his mouth lifted, though it wasn't a smile. "Names aren't worth much here. They fade fastest."

The words chilled her. Because suddenly, she could imagine a market where even he would vanish, piece by piece, until nothing remained but the stall, the vials, the scent of rain in the air.

And yet...she wanted him more fiercely than ever. Even if it meant paying with the scraps of herself she had left.

Somewhere deep inside her, a thought began to take root, sharp as glass:

If he could give up pieces of himself to meet her, then there must be a price high enough to keep him.

But she didn't yet know what it was.

* * *

The sky was a deep black velvet stretched taut, pierced by two moons locked in an unyielding embrace. A double eclipse. The rarest of nights, an event so powerful, the floating market had never appeared for more than a single evening before. Now it would linger for three.

Adeola felt the weight of the moment before she even stepped onto the creaking wooden platform that seemed to breathe beneath her feet. The air shimmered with lantern light, golden and soft, each glow whispering secrets in tongues she almost understood. The market swayed gently on dark waters that reflected the fractured moons above, a mirror to a world both strange and achingly familiar.

In the waking world, Adeola was unrecognizable even to herself. Her reflection was a stranger – hollow eyes framed by tired skin, lips parted as if to speak a name long lost. She could not remember the city she called home, nor the faces of those who once laughed beside her. The comfort of her job, the rhythm of her days, all evaporated like mist in the dawn.

Only one memory burned bright and clear: the Merchant.

He waited beneath the lantern-lit archway, his eyes deep pools of ink spilled into water, calm and infinite. His hand stretched toward her, unwavering.

Adeola swallowed the lump in her throat. The choice had come, heavy as the eclipse's shadow: remain tethered to a fractured waking world that no longer felt like hers, or step beyond the veil and lose everything but this dream, this impossible love.

"I want forever," she whispered, voice fragile but steady, trembling with the weight of everything she had sacrificed to arrive here.

The Merchant's face softened, but his eyes flickered with a quiet sorrow. "The price is more than you know," he said. "Once you drink, there is no turning back."

Adeola met his gaze and reached into the folds of her spirit, pulling out the last piece she held tight, the memory of how to return to the waking world. She offered it with open hands.

The Merchant's fingers closed gently around the fragile gift, the memory flickering like a dying candle flame before vanishing entirely. He handed her a vial shimmering with silver liquid – *Tomorrow's Forever*.

Heart pounding, Adeola lifted the glass to her lips. The liquid was cool, tasting like moonlight and jasmine, flowing like liquid time through her veins. A warmth blossomed from her chest, spreading through her limbs until she felt as if she were dissolving, weightless and unbound.

Around her, the market transformed. The wooden planks beneath her feet became clouds, lanterns burst into constellations, and the music of invisible strings wove through the air, a melody older than memory, filled with longing and hope.

She took the Merchant's hand. His touch was a promise, a tether to this place where hunger, pain, and fear no longer held sway. Here, she could live forever in the dreamscape where love was constant, where the impossible bloomed beneath eternal moons.

A single tear escaped, tracing a silver path down her cheek, shimmering in the golden light.

Adeola closed her eyes and let herself fall deeper, knowing...feeling...that she would never wake.

Because some loves are bound not by life, but by the surrender of all that once was.

The market swayed gently, the double moons casting long shadows, and somewhere between the lanterns and the stars, the whisper of a trade completed echoed – a love forever sealed, a price forever paid.

* * *

Adeola drifted through the market, endlessly weaving between stalls that shimmered like distant stars. Her feet made no sound on the wooden planks, worn smooth by centuries of whispered trades and silent bargains. Time had no claim here. The weight of years, the ache of hunger, the sharp edges of loss – all were softened into a gentle haze, a golden glow that wrapped around her like a second skin.

She smiled, touched a lantern glowing with a fragile light, and moved on. The market's song played softly, a melody she could no longer name but knew in the marrow of her bones. The stalls offered wonders – bottles of forgotten dreams, shards of laughter long past, and fragrances that teased memories she could no longer reach. She passed one selling *Yesterday's Laughter*, its glass catching the moonlight, casting rainbows on her skin.

The Merchant stood nearby, watching the crowd with quiet eyes. When Adeola's gaze met his, he looked away, as if the weight of her name was a debt he could not pay. Did he remember? Or had he traded her identity away to hold her forever in this dream?

Adeola did not wonder. The question no longer mattered.

In the waking world, her apartment was silent and still.

The door stood ajar, swinging slightly in a breeze that did not come. Inside, the bed was made with careless neatness, the pillow plumped as if waiting for someone who would never return. A mug sat on the table, steam curling in the pale morning light, forgotten warmth in a cold room.

Friends had called, again and again. Police searched, rumors spread. No leads, no answers. Adeola was a ghost who had slipped through the cracks of time, swallowed by the market that only appeared under eclipsed moons.

Her life was a story half-told, a song cut short.

Back in the dreamscape, Adeola's footsteps echoed softly, a whisper beneath the eternal moonlight. She moved through a world suspended between sorrow and joy, a place where the ache of perfect love came with the price of everything she once was.

The market continued, timeless and merciless. And somewhere between the stalls, the Merchant kept watch – keeper of memories, trader of tomorrows, and, perhaps, the last guardian of a love that could never truly be free.

The silent question hung in the air, fragile as a breath:

What becomes of a soul traded for forever?

The ache of beauty lost, the hollow echo of choices made. Adeola's fate is a tender wound that refuses to heal, a reminder that the deepest love may demand the severing of the self. The story closes with a haunting ambiguity – love eternal, but at what cost?

The Severance Pact

Victor W. Clubb

The first time Kael coughed blood, Sira tasted iron.

That was the problem with sharing a soul – when one bled, the other choked on it.

They had not been born together, but the magic had decided otherwise.

War orphans from different clans, lifted from the ruins on the same night. The healers had said they wouldn't survive the plague alone – too small, too weak, too full of the old sickness. So the elders bound them with blood magic: heart-linked, pain-shared, soul-knotted.

The spell took. And for twenty years there was no me, only us.

They moved like two hands of the same body. When Kael bent to lift the water jars, Sira was already steadying the rope. When she turned the drying racks in the herb shed, his shadow fell beside hers. Sometimes their eyes met by accident – lingering too long, with a flicker of something neither dared name.

It was easy to pretend it was just the bond.

Until the coughs worsened.

The first time, she thought it was berry sap staining his palm. The second time, the sound of it tore her from sleep, clutching her own chest where the ache bloomed in perfect sync. By the third, the village healer could not look either of them in the eye.

"It's the bond," the old woman said, voice low. "Too much magic for too long. One body's failing, both will pay."

Her nails, blackened at the tips, traced a rune on Kael's wrist. The skin blistered instantly. "See? Even a ghost of the bond burns."

Sira's stomach hollowed. "Then we fix it."

The healer hesitated, then whispered a name neither had spoken aloud since childhood stories: the Severer.

They found her beyond the swamp, in a hollow tree slick with moss. The air was heavy, breathing slower than it should. Her skin was crosshatched with runes no longer spoken, and when she blinked, the pupils seemed to catch in the air before sliding back into place.

"I can cut the cord," she rasped, eyes gleaming like wet stone. "But it will not come clean. One will forget the other entirely. The other will carry the memory – and the pain – alone."

Sira's answer was ready before the words finished. "Take it from me. Let him remember."

Kael's head snapped toward her. "No. If you forget, it'll kill me anyway. You're the one who dreams in color. You need those."

Her throat burned. "I need you."

Something flickered in his gaze – tender, aching, dangerously close to the edge of the bond's safety. "Then let me forget. You've carried me long enough."

They argued in whispers, forehead to forehead, until the Severer's patience thinned. She slit her palm with a bone knife, letting blood drip onto the roots. The droplets hissed as though the earth disliked the taste.

"Decide now," she said. "No bargains. One forgets. One remembers. And know this—" Her voice thinned to a whisper that wormed into the marrow. "When love crosses a severed bond, it will heal or it will kill. But it will not be quiet about it."

Kael's breath hitched. His hand found hers, fingers tightening once – just once – before he closed his eyes.

"Let me forget."

The ritual split the sky.

Lightning ripped through the swamp, striking the hollow tree. Roots shuddered underfoot. The thread between them, invisible but constant for two decades, pulled so taut Sira thought it would split her spine.

Then it snapped.

The sound was not a thread breaking. It was a soul.

Kael screamed once, a raw and empty thing, then went still.

When his eyes opened, they were clear – too clear. He looked at her like she was a stranger with dirt on her cheek.

Sira's lips curved into a smile she didn't feel. "You'll be fine," she said softly.

And she tried to believe it as the swamp wind carried the last echoes of their bond away.

* * *

The market always smelled like oranges and river mud. Kael stood by the fishmonger's stall, sleeves rolled, laughing at something the netters said about last night's storm.

The sound startled Sira. It was so light. Untethered.

She had come for salt. She stayed for the sound of him.

He glanced up mid-story and stilled – not fear, not recognition, but the look of a man catching a half-forgotten word before it slips away.

"Do I…know you?"

Her pulse jumped. Say no. Say it. "Only if you like bargains," she said, turning toward the stalls.

He followed. At the salt merchant, their hands met over the same sack.

A static hum prickled across her skin, faint but real.

Nothing visible, no lightning. But her heart kicked once, hard.

"Sorry," he said, pulling back. "Been forgetting things lately. Names. Streets. Dreams."

"Dreams don't like to be named," she said.

He smiled faintly. "There's one that keeps coming back. A field. Not grass – threads, thousands of them, stretching to the horizon. Each whispering the same name. Yours, I think. When I try to touch you…" He shook his head. "You turn to river fog."

Sira swallowed the ache and gave him the only gift she could. "Then you've got the wrong girl."

They crossed paths again two days later – small village, smaller excuses.

At the kiln, she traded willow bark for clay jars. He arrived with a carved toy horse, wheels squeaking on its axle.

"For Mara's boy," he told the potter. Then, to her, almost shy: "I thought you'd like the grain on this one."

"You're good with a knife."

"Hands remember what heads forget."

"Isn't that dangerous?"

"Maybe that's why I can't stop carving."

They left together, baskets between them. At the lane's fork, he gestured left. "I'm this way."

"I'm not."

A pause. "Would you like to be?"

She should have said no. The Severer's warning pressed cold between her ribs: When love crosses a severed bond...

But the sun was kind, and he was looking at her like a caged bird seeing sky.

"All right," she said. "For a while."

They began collecting 'for a while's the way children collect river stones.

A shared loaf beneath the fig tree. Mending a net that wasn't hers to mend. Walking the twilight road until the air turned copper.

And with every meeting, the hum returned – soft at first, then sharper. Once, after brushing against him in passing, her fingertips ached with heat for hours.

"What about you?" he asked one night when the road was empty and the only witnesses were night birds in the hedge.

"I dry herbs. Make tea for headaches, paste for burns. I listen."

"To what?"

"The space around words."

"What does it say about me?"

"That you're learning to breathe in a room with all the windows open."

He considered this. "And you?"

"That I'm still closing mine."

The dreams grew teeth.

He came to her door at dawn, hair wet, shirt crooked. "You were in it again. The field of threads. The river. A hollow tree humming like it had a heartbeat. I touched you and the roots shook."

She gripped the doorframe. "Dreams don't hurt you."

"This one does." He flexed his fingers like they still burned.

Sira touched the charm at her throat – twine and a bit of blue glass, their childhood talisman. Her pulse fluttered against it like a caught moth.

"Sometimes," she said, "dreams are just seams in the world. Best not to pull at them."

He stepped closer. "What if it's already fraying?"

That evening, the midsummer river wore jewelry – gold lanterns rocking on black water, children with sparklers, old men arguing about nothing.

Kael found her in the half-light as if there was a string tied between them. Maybe there was. Maybe there always would be.

They didn't dance at first. They stood shoulder to shoulder, watching the lanterns drift. He told her about carving spoons from storm-fallen branches. She told him about a plant that only bloomed at night.

"How do you know which branch will make a good spoon?"

"It tells you. You just have to want to hear."

The music slowed. He held out his hand – unsure, brave.

They moved like people trying not to wake something sleeping under the water. His hand found her waist as if it had always been there. Her cheek brushed his shoulder, and the hum flared – stronger this time, carrying the faint taste of iron.

His breath caught. "Sira."

She smiled a smile that knew about knives. "I know."

When he walked her home, they didn't touch again. But the hum lingered under her skin like the promise of rain.

* * *

The midsummer night should have been nothing – a dance, a river, lanterns drifting downstream. But in the week after, it rooted between them like something planted in secret.

Kael began showing up without pretense – returning a borrowed jar, asking if she knew where the fishing was good, pretending to be passing by. Sometimes they spoke in her doorway. Sometimes he stepped inside.

Once, he came in the rain, hair slick to his forehead, smelling of cedar and storm.

"I was working near the ridge," he said, setting a wrapped bundle on her table. "Saw this and thought of you."

Inside was a length of pale wood, grain curling like windblown sand.

"It's perfect for carving – soft enough for a spoon, strong enough for a handle."

Her fingers traced it before she could stop herself. The hum of the bond pulsed faintly under her skin, then spiked. She flinched.

"You all right?" he asked.

"Just a splinter," she lied, though there was no splinter – only the ghost of a thread that should have been severed.

The dreams changed.

No longer glimpses – they came whole, heavy. She stood in the field of threads, each one trembling in the windless air, each whispering her name. Kael walked toward her, the threads catching on his sleeves, staining him with silver light. When he reached for her, the air thickened like water, pulling them together and holding them there until the tree's hollow opened behind her.

In waking, she could still feel the threads dragging across her skin.

One evening on the orchard path, he stopped her with a hand on her sleeve.

"When I'm near you…there's this pull. Not like wanting something. More like remembering it."

"And if you remembered?"

"I think I'd want to keep it."

"That's dangerous talk."

He smiled faintly. "Everything worth anything is dangerous."

The first kiss came by accident – if accidents are just choices without courage.

They were mending a fishing net in her garden, the last of the evening light turning his hair to bronze. She leaned past him for the shuttle, and he turned to speak.

Their mouths brushed – barely a touch, but the hum roared through her like wind through a struck bell.

He froze, searching her face. "Sira..."

She shook her head, though her hand stayed on the edge of the net instead of pushing him away. "You don't know what you're doing."

"I know enough to know I don't want to stop."

When he kissed her again, properly this time, the bond flared hot and bright – so sharp she gasped into his mouth. He jerked back, startled.

"What was that?"

"Nothing," she lied.

But the taste of blood-slick heat was in both their mouths now.

That night, she dreamed the hollow tree again, only this time it wasn't empty. Its roots were wet with blood, and every drop carried a memory – his laughter, his hand on her cheek, his voice whispering her name in sleep. The Severer stood behind him, rune-marked fingers in the soil, smiling like someone watching two moths circle a flame.

She woke to find her pillow damp with sweat – or was it rain? The window was closed.

And somewhere across the village, Kael woke choking on a cough he hadn't had in years.

* * *

The first memory came in a dream so sharp it cut him awake.

Not the vague, watercolor dreams he'd been having for weeks. This was vivid, absolute – the smell of swamp water and smoke, a hollow tree thrumming like a drumbeat under his ribs, Sira's face streaked with rain as lightning split the sky.

When he woke, the taste of iron coated his tongue. His chest ached faintly. The cough he thought gone forever whispered at the edges.

* * *

The next day, he found her at the market, hands deep in a basket of fennel.

"Tell me what we were," he said.

Her hands stilled. "Kael—"

"I dreamt of you. And the tree. And something breaking inside me. I need you to tell me."

"Some things aren't meant to be remembered."

"That's not your choice to make."

The silence between them held the pressure of a coming storm.

She led him to her herb shed. The air was thick with drying lavender and mint.

"We were bound," she said. "Not by blood. By magic. They did it so we'd survive. We shared pain, breath, dreams. You were dying, and it was killing me too. The Severer said one of us would forget. I wanted you to remember. You chose to forget."

"And now?"

"Now you're free. Healthy. But if we keep going…" She hesitated. "The bond might come back. And it might kill us. Or both."

He took a slow step forward. "You knew this was happening."

"Yes."

"And you let me—" His voice cracked. "You let me fall in love with you again?"

Tears filled her eyes. "I've been in love with you every day since I lost you. I just didn't think I'd get another chance to breathe the same air without paying for it."

For a moment, neither moved. The scent of mint felt too sharp, too green.

"What happens if we stop?"

"You go on. You live. You carve spoons and laugh with your friends and sleep without dreams of me."

"And you?"

"I keep watching from doorways until I can't anymore."

He stepped close enough that the hum between them roared in her bones. "And if we don't stop?"

Her voice was barely a whisper. "Then we find out what kills us first – magic or time."

"Magic or time," he murmured, cupping her face. "I'd rather choose the thing that lets me keep you."

When he kissed her, the bond slammed back like a door on its hinges. Heat lanced her spine. The iron taste bloomed on both their tongues – the same sharp tang she'd swallowed in the swamp the day he forgot her.

They broke apart, breathless. His hand pressed to his chest. Her fingertips tingled painfully. Somewhere under her skin, she swore she felt the thread pulse again.

Outside, the wind rose suddenly, carrying the smell of rain from nowhere. Dark clouds knotted in the distance.

"Maybe it heals," he said.

"Maybe it kills."

"Either way," he said, voice rough, "I won't forget this time."

The first drop struck the threshold. Then another.

By the time they stepped out into the downpour, it was impossible to tell if the water on their faces was rain or the bond bleeding back into the world.

The Whisper Tree

Irene W. Collins

The first time the tree whispered her name, it came like a breath through silk.

Onaedo stirred in sleep, her lashes fluttering as the syllables unspooled around her like mist: *Ona-e-do... Onaedo...* The voice was neither male nor female, neither old nor young, and it curled around her like the scent of first rain on parched red earth.

She stood barefoot in a clearing she had never seen, yet knew in her bones. The earth pulsed beneath her feet – warm, humming, as though the land itself remembered something her waking mind had long forgotten. Before her loomed the tree.

It was massive, ancient, silver in the moonlight. Its bark shimmered with etchings that moved as she watched – glyphs and faces and patterns that reminded her of the *uli* symbols her grandmother once painted on calabashes before the river came and took her. From its branches hung vines like braided hair, each swaying, though there was no wind.

And beneath the tree, he waited.

He sat with his back against the trunk, one knee raised, clothed in what looked like cloth woven from shadows and dew. His eyes were the color of ash after fire – pale, glowing faintly, and when they met hers, something inside her chest tightened, as though a string had been plucked in the hollows of her heart.

"I've waited lifetimes," he said. Then nothing more.

She reached for him, and woke up.

The ceiling of her aunt's mud-brick house greeted her, cracked and familiar. A rooster cried. Morning light filtered through the raffia blinds. But her fingers still tingled as though she'd touched something that breathed.

* * *

She didn't speak of the dream. In Amube village, dreams were either *nonsense* or *omens*, and both were better left alone. Her aunt Mama Onya, who still left coins at the shrine by the river despite calling herself a church woman, had warned her many times not to play with 'spirit things.'

But the dream did not let go. Not that morning, nor the next.

Each night, Onaedo returned – to the whispering tree, to the silver light, to the stranger who waited and said little, only watching her as if trying to remember something from a long time ago. Sometimes, he would hum a song with no words, and the tree would sway to its rhythm.

Sometimes, she would speak, and he would listen – about her loneliness, her memories of her mother's voice, about the ache in her chest she couldn't explain. When she cried, he placed his hand on the earth between them, and the grass glowed blue.

In waking life, Onaedo began to change.

She stopped helping at the stall. She forgot to buy kerosene. She would sit for hours behind Mama Onya's compound, sketching the tree again and again in charcoal, the stranger's face taking shape with each pass. When her aunt scolded her for laziness, Onaedo smiled and said nothing.

She hid her sketches under her mattress, beneath an old wrapper and the Bible her mother had left her.

One evening, Mama Onya found her humming the dream-song beside the well. The old woman stared at her with a look Onaedo could not name – half worry, half knowing.

"You dream too much, *nne*. Dreams are not for girls with no husband," she said. "Dreams do not fill a belly."

Onaedo wanted to say, *But what if they fill the heart*? But she said nothing.

Because how could she explain what she now suspected?

That the tree was more than a dream.

That the man beneath it was more than a figment.

That each night, she was being *called*.

* * *

The second dream came heavier, like dusk slipping into her bones.

Onaedo stood again in the moonlit hush of that otherworld clearing, barefoot in dew-soaked grass, her breath weaving frost into the air. The tree was even taller now, branches arching like the ribs of a sleeping god. Its bark shimmered with faint symbols, glowing amber beneath her touch. This time, it did not whisper her name, it whispered others.

"Obianuju. Mgbeke. Nneora. Ukandu."

Ancient names. Familiar but unknown.

"They walked before you. You walk because of them."

She blinked. Her heartbeat fluttered in her throat like trapped birds. She turned, and he was there again.

The stranger from the first dream, waiting beneath the tree, knees folded, hands resting gently over each other like a priest at a shrine. His eyes were the color of ash left after sacred fire – white, yet full of heat. He wore a robe that clung to the wind, though no wind blew. His skin shimmered faintly, as if caught between worlds, candlelight flickering on water.

"You came back," she said, or thought. In dreams, the two often tangled.

"I have waited for you," he replied, in a voice like distant drums echoing through fog. "I always do."

"What is this place?" she asked, not sure she wanted an answer.

"Some call it the Between. Some call it the Remembering. But this..." He looked up into the branches where starlight threaded through leaves. "This is the Whisper Tree. It remembers all who were forgotten."

"And you? Who are you?"

He smiled then, gently. "I am Chika. I once lived, long before you. And now, I dream."

Something about the way he said her name...*Onaedo*... carried the ache of a lullaby and the weight of a funeral chant. She sat beside him without knowing why. Their arms didn't touch, but the space between them pulsed like a held breath.

"Am I dreaming you?" she whispered.

"Or am I remembering you?" he answered.

They spoke for what felt like hours, though time had little meaning there. She asked of her parents, of the flood that had taken them, of her childhood memories that came in flickers. He asked of the waking world, what music sounded like now, how the yam flowers bloomed this year, what names the children bore. When she tried to ask more of him, what village he came from, how he had died, his answers turned to riddles.

"I was born where rivers split. I died before the war you don't remember."

"What war?"

But he only turned back toward the tree and began humming a tune that stirred something deep inside her, like a lullaby her mother might have sung before the rains.

The third morning, Onaedo woke with soil beneath her fingernails and the scent of bark on her bedsheets. A single white leaf, thin as breath, lay beside her head on the pillow. She held it up to the window. It crumbled to powder in the sunlight.

Her aunt was pounding cassava outside. The mortar echoed through the compound like warning bells. Onaedo stared at her fingers. They still tingled. Her sketchbook lay open beside her bed, the Whisper Tree now drawn a dozen times in pencil, ink, and charcoal. In some pages it was burning; in others, it bled.

She hid the book under the mat before her aunt could come in.

At the village stream later that day, an old herbalist woman named Mama Isioma stopped and stared at Onaedo's drawing, which she'd accidentally dropped from her bag.

The woman's voice turned thin. "Child…where did you see this?"

"It came to me in a dream."

Mama Isioma's lips tightened. She crossed herself with a kola nut she carried. "That is the Whisper Tree. That tree grows only in the land of the forgotten dead."

Onaedo felt her stomach tilt.

"Be careful," the old woman said, not unkindly. "Some trees do not only whisper. They remember. And remembering too deeply can pull you in."

That night, she did not sleep. Not truly.

She waited.

And just before dawn, the clearing bloomed again behind her eyelids. The tree stood tall, arms open. Chika stood beneath it, his eyes soft with longing.

"I missed you," she said without shame.

His answer was a breath: "Then stay."

* * *

The night Onaedo kissed a ghost, the sky turned violet.

It began again in the hush between sleep and waking, when the mind forgets its edges. She stood beneath the whispering branches, her toes curled into silver grass. The air shimmered like a held breath. And there…as always…was Chika.

But tonight, he looked older somehow. Not in face, which remained lit by the ageless hush of twilight, but in soul. His smile was smaller. His eyes – moon-pale, rimmed with sorrow – waited longer before meeting hers.

"You're slipping," he said, his voice soft as kora strings. "The more you love me, the harder it will be to return."

Onaedo did not answer. She stepped closer instead, placing her palm against his chest. His heartbeat was slow, distant, like drums played in the next village over. Still, it beat.

"Tell me the truth," she whispered.

He closed his eyes. The wind stirred the tree, and with it, voices rose like wind-chimes, names of the old ones, the forgotten dead.

"My name," Chika said, "was the last word your mother spoke before the river took her."

Onaedo froze. The tree swayed above them. Her breath caught like a bird in a net.

"You knew her?"

"I loved her."

"No," Onaedo said, backing away. "No, that's not possible."

"I was a boy then. Seventeen. The year the river spirit rose in anger. It came to swallow the village. The gods demanded one heart."

Onaedo's hand trembled. She'd heard this story as a child, in whispers after nightfall: the great flood, the boy who vanished into the waters, nameless.

"They never said your name," she murmured.

"Because names hold memory," he said, bitter and sad. "And forgetting is the village's greatest magic."

The dream pulsed around them. The sky bruised violet. The tree leaned in, listening.

"I wasn't just offered to the spirit," Chika said. "I walked into the water willingly, because she was already drowning. I thought, if I gave enough of myself, I could hold back the river."

"But you died."

"I changed," he said. "I became part of the in-between. The roots. The remembering."

Onaedo reached for him again, this time not with fear, but aching wonder. When her lips met his, the air around them fractured like glass touched by thunder. The tree pulsed. The sky cracked open.

And in that instant, she remembered every dream at once.

She woke gasping. Her bed was soaked, not with sweat but with dew. Real dew. Moon-washed and cold. Her blanket smelled like bark. Beneath her nails, flecks of earth.

The sketches on her wall had changed. Where before the tree stood alone, now a figure sat beneath it, his back turned, silver eyes faintly glowing.

She ran to the mirror, only to find her own face blurred. She blinked. Focused. It cleared.

But when her aunt called her from outside, Onaedo hesitated before answering. The name felt distant.

Later, she sat in the herbalist's shrine, silent, trembling. The old woman stared at the sketch Onaedo had brought – the newest one, drawn not with pencil but with charcoal scraped from the hearth.

"You've seen the Whisper Tree?" the woman asked, voice barely above a hiss.

Onaedo nodded.

"You should not have gone," the woman said. "That tree only grows in the land of the forgotten dead. It does not whisper, it remembers. And once it remembers you, it will not let go."

Onaedo tried to speak, but her mouth was dry. The herbs hanging from the rafters seemed to wilt in the silence. Somewhere behind them, a gourd cracked with no one touching it.

"I thought I was dreaming," Onaedo whispered.

"You were. And you weren't," the herbalist replied. "The spirits choose those who still listen. Your mother heard, once. And now you carry her silence."

Outside, thunder murmured on the horizon. A storm was coming, slow and certain. The past rising like water. And in the pit of her stomach, Onaedo knew: she wasn't only dreaming of Chika – she was remembering him.

And the remembering had only just begun.

Therefore dreams come faster now. No longer just at night. At the market, Onaedo touches a cowrie bead and sees the Whisper Tree blooming in her mind's eye. In the kitchen, the smell of boiling yam fades, replaced by the soft rustle of dream-leaves and the sound of drums rising from roots.

Chika stands beneath the tree, wrapped in twilight. His presence is different this time. Still radiant, still burning with some memory of breath, but quieter, heavier, as if he carries the weight of a goodbye.

"You must choose," he says, and his voice carries the hush of wind through the hollows of bones. "The tree blooms once more. After that, the door closes. Either you come fully…or you forget."

She doesn't answer. Not yet. But her heart already leans.

By daylight, Onaedo walks to the riverbank where her dreams always begin. The soil is soft beneath her bare feet, soaked with August rains. And there, nestled beside the mangroves, is a tree stump, half-eaten by time.

She kneels. Her fingers trace the spiraled rings of wood, cracked and crumbling, but familiar.

She knows this shape.

She's drawn it over and over in her notebooks. Not from life. Not from memory. But from the other place – the dreaming.

The Whisper Tree was real. It once stood here, rooted in the waking world, before time or tongues forgot.

That evening, she returns home late, hair wet with dew though the sky held no rain.

Aunt Onya waits by the hearth, arms crossed, eyes hard with fear and something more fragile.

"I was going to tell you," she says. "When you were older. When it wouldn't matter."

Onaedo sits on the floor. Something inside her already knows.

"You were born after your mother's first child died," her aunt says. "She was eight months pregnant when she went into labour. The baby was lost. Your mother nearly followed."

Silence.

"But in her fever, she kept whispering one thing again and again. 'He's coming back for her.'"

Onaedo's mouth dries.

"He who?"

"I don't know," her aunt says. "But she said it like a vow. Like a truth older than words."

In the dream, she returns to the tree, but this time the air is thick with transition. Petals bloom like moonlight from every branch. The leaves hum.

She touches her own chest and feels it: time is bending.

She is no longer just Onaedo.

She is the echo of someone who once loved.

She is the breath of a promise made between death and dawn.

And Chika waits for her with both sorrow and hope in his eyes. His hand is outstretched. The bark of the tree pulses beneath their feet like a heartbeat remembered.

"You were never just dreaming," he says.

"I know."

"If you cross, you will never wake again in the world of clay and dust."

"I know."

"Your name will fall from their mouths. You will vanish from memory."

"I know."

"And still?"

She reaches for him.

But just before their fingers meet, she hears her name… whispered like a cry…from the real world.

She turns.

Sees the faintest image of her aunt, kneeling beside her real body, praying, weeping.

Onaedo stands between two worlds – spirit and skin, longing and lineage.

One step, and she is his forever.

One breath, and she wakes, alone.

* * *

She doesn't choose.

Not yet.

Instead, she opens her eyes with tears blooming in her lashes, the scent of bark still in her hair, and her heart a pendulum between centuries.

But she knows the tree will bloom once more.

And when it does, it will not wait.

* * *

The moon hung low, wide as a watcher's eye, over the clearing where the whispering tree had always lived – in dreams, in sketches, in shadows cast by memory. Tonight, it stood full once more, branches glowing with soft white blooms, petals trembling like breath.

Onaedo stepped forward barefoot, the dream pressing against her skin like warm wind. She wore the wrapper her mother had once hemmed for her, the one that always felt too old, too sacred. The fabric fluttered, stitched with whispers.

Chika stood beneath the tree, radiant in a quiet, impossible way – like starlight held in human form. His eyes shone with sadness and hope. The air shimmered between them.

"All things," he said, voice hushed as rustling leaves, "must root or wither. It is time, Ona."

From every branch, the voices of ancestors rose. Some mourned. Some hummed songs her mother once sang while grinding ogbono. Others called her name the way her father had when she was learning to walk – *Nne, nwam, come home.*

But which home?

Onaedo's heart beat hard against her ribs. She reached for Chika. His hand was warm. Real. She remembered the first time he had kissed her, how the sky had turned the color of bruised plums, how the tree had pulsed like a second heart. That kiss had bent time. This one would bind it.

She leaned forward.

Their lips met, soft and searing, a farewell cradled in longing.

Then she pulled away.

Chika blinked. His smile didn't fade, but something in it fractured.

"I will always love you," she whispered. "Even if I forget the sound of your voice. Even if I grow old and no one believes this ever happened. I will carry you in the songs I sing to my child."

His eyes glistened. "Then I will bloom where your memory allows me."

As the words left him, the tree's petals began to fall – slow, weightless, like ashes. The clearing dimmed. The soil sighed. And everything folded inward.

She awoke with a gasp, curled on the floor of her room. The sketchbook lay open beside her. Pages fluttered in a wind that wasn't there.

She reached to close it.

It caught fire in her hands.

The flames did not burn. They kissed her skin like goodbye.

By morning, nothing remained of the book. Not the tree. Not Chika's face. Only the scent of smoked jasmine in the air.

Her aunt found her staring at the window. "Are you well?"

Onaedo smiled, the kind of smile that held both ache and peace.

"I'm here," she said.

Life stitched itself back together. Slowly. She returned to church. She learned her cousin's name again. She helped her aunt harvest yams, laughed when goats stole the cassava peels, sang lullabies to herself as she swept the compound at dusk.

And then, one night, years later, with her daughter cradled against her chest, she hummed a tune no one had ever taught her. A melody like wind in leaves. Like a name forgotten and found again. The baby cooed, reaching up as if to pluck stars.

Onaedo sang softer, words blooming in her mouth: *Ndo, my love. Sleep deep, my seed. Beneath the tree where dreams still feed…*

Far off, at the old riverbank, a stump sat where no one remembered planting a tree. Moss-covered. Weathered.

Under the moonlight, it glowed – faint and pulsing, then bloomed.

Just once.

The Silent War

K.S. Dearsley

Rachel woke with a sense of loss. The familiar objects in the bedroom were just beginning to be edged with light. The wardrobes, the dressing table, the chair; all were in their place. Beside her, Bob was breathing evenly, peacefully asleep. If she moved closer, Rachel knew his arms would automatically curl around her and he would snuggle up until they fitted together like two pieces of a jigsaw puzzle. Rachel needed the security of being held in his arms, but did not move. She tried to push away the thoughts that had haunted her waking moments for the past two days and relax back into sleep. That was the only place she was able to find peace. Her dream had been full of it; peace and contentment.

There had been deep, undisturbed snow around a straggling village of wooden houses, turning the countryside to monochrome. Only the village inhabitants had given the place colour. Rachel had watched them as if through a telescope, seeing a dog barking and the puff of frozen breath, but hearing nothing. Yet she felt the sharp cold of the frosty fields and the pale warmth of a sun only an hour or two above the horizon on her back.

A fair-haired girl, Rachel thought she could be no more than sixteen or seventeen, stood with her arms folded across her middle, wrapped in a rough woollen cloak, watching the empty countryside. It was her back that felt the warmth, and Rachel knew that what she saw and felt was what the girl saw and felt, although she was apart.

One or two hens pecked hopefully in the muddy area outside the stable where the girl stood, but she was hardly aware of them. Rachel felt the girl's surge of excitement as a group of figures emerged from a distant stand of trees. The girl cried out and, heedless of the snow, ran to meet them while the other villagers looked on with shaded eyes.

A rider broke away from the rest of the group and cantered towards her. The chestnut horse laboured as if running through deep water. Rachel's heart jumped as the two met. The bearded rider had a smile to break hearts. Rachel imagined she heard his laugh as he swung the girl up to sit before him. She nestled against him, her eyes never leaving his face. He teased her, pulling her plait, and told her all that had happened since he had left. Although Rachel could not hear them, she knew he had returned from the hunt successful.

And then they were in the house, beside a silent fire which scorched Rachel's cheeks, as she slowly relieved the rider of his clothes. He smelled warm and clean. The girl ran her hand lightly over his now bare chest, and Rachel felt her fingertips tingle. He smiled lopsidedly, then undid the girl's long plait with shaking hands. Rachel became aware of the soft touch of fur, and realised she was sitting on a couch covered in skins. The girl was trying to tell her husband something, but he was covering her face with kisses and would not listen.

"Later," Rachel knew he said.

The girl laughed and told him, "Later you'll be asleep."

With a certainty that needed neither the look of awe on the man's face, nor the gentle kiss he placed on her forehead for confirmation, Rachel knew the girl was pregnant. They lay back in each other's arms, and their happiness was hers.

* * *

The touch of a real arm around her made Rachel tense like a sudden drawing in of air.

"Can't you sleep?" Bob was looking at her with serious eyes. Returning his gaze, Rachel felt a twist of pain.

"How long have you been awake?" She spoke sharply, unhappy at being caught out.

"Only a minute or two. I was watching you."

Rachel felt unable to cope with the plea she saw in his face. "I might as well get up. It's almost time now, anyway."

Bob withdrew his arm. Not daring to look at him, Rachel rose.

"I'll bring you some coffee."

"There's no need." Bob turned over, so his back was towards her, and pulled the covers more tightly around him.

In the kitchen Rachel tried to be businesslike, but she got no further than filling the kettle before her thoughts stopped her. She gazed out of the window, at the slowly lightening sky. Her coldness hurt Bob terribly. Touch had always played such an important part in their relationship. The comfort of feeling another back pressed against hers at night, holding hands when they went shopping.

Her fingers touched the place on her right breast. There was nothing to be seen, but she could feel it. She could not let Bob touch her. If he did, he would know, and she could not cope with that. Not yet, perhaps never. Never might not be so far away, she thought with a shiver. If she did not find the courage to do something soon, there might not be a decision for her to make. She had always thought the women who tried to hide from reality, instead of seeing a doctor, such fools. Now Rachel was faced with the situation, all she could think of was Bob looking at her, incomplete. She would rather leave him than face that.

* * *

Rachel tried to make small-talk with Bob over the breakfast table, but his answers were kept to the minimum. Only a restoration of physical contact could dispel the barrier of coldness she had placed between them.

Throughout the day, Rachel struggled with the problem. All she had to do was pick up the telephone and make an appointment. Somehow, she could not bring herself to do it; she could call in at the surgery on the way home.

When the time came, Rachel found that that was equally as bad. She walked up and down the road outside. Mentally, she argued with and insulted herself, but by the time she had worked up sufficient courage to go in, she found her feet had already taken her home. The battered sports car that was Bob's pride and joy was already standing on the drive, and Rachel knew another layer of ice would have formed between them.

"Hello! Sorry I'm late, I missed the bus." Rachel was conscious of the lie, and could tell by the look on Bob's face that it showed.

"I'll put the supper on."

"Rachel, I think we…"

"Yes, in a minute. Let me get organised."

It was easy to find ways of not being organised all evening. After supper there were the dishes, then ironing. Finally, Bob gave up and went to bed.

"Coming?"

"In a minute."

The way he shrugged and the heaviness in his step as he went upstairs brought Rachel to the edge of tears. She sat on the sofa with her legs drawn up, like a foetus, and tried to think of happy outcomes. Gradually, her arms relaxed around her knees.

* * *

The air had lost its bite. Where there had been snow there was now grass and a scattering of delicate flowers. The girl stooped and picked one. She held it to her nose, but Rachel could catch no scent. Of course, it was a buttercup, a vibrant coin of gold without perfume. Rachel felt a heaviness that was new to her. Looking down with the girl's eyes she realised the difference the few months from deep winter to spring had made to her figure. But the heaviness was more than just the growing child.

The girl let the flower slip from her fingers as she gazed into the distance. No riders appeared. Only a crow, flapping purposefully across the spring sky, disturbed the stillness. The watchfulness was different now, Rachel could sense an air of waiting hanging over the settlement. This time the men were not on a hunt.

* * *

"Rachel!" Bob had only shaken her gently, but Rachel jumped as if she had been slapped. "You can't sleep down here."

For a moment, Rachel was not sure where she was. Bob reached out to help her up, but she knocked his hand away.

"No!"

Bob sat back on his haunches, his face a mixture of emotions. "If you don't want to share our bed, I'll move out of it."

"Don't be silly!" Even Rachel didn't know why she was so angry.

"Is it silly? Something's wrong."

"You're imagining things."

Bob reached out to touch Rachel's cheek. Involuntarily, she pulled away. "Of course."

"There's nothing wrong. I'm just tired."

"Come to bed then."

Rachel hesitated.

"Whatever it is, we ought to talk about it. I'm a big boy, you know. I can cope with bad news."

The tension boiled over. How could he blithely say he could cope, when she could not?

"For goodness sake, leave me alone! All I need is some sleep."

Bob nodded. "Whatever you say."

He left the room, and a moment later Rachel could hear him moving about upstairs. She waited until there was silence, then followed. Bob's pillow was missing from their empty bed. Without undressing, Rachel crawled onto the bed. Hugging the pillow that was left, she cried herself to sleep.

* * *

Almost immediately, Rachel was back in the village. If it had not been for the fact that the grass was taller it would have seemed that no time had passed. Then Rachel noticed the girl. She was standing outside the stable where Rachel had first seen her, clutching at her gown where her heart thudded against her ribs. She felt no excitement, only an almost unbearable tension.

From over the horizon there rose a curly black wire of smoke. Instinct told her this was no camp fire, no cosy friend to cook on, or stretch her hands out to. This was the smoke of war. All she could do was wait, while the sun climbed higher in the sky, as if nothing was wrong.

Rachel felt as if she had stood there, inside and outside the girl, all her life, yet the shadows were still short when the first of them began to arrive. Men, weary and stumbling. Some with bloody rags tied to wounds, some using their comrades as crutches, some borne on makeshift stretchers about to see their homes for the last time. The girl could no longer run to meet them, her figure was too cumbersome, but she scanned each face anxiously.

Rachel imagined her questions.

"Where's my husband? You must have seen him, riding a chestnut horse. You must have seen him!"

Each one shook his head, too tired to feel pity. They had won, as far as a battle is ever won, and they had strength for nothing more. With the passing of each one the girl felt more numb. She was hardly even aware when her knees gave way, that she was on the ground. All her energy and youth seemed to flow away from her.

"No! No! You mustn't give up!" Rachel heard her dream self shouting. No one gave any sign that she had made a noise.

Suddenly Rachel felt herself soaring upwards. The village and all that surrounded it looked as if they were drawings on a map. All Rachel had to do was think of it, and she was speeding in the direction of the smoke. When she was above it, she slowly wheeled and circled downwards, feeling herself to be a huge black bird with powerful wings.

Rachel felt eyes on her, though she knew his thoughts were far away with the flaxen-haired wife who was soon to bear his child. He would have struggled to free himself of his horse which pinned him where the berserker's knife had felled it, but he was tired and his crushed leg no longer hurt. Only the great black bird kept him from slipping away. He did not want his pretty wife to see him after the scavengers had found him.

It was impossible, but Rachel was in two places at once; hovering over the fallen rider, and shrieking abuse at his numbed wife. She tried shaking her, but could not grasp her.

"I know where he is! What's the matter with you? You're afraid of what you'll find, aren't you? I know what that's like, it's the worst thing in the world. You must do something or it'll be too late!"

The girl stirred, as if she had felt a fresh breeze, and looked about her. With an agility that astonished Rachel, she got up and ran into the village. People were milling about, tending the wounded, resting. The girl chivvied and pulled at them, until two of the villagers got up and followed her.

* * *

There was a tremendous release. Rachel's jaws ached where she had clenched her teeth. Her limbs felt weak and shaky, but she was happy. It would be all right now. The girl would find her husband. Their winters would be spent together in front of the fire. Rachel felt it all as if it was recorded history, rather than a troubled dream. The girl had found the courage to act.

* * *

Without pausing to think what she would say, Rachel padded through to the spare room. The instant she stepped through the door, Bob's eyes opened. Rachel knelt at the side of the bed and took his hands in hers.

"I don't know how to tell you."

"Just say 'I don't love you any more'."

Caught between laughter and tears, Rachel could only shake her head. With a calmness she had not thought possible, she placed Bob's hand on the lump. Understanding leapt into his eyes.

"It's going to be all right," Rachel said, suddenly confident that it was the truth. "It's going to be all right."

The Glass Ghost

H.L. Docherty

Like all dreams, this one had no beginning.

An acoustic guitar's musical notes tasted of honey and held the earthy scent of wildflower meadows. Ahead, a stone bridge arched a churning river devoid of sound. Same bridge, different life. The same terrifying tug-of-war between longing and caution.

I tried to use my magic – to teleport away from this place in a blink. It didn't work here – proof enough I was dreaming. Out there in reality, magic was a death sentence. Here, it wasn't allowed. I scoffed. Regardless, others controlled my magic, be it government or Fate.

The music coaxed me forward like an invisible string, each step glowing with a white light refracting in faint rainbows. I paused at the weathered bridgehead, heart clattering.

Beyond it was a choice my soul recognised: remain, or step forward towards someone Fate had shackled me to. My chest ached. Every time I'd crossed bridges like this in other lives, I was left burying a body. Over the years, I'd fractured. Became broken and bitter from the same ruin Fate had dealt me time and time again. Perhaps it had been too much to hope that in this life I'd be spared.

I'd rather have faced a firing squad than this bridge.

Still, there was an easy lie to believe; the air tasted sweeter when I stood at the edge. I could pretend the other side was everything I'd ever wanted.

The melodic notes formed silver droplets of rain that didn't touch me, drumming off cobblestones that hadn't existed mere moments ago. The deluge painted a landscape until I stood alone in a city resembling my own – colourless concrete high-rises that sparkled like stars.

An imitation, yet home nonetheless.

The notion was absurd; I hadn't had a real home in a hundred years. But as lamplight blurred the city into pewters and golds, I fantasised this could be.

Perhaps I didn't need reality; dreams would be enough.

Foolishly, I told myself that this time, the man beyond the bridge might bind his soul to mine forever.

Love or ruin. That was always the choice.

I'd only ever found ruin. Still, I stepped forward—

I jolted awake. Gooseflesh thundered over my skin as my body registered the rupture of Fated magic.

I inhaled the calming scent of lilacs on my bedside table until my grip loosened on the silk sheets. Above me, chandeliers reflected muted sunlight struggling through the morning clouds.

I hauled the blanket over my head to stop the spiral. My life was perfect; I was Elite, adopted from the slum streets to nanny for the richest people in the country – the closest thing I had to family. In exchange for my services, my reality was diamonds and mansions and gold.

And with one step over that bridge, I had ruined it all.

* * *

The dreams he haunted didn't happen often at first. Within them was a land unlike anything I had witnessed in my polished life. His music painted faceless people who filled every crevice. It rendered the mountains, meadows, woodland, and marketplaces. Beyond the dreamscape bridge, I explored his world, ignoring the pull that led to him.

He lived a life untouched by me. I lived a life wondering what might've been; experience had taught me the *if-onlys* were sweeter than knowing. As long as we didn't touch, nothing could begin or end. I kept my distance, living in the optimistic warmth of his dream-world.

In waking life, I found myself staring off into nothing for too long when tidying the children's playroom. The ache to know seared through every muscle, every nerve, until resisting his pull drowned me in a sea of *not knowing*.

It took a year for me to give in.

Risking everything, I teleported along the golden thread connecting us, and ended up not in a vibrant market of colour, but in a slum.

Cobbled together with rusted metal and rotted wood, a concrete building stretched ahead, each level precariously balanced on the next with laundry hanging from its upper floors. Sprawled before it was a shanty awning, creating a marketplace that held nothing in comparison to the oil-painted scene in my dreams. I'd come looking for that dream, but once again, my curiosity had killed it.

In my finery, I stood out like a diamond in coal. Breath clouding in the frozen air, I covered my nose to evade the stench of sewage. Stepping away from a questionably yellow puddle, a man with unwashed hair blocked my way, flashing a gap-toothed grin.

"You're far too pretty to be hangin' round here on your own." He stepped closer, and I nearly gagged on the stench of his breath. "How about you hand over that bracelet, and I help you out?"

My lungs seized. I had nowhere to go without turning my back on him, and I could hardly be spotted teleporting away.

A second man – a teen no older than me – appeared, towering over the first. His solid frame was relaxed, yet the way he slammed his hand onto the first man's shoulder suggested he was anything but.

"Ian, I need a super illegal favour—" He stopped, Fate shoving me into his peripheral.

When his gaze met mine, my world came apart.

The silver lighting his eyes was the same silver that painted my dreamscapes. No doubt, the guitar strapped to his back created my melodies. A giddy panic rose from my stomach. Fate had outdone herself with him – handsome, creative… and doomed.

His grey eyes narrowed, perfect lips pulling back into a snarl. That was all it took to know this man would one day kill me.

Seizing my arm, he dragged me away from the crowd. While I was brazen enough to teleport here, I was unskilled at teleporting *out* of someone's grasp.

"Let go of me!" I writhed against him, clawing at his face and neck. "Get the fuck off me!"

He shoved me down an alleyway and rubbed at the red gouges I'd left upon his pale skin. "You gotta death wish? What are you doing here dressed in *that*?"

My jaw slackened. "Your concern is with my clothes?"

His brows drew together. "You think I make it a habit of dragging tiny women into alleyways? Yeah, your clothes – you're gonna get mugged here."

I blinked; he had no notion of who I was.

That meant he held no magic.

That was new.

He stepped close enough that his shadow swallowed me. "What's Elite scum like you doing in the slums anyway?"

I opened my mouth. Closed it. I pretended to belong with the Elites, yet I didn't; the right family found me on the right street. But I didn't belong here either. I was the bridge in my dreams – stuck between two worlds and belonging to neither.

Flashing a smile and using a charm offensive worked on normal men. Wholly unprepared for him, I spun on my heels, trying to hold my balance on cobblestones which were unlike the clouds I'd grown accustomed to walking on in my dreams.

"Whoa!" He ducked under an awning to reach me. "You don't need to run off. I didn't mean to scare you or nothin', you just have to be careful here."

"Yes, quite clearly." My face burned, finding the end of the alley he'd trapped me in.

He rubbed the back of his neck, a coy smile stretching over his face, and he looked down at his well-worn boots. "Yeah, okay. Maybe calling Elite scum *scum* to their face wasn't smart."

I blinked, unsure what to do with that.

"I'm not Elite." It was technically true. "I'm…not from here."

He raised an eyebrow. "What's your name?"

Coming here was dangerous. Imbecilic. Juvenile.

Pushing past him, I rushed from the deserted alleyway. He still called after me.

Rounding the corner, in the blink of an eye I was gone.

* * *

My dream that night was different. There was no bridge. No platinums and golds of my city or oil-painted marketplaces laced with meadows. Black stretched endlessly, lit only by a prism that followed me like a shadow.

And another light.

This one was darker. Glowing red. It smouldered.

Embers and smoke bound into the outline of a body, bleeding heat into the air. He had no discernible features apart from his shape. The maroon glow inside him pulsed with each note he coaxed from the guitar in his lap, spreading to me. The refracted light around me danced.

He stopped playing when I approached. "What are you?"

I arched a brow, surprised he could see me. "What do you think I am?"

He chuckled, playing a fresh tune. "A ghost, maybe."

"Yes, I think that's accurate." My lips pressed tight.

"How'd you die?"

"Which time?"

"You died more than once?"

My laugh came out cold. "I've died many times."

His fingers stilled on the guitar, yet his melody carried in the air, wrapping me like a blanket. The closer I came, the more detail emerged in the embers – his narrow eyes, the rise and fall of his chest, the curve of a mouth I'd never touch.

"That sucks. Who killed you?"

I was silent for seconds, minutes, hours. Who knew? There was no *time* here.

Eventually, I said, "People like you."

I awoke, staring at the frescoed ceiling, quite sure he would never return.

How wrong I was.

The very next night, argent semiquavers and crotchets inked a forest, painting trees which dripped gold. He was sitting cross-legged beneath one with his guitar.

"What's *people like you* mean?" he said at once.

I smiled. "You're like a dog with a bone."

"You left halfway through a conversation. Rude if you ask me."

My laugh here was musical.

"Well?" he pressed.

He couldn't judge me, couldn't tell the guard about my magic, they couldn't drag me to the gallows; I was a ghost.

"I find people in my dreams. Most of the time, they turn out to be bad people."

He brushed off the severity of my words, more intrigued by my magic. "That's cool. I know a couple of people with magic. Nothin' as good as walking in people's dreams, mind."

He went back to playing, though the melody in the air didn't match the chords his hands were making.

"You're not playing." I folded myself onto the ground opposite him.

"Apparently, I don't need to here." He smiled. "Plus, I'm still pretty shit. Since I turned sixteen I've been forced into work camps so don't get much time to practise." Sparks skittered where he ground his teeth. "I swear, I don't sound as good as whatever this place is making me out to be."

"Do you glare at the strings until the notes sound good?"

It was a pathetic attempt to brighten his mood, yet it succeeded. He narrowed his ember-lit eyes, and the next chord he played was so discordant I choked on a laugh.

He sang, or more accurately, yowled like a cat, until I was forced to cover my ears.

"That should be illegal."

"You've got no taste." He leaned forward until the tips of his smoke-edged fingers hovered just shy of my knees. "I could teach you."

"I hated guitar. The strings hurt my fingers."

He grinned. "Wimp."

"You're full of compliments, aren't you?"

"You took the piss outta my playing; as far as I'm concerned, you earned it."

With that, he launched into a rendition wildly off-key. I couldn't help giggling again.

For the first time, I was sad to wake.

* * *

The desperate need to see him had grown into a fire that consumed me. But to risk meeting in reality was foolish. The class discrepancy between us, the fact he was a mortal, and I had magical blood all meant that even if he didn't seek my destruction, we still couldn't be together.

So I let the searing ache consume me and waited for sleep.

But Fate had a tricky sense of humour. She provided me with no more dreams.

Another year passed with no cityscapes of silver. No guitar melodies. No him.

My resolve crumbled once again.

The moment I arrived in his wretched market, I spotted him across the cobblestones, busking with an older man who was so much his double, I assumed him his father. As I neared, I spotted a little girl with his matching auburn hair. She sang a sweet tune to the crowd while he harmonised.

My dream man ignored the presence of soldiers in uniforms of grey and navy, his rusty hair hung across his face. Even without their guns, the way people flinched at the guard told me everything. But the music numbed their chaos. In dreams, his playing painted worlds. Here, it did much the same, his voice smouldering. He'd lied about his talent, or perhaps he simply didn't know how good he was.

Like the first time I'd come here, his steely eyes found mine without provocation. Then they darted to my left. I followed his gaze to a guard with narrowed time-creased eyes and lips pressed flat.

"You all right, Miss?"

To my right, the unmissable sound of a guitar being dropped echoed. My dream man was between me and the soldier before my words formed.

"She's not from here." His voice was a menacing growl. "Leave her alone."

The guard raised an eyebrow. "You giving me orders, boy?"

The steel in his eyes flashed, fists curling in a way that suggested he was about to say something monumentally reckless. I grasped his arm, and his mouth snapped shut.

"I'm lost." I said to the guard, letting relief soften my features. "Would you escort me to the main road? I'd feel much safer."

But the dream man's arm cinched my waist, muttering against my temple, "You gonna tell me your name yet, stranger?"

Butterflies fluttered through me; he didn't recognise me from our dreams.

I winked and stepped towards the guard, allowing myself to be led away.

At the market gates, the soldier spoke, and a glacier formed in my stomach. "Don't you work for the governor?"

I started. "That would be nice, wouldn't it? You know? I do think my purse has been stolen."

When he turned back to the marketplace, I blinked into oblivion.

* * *

I caught myself humming as I straightened my youngest boy's tie – the same melody that my dream man had played each time we met in our space between worlds. Three years had passed like this: a handful of scattershot encounters in the waking world. I'd learnt to blend in. Rougher clothes, emptier pockets, an invented accent that matched his. I never gave him my name. I never asked for his.

In dreams, I wasn't as careful. He couldn't see me, not in our world of flowing mercurial music where I danced, sang, and wove rivers from wildflowers. There, I was more *me* than I'd allowed myself to be with anyone for years.

I lived.

"That's a pretty song," the child said, vying for the attention I always showered him with.

"Thank you." I continued the tune, mind back in a land of moonlit rivers and invisible rain.

The eldest practised piano, notes bleeding into my daydream. I corrected his finger on the keys and—

An invisible weight slammed into my chest, murdering my tune and stealing my breath. I staggered as the world tilted, and my boys looked up, their foreheads puckering.

"Are you all right?" the eldest asked.

"Yes – I mean – I'm a bit dizzy. Can you mind your little brother if I lie down?"

"Of course." He smiled in a way which indicated he was about to torment his sibling for the time I was away, but my thoughts had scattered to the wind.

Only one thing filled my head.

My Fated match was in danger. I knew the sensation. I'd felt it before, yet this wasn't like the others who had come before him. To let him die – living without half of me – the world swam again, whitewashing out my vision at the edges.

The moment my bedroom door closed behind me, I blinked along our golden thread.

My next inhale was of smoke.

Shouts ricocheted between stalls of the market, chased by the thunder of boots on wet cobblestones. Not wet with water. Slick with blood. Somewhere close by, gunfire ricocheted off the concrete building.

Through the chaos, auburn hair and storm-tossed eyes caught my full attention. A snarl twisted his mouth – murder in his eyes – before he lunged at a guard. He moved like a force of nature, hands closing around the soldier's rifle as if he could hold a bullet back with his bare hands.

The soldier drove the butt of their rifle into his face, knocking him flat. His father swung for the guard, flattening him into unconsciousness.

"Get your sister home!" his father shouted, rushing off into the crowd to try to intercept another beating.

Without thought of my finery, I shoved through the tangle of bodies. When I reached him, I saw that blood streaked from his temple to his jaw. I heaved him by the arm. His balance swayed into mine until we reached the cover of a narrow alley, the noise muffling behind us.

"Are you all right?" I asked.

He pressed the heel of his hand to his brow, smearing the blood. "I've been worse. This happens all the time. First time I tried fighting back though."

"Oh." That was why I'd felt him in danger.

He raked his gaze over me, noticing that my clothes were far too rich for where we were. "You shouldn't be here."

I swallowed and brushed my thumb through the blood at his temple to see the wound beneath.

He stilled under the contact, flashing a crooked smile, though his eyes remained cold. "You save people as a hobby, or am I special?"

I stepped back before the bond could pull me any closer. He captured my hand in his. For a moment, the riot felt far away, like the dreams but not. Reality smelled of copper and refuse, not pine and wildflowers, and the air was filled with screams, not guitar melodies.

Someone shouted nearby, and his gaze slid past me, back toward the chaos.

"I gotta go," he said. "Don't come back, you're not safe here."

I nodded, a piece of me breaking away.

He hesitated to release my hand, then pushed away from the wall and melted into the crowd. He shouted at the auburn haired girl, no older than twelve, who was being shuffled out of harm's way by the crowd.

Every guard was paid by the same people who dressed my bed in silk, while these people bled in the streets. My comforts were built on the ruin of this place, and that weight was heavier now than it had ever been.

I couldn't find it in myself to leave. Instead, I let the screams drown me.

* * *

Weeks went by. We next met in dreams. There was no music. Only silver drizzle which never touched the ground.

He was waiting in a shadowed alley where the walls bled, and the marketplace bleached to greys and browns. Food rotted in baskets, iron and smoke choking as it curled in the back of my throat. Whatever magic enriched this place had bled away. He leaned close enough that the heat of his smouldering form caressed my skin.

Like this, he was a roaring blaze.

I swallowed. "What's wrong?"

"Someone got shot dead in the marketplace today." His fire glowed brighter. "A mate of mine."

I gasped, reaching for him before I could think better of it. My hand cupped his cheek, rubbing a thumb beneath his eye, though no tears fell. He didn't burn me, nor did he shy away from the touch. Rather, he leaned into me as though I were the flame and he were a moth.

"I wanna live in here. I fucking hate it out there. Elites treat us like slaves then kill us, just because we live on the wrong side of a wall." His voice was hoarse. "And there's a girl out there – she's one of them. I don't see her a lot – I think she avoids me. But then, she doesn't. She finds me. She's there and she's funny and stuck up and looks at me all cute with big blue eyes."

A lump grew in my throat.

"But she's one of them."

"Why does that matter?" I begged for my fantasy to remain intact after he spoke. Begged that he wouldn't ruin the fragile peace that had taken so many years to garner.

"Because one day, I'll burn her city down. I don't think she'll like that."

My voice withered to a whisper, hand dropping to my side. "I don't think she will either."

Like our dreams were prophetic, fire spread from him, burning the city behind me to nothing but cinders. Only then did his world colour. Only then did the silver rain's magic restore the marketplace to its beauty.

The meaning was clear: for his world to thrive, mine needed to be destroyed.

Ice curled around my lungs. I squashed the sensation until my fear tasted like wildflowers and honey again.

He didn't move away. The blaze inside him wavered, light flickering through the cracks of his silhouette until it was softer.

"Strange thing, though." The coals of his eyes narrowed. "When I'm here with you, it's like she's here. Except she's real, and you're a weird glass ghost."

I chuckled. "A glass ghost?"

"Yeah, like a broken window or something. But you make light."

He pointed to the prisms on the pewter cobblestones.

It was me.

"Oh."

His head tilted. "You've been smashed to hells, but the cracks glow. Not in a pretty way – in a *warning* way. Like you'll probably cut me if I don't stay away."

I huffed a laugh. "You've got a talent for flattery."

"Didn't say it was bad." His gaze dragged over me. "I can't stop looking. Maybe that's why you remind me of her."

The air thickened, hot with his blaze and the pull between us. I stepped closer, because here, I could, and the light inside my fractures pushed into the heat coming off him.

His hand came up to my face.

"Do I cut you?" I asked.

"No." He let his thumb float across my cheekbone. "You feel warm." He paused. "Not a ghost. Alive."

The heat between us swelled until I could feel it over every inch of my skin. If he burned my city, it was foolish to believe he would spare me. But for now, he tilted his head, caught in the same pull that had wrecked me for years. His other hand slid into my hair. I pressed onto my tiptoes, and he dipped his chin, his lips meeting mine with a sensation that could have destroyed worlds.

The blaze inside him seared into me until my light burst free. I grabbed hold of the front of what must have been his shirt, dragging him closer until there was nothing between us. Greed sharpened into something desperate; he tasted of smoke and honey and freedom. His hands curved over my hips, brushing the light spilling through me, mapping the places I came apart.

Rain hissed into steam where it finally touched us. The silver cobblestones flared brighter under our feet, scattering prisms far and wide. His blaze longed for destruction. I felt its hunger. But the light pouring from my cracks caught the flames, binding them to me, refusing to let them spill. I was stopping them. Holding them.

When he pulled back, his forehead stayed against mine. "Are you real?"

I swallowed, heart breaking in two. "I'm real here."

"Then let's stay here."

I had spent lifetimes running from the ruin he promised. But if ruin was my fate, then I would shape the flames. Teach him restraint.

Even if I had to trade riches and family for bloodstained cobblestones, I chose him.

"What if I could be real out there?"

His wicked grin dazzled. "Then you're stuck with me forever."

"Until the fire takes us, darling." I curled myself around him. "And when that happens, I'll keep you safe and sound, I promise."

"I'm Ben." He brushed his lips to mine.

I took a steadying breath. "I'm Magdalena."

No Regrets

Philip Brian Hall

Hell is other people, the philosopher Sartre once said. But I don't think he was right. You see, for the average Joe and Jill, Hell involves nothing more than a life of missing out. We are just timid people who recognise opportunities but are afraid to take them. And it isn't other people who reproach us. How could they? They've no idea of what we've not done.

No. We blame ourselves. We make our own Hell. It's called Regret. "If only," we sigh, looking back wistfully, when it's too late, and our dreary life has continued along its regular, unromantic course towards the grave.

For most of us, it wasn't that we failed to do something big – say, contribute to world peace or the sum of human happiness. No. More than likely, we just passed up some forbidden fun. And rather than enjoy ourselves at the time, we settled, as usual, for fantasies about what might have been.

And why, you ask? I'll tell you. It was a premonition of the guilt we'd feel afterwards. A relic of our ancestors' puritanism. "Thus conscience does make cowards of us all," as the guy says in the play. Our imaginations are a safe, private place for all manner of sinful conduct, but our reality is stalked by fear.

Well, my friends, I'm here to tell you it needn't be so. Not any more. Carlos, head barman on the lunar cruise ship *Lethe,* has the solution. He has perfected an extraordinary nanobot-based liqueur that he's named, in honour of the Greek legend, *The Waters of Lethe.* It leaves the drinker perfectly clear-headed, though remarkably uninhibited, during an evening of pleasure but, the morning after, completely without memory of the night before. You can't regret what you can't remember, so there's no cause to feel guilty.

At least, that's what Augustus Pennyfeather figured, not long after he first laid eyes on Pandora. Now, as a classically educated man, Augustus should have realised that the lady was named after the source of all the troubles in the world. But Augustus was the wrong side of sixty years old. He'd quite forgotten having been once thought moderately attractive to women. He'd been married for forty years, and romance, as is often the way, had long since given way to pragmatic partnership. Augustus was neither ungrateful nor particularly wistful, and he was, in any case, pretty set in his ways. But apple-carts, these days, serve no other purpose than waiting around for someone to upset them.

Pandora astonished him. She reminded him that he had once supposedly possessed sex appeal by a very simple expedient: claiming to believe he still possessed it. She certainly possessed it herself, and in spades.

It was true that Augustus's ideas of feminine beauty had matured along with himself; nevertheless, he was quite sure Pandora was one of the most beautiful women he had ever seen. Some might have cavilled at that: she was, after all, a dress size larger than the typical movie star, or a good two sizes bigger than a catwalk model, but Augustus's taste was that way inclined. He didn't appreciate stick insects.

After dinner on the second evening, towards the end of the first full day of their lunar cruise, his wife, as usual, retired to their stateroom to read. Augustus made his way to the lounge bar situated on the observation deck. He still liked dancing, even if his best moves were somewhat less lithe than they had once been. Seeing Pandora alone, he naturally engaged her in conversation, and, being an old-fashioned gentleman, at some point he got round to complimenting her appearance.

"Guess how old I am," she said bluntly.

Now, unprompted, Augustus would not have dreamed of offering such an estimate. He found judging female age difficult at the best of times but, in response to a direct question, he was obliged to make an embarrassed effort.

"Thirty?" he suggested. "Thirty-five at most, I'd say."

"I'm fifty," she said. Was that a look of regret in those lovely eyes, or did the lack of focus result from an excess of booze?

"Never!" he rejoined.

"Next birthday," she clarified.

Augustus reflected that a single word from him had already negotiated a whole year off the lady's age, and idly speculated on what rejuvenation his utterance of a whole sentence might have achieved, but since Pandora was much his junior anyway, he did not press the matter.

"Well, ma'am," he said. "It sits lightly upon you."

"Come and dance with me," she said, taking him by the arm and propelling him towards the dance floor.

Lethe's observation lounge boasts a three piece band, and a dance floor comprising all of a hundred square feet, surfaced in real imitation wood. It was already quite crowded, with six couples engaged in the desultory shuffling that, on expensive cruises, passes for dancing, usually after everyone concerned has consumed far too much alcohol.

Augustus's idea of dancing, requiring enough space to perform actual steps, was sadly not an option. Pandora's idea of dancing involved a tight hug, both arms wrapped around her partner's waist, which not only eliminated any danger of the stylistic fault known to experienced ballroom dancers as 'gapping' but also restricted her partner's ability to perform a rather more fundamental manoeuvre, often referred to by experienced ballroom dancers, and others, as breathing.

The lady's décolletage presented Augustus with the opportunity for an intimate inspection of the ample bosom jammed into his ribs, while her hips, firmly pressed against his body, ensured she could hardly fail to perceive a certain involuntary, responsive firmness on his part. After some minutes more resembling staggering than dancing, she brazenly removed one of his hands from around her waist and pressed it against her right breast.

A shocked Augustus was much confused as to how to extricate himself. Yet at the same time, he was sorely tried by a sudden revival of certain primitive urges, long-supposed extinct. He was spared further immediate temptation by the arrival at his elbow of a waitress, bearing a tray on which were perched two slender glasses.

"Your *Waters of Lethe*, sir," she announced, studiously averting her gaze from the couple's unorthodox dance hold.

"Er...I don't think I ordered drinks," said Augustus.

"Compliments of your head barman Carlos, sir," the waitress replied. "He thought you might be in need of a restorative."

"Good idea," exclaimed Pandora, seizing one of the glasses and downing half the contents in one gulp.

"Th–thank you," stammered Augustus, following Pandora's example. "A–and please convey my appreciation to Carlos, would you?"

"Certainly, sir. The *Waters* are his own speciality, you know. Oh, and he asked me to tell you that, as a personal favour, since it's your first time on board, he's backdated them ten minutes."

"Eh?"

"That means they'll take effect ten minutes before you drink them, sir."

"Will they indeed?" Augustus marvelled at what he took to be an outrageous marketing exercise rather than a statement of scientific fact. "Well, that's ingenious, that is."

"Very talented is our Carlos, sir. Enjoy." And with a grin on her face, the waitress departed.

"Finish your drink," said Pandora. "I think we should go to my cabin."

* * *

The next morning, Augustus woke up in his own bed, in his own stateroom, suffering less of a hangover than would have been amply justified by the volume of alcohol he'd imbibed the previous night. His muscles were a trifle sore, as they usually were after his increasingly rare expeditions to the dance floor.

"Ah, you're awake," his wife Irene observed, as she busied herself preparing coffee.

"Just about," Augustus conceded.

"Was the band good? Did you find someone to dance with?"

"Er…I suppose I must have done. At this precise moment in time, I find I can't actually remember anything after the two of us parted on the stairs after dinner."

"That," Irene laughed, "is the natural consequence of drinking yourself into a stupor. Given the amount of single malt you consumed before dinner, the quantity of rare Bordeaux you consumed during dinner, and the well-aged cognac you consumed after dinner, I was amazed you were still able to stand, let alone dance."

"We Pennyfeathers come from staunch yeoman stock," he protested. "I'm sure my ancestor Wilfred, the one who fought at Agincourt, consumed far more booze on the night before the battle."

"Fortunately for Wilfred," Irene retorted, "the French that day were even more rat-arsed than the English. That's why they rode full-tilt into a bog!"

"Humph! Serves them right! Should have gone to the loo before they put their armour on," Augustus quipped. "Getting all your ironmongery wet causes your joints to seize up, so you can't wield your weapons. Everyone knows that."

"Not much has changed there then," Irene giggled. "Are you getting up for breakfast? Today's the orbit of the moon, remember, and I want to be in the observation lounge in time to get a good view."

* * *

The lunar orbit being the sightseeing highlight of the cruise, all of the *Lethe*'s passengers were on the observation deck, all dressed as if for a day out at Ascot Races. A sumptuous buffet was on offer, and a party atmosphere prevailed.

Pandora wore a white trouser suit over a black shirt with a white string tie. She resembled a technology millionaire, or perhaps an actress auditioning for the part of the glamorous senior detective in some unrealistic police holodrama.

"I've a feeling we may have met before," she said, introducing herself to Augustus and Irene.

"Probably the Captain's welcome-on-board drinks party," Irene said.

"Oh, sure," Pandora nodded. "We all met there, didn't we? Anyway, you'll be looking forward to seeing the moon close up, I expect."

"The main point of the cruise," said Irene.

"I know, especially the so-called dark side," Pandora enthused. "It's really odd, all this time after the first moon landing, that we still have so few good images of the dark side, don't you think? I reckon there ought to be holodramas set down there by now."

As Pandora and Irene continued to chatter happily about the voyage, the moon, and assorted topics of no interest to him, Augustus found himself drawn back to Pandora's remarks about having met before. The thing was, he'd been feeling the same way. He couldn't put his finger on where or when, any more than it appeared she could, though surely he would not have forgotten someone so striking. But if he hadn't met her before, he would certainly like to get better acquainted now. Though possibly not while Irene was around.

Excusing himself from the two ladies, who scarcely noticed his departure, he walked over to the bar, where Carlos was polishing glasses in anticipation of heavy demand later.

"Good morning, sir," the head barman smiled. "I hope I find you well, today?"

"You do, my friend. But why do I get the feeling you might have expected otherwise?"

"Me, sir? Oh, no, sir. No one feels bad the morning after finishing their evening's drinking with a *Waters of Lethe*."

"Is that what I did? I don't actually remember."

"No, sir. You wouldn't. That's also the consequence of taking the *Waters*. In fact, that's the main point."

"To forget having drunk it?"

"No, sir," Carlos smiled. "To forget whatever you might go on to do *after* drinking it."

"Is that right?" Augustus looked puzzled. "I did wonder. I don't usually suffer memory blackouts."

"Ah, no. You see, sir, it's this way. We Mexicans are relaxed about…certain things, as a general rule, but if we are really upset with ourselves we go and confess to the priest, and he forgives us our sins, tells us to say ten 'Our Fathers' and behave better in future. But you British belong to a Protestant tradition, where you just go on and on beating yourselves up about things in the past that you can't change. You know what I mean? Telling yourselves you shouldn't have, even though at the time you enjoyed it."

"That's true, unfortunately," Augustus conceded. It was something of a national trait among the British, he thought.

"So, just for people like you," Carlos smiled, "I came up with the *Waters of Lethe*. All sense of guilt is removed very simply, by the loss of a very precise section of short-term memory."

"A drink can do this?"

"Not just any drink, sir. Each *Waters of Lethe* is nano-engineered to a fine degree of precision. I've had it tested under laboratory conditions. When calibrated correctly it is accurate to plus or minus one second."

"You mean it excises a particular piece of memory and nothing else?"

"Just so, sir."

"That's astonishing. You are clearly a public benefactor, Carlos," Augustus grinned conspiratorially. "I shall bear this service in mind. In the unlikely event that I ever need it, that is."

"Always happy to help, sir." Carlos beamed again. "Sadly, some people are really determined to make themselves miserable, and so they will eventually find something else to be miserable about. But my policy is, no regrets about your holiday, right? While you are on my ship, at least, you can be Mexican too."

Augustus reflected that there was much truth in the head barman's philosophy. Granted, he himself was deep into middle age, but a tendency to be his own fiercest critic had for so long been an integral part of his personality he found it hard to envisage what an alternative attitude to life might be like. As far as he was concerned, there was no way known to man, or at least pre-Carlos man, of combining the lusts of Casanova with the conscience of Calvin. At least not without extensive psychiatric help afterwards.

* * *

The orbit of the moon was probably the only time during the cruise that the passengers aboard the *Lethe* paid more attention to what was outside their craft than what was going on inside. Having paid so much for the experience, it was, of course, compulsory for them to "Ooh!" and "Ah!" with everyone else, point fingers, publicly display a little knowledge, spread too thinly and containing significant involuntary disinformation, explain proudly and repeatedly, sometimes to the same person, that their second cousin had once designed an astronaut's pied-a-terre, and generally behave in the asinine way a tourist is expected to behave.

Later, as the moon receded into the ship's wake, the crew made an attempt to maintain a carnival feel. The observation lounge, and the concert hall immediately below it, were each converted into a themed, wholly immersive entertainment venue: an Australian beach barbecue above, a Parisian restaurant and nightclub below. Guests, invited to dine in the location of their choice, returned briefly to their cabins beforehand to rest and to change into appropriate clothes.

"Paris for me," said Irene. "How about you?"

"Oh, I'm happy enough with Paris," Augustus responded. "I'll maybe take a look in on Australia after dinner. Not often you get to visit two continents in one night, is it? Though it could be tricky to figure out what clothes might be appropriate in both places."

"Easy," said Irene. "Wear your blue and white Breton T-shirt and your grey slacks. You can be an Apache dancer in Paris and a beach-bum in Bondi. You simply need to wear your flat cap, with that big red handkerchief of yours tied round your neck, for the Apache. Leave them with me when you visit Australia; I'll bring them back to the cabin for you when I come back down after dinner."

"A true stroke of genius, that is," Augustus laughed. "Apache dancing, eh? I remember it, though I haven't seen anyone actually *do* it for ages."

* * *

To say that Pandora was dressed for the Australian beach would be an overstatement. In fact, to be honest, to say that Pandora was dressed was a bit of an overstatement. Augustus wasn't sure whether she was wearing a longish, belted blouse or a very short dress. Either way, the gauzy blue-flowered chiffon extended scarcely a foot below her waist, and her every move sent it floating up to reveal what looked like a matching pair of briefs, but was probably the bottom half of a bikini.

"There you are!" she exclaimed, slurring her words a little. "Dansh with me."

Dragged on to the tiny dance floor, Augustus again found himself clasped tightly against her body, but this time with considerably less fabric in between the two of them. It was obvious she was not wearing the top half of her bikini under her blouse.

"You're as squiffy as I am," she giggled, as he stumbled over his own feet. "Here, have something to hold on to." And, once again, she placed his hand on her breast, only this time there was nothing to prevent it sliding down inside her top. Instinctively, because he certainly wouldn't have done it if he'd retained any capacity for rational thought, Augustus responded by flipping up her tiny skirt and pushing his free hand down inside her bikini bottom until it rested on her rump. Something not unlike an electric shock ran through his whole body from his left hand to his right, leaving him semi-paralysed, terrified with sheer excitement. It was as well for him that his heart, though ageing, was strong.

"Ooh, steady tiger," Pandora grinned. "Leah you n'me go grab ourshelves a couple of *Waters*, and then we can go to my cabin. Wouldn't do to make an exshib…exshibith…show ourshelves up, would it?"

Managing to lift his head sufficiently from her shoulder to glance around him, Augustus observed that everyone else on the imitation beach was at least as far gone as the two of them, if not worse, and in no position to comment on anyone else's behaviour.

In other circumstances, he might have been disconcerted to learn that Carlos was rushed off his feet and could only offer them regular *Waters* rather than backdated ones.

* * *

The next morning, Augustus found himself once again in his own stateroom, but this time with quite a few extra aches and pains, and feeling more than a little exhausted. He didn't know why. He did not recall what had happened after he'd drunk his *Waters of Lethe*, but he did recall going further in fondling Pandora beforehand than was strictly proper for a happily married man.

He felt a little uncomfortable as he saw Irene busying herself making coffee again, a picture of devoted domesticity. While the cat's away, and all that, he thought, and she'd not even been very far away. Maybe he did not feel guilty enough to confess; it had only been a drunken fumble after all, but he certainly felt guilty enough to deprecate his own conduct. It's all very well saying you were drunk, he said severely to himself, but whose choice was it to take so much drink, eh?

"Morning, Irene," he said hesitantly. "You're looking cheerful today."

"Any reason I shouldn't be?" she responded.

"No, none at all. Er...Did anything happen in Paris after I left, or did you just come back here to read?"

"Do you know something?" she said. "I never knew amnesia was infectious. You had it yesterday, didn't you? Well, last night, I remember asking the bandleader if he could play 'Je Ne Regrette Rien' for me. A very nice man called Marcel, he is. Handsome. Reminded me of that old -time singer Maurice Chevalier. I always fancied him in the old movies. Anyway, Marcel was delighted to be asked to play a real French tune. "*Cinq minutes, ma chère madame*," he said. So I decided I'd just have one of those specialities of the house they call *Waters of Lethe* while I was waiting. A pity to come on this cruise and not try their famous liqueur, I thought. And after that, guess what? I can't remember anything. Not one blessed thing."

Where the Moths Burn Gold

Diyora Kabilova

Callista had not dreamed in fourteen years.

Not safely.

Each time her mind slipped into that golden hush – the breath before the first dream-note unfurled – something in the world vanished. Not metaphorically, not gently. Gone.

Once, it had been a forest of sycamores that grew upside down. Another time, a kingdom whose towers sang. Most recently, a village that spun glass rain into thread – now remembered only by the smoke that still drifted where its people had once lived.

So the scholars gathered, with their copper flutes and mirrored gloves and gentle poisonings. They built her a tower of sleepglass – a shimmering column that tilted slightly, like it was resisting its own existence. And inside, they placed the girl who couldn't dream.

Callista.

She was sixteen now, though her days moved like honey and her hours fell soundless. Pale-eyed and too thin, she paced the inner sanctum, barefoot on chilled stone, her long nightgown stained with tinctures. Every night, they brought her lull-root tea in porcelain bowls. Every night, she drank it.

And every night, she remembered less.

The Moonwater Dominion had passed laws for dreamers. Taxes on dreams, fees on fantasies, permits for prophetic sleep. Nightmares, if caught early, were weaponized and sold. But Callista was different. Her dreams were apocalyptic.

They didn't just kill people. They unmade places.

So they trapped her in the tower and placed votive candles along the halls, which never melted. They pressed tiny suction flutes behind her ears, to siphon her sleep into bell-jars. When she slept, her dreams were funneled into crystal – studied, sterilized, buried.

And yet.

There were days when her skin itched to be touched by sleep. Nights where her breath curled like a moth at the edge of a flame, trembling for that first descent. She dreamed of dreaming – which was cruel, perhaps, or simply human. To ache for the thing you're cursed to ruin.

And lately, the lull-root tea no longer worked. Her mind wandered. Her body drifted. Her soul – if she still had one – stirred like fog behind frostglass.

That's when the moths began to arrive.

No one knew why. They weren't part of the Dominion's registries. They weren't licensed dream-kin. They weren't even alive, technically – bone-thin, gold-lit creatures with wings that shimmered like old parchment, always burning faintly at the edges.

They came every dusk, brushing the glass with their wings, thousands of them, all drawn to her. When she pressed her hand to the pane, they scattered, then returned.

Once, she let her finger bleed across the sill. The moths drank from it.

"You are not cursed," one scholar whispered nervously. "You are...chosen."

Chosen for what, he never said.

That night, as the sleepglass turned dark and the moon curled like a claw above the sea, Callista sat cross-legged on her stone bed, hands resting in her lap, and watched the moths gather.

Something inside her chest felt unfinished.

The scholars had told her: Your dreams break the world. You must not sleep. You must not feel too much. You must not love.

But she had begun to wonder:

What if the dream wasn't the curse?

What if the world simply broke too easily?

She had begun writing, in secret – not letters, but dream-maps. Flickers of images on the inside of her wrist. A boy with a lantern. A field of golden moths. A flame that sang. She etched them lightly with a blunt needle, not deep enough to scar, but just enough to make them real.

And then, on the fourteenth night of the blue moon – when the wind blew salt through the tower and the sky above the Dominion cracked with a distant, hollow thunder – she dozed off.

Only for a moment.

The moths buzzed against the glass like struck bells. Her breath slowed. Her body folded in on itself like a wilted flower.

And one moth – smaller than the rest, ash-white, its wings torn – landed softly on her wrist.

It did not drink her blood.

It whispered.

A name.

Cassian.

And just like that, Callista began to dream.

Cassian moved like memory through the world – something no longer quite alive, but still present, still burdened. His lantern hung from one hand like an old sin, flickering with mourningflame – a pale and breathing blue. In it, dreams twisted like moths caught mid-prayer, their wings curling inward with regret.

He was a dream pyre.

Not by choice.

He had been raised in the shadow of ruin, taught that dreams could rot a city or flood a kingdom. That some dreams were not made to be dreamed. That some souls, too beautiful, too strange, too soft for the world, had to be burned before their sleep turned into plague.

He had burned cathedrals made of children's sleep. Cities stitched from a single nightmare. Once, he burned a garden that had grown from a girl's last wish – it wept flowers even as it died.

And every time he burned a dream, something inside him withered too. Not visibly. Not with sound. But slowly. As if breath by breath, he became less of a man and more of a silence.

The summons came in silver parchment, sealed with moonwax. Royal. Urgent. Addressed only to him.

Come to the Moonwater Dominion. A sealed dream has broken. You are the last fire.

He did not want to go. And yet, he did.

The Dominion was a pale city carved from frost and sleepglass. The towers bent slightly, as if leaning in to hear a lullaby still echoing from centuries past. Every window blinked like an eye watching its own dream. Here, dreams were taxed and traded. Nightmares distilled into weapons. Children were weighed for the gold in their sleep.

He hated it instantly.

He was led by silent scholars down corridors slick with silence. They wore masks of old saints, their voices slow as syrup.

"A dream has woken," they whispered. "We believe it cracked its seal three nights ago."

"What form?" he asked.

They glanced at one another. "Not what. Who."

He followed them to a tower veiled in soft snowlight. Inside, glass walls shimmered faintly, carved with lullabies in dying languages. A girl slept in the center, her wrists bound with ribbons soaked in lull-root. Her hair was the color of soft caramel turned ash. She looked like someone remembered by the world only in grief.

"She is the dream," they told him. "Every time she sleeps, a piece of the world vanishes."

Cassian stepped forward, lantern trembling in his grip.

And then he saw her – not just with his eyes, but as if she was something once seen in the smoke of another dream. His knees nearly buckled. His breath fled. Because he knew her.

Years ago, a dream had nearly drowned his homeland. The rivers reversed. The lakes bloomed with blood and light. His sister vanished mid-laughter, leaving only her dress and a song she had once hummed. Cassian traced the dream back to its source, but by the time he arrived, it had already vanished.

He remembered nothing of the dream except its scent – salt and ash and violets – and the unbearable sound it made when it tried to cry.

Now, standing in the moonlit hush of the tower, he smelled it again.

The girl stirred. Her lips parted. Her lashes fluttered. And for the briefest moment, her gaze found his. The whole room held its breath.

Her eyes were not made for this world. They were made for something older, softer. They seemed to remember him, though they had never met.

A moth clung to the inside of the glass, its wings burning faintly gold.

Cassian stepped back.

"She is not a dream," he said. "She is a girl."

The scholars tilted their heads in unison. "There is no difference."

He felt it then – the shape of fate sharpening. The old ache in his chest, the grief that had never healed. The smell of violets and blood returning. A dream he had once failed to catch had grown into a girl. And now, they asked him to burn her.

No.

Not again.

The moths stirred. The flame inside his lantern bowed its head.

Hooked by something he could not name, Cassian turned back toward the glass. She watched him now, as if through sleep or snow or centuries. She did not smile. But she did not look away.

Her name came to him then – not from memory, but from bone.

Callista.

And though he said nothing, the lantern flared.

He did not destroy her.

The order stood like a blade across his chest but Cassian sheathed it behind a silence of his own. In her presence he found not a curse but a contradiction. She was not madness, not even danger in the way scholars imagined danger – she was stillness, like snow falling inside a ruined chapel. She sat without speaking for hours, her breath so light it barely disturbed the dust. And he, who had buried kingdoms for less, sat with her.

The days unfolded like a study in restraint. She moved softly through the white-marbled chamber the royal scholars had sealed her inside, trailing dreams behind her like shadowlight. He watched from the corner of the room, holding his bone lantern close. The mourningflame inside it burned low and silver, casting long shadows on the walls as if listening.

Their conversations began like this:

She: "Do you dream?"

He, after a pause: "Not anymore."

Then silence again. Not awkward silence, but the kind that throbbed like a wound learning to heal. They spoke in fragments, in philosophical riddles, in questions that echoed long after they ended. She never asked why he was there. He never told her what she was.

"I like your moths," she said one day, tracing a fingertip against the lantern's glass. The mourningflame stirred and the tiny silver moths within twitched, wings flecked with dust and ash. "They look sad."

"They carry what the dreams leave behind," he said. "Some burn. Some forget. Some beg to be remembered."

"And you?" she asked.

He could not answer.

She grew curious about his scars, though she never asked directly. Once, when he had dozed beside the wall – eyes half open, pretending he was not watching her – she reached out and touched the side of his throat, just where an old dreamfire mark bloomed like dried roses on his skin. He did not flinch. He had been burned before. But her fingers were cold, and clean, and felt like snowfall.

"It hurts?" she whispered.

"Sometimes," he said, though what he meant was: only now.

Every day she asked more of him. Not in words, but in the way her gaze stayed longer. The way her dreams left shapes behind in the frost of the windows. The way she hummed lullabies she had never learned. The girl was not a girl – she was a cathedral in collapse. He told himself he was only studying her, that it was all calculation, containment, duty. But every time she smiled, some small light cracked inside his ribs.

And yet – she did not know.

She did not know that her dreams drowned entire cities. That her sleep cracked kingdoms open like porcelain cups. That she was the flood that nearly ruined his homeland.

She did not know and he did not tell her.

Instead he brought her candied violets and told her they were snowflakes that survived. He taught her to fold paper into birds. He told her that her dreams – if she ever remembered them – might be nothing more than the body grieving its own silence.

Sometimes he wanted to tell her. Sometimes he nearly did.

But then she would ask something small and holy like, "Do you think dreams are alive?" and he would forget his name for a moment.

And then – one night—

She spoke in her sleep. No words. Just a sound – low and shivering like a harp-string breaking. And the flame inside his lantern – the mourningflame that had never changed, never wept, never stuttered – turned blue.

Not sky-blue. Not ocean.

Blue like bruises after drowning.

And then the moths within it rose in a spiral and began to sing.

It began with the moths. Not many. Only three. One landed on her fingertip in the hour before dawn and would not leave. One fluttered against the dreamglass pane above her bed. One circled the lantern Cassian had hung from the ceiling beam like a silent watchman.

She followed them.

Barefoot through the spiral corridors of the sleepglass tower, past abandoned rooms filled with gold dust and broken dreaming-masks, down into the hollows where the air tasted of salt and ash and buried memory. Cassian followed, half in fear, half in awe, the lantern clenched in his fist but dimming with every step. The moths knew the way. Their wings did not beat but shimmered, as if pulsing with a memory older than breath.

At the base of the tower there was a door made of bone-white stone. Behind it, a stairwell descending into silence.

And there – beneath all memory – was the temple.

A ruin of impossible beauty. Dreammosaics collapsed in heaps of color. Archways grown over with thorn and moonvine. Statues of the first dreamers slumped in reverence or ruin, their faces blank, their palms open as if asking to be remembered. Here, once, the first prophets dreamed the world into being. Here, once, the gods listened.

The moths flew ahead, their wings catching fire one by one.

Callista walked like one remembering something from before she was born.

In the center of the chamber stood a mirror. Cracked from the top down like lightning had struck it. She approached it slowly. Cassian did not speak. His fingers were wrapped so tightly around the lantern that the handle bit into his palm.

She touched the mirror.

The moment her skin met the glass, she convulsed.

She did not cry out, but her knees buckled, her mouth parted, and the air shifted – a windless tremble, a shudder across the marrow of the world. She saw it. All of it. The dream she carried in her skull like a silent star. What it would become. A golden apocalypse. A cathedral of burning silence. The ocean peeled back. The moon split like fruit. Cities wept. Trees bowed. Moths fell from the sky like snow. The world did not end with fire or scream but with unbearable light and the hush of no one left to listen.

She fell against him.

"Burn me," she whispered, eyes wide and wild and full of ruin. "Please. You have to."

He caught her.

She tried to rise again but her limbs failed her. She clutched his wrist with both hands and pressed her face into his shoulder, her voice trembling like a bird trapped in the throat.

"I am the end. Burn me before I dream it."

Cassian looked down at her. She who did not know what she was. She who had asked what dreams felt like. Who had traced the ridges of his scars like holy script. She who laughed quietly once and it nearly shattered him.

He could not do it.

"You are not the dream," he said slowly, voice shaking like a prayer forgotten. "You are the fire inside it."

She looked up at him with wet eyes. Then she kissed him.

It was not gentle.

It was the kind of kiss that cracked centuries. That did not ask for permission. That bloomed out of the spine like flame. And the moment her mouth touched his, the lantern shattered. The moths erupted into white fire. The statues groaned. Reality itself tilted slightly off its axis, as if the laws of nature had briefly forgotten themselves.

And just before the world began to collapse, he thought:

So this is what it means to be human again.

The world began to split at the seams.

Hairline cracks shimmered through the air like veins of glass, as if reality itself had grown tired of holding its shape. Beneath Callista's feet, the stone floor shivered, not from movement, but from something deeper – like memory surfacing from beneath centuries of silence. The dream was stirring. And for the first time in her life, she was not running from it.

Cassian saw it before she did. It wasn't in her eyes or voice, but in the way the air bent around her. The gold of her hair seemed touched by a softer fire, the moths clustering like haloed stars near her shoulders. She was beginning to dream. Not in half-whispers or glimpses. This was full. Whole. Awake.

And the dream was not passive.

It curled around her like smoke, watching her with a jealous devotion only gods once knew. It adored her. It ached for her. It wanted her entirely. And it hated that she was not alone.

Cassian felt it then – some great ancient awareness pressing against him like a door refusing to open. The dream had no shape, no face, no voice. But its loathing of him was almost tender in its violence.

They stumbled forward into the broken temple, and time fractured with them.

The first shift came like breath drawn too sharply. Then, like mirrors falling one by one, the air split into versions of what could have been. He reached for her hand – and saw not one, but many.

A hundred lives bloomed around them. Some cruel. Some kind.

In one, they were strangers passing in a moonlit bazaar – she selling woven silk, he buying a lantern for a girl he did not yet know he loved.

In another, she was a seer behind prison bars, and he the guard who left the door open.

In yet another, they were children, sitting on a carpet of indigo sand, trading riddles for dreamfruit, their laughter caught in bottles they swore to break only when the world ended.

Lovers in one life. Enemies in another. Twin stars in one sky. Twin swords in another.

Callista's breath caught in her throat. "Is this what I dreamed before?"

"No," Cassian said, his voice rough. "This is what the dream remembers of you."

She turned to him, her expression lit with something like grief and wonder braided together. "It remembers us?"

He nodded, barely. "It loves you. And it cannot bear that you love me."

And then the dream tightened its hold.

The lantern at Cassian's side began to flicker, the flame inside it shrinking, shrinking, flickering as though gasping for breath. A voice began to hum around them – low, steady, ancient. Not spoken in any tongue, but woven through marrow and memory. The dream was trying to pull her under. Back into sleep. Back into its arms.

Cassian stepped between her and the mirror of light, his eyes dark with resolve.

"Let me take it," he said. "Let me hold it. I'll bind it into the lantern. I'll burn it into myself. I'll carry it until there's nothing left of me to carry."

She stared at him. "You'd burn yourself for me?"

His voice broke. "You think I haven't already?"

Callista's eyes shone wet with something deeper than sorrow. "No," she whispered. "You are not my martyr."

"I don't want to be your god," he said. "Only your witness."

"I do not want to end the world," she said. "I want to wake it."

And with that, the dream paused.

For the first time since the world began to fracture, it listened.

Cassian held out his hand.

Callista took it.

The dream shuddered. Moths scattered into gold. The walls pulsed once and then stilled.

Together – unburned, unconsumed, unbecoming – they stepped into her dream, hand in hand. Not as sacrifice and salvation, but as two who had chosen each other again and again, in every life, every version, every flickering pane of time.

Whatever came next, they would meet it not as fire and fuel but as dreamers who dared to wake.

There is no sound in the dream. Not at first. Only a shimmer. A weightless golden hush that breathes like the air before a church bell tolls.

Callista walks slowly, barefoot, across a field that glows with something older than fire. Gold, yes. But not the kind that sleeps in coins or crowns. This gold moves. It flutters. It flies.

The moths drift from the dust like sparks from a sacred pyre, rising in waves around her. Thousands of them. Each wing veined with flame. They burn without dying. Light without smoke. Fire without pain. Their glow so gentle it feels like memory.

All around her, the places she once destroyed have returned. But not as they were. They flicker like mirages, half-built from dreamstuff. A ruined cathedral opens its arms to the sky. A river runs backward, folding light into itself. A burnt garden blooms again, not from soil but from prayer. Every city she ever lost is here. Not whole. But forgiven.

And at the center of it all, Cassian.

He is kneeling. His hands slack. His body bent forward as though the flame inside him is too great a burden to hold upright. He does not cry out. He does not tremble. But his skin is glowing, and it is the kind of glow that comes just before something disappears.

She runs to him. Or tries. Her limbs are heavy. As if the dream is resisting. As if even now, it wishes to protect her from what comes next.

But she reaches him. And when she touches him, she feels it. The fire inside his chest. Not hot. Not cruel. Just infinite. And breaking.

"Cassian," she breathes. The sound of his name almost makes the dream collapse. "Please. Let me carry it now."

He lifts his head, and there is no hate in his eyes. No pride. Only a quiet, exhausted devotion.

"You were never meant to," he whispers. "But you always would."

He takes her hand. Places it to his chest. And she feels it. The flame. Pure. Ancient. Dying.

"I was only ever the vessel," he says. "But you. You are the dreamer. The world bends to your sorrow. It will listen to your love."

She does not cry. Not yet. Instead she leans in and kisses him. Again. Fiercely. As if trying to kiss death away. As if she could breathe life into him through her mouth. The moths stir. The dream deepens.

She places the last moth – the one from her childhood, the one that waited all her life to be released – into the hollow of his chest. And the moment she does, the dream holds its breath.

She says it then. The final wish.

"Let me dream the world not as it ends, but as it begins again."

The field erupts.

Not in violence, but in surrender. The sky splits open. The moths rise like stardust, lifting the ruins with them.

Everything turns to gold – the flame, the boy, the dream – and then dissolves. Not into ash. But into morning.

She wakes.

He is beside her. Breathing. Pale and fevered, but real. His hands are warm. His lips bloodless, but alive.

The world is quiet. Outside the window, the sky does not weep. It shines.

She touches her chest. No wound. No weight. Just the echo of something holy. A silence that does not crush but comforts.

She closes her eyes.

And for the first time since childhood, Callista dreams.

Not of fire.

Not of ruin.

But of spring. Of cities blooming from rivers. Of love that does not end in ash. Of Cassian, not as a ghost, but as a man with his arms around her.

And the dream does not shatter.

It begins.

It was months later or perhaps a moment after. Time had lost its edge here. The temple stood where it always had, though no one could agree on where that was. To some it rose on a hill above a vanished city. To others, it bloomed in the hollows of sleep, between silence and sky.

Inside, the air was thick with golden hush. Dust turned gently in the columns of light, as if the world now breathed slower, softer, not to wake what had once nearly died.

Callista no longer trembled when she closed her eyes. Her hands were steady now. Her dreams small, careful, luminous. Moths, stars, fireflies. The familiar faces of a world that would never again slip away from her. She no longer destroyed what she loved. She stitched it back into being.

Cassian lived beside her in that quiet miracle, his laugh low and tired, his eyes forever watchful. He had not left her side since the world collapsed and reformed in her arms. When she dreamt now, he held her wrists until they stopped shaking. He lit candles at the edge of her bed and sat until dawn listening to her breathe. When she turned toward him in the dark, their foreheads would meet like a vow.

In the mornings, villagers came. Wandering souls, battered by their own ghosts. They brought folded notes, songs, fragments of dreams they had long since buried. She took each offering into her palms like a prayer. Some she held to her heart. Others she laid beneath her pillow. And when she slept, she rewrote them – not to be perfect, but to be gentler. Less cruel. More bearable. She did not banish their sorrow. She only taught it to kneel.

Cassian watched her become what she had feared most. Not a destroyer of worlds but a steward of small mercies. Her voice was softer now, but there was a stillness in it that made people listen as if hearing their own name spoken for the first time. He had loved her before she knew who she was. But now he loved her with a kind of reverence, as one might love fire after it has spared them.

And in quiet moments, between the ink and the golden dust, between the lamplight and the drifting wings, they would sit together. Not speaking. Just breathing the same breath.

Sometimes, she would lean against his shoulder and say nothing for hours. Sometimes, he would kiss the inside of her wrist where the burn mark still shimmered faintly, like an echo of the beginning.

She no longer asked if it would last. He no longer promised anything he could not hold in both hands. They had seen how easily eternity could turn to ash. So instead, they loved as if the world was ending at any moment. And perhaps, in that, it finally wasn't.

It is said that no new wars came from that place. That people forgot how to speak in hatred there. That when they left, they remembered something they had never known they were missing.

And no matter how many came or how many left, the temple remained. Light flickered at its threshold, and moths brushed their wings across its stones like the hush of ancient songs.

They lived simply. Cassian sometimes vanished into the woods to gather moss and roots. Callista lit lamps made of glass and slow fire. And at night, when the world folded in on itself, she laid her head on his chest and said, I am not afraid anymore.

He would answer, You never were. You only needed someone to believe it first.

And they would fall asleep beneath the whispering wings of moths that glowed with gold. In that place where endings once bloomed like fire, two broken dreamers had built something else entirely.

Not heaven. Not paradise.

But a world that could bear them.

When Love Lies Dreaming

Shona Kinsella

Nicnevin woke slowly, dragging herself up through the layers of sleep as a swimmer rising from the deep. She opened her eyes, wincing against the sunlight flooding into her room through the open window.

"I brought your breakfast tray, my lady." Her maid stepped into her field of vision, holding a simple silver tray, topped with delicate dishes.

Nicnevin groaned and pushed herself up to rest on her elbows. "Thank you, Aliv," she said, her voice thick with sleep.

"I can bring it back later, if you prefer?" Aliv said.

"All is well. I'll take it now."

Aliv moved across the room and carefully set the tray down on a gleaming heartwood table beside the open window. Nicnevin sat up and swung her legs over the side of her bed, waving a hand in the direction of a spider-silk robe which hung from a hook on the back of the door. The robe disappeared and reformed wrapped around her.

"Are you well, my lady?" Aliv asked, looking at her with a frown. "You do not seem quite yourself this morning."

Nicnevin stood up and stretched languidly before padding across the room on bare feet. "Just tired," she said, stifling a yawn as she sat down at the table. "I had the most realistic dreams. Almost like being awake."

"Perhaps you're worried about something?" Aliv suggested, lifting a silver jug as she spoke and pouring nectar from it into a glass made from an iris flower.

"It was not that kind of dream," Nicnevin said, feeling colour rise in her cheeks even as a smile graced her lips.

"Oh?" Aliv raised an eyebrow, her shimmering dragonfly wings twitching with amusement, making the air hum silently.

Nicnevin looked up at Aliv and considered for a moment, before using her foot to push out the chair opposite. "Join me?"

Aliv dropped into the chair and Nicnevin gestured, calling a plate out of the air for her. She handed it over and pushed the tray between them, inviting Aliv to share the food.

"So, the dreams were...pleasant?" Aliv asked with a knowing smirk, while they both filled their plates from a serving dish which produced anything they wished for.

Nicnevin thought of bread with honey, spiced nuts, and baked fennel-stuffed trout, and it all appeared. Aliv chose a selection of sliced meats with berries and lavender flowers.

"Pleasant is certainly one word for them," Nicnevin said. She speared a forkful of fish and ate it, letting the taste bring her fully to wakefulness, before continuing, "Several times a week for the last quarter-year, I have been dreaming of the same woman."

"Anyone I know?" Aliv asked.

"I don't think it's even anyone I know. I'm sure I've never seen her before."

Aliv frowned. "Is she a witch?"

Nicnevin shook her head. "I don't think so. Or at least, she's not one of mine. I don't feel that connection with her that I usually have with witches."

"What happens in these dreams?"

Nicnevin looked down at her plate, oddly bashful. The fae were, as a rule, very open when discussing their lovers, and Aliv was as much a friend and confidante as a servant. "We make love," Nicnevin said, still not looking up.

"Is that all?" Aliv said with a tinkling laugh. "We all dream of mysterious lovers now and again. It's harmless fun. Why does it bother you so?"

Nicnevin struggled to pull together the words to explain how this woman made her feel. The sense of peace and safety she found in her lover's arms. How she woke to a body which remembered every caress, every meeting of their lips, every moment of overwhelming pleasure, as if they had truly occurred.

"I'm not certain she's just a dream."

"What else would she be? You said she's not a witch, so it's not magic."

Nicnevin shrugged. "At least not of a type I'm familiar with."

"Why not just enjoy it while it lasts, whatever it is?" Aliv licked berry juice from her fingers.

"I think…I might be falling in love with her."

Aliv sat back and looked at Nicnevin intently. "Well, that does complicate things somewhat. Do you know anything about her at all?"

"Only her name – Arehtu. The language she speaks is beyond my understanding."

"I may be able to help with that."

That night, as Nicnevin prepared for bed, she carefully looped the knotwork spell she and Aliv had crafted that afternoon around her upper arm. Aliv was a natural linguist and spoke most of the languages known in Faery and a number from other realms too. She was confident that if Nicnevin could capture Arehtu's words, she would be able to at least identify the language and perhaps begin some sort of translation. All Nicnevin had to do was get Arehtu talking and the knotwork spell would capture the sounds and release them for Aliv the next day.

Nicnevin could only hope that the recorded words were not too intimate in nature.

She climbed into bed, wearing only the sheerest of nightdresses, and recited her own quick spell to make sure that she retained enough awareness of her waking self and her purpose to remember that she needed Arehtu to speak enough words for Aliv to identify the language. Her usual soft exclamations of pleasure were unlikely to be sufficient for this task.

Nicnevin tossed and turned as she waited for sleep to claim her, her body already anticipating the caresses and attentions of her lover. *Please let her be real.*

When birdsong woke her the next morning, Nicnevin was refreshed but disappointed. Her beloved had not made an appearance to her sleeping self. She did not dream of Arehtu every night and had not been able to spot any discernible pattern to when she did. Sometimes, Arehtu would appear in her dreams three nights in a row, only to make her wait for six before returning.

She sighed and got out of bed, dressing before Aliv arrived with her breakfast. This morning, there were two plates on the tray and Aliv seemed eager to hear if the knotwork spell had worked. She was almost as disappointed as Nicnevin to learn that there had been no opportunity to try it.

Ten days passed. Each night, Nicnevin wrapped the knotwork spell around her arm as she prepared herself for sleep, and each morning she unwound it sadly. This was the longest stretch she could remember not dreaming of Arehtu since the experience had begun.

On the tenth day, as she walked the boundary line of her holding, Nicnevin began to wonder if perhaps Arehtu had been nothing but a dream the whole time. Perhaps her below-mind was simply trying to tell her that it had been too long since she allowed herself to truly love another and accept their love in return. Even in her dreams, she had fallen for someone unobtainable, someone she could only share so much of herself with before the language barrier prevented them from achieving true emotional intimacy.

That night, as she prepared for bed, she lifted the knotwork spell and looked at the delicate weave of it. In the working of this spell, she could feel Aliv's friendship and deep respect, as well as the low hum of the other fae's magic. Could this be somehow keeping Arehtu away? Nicnevin placed it on the bed and stared at it, thinking through each step of the process they had come up with to make it. There was nothing in the magic that she could imagine would have had that effect, but the dreams had stopped when she started wearing it.

If all of this was just a dream and meant nothing, then the spell would make no difference to its occurrence. If Arehtu was somehow real and existed in some other place, then nothing in the formulation of the spell should prevent her from appearing to Nicnevin. Either way, there was no reason to assume the spell was a problem. Nicnevin bit her lip then grabbed it up and swiftly wrapped it around her arm, before climbing into bed and settling herself beneath blankets of petals woven together with threads of moonlight.

She was in a room full of mirrors, which bright violet water trickled over, shimmering under rose-coloured light coming from elaborate chandeliers suspended above her. Everywhere she looked, her own image was reflected back at her, but these images did not only reflect who she was now. Here she was as a child, dressed in the furs of the people she called family so many years ago. There she was reflected in her ceremonial robes as a priestess. And so many more, taken from the years in between and the countless years since she became the fae that she was now. She turned and turned, looking for some way to leave this place, and escape the many versions of herself. She had been there; she did not need to be reminded of her past life.

One mirror caught her eye, not because of what it showed, but what it didn't. It held no reflection – not of her at any stage of her life, nor of any other mirror in the room she was in. She stepped towards it, tentatively reaching out to touch the water-covered glass with the tips of her fingers. A hazy smudge appeared in the mirror, growing larger as she watched. She stepped back, raising her hands defensively, feeling some other presence approach. Details began to form in the haze: dark flowing hair, sun-kissed skin the colour of heartwood, shimmering through the drape of sheer orange and red fabrics she had no name for.

Arehtu.

Nicnevin stepped forward again, pressing her hands to the glass, while Arehtu did the same. Though they were hand to hand and nose to nose, the glass between them remained solid and prevented the warm caress of skin that Nicnevin longed for.

"Arehtu, my love. Oh, how I've missed you," Nicnevin said, pressing her forehead to the glass which separated them, caring little for the water which cascaded over her.

On the other side of the barrier between them, Arehtu's lips were moving, but try as she might, Nicnevin could not hear the warm and honeyed sounds of her voice. Arehtu began to bang her hands against the glass, the skin of her hands blanching from the force, but the barrier remained resolute and still no sound crossed between them.

Remember who you are, Nicnevin admonished herself. *Think like a witch, not a pining lover*!

She pressed her hands to the glass once more, but this time, instead of trying to reach through it to Arehtu, she sent her magical senses into it. Now, studying it as a witch, she could feel the lattice of magical threads woven through it, creating this barrier. Someone had purposefully erected this, someone powerful, by the touch of their magic. Nicnevin sent her senses racing along each thread, searching for a weakness, anything she could use to break through. There was nothing. It had been deftly woven by someone who clearly knew what they were doing.

Frustrated, she pulled back to herself and looked through the glass again to where Arehtu leaned against it, tears filling her eyes.

"I will find you," Nicnevin said, knowing that her lover could neither hear nor understand her, but needing to say the words aloud anyway. "Somehow, I promise, I will find you."

* * *

When Aliv brought the breakfast tray the next morning, Nicnevin was already dressed and seated at the table surrounded by piles of books and scrolls. She pushed out a chair for Aliv without looking up, even when the silver tray was placed on the table.

"Has something happened?" Aliv asked, taking the offered seat.

Nicnevin finished scanning the lines of text she was reading, then slid the scroll aside before answering.

"She's real," she said, finally looking up at her room maid and friend. "Arehtu is real. I'm sure now."

"You dreamt of her again? Did our spell work?" Aliv asked eagerly. Her eyes scanned the room, most likely seeking out the knotwork spell cord.

"I didn't get a chance to test it."

Aliv smirked. "Too eager to reconnect?"

"No, she was trapped." Nicnevin reached for the tray and poured herself some nectar, then changed her mind and summoned coffee instead. "There was powerful magic involved. Someone was deliberately keeping us apart."

Aliv leaned forward, frowning. "You're certain?"

"Positive."

While they were eating, Nicnevin told Aliv all about the hall of mirrors and the spell she had found woven through the glass that separated her from Arehtu. "There was something familiar about the magic," she said. I could swear I've felt it somewhere before.'

"You don't think Alethea—"

"No. I would know her magic anywhere."

"Another fae then? Or one of your witches?" Aliv used a piece of bread to wipe honey from her plate.

"It was definitely fae magic," Nicnevin mused, turning to the window and gazing out across the landscape. Beyond the fields of her holding, birds swooped over the marshes, only to scatter when a firedrake soared overhead, its shadow sending many smaller creatures into hiding, no doubt. On the other side of the marshes lay a dense forest, in the centre of which sat the Seelie Court.

"Somewhere out there, Arehtu is real, and she's trapped." Nicnevin turned back to look at Aliv. "I have to help her."

Aliv nodded thoughtfully. "Where do we start?"

"I've been looking for any mention of magic like this used before so I can figure out a way to undo it. Or identify who set it up in the first place." She gestured to the piles of books and scrolls. "But there's so much to go through."

Aliv pulled a scroll over and unrolled it. "Describe the magic again?"

Two nights passed before Nicnevin found herself in the hall of mirrors again, but this time she had a plan. She ignored all of the reflections of her past and went straight to the blank mirror, sinking her hands into the violet water which streamed over its surface and placing them flat against the glass. She knew she should start straight away – every moment could count – but she couldn't settle herself until she had seen Arehtu and knew that she was safe, so she stood there, waiting, her heart in her mouth.

It seemed an age before the hazy smudge appeared and eventually coalesced into Arehtu, gazing at her from the other side of the glass. She looked tired. Weakened. The gorgeous, silky hair that Nicnevin had run her hands through so many times, was dry and unkempt. A bruise bloomed above her eye and her lower lip was swollen and cracked.

Nicnevin's heart ached. Who had done this? And why? She accepted that she could not truly know Arehtu when they shared no language, but all she had ever felt of the other woman's heart was kindness, a gentle spirit, and a deep reverence for life. What could she possibly have done to deserve such treatment?

"I'm going to get you out," she whispered, her throat clogged with emotion.

Arehtu lifted her hand to the mirror and sadly traced the shape of Nicnevin's jawline.

Nicnevin blinked back tears and closed her eyes, taking a few deep breaths and centring herself. She reached for her own magic, bolstered by the strength that Aliv had woven into the new knotwork spell around her arm. Sending her senses into the barrier once more, she traced the lines of force that had been woven over and under each other to create the latticework of power. Only when she held the full pattern of the barrier in her mind did she begin to direct her own magic, coating every strand in the power she and Aliv had built between them. When her magic covered each strand of the barrier, she began sending pulses of power through it. Heat built and the violet water coating the mirror began to turn to steam. Sweat beaded on Nicnevin's forehead, but still she pulsed her power, faster and faster in a building tempo that made the barrier begin to vibrate.

She wanted to check on Arehtu, but could not pull her focus from the magic for even a moment without losing the momentum. She hoped Arehtu would realise that something was happening and move away from the barrier. If this worked, Nicnevin had no idea if the barrier would come down with a fizzle or an explosion.

Heat built in her body as she began to feel the strain of channelling so much power at once. She gritted her teeth and pushed harder, pulsing the magic so fast now that it created a steady thrum. Her heart thrummed along with it. She thought of that bruise over Arehtu's eye and pushed harder again, screaming with the effort of it.

The magical barrier vibrated so hard and fast that it chimed, the note loud and long and clear, rattling Nicnevin's teeth together in a most unpleasant manner.

Suddenly, the barrier collapsed in on itself, pulling everything in towards it, mirrors, water, Nicnevin, all were pulled into its nexus, before the direction reversed and they were blasted out and away.

Nicnevin's power slammed back into her just as her back slammed against the opposite wall of the vast space and she knew no more.

Nicnevin woke slowly, her body feeling as if it were crushed beneath the entire weight of the Seelie Court, her eyes gummed shut, the skin across her face tight and painful. She could hear the soft sounds of someone else breathing deeply as if in sleep. She shifted carefully, unsure of where she was or what had happened, lifting her hands to wipe the crust from her eyes.

The skin there was tender and she hissed in pain from the light pressure.

The soft breathing stopped.

"You're awake!"

Nicnevin peeled her eyes open and blinked a couple of times to clear them. Aliv was leaning over the bed, a relieved expression on her face.

"Don't try and move yet," she said. She disappeared from view and returned a moment later holding an iris glass filled with nectar. She helped Nicnevin to sit up enough to drink and held the glass for her.

Nicnevin felt the cool elixir begin to work its magic even as it slipped down her throat. "What happened?" she asked as soon as Aliv moved the glass from her mouth.

"I'll tell you everything in a moment. Let's get you comfortable first." Aliv fussed around her, sitting her up against piled cushions, giving her more nectar to sip, dabbing a cool ointment over the burned skin on her face.

Nicnevin tolerated her attentions for a few moments before pushing her hands away. "Enough. Tell me what happened."

"There's someone else who can explain it better. Let me go and fetch them."

Nicnevin's heart started to beat faster. Why was Aliv being so evasive?

Aliv hurried from the room, only a slight tremble in her hand as she turned the door handle giving away that something was amiss.

Nicnevin reached for her magic and groaned at the pain that slammed into her when she did. Hazy memories began to form, of expending a huge amount of power, and being sent flying. Before she could chase the memory down, the bedroom door opened and Aliv stepped back in, followed by another woman.

The bruise above her eye had turned to the sickly shade of yellow that comes with healing, and she was wearing one of Nicnevin's dresses rather than the orange and red outfit she had worn on the other side of the glass, but there was no mistaking her.

Arehtu was standing in her bedroom. Nicnevin's brain froze, not quite able to process what she was seeing. She was so filled with emotion that it felt as if there was no room left to breathe.

"You…you're here!" she stuttered at last, staring at this woman she knew intimately and had never met. "How?"

Arehtu was studying her just as intently, a frown creasing the smooth skin between her brows. She spoke in that musical language that Nicnevin did not know and turned to Aliv, who smiled.

"She wants to know if you're well."

"I'll be better when you tell me what's going on!"

Aliv perched on the side of the bed. "How much do you remember?"

Nicnevin answered without taking her eyes from her dream lover who was somehow standing right here in her bedroom. "Arehtu was trapped. I went into the dream to help her, I think there was some backlash when I broke the barrier but I'm not sure."

"Somehow, the force of the barrier collapsing pulled Arehtu through to your side, and you managed to bring her back with you. She came running through the hold, trying to find help for you. You've been unconscious for two days. You must have really overextended your magic."

Nicnevin nodded slowly, bits and pieces coming back to her. "Can you speak with her? Arehtu?"

Aliv grinned. "I can! She speaks one of the dialects from the islands on the other side of the Crimson Sea. They are Fyrefolk, though Arehtu has no fire powers. She has been something of an outcast her whole life, but for her mother being one of their most powerful seers. When they discovered that Arehtu had the ability to dreamwalk, they became frightened of her, and her mother erected that magical snare to prevent her from using her gift. Otherwise, they were going to expel her from the island and put her to sea in only a coracle, with nought but bread and water."

"She's been through so much," Nicnevin said sadly. "Please tell her that she is safe here. That she can stay as long as she wishes, and will have anything she needs." She swallowed, her heart thrumming at the base of her throat. "Tell her that she has no obligation to me here."

"I don't think that will be a problem," Aliv responded with a wry smile.

"Just tell her. Please."

Aliv translated, answering when Arehtu asked a question. Nicnevin pulled her eyes away from Arehtu, desperate not to put any expectations on her. She couldn't bear it if the other woman felt that she had no choice but to share her bed in order to be safe.

Aliv stood and gestured to the bed and Arehtu closed the distance between them in three quick strides. She perched beside Nicnevin, reaching for her hand and stopping short of touching her, raising her eyes in a questioning look. Nicnevin tentatively reached out, touching the tips of her fingers to Arehtu's.

Arehtu began to speak, pausing every few words for Aliv to translate.

"All my life, I have been lonely," she said, through Aliv. "Every night I would pray to meet just one person who could see me for who I am and not what I lack. When I began to dream of you, for the first time in forever I felt seen. Whole. Loved. And now you have saved me. I cannot…" She began to cry softly and Nicnevin ached to lean forward and put her arms around her, but still, the witch queen did not want to take anything for granted.

Arehtu smiled through her tears. "There would be no obligation," she said, translated by Aliv. "I could spend every day loving you until the end of time and still want more." She leaned forward, stopping inches from Nicnevin's face, her breath warm on Nicnevin's lips.

Nicnevin lifted her hand and cupped her dream lover's face, then closed the distance between them.

The Dream-Eater's Kiss

Vanessa Ziff Lasdon

Prologue: Riven

The young woman's soul shone like a starlight beacon through the rain-drenched murk of her nightmare. If Riven could see it, so could all the rest of his accursed kind. Make enough cosmic noise in the Endless and the Old Ones always turned their gazes.

Gods, they'll come after her. The thought made Riven's pulse pound and his chest ache.

He could already sense them. The ancient, cloying stink of myrrh and crushed roses. Desire's pack of lust-crazed, parasitic freaks always caught the scent first. Riven couldn't get the woman out of his damn head; gods only knew the depraved minds of Desire's feral Dream-Eaters. Hell, they'd feed and feed and feed until...

I'll get to her first, Riven decided. *Warn her.*

Shame he'd never mastered self-deception. Riven had been fantasizing about the woman all night: what it would feel like to consume her pure spirit, to press his mouth against hers and taste freedom on her lips, to devour her perfect pain. His breath caught at the thought. *Some protector. Riven, you fool.*

She was devastatingly beautiful. Luminous. Divine. He'd wanted to ravage her from the second he saw her, glowing with all her exquisite humanity. Mortals shouldn't burn this bright.

Riven swallowed the gnashing hunger. *Peace*. That's what he could give her. What she deserved.

He'd only take a little. Just her worst terrors and despair. Just enough to silence her tumult and stave off the hollows creeping in at the edge of his vision.

Fuck, who was he kidding? Starving as he was, he'd rip her open if she let him. *Nyx jabbed ice into my bones; Inanna left fire under my tongue*. He was just as much of an irredeemable, soul-sucking, dream-eating asshole as all the rest.

And the depth of his dark hunger was unbearable against the brightness of her being. Riven was already walking a tightrope above the hollows; he'd rather take his chances with a savage cabal of soul-cannibals than claw his way out of that gods-forsaken abyss.

But he would draw the line at her desire. No matter how desperate his craving. *I will not touch desire, even if it kills me*, Riven vowed.

And she will be mine. No. Matter. What.

1

Elara knew the dream was wrong before she even opened her seeing eye inside it. She stood in a murky, roofless corridor that was filling like a bathtub around her bare legs from the sheets of rain pounding down. Fucking. Cold. Soaking wet. And *definitely not* in control.

Why the hell was she here?

Her teeth were chattering so loudly as she stared with furious intent down the dim corridor that she didn't notice the man with the umbrella and trenchcoat behind her until he called her name and she jumped.

"Elara."

"Holy mother!" Nightmare, hands down. They talk now? *How*? Elara's pulse hammered and she stumbled – out of his shelter, out of his grasp, back into the torrent that was now up to her knees.

The not-a-figment grabbed for her flailing hand just as she felt her feet slip. "It's not safe for you here," he said, setting her steady before releasing her wrist. She stared at him, stunned. His heat on *her* wrist. *How*? He parted the water around his every step forward as she took one after another back. "Predators are on the prowl. You should go, Elara. Now."

Go? Great idea. *Run*! But where? Sloshing to nowhere in near-freezing water that was already numbing her senses wasn't a smart option. And was she seriously taking orders from a *dream*?

Elara felt along the wall, willing a door from her mind's eye into existence the way she used to draw 11s on paper, though that was to fall into sleep, not out of it. *Come on, Lucky Number 11. Any day now…! This* predator right here – this beautiful, imposing asshole that knew her name, who might be 20 or 200 – he and his steel-blue stare and rainy-day gear could fuck right off and meet Death himself. Elara's anger spiked. Somehow she knew in her soul he was more dangerous than all the rest.

"The name is Riven." He glanced up warily at the sconces that were now flickering off, on, off.

Down the hallway, a pack of shadows cut from darkness suddenly materialized from paintings on the walls, each taking human shape in the form of living dread. They stalked toward her like savages hunting prey, eyes burning with lustful malice as they ripped the walls inward behind them to trap her inside this watery tomb.

Terror seized Elara at knifepoint. She reached for her sheaths. Empty? Shit, shit! They'd be here in twenty heartbeats…fifteen…*Fucking door*! A flash of memory – an alleyway, a futile knife fight – froze her in place. A scream gripped Elara's throat tight. She'd die drowning. Or suffocating. Or torn to shreds. Or—

Riven was all at once everywhere: enveloping her in his embrace, blocking everything out but *him*. Tucked into his trenchcoat, safe from the elements, heat and strength radiating from his body into hers, Elara felt paradoxically shielded and ensnared. What the fuck was going on?

That's all Elara had time to think before Riven's lips collided with hers and the world went – silent. Defying logic or license or the laws of dreamwaking, Elara's mouth responded on instinct, sending a psychic spark one direction and a jolt of need in the other. Riven took the invitation with a hunger so terrifying it made Elara shudder. Time ceased to exist as his tongue consumed her world in a sensory overload, draining and drinking in every trace of her terror to feed a whole new form of desperation deep in her core.

Danger, Elara! A tiny voice screamed from far, far back in her psyche. *Wake*!

As if both of them had heard the voice, Elara and Riven pulled apart with twin gasps. She felt the absence acutely. Riven's steel-blue eyes held hers with rapt fascination as the dreamscape collapsed in on them. Only then did Room 11 appear, and with her hand already on the doorknob, Elara fled for her life.

* * *

Two things were on Elara's mind as she shot awake in bed, clutching her sheets, heartbeat ragged: changing her underwear and checking her face. It had been the hottest, strangest, scariest dream in her 20 years of existence. *From a single fucking kiss*, Elara. Gods, she needed to get laid.

Once in front of the mirror, though, staring at her swollen lips, Elara dropped her smirk in a state of shock. Had the kiss been real? Her fingertips traced the tender, bruised curves up and around, remembering Riven. And that wicked mouth.

Remembering other things too, now that the burn of desire had cleared. Details that should have come in first, not last, because they were *so damn real*. The corridor. The rain and rising water. The menacing stalking shadows. The door and knives that wouldn't materialize. The panic and despair. The certainty of Riven's predatory nature. The peace and pleasure he wrapped her in when she should have felt peril.

The *sheer-overwhelming-paradoxical-wrongness* of it all. That was something new.

Elara's gaze fell to her palm where a faint ash star was imprinted like a kiss. She added it to the list.

"Terror tells no lies. Wield it. – C." Elara read the index card on her mirror for the umpteenth time. "Yeah, Aunt Cass. Thanks for the tip."

How had Riven known her name? Who was he? *What* was he? How was he the only one dressed for the rain? And why had he kissed her like… *that*… like he was wielding a weapon, and with such lethal grace?

Why had none of her lucid power *worked* right?

Elara grabbed her robe off the hook, feeling suddenly cold and exposed. She shivered into its warmth, recalling a similar sensation wrapped in Riven's arms, shielded by his strength…and the tiny slice of intuition that had spied the truth of her entrapment. She'd succumbed to his control.

Oh, hell no. Fury and defiance rose inside Elara. She'd survived nightmares her whole life, endured visions that no one else could see, and never once had she yielded. Whoever Riven was – whatever he and all the others thought they could take from her – she would not be cowed.

Elara hadn't spent seven brutal winters at the mercy of crazy Aunt Cassandra and her self-taught dream 'therapy' sessions to start sliding back into delusion and defenseless naiveté simply because a tall, dark dreamboat swooped into her psyche out of the steel-blue, intent on stealing kisses like they'd save his soul.

She'd given as good as she got with the mouth-to-mouth, but conjuring had been a complete fail, and dropping her own defenses so completely that Riven's kiss seemed like the only mercy possible was also a monstrously wrong move. *Terror tells no lies.* Elara could practically hear Aunt Cass tapping out every word with her bejeweled nails from beyond the grave. *When nightmares come alive, wield fear like shield and scythe.*

Setting her jaw in a firm line and staring herself down in the mirror, Elara swore that surrender was not happening a second time.

2

Riven stuck to the shadows as he skimmed the underbelly of the Endless, where dreams stacked like the glass panes of skyscrapers, each reflecting a life. He learned long ago on these patrols to avoid looking too closely; mortals had a way of staining him with their appetites for ecstasy and ruin, and a soul's torment was just as seductive as its devotion.

Nyx's cold hush threaded his bones; Inanna's heat braided his hunger. And tonight, Riven's restraint was as likely as a cracked window in a gale: fifty-fifty at best. Elara had lodged in his dark heart like a shard of light.

Two brands. Two leashes. Two gods who would never forgive him for refusing to be only what they made. Fuck 'em.

He found her again in the rain-corridor dream before it built itself, like she'd been waiting for him. Had she? Riven tried to make his touch gentle – he'd gone way too far last night and now meant to make good on his promise, taking only the edge of her fears, leaving her shield mostly intact. He was halfway to convincing himself of this mercy when Elara spun around and shoved him.

Not with her hands. With her will.

Light knifed from her sternum in a white flare that slammed into his chest. *Holy shit.* Riven staggered, shocked laughter cracking in his throat. "Ouch," he said, impressed despite himself. "That burned."

"Get out of my head," Elara snapped. To which Riven guessed she meant *get out of my dream, out of my personal space. Out of my life*. It was a fair request.

"Can't," he lied, drawn to the wild storm in her eyes, the stubborn flush of her cheeks. Then he reached. Her fear and fury rolled over his lips – intoxicating, essential – then stung. *Hot. Fiery hot.* Sparks flared again between them, heating the corridor until steam rose in the rain. Riven smelled the singe of Elara's resistance on his skin beneath the umbrella, a clean ash sensation that should not exist in this place.

His heart jolted and he jerked back. Across Elara's dreamscape, reality rippled like a desert mirage, a fever wave that melted the corridor paintings and bent the walls to her will. All at once, Riven urgently wanted to strip off every layer of artifice and fall to his knees bare before this woman. If he wasn't so shaken by her visceral effect on him, he might have laughed. Or cried.

Riven felt attention turn upon Elara – old, avid, smiling with too many teeth – and his burning blood instantly chilled to ice.

Ancients.

With a calm he did not possess and a smirk that masked his dismay, Riven tipped an invisible hat and bowed mock-courtly at Elara. "You're causing a stir."

"Good," Elara said with a willful tilt of her chin. "Let them come."

Riven's eyes flashed and he scowled. Reckless woman. *Does she have a death wish*? He wanted to shake the cosmic sense back into her. "Be careful what you wish for," he warned.

Elara's own fiery eyes flashed back: green around the rim, amber within. *A starburst*, he thought. As if through those golden eyes, Riven might find a door to a hidden galaxy.

He vanished before she could see the fear filling his.

* * *

Elara woke with a deep, charred print in the shape of a starburst on her palm. To her surprise, the only thing that hurt about the mark was the memory of Riven's smartass response and infuriating smirk before they played a game of whose-eyes-tell-the-most-lies that even now made Elara's cheeks sting.

Or maybe that was from allowing him to kiss her again with those perfect, poisonous lips.

Or realizing that she'd actually hurt him, first when she'd burned him summoning the flares that split them apart, then again when she threw his ominous warning back in his beautiful face.

"*Let them come*." *Ugh*. Elara wiped her hand down her face. *Do I have a death wish*?

Still. The fact that Riven could be hurt meant she could fight back. That was no small feat. Even by defying his will or denying him…whatever it was he craved. *Denial itself is a weapon*. The realization snapped like a burst of sparks at the back of her brain.

Fear had always been Elara's shield and compass in the chaos of dreaming. Without it, she found her body flooded with a far more dangerous force when it came to Riven: a ravishing heat so hungry, so seductive, so *sublime* that with every second their mouths aligned, the bonfire coursing through her veins sent Elara careening further down a fated path from which there was no return. That was why she had shoved him away. Because the alternative was so wildly out of her control that tasting him another moment meant surely drowning in the shape of his soul.

"Room eleven," Elara whispered to the ceiling with a shaky breath, testing her command of the number. Nearby, the heater ticked. Far off, a siren wailed. In her breast, the drumbeat of war.

"Let's go," she told the dark, and her heart. "Round two."

3

Aunt Cassandra's journal smelled like cedar and ink and old thunderstorms. Elara spread it on the kitchen table, the teacup leaving a ring that would have earned her a lecture. Cass had written as if she expected Elara to read this one day and either forgive her or curse her name.

"Five wear the masks we call gods.

Night (Nyx) binds the boundary. Desire (Inanna) lights the wanting. Vengeance (Furies) keep the tally. Rebellion (Lilith) breaks the leash. Death (Thanatos) closes the door.

Eaters are their hands. Ancients are their teeth. Endless is their reign and realm."

A sketch followed – doors with numbers, and a note scrawled: *Thresholds obey will.* Another page: *Hybrid Eaters exist. There is always a price.*

"Numbers are not arithmetic here. They are thresholds. Each door is a covenant between soul and Endless, shaped by need. Eleven is the threshold of beginnings. Thirteen is the threshold of transformation. But the higher sequences – 2213, 9933 – these are not chosen. They are given. When such a door appears, it means the dreamer has crossed into the notice of powers greater than gods. The door is both sanctuary and sentence."

Elara took two deep breaths and built a controlled dreamscape.

The corridor came, but dry and still, and not a single soul around. Elara imagined a hallway runner, forest-green, and pictures that didn't peel. At the far end: Room 11 in polished brass. She laid her palm to the wood and felt the click of tumblers she had not known she owned.

"Come," she said to the empty air. "If you can."

He arrived without a ripple – simply there, as if he'd always been there, leaning against the wall. No trench coat or umbrella. Just the deadly beautiful mouth that had dismantled her. Riven took her measure and grinned. *Asshole.*

"You called?"

"I did," she said, proud that her voice didn't quake. "We need to lay down some terms." *Activating Boss Mode.*

Riven's gaze flicked to the door. "You can't let me in there."

"Watch me."

Elara opened 11 to find a small, lamplit room: a table, two chairs, a window with the rain on the outside this time. A sanctuary. Riven's kind could unmake castles. *But rooms with numbers answer to different laws.*

The Dream-Eater hovered on the threshold, head tilted. "This is yours." His eyes flashed with a wary curiosity that brightened their blue steel.

Elara's pulse thrummed. "Everything in here is," she said. "Including what you take."

He stared for a long while. "So you would leash me."

She stared right back. "I refuse to be prey."

The hunger in him flexed; so did something softer. Riven inclined his head as if accepting terms of surrender after a surprise battle.

"My dream, my rules," Elara said, counting on her fingers. "One: you feed only when I consent. Two: you touch fear only. Never desire."

Riven flinched as if she'd stripped off his mask and struck him with it. "You know what I am, then."

"I know enough."

"Three," he said, drawing a rough breath. "I never feed while angry."

Elara blinked. "That's…your rule."

Riven nodded slowly, his gaze intense. "It is if I'm stepping into your room."

Elara's heart skipped a beat. "So you're...stepping in?"

"I am starving, Dream-Weaver."

He crossed the threshold. The room held – solid, humming. Riven stopped an arm's length away, eyes on her mouth like a pilgrim before a reliquary.

"Say it," he said. "Or I won't touch you."

Elara swallowed. Power pooled low in her belly, different from fear. "You may feed."

Riven moved with terrible gentleness – one hand at her jaw, the other hovering in the air like an apology. His lips found hers with desperate need, and this time she felt the pull but didn't fight it as fear unspooled from her like a ribbon. Beneath it, something else stirred, and he… stopped. Held still, trembling.

"Only fear," he whispered against her, their mingled breath causing an involuntarily shiver to ripple through her. "I will not take what I will not give back."

Elara would have asked what that meant, but the kiss changed, tilted, and a rush of images pressed into her: a young man kneeling in a temple of stars; two goddesses in shadow and gold laying their hands on either side of his throat; a voice that was heat and honey, another that was velvet and night. Riven, torn neatly in two.

She gasped, and he pulled away as if scalded.

"You're…spilling," she stuttered, confused and breathless. "Pieces of you, I mean."

Riven was shaking. "Only with you." His voice was barely a whisper.

Outside, the rain smelled suddenly of myrrh and roses. Elara shut the window. The lamplight flickered. Hairline cracks traced the room's ceiling like constellations trying to rearrange themselves.

Riven stared upward. "Fuck. They're close."

"Who?"

"The ones I warned you about." He met her eyes with a gravity that stole her breath. "Ancients. And they've decided you taste like war."

4

Riven pushed Elara behind him the instant the wallpaper buckled, its seams ripping open like flesh. Shadows poured in like a tide, and from its rush stepped Korathis – wearing a gentleman's ruin like a suit: silk shredded just so as though torn at some endless frenzied feast. His mouth, too, was a ruin of roses and blood, smiling too wide, too red. Every inch of him gleamed with hunger restrained only for effect.

"Brother," Korathis crooned. The word was sweet rot, a caress sharpened to cut. "She's exquisite. Give her, and I will be merciful."

Riven's laugh scraped. "You don't have mercy."

"True. But I could stop with her." Korathis inhaled fiendishly. "Desire burns bright in this one. Imagine the silence after." His laugh was music warped, like a love song played backwards. "And, oh, how I would savor her. You'd be proud."

Riven lunged. They met like storms – shadow and heat, hunger against hunger. The numbered room shuddered, its laws straining. Elara tried to stay tucked behind as Riven slammed Korathis into the table, chairs splintering, window holding by faith alone. But even Riven felt small against Korathis's ravenous grace.

* * *

The temperature dropped then. The lamplight guttered blue. Another presence slid from the corner like frost. Elara knew it before she turned, because her breath had stopped moving in her chest.

Another Ancient stood there, no monstrous teeth, no grotesque form, only the unbearable reflection of...*her*. He wore her memory, her worst *failure*, like a cloak: the alley, the siren-red wash, her mother's scream trapped in her throat. That was his feast: not blood, but the seconds in which she froze. He smiled with her own helplessness. Fear was not his weapon; it was his scripture, and he read her soul line by trembling line.

"Elara," he drawled, "last descendent of legendary Elarion, the Master Builder!" *It's my voice*, she realized.

My fear, speaking back to me. "You know who I am. You always have. *I am* Umbryss. A pleasure to finally meet."

Elara's mouth dried. The old paralysis slithered up her spine like ice water. In the corner of her eye, Riven and Korathis blurred – blows, snarls; that red, obscene mouth. Umbryss stepped closer, waiting for Elara with the promise of endless night. He didn't need to strike; he only needed her stillness. *Because Desire devours where Fear endures. And between them, mortals are never free.*

"You'll freeze again," Umbryss cooed. "And when you do, you'll lose him, as you've lost those you loved before. And I'll wear your terror again like an All Hallows' Eve mask."

Elara's fingers clenched, nails cutting skin. *Do something*. The words tolled in her skull. *Do anything*.

"I see you," Umbryss purred. "And I will keep you."

"No," Elara whispered. Then louder: "No."

* * *

Korathis had Riven pinned against the splintered table, silk brushing like nettles. "Taste her," the Ancient taunted. "One mouthful of desire and you'll remember what it is to feast. Do it, and I'll even call you my equal."

Riven snarled, straining. "I'd rather starve!" His vow burned acid in his throat.

"Then you'll die hollow, while I drink her dry." Korathis's gaze flicked toward Elara, and his smile widened.

Rage surged, but so did terror. Riven caught sight of Umbryss behind Elara, cloaked in her stillness. Both Ancients, circling. Both gods' teeth closing.

He was losing.

* * *

The walls bowed with the weight of two battles: Korathis's frenzy, Umbryss's silence. Elara pressed her palm to the nearest wall and *willed.* Numbers stirred under her skin, searing: 11, bright as fire. It hurt now – a good hurt. But not enough.

Her terror spiked, and she refused to let it stop her. She shoved the fear outward, weaponized it, and the wall split. Brass gleamed through. A door waited. *Double or nothing.*

2213. The air smelled suddenly like winter stars.

"Elara—" Riven's voice broke across the room. He was staggering, body wrecked with want, blood-black shadows staining his jaw. His eyes locked on hers, desperate, starving, still fighting for her, *with her*.

She grabbed his arm. "With me."

Korathis moved like a knife. Umbryss like a night tide. Elara didn't let the fear flood her; she used it, body shaking with power she did not understand. Fear drove her legs; defiance drove all the rest.

"Consent," she said to Riven, because the room listened to that word, and dragged him through the threshold. The door slammed behind them with the weight of eternity.

5

Korathis's howl clawed the air, fury and lust entwined. Umbryss's whisper slid after them, colder than death. Brass still glowed in Elara's palm: 2213. She didn't know why that number had come, only that it was *more*: more final, more binding, more hers.

The chamber was vast and cathedral-dark, lit by constellations that shifted restlessly overhead; they didn't belong to any sky Elara knew. An altar waited at its heart. The air tasted of iron and roses and frost, both Ancients pressing at the walls, their wills colliding.

Riven sagged to his knees in front of the altar. Shadows crawled over his skin like parasites. His lips pulled back from his teeth, hunger and shame tearing him open. "I can't…can't stop it," he rasped. "If I touch you now, I'll take everything."

And Elara saw how this ended. If he fed like he had to, he *would* take everything. If he didn't, he'd die. Either way she'd lose him. "Look at me," she said, crouching before him. He did. Those steel-blue eyes were still his to command. "If you take, you take because I give."

"Elara…" Riven's whisper was half plea, half prayer. His starving eyes locked on her mouth and her heart hammered. "If I taste desire—"

"Then taste what I offer. All of it. Nothing else." She pressed her hand to his chest, where his heartbeat still stuttered under withering hunger, its wild pulse echoing her own. "You left pieces of yourself in me, remember? And I've kept them. Safe. Now I'm giving them back."

Riven stared, stunned. He clutched her hair fiercely and pressed her close like he was holding onto her with the last shred of his soul. "Say it," he rasped, breath ragged and hot against hers. "Please. Let me in all the way, Elara."

Swiping her tongue along the seam of his lips, Elara whispered. "Kiss me, Riven."

And together, they broke.

* * *

Those words. Those three words coming out of those perfect lips. Those lips that set every part of me to rising. Lips I would make love to for an eternity. An eternity of anything, *everything*, she dreamed.

I was *hers*. *Endlessly*.

When I disappeared into Elara's wet warmth and soft moans, it all fell away. She melted into me, and fuck, I moaned too, drunk and drowning in her breath, her body, her soul. This close, nearly skin to skin, I could *finally* touch her, taste her, hear her, watch her, *worship* her.

We held each other; opened each other; filled and surrendered ourselves to one another. Everything we'd hidden away. All of it laid bare. Loving her was electrifying, and I wanted more. *More*!

Gods help me, I fed. I fed and I fed, until I was fucking destroyed.

The world split. Fear streamed out of Elara first – bright, clean, searing sweet – and I drank with a care that nearly killed me. But beneath it burned desire, molten and inexorable, and when it surged, I nearly tore away. Until – she pushed memories into me.

Not hers. *Mine.*

I saw them spill across her kiss: summer fields, blackberry wine, a woman's laugh like church bells, the temple of stars where Nyx and Inanna bound my throat, cursed my name, split me asunder. I had been human before they made me into hunger. I had loved. Been loved.

Riven. Elara's luminous soul sang across the ages.

Elara! I called back, reaching, reaching.

She had miraculously caught those pieces of me and pushed them all back into our kiss, the way you push air into drowning lungs. I had never known fullness without ruin. Never known a kiss that didn't end in absence. Her mouth remade me with a violence as gentle as rain.

The hunger buckled. Consent rewrote laws older than gods. Where feeding had always hollowed, now it *filled.* The leash around my throat loosened a notch – enough to breathe. And for the first time, I wasn't devouring, I was… *exchanging.* I kissed her as I sobbed into her mouth and fed not as a predator, but as a man, savoring the pleasure of vulnerability and the thrill of love.

I was gone. Completely undone. And when the world righted itself, it all felt different. *I* felt different. Like I'd been remade in the cathedral of her heart.

* * *

Constellations wheeled. Korathis seethed outside, a storm denied its ravage. He heaved his frenzied body through the doorframe, but 2213 burned to the quick. His silks caught fire; roses blackened on his lips. "Why won't you starve!" he shrieked.

Because she chose me, Riven thought, *and that changes all the rules.* He drove Korathis back through the threshold – not with hideous hunger, but with humanity as his blade: berry-stained fingertips, laughter and loving eyes, a name rewoken, a soul remade whole. Back and back and back Riven hurled Desire's Ancient into the hellscape that waited to devour him.

Umbryss seeped low across the ceiling, wearing Elara's worst terror intensified: her frozen hands, the scream locked in her chest, her mother's lifeless body. The Ancient bent close, whispering with her own voice: "You'll fail him. Just as you failed before."

Elara's entire body shook with the effort it took to push past her icy pain and step toward her greatest torment as fire swayed in her palm. "My fear is my own. I wield it like shield and scythe. And terror tells no lies."

Riven watched transfixed as Elara's words flared through the chamber like commandments. Umbryss froze for once, cracks splitting his shadow-skin as though he'd been named and unbound. Night's Ancient smile faintly, almost…proud, before collapsing into murk and starlight.

* * *

Now Riven stood before Elara on the threshold of 2213 as if waiting his turn to be sentenced. She stepped closer and took his hand. He looked radiant to Elara's eyes. Positively exquisite. A glint in his dangerous blue gaze.

"They will keep coming," he warned.

"Then we build more doors," Elara said. "New numbers. New dreamscapes. But this door? It's ours."

Riven brought her palm to his lips and kissed her reverently, as if it were the first sacred thing he'd touched since he was a young man in truth.

"Will…will you wake with me?" Elara asked, startled by her own courage.

Riven's smile was a broken thing mended. "Always, if you'll have me. Elara." Her name on his lips was a vow. He kissed her again with a love sweet and full, a love that gave and gave and gave, pressing grief and memory and devotion into her mouth because he trusted her with his soul as she trusted him with hers.

When Elara woke in her own dark room, her palm still bore the sigil 2213. On the windowsill, a single black button glimmered in the moonlight – a relic from a trench coat Riven hadn't been wearing when they last met.

In the corner, the air shifted the way a door does when a key turns – an almost-sound, a promise. For the first time in years, Elara breathed into the night and grinned, snuggling back under her blankets to summon her dreams with lusty anticipation.

Seduction and Shadows

Corina Lee

Clouds, dark and swollen, cast shadows over the hillside, and an ancient oak leered down from the top, its skeletal branches twisting grotesquely. Beckoning. Daring me to enter through the doorway carved by elves in yestertimes.

It was a death sentence to enter.

Why did I think I could succeed when everyone else had failed? I wasn't a hero. I had no magic – I was a Regular.

A thief.

My hand curled around the treasure hidden inside my pocket, guilt twisting like a serpent in my chest. Only Rila knew what I'd done so long ago. I was foolish.

My umber skirt slapped my ankles, and winds thrashed the silver strands of my hair across my face, as if whipping me for my past transgressions.

I had to try. I could no longer cower, safe in my village.

The King was dead.

The Prince, lost.

The traitorous Valiha would claim the crown unless someone rescued Prince Aether. Many tried, and failed, including my poor sweet lovestruck friend. Rila accepted the Sorcerer's challenge – walk into shadow to save Prince Aether. Anyone who failed would become a slave in Valiha's dungeons.

Rila hadn't hesitated, but Rila hadn't returned.

She'd sacrificed herself to rescue the Prince.

An image of the Prince took life within my mind. His youthful smile, joyful and teasing, his eyes, sharp, like a crystal storm. And those perfect, pointed ears.

We met. Once. That moment was burned into my memory. We were but elflings when he and the King traveled to our village to meet with the elders.

The Prince had been kind.

I stole from him.

That was a dozen lifecycles ago. If it weren't for Rila, I'd still be cowering in my village. Our friendship was too precious to cast aside. I wouldn't forsake her. I had to go after her and face my shame.

Rain fell like tears from the sky, as if grieving my demise even before I began.

Taking a steadying breath, I approached the door and knocked on the ancient wood. It opened of its own accord, as if expecting me.

The area inside the tree was much larger than I'd expected. Silver lamps dripped from the ceiling, casting a harsh marigold gloom over the room. Chairs made of antler and bone surrounded a table of polished ebony.

Valiha himself stood behind a desk. Severe eyebrows rose above his dead orbs. "What is this? A drowned rat on my doorstep?" His voice was harsh, like the winds of the Naavian Desert. "What could you possibly want, I wonder?"

Courage Kiera. I lifted my chin. "I've come to accept your challenge."

His lips curled into a snarl. "You get one chance to rescue Prince Aether, and if you fail, you'll be trapped, bound to an eternity of servitude. No one has bested me yet."

Molten hatred quickened through my veins. I would return Prince Aether to his rightful place and rescue Rila.

Valiha would fall.

"I'll beat you at your own game."

"Big words for a little elf." A parchment and quill magically appeared in his hands. He slapped them on the table. "Sign here. A binding contract. If you fail, your soul is mine for eternity."

I grasped the quill, and without hesitation, signed my name.

Kiera Marivel.

An evil gleam brightened his eyes. "I look forward to adding another slave to my collection, and such a pretty one."

"I'll prove you wrong."

One eyebrow rose, as if questioning the resolve in my tone. "We shall see."

Valiha raised his staff above his head and lightning flashed.

BOOM.

The walls of the tree shivered.

Valiha chanted foreign words, his tone deep and steady, weaving a tapestry of lethargy through my brain.

Dark grey matter swirled into a vortex of dust and shadows. Gripping the stolen treasure for courage, I stepped into the cloud. My calves lost their strength, and I slumped to the floor.

An abyss opened beneath me; the air shifted – then bent. I fell. Tumbling. Twisting through a haze of starlight and fog.

Fear squeezed the air from my chest and nausea churned my stomach. *Don't look.* I slammed my eyes shut.

"Oomph." I landed on my back, my head resting on something hard. Smells of sea mist and tanglo berries surrounded me.

Warm fingers caressed my forehead. "Hello there beautiful."

My eyes snapped open. Something hard was someone's lap. No, not someone…

"Prince Aether." My voice was a breathy whisper. It had been forever since I last saw him, but I would recognize that smile anywhere. Eyes, the color of newly formed crystals, studied me.

His fingers trailed softly across my lips. My breathing deepened. I brushed aside the dark hair curling across his forehead. An intense craving came over me. I yearned to touch his perfect pointed ears, but it was something reserved only for thiramin – *soul mates*.

A low vibrating moan whistled through his lips. Did he wish for it too?

What was I doing? I'd lost all reason. I pressed against his chest and scrambled out of his lap, my silken blouse gaping at the neck. I grasped the thin fabric tight with one hand as my gaze swept the space, looking for danger.

The walls and floor wavered, as if they had no substance, but I'd stopped falling. I jerked my hand in front of my face. My long slender fingers were solid. I was real.

Prince Aether, he was too. But the overstuffed velvet chair he sat on was nearly invisible. Otherwise, the room was empty.

Where was Rila?

Disappointment thick and heavy squeezed my chest. I'd imagined all sorts of scenarios I'd be walking into, but this was the last thing I'd expected.

Aether rose from his seat. "You run from me too quickly Titta Nénar."

Little Star.

"Why do you call me that?"

"Because you fell from the heavens and into my arms." His words were low, like a caress. "You were meant for me. Come here so I can properly ravish you." He grasped my hand and drew me close. His breath was but a whisper on my neck. Was he crazy? He knew nothing about me. Then his warm lips met the soft skin below my ear. My pulse jumped. Lips parted.

"You're a temptress sent here to ensnare me." His warm breath caressed my neck, and desire coiled between my legs.

No! This was a distraction. A seduction.

And he was a little too cocky for my liking.

I yanked from his arms. Focus.

"Prince Aether." I dropped to one knee. "I am Kiera—"

"Why do you kneel?" His eyebrows furrowed in confusion. "I'm not a prince." He grasped my hand and lifted me from the floor.

"You are Aether of Elmore. Valiha trapped you here. We must find a way to escape."

"Where would I go?"

"To your kingdom."

Clouds gathered in his eyes.

"Don't you remember what happened? Valiha captured you ten moon cycles ago. You've been lost. Others have come, searching for you. Haven't you seen them?"

"None of this is familiar, but you…do I know you?"

Dread knotted my stomach. Did he remember our meeting? That I'd stolen from him?

"We met once when we were young."

Confess. Now.

My hand fisted around the treasure and started to pull it out, but hesitated, and released it back to the folds.

You're a coward, Kiera.

"Will you come with me? Please?" I asked. "Your people need you—"

"You talk nonsense." He held his finger to my lips. "But if you want me to be a prince, I can be anything you want me to be."

"Valiha must've stripped your memories."

"It's you whose mind must be muddled from the fall." Aether grasped my hand. "Come with me. I'll get us some elderberry wine. It'll clear your head."

The lights flickered.

A table of food appeared before us, overflowing with meats and puddings, berries, and other sweet treats. A fountain with lavender liquid flowed in the center. My mouth dropped. "How did you do that?"

He swiped a goblet from the table and held it beneath the flowing liquid and took a sip. His clouded, crystal eyes considered me over the rim. Another goblet, already filled, snapped into his other hand. "Try this. It's delicious."

I accepted the glass and took a sip, the sweet, fruity liquid coating my tongue. My reflection stared back at me from the amber liquid. It, along with the glass, was almost nonexistent. I dipped my finger into the liquid. Cold. But it did not cling to my finger as it should.

"This isn't real." The goblet, the chair, even the people were but shadows, and Aether acted like he was in a daze. "Is this a dream?"

"You're my dream, sent here to seduce me."

The lights flickered again.

We stood in a ballroom. The walls wavered, like a mirage in an elfling storybook. Fairies and gnomes, pixies and elves twirled across the dance floor, the music, low. Pulsing. Wood sprites and topless sea nymphs gathered around tables. Everyone lacked substance.

Like ghosts.

"Dance with me, Titta Nénar." He swept me into his arms, gold dust coating the dance floor.

The pulsing music infused my soul with a desire to dance. Prince Aether lifted me, and we twirled. Then we were gliding across the floor, his arms securing me tight against his chest.

Glitter and gold, velvet and starlight. Couples danced closely, lost in the deep, throbbing rhythms. My skirt was no longer the color of mud, but a deep rich violet, and my blouse was made of the softest pearls.

Time slowed to a blur. Our bodies molded as we moved; his hard body pressed to mine. His lips, so close. His breath, hot on my neck. He smelled of exotic spices and rich cocoa. My pulse jumped. We twirled and dipped, and when he brought me up, my arms slid around his neck.

"You're an enchantress." His hot breath tickled my ear.

Me? "No, I have no magical abilities—"

"You don't realize the power you exude. You're out to seduce and trap me."

The fog muddling my brain cleared. "You're the one who's trapped here." I stepped out of his arms. "Please remember. Your home is by the seaside; a majestic castle made of sea stone and marble. There are stables. You love horses. Everywhere you visit, you ride a dapple grey – Lightfoot is his name. A gift from your mother. She was a Seer and the kindest, most generous queen, and the entire kingdom mourned her death. She had hair the color of spun gold, and eyes the shade of the sea. And the King—"

"My father."

I held my breath. "Do you remember?"

"No, I don't have a father."

I grasped his arms and stepped close. "Aether, please, wake up. This isn't real."

His face was millimeters from my own. "Oh, but this is real."

His lips brushed mine. Soft. Tender. Then – crushing.

His arms pinned me to his chest, and my mouth moved against his. He tasted like elderberries and sweet nectar.

A deep groan rumbled from his chest, his hand gripping the hair at the nape of my neck. Blazing a trail of kisses across my throat, to my ear—

"No, we mustn't." I yanked away, gasping. He'd kiss away my memory and I'd forget my purpose, as he'd forgotten his.

Would it be so bad to be stuck here with Aether?

"I'm sorry…I…I need a minute." I elbowed my way through the sea of dancers. All my attempts at convincing Aether had failed, but I didn't have time to waste dancing. I had to find a way to escape this place.

I approached one of the walls and put my hand to the wavering image. It stretched – elastic and springy.

It didn't break.

Light flashed, reflecting off the wall. *BOOM.*

The light flickered.

I twirled and gasped. The ballroom vanished, and in its place was a meadow bursting with colorful wildflowers. Aether stood on the far side, and a woman in a forest silk gown, with hair the color of copper appeared between us. She was not a mirage, like the dancers had been, but solid. Real.

"Rila! I was so worried. Where have you—"

"You kissed him. I saw you." She stalked toward me, her face purple with fury.

She'd seen? My heart dipped into my stomach.

"He's mine." Her voice was low and threatening. "Valiha promised if I returned, he'd release me from our contract, and I could stay with the Prince. You can take my place in the dungeons for all I care."

Storm clouds swirled in her eyes.

I took a step back. "What has come over you?" In all our years of friendship, Rila had never said an unkind word, to me or to anyone. Jealousy had transformed my friend into a monster I didn't recognize.

"You know how I've always felt about him."

"This is all a misunderstanding," I said. "I was worried and came searching for you. We're friends."

"You're no friend of mine. You're a thief and a coward."

She turned her back and stalked away.

Pain exploded in my chest. I doubled over, hugging my sides. She knew what I'd done all those years ago, and never once threw it in my face. Until now.

I cupped my head in my hands. Rila spoke the truth.

I am a thief. A coward.

And I kissed the prince, knowing how she'd always pined for him.

But so had I.

Everything was unraveling. I'd been hiding away from doing the right thing for years. How did I think now would be any different?

But you've changed. I faced Valiha, didn't I? That alone took courage. That little nugget bloomed inside my head. I didn't want to be a thief or a coward.

And I wouldn't let Rila ruin everything.

I raced across the meadow after her.

Rila moved to Aether's side, resting her hand on his arm. The same lusty look he'd given me was now directed at her.

"Hello beautiful. Who are you?"

"I'm Rila, remember?"

"Rila. Where have you been all my life?" Prince Aether cupped her chin with his fingers and held her gaze.

"I'm here now."

A spark of something dark and dangerous snaked through me. He looked as if he wanted to kiss her.

Was he going to kiss her?

"Stop!"

Prince Aether's gaze slid from Rila, and his eyebrows dipped. "Do I know you?"

A sharp pain pierced my heart. He'd already forgotten me.

Rila blocked my view of Aether. Her voice was low and menacing. "I'm warning you. Leave us, now." Her eyes flashed fire and I stepped back. Rila's eyes were clouded. Unnatural.

Had Valiha cast a spell on her too?

Rila led Aether away like he was a unicorn on a leash.

He wasn't getting away that easily. If I didn't do this now, I'd never have the chance. I yanked his arm, spinning him so we faced each other. "Aether, please…wake up, this is a dream."

"Hello, beautiful. Do I know you?" He squeezed his eyes as if trying hard to unravel a puzzle.

"I'm Kiera. Little Star. Don't you remember?"

"Titta Nénar."

"Kiera, stop." Rila grabbed my arm and yanked. "Don't–"

"No, you stop, Rila." I pushed her with everything I had. She fell to the grass in a pile of crinoline and lace, a look of disbelief on her face.

Do it now. Show him.

My hand gripped around the treasure and I withdrew it from my pocket. "Don't you remember? We were just kids when we met. You teased me about my freckles. I got angry. So angry I did something awful. I stole this from you."

"Kiera, no!" Rila struggled to rise from the ground.

Ignoring her, I held my hand out to Aether and relaxed my fist. A small, perfect acorn rested in the palm of my hand.

Confusion clouded his eyes. "Why do I recognize this? It's familiar." I dropped the treasure into Aether's open palm. "I know this." He held the acorn to his ear and closed his eyes, and an Elvish song burst from the small trinket. "This was my mother's."

"No!" Rila put her hands over her face, her shoulders shaking as she sobbed.

"I'm sorry," I said. "I never should've taken it. I knew how much it meant to you, but…I just wanted to have a little piece of you, because I knew I could never have you."

Lights flashed, bright and blinding.

The ballroom reappeared, but this time the music was too loud. The dancers spun wildly, manically, their harsh laughter looping endlessly.

Sparks rained from the sky, and the dancers disappeared.

Prince Aether tore his gaze from the acorn. His eyes locked with mine.

The lights burst into a waterfall of colors. The walls shook. The dancers were back.

The clouds cleared from Aether's eyes.

"I remember."

BOOM!

The floor fell away. Screams echoed as the dancers around us vanished into a dark abyss. Rila crouched low, her fingers splayed as if searching for something to hold on to. But she didn't fall. Neither did we.

"I should've returned your acorn long before now, but I was a coward. I'll accept any punishment I have coming."

"No more explanations needed, Titta Nénar." He held his finger to my lips, silencing my words.

My heart lifted. "You remember me."

"How could I forget the little girl with stars misting her cheeks? You didn't steal this acorn. I misplaced it on purpose, hoping you would find it."

"But...why?"

"My mother was a Seer. She said a girl with silver starlight in her hair and a constellation on her cheeks would fall from the sky one day, returning something I'd lost. Although we met only briefly, I wished that girl to be you. Because of you, I've regained my memories."

The walls disintegrated, and the last of the illusion broke. The ancient oak stood before us, its door open to the outside world.

The earth shook and I stumbled. Aether grasped my arm, keeping me from falling.

Rila struggled to stand. I hesitated, but grasped her hand.

"I'm so sorry," she sobbed. "I don't know what came over me." Her words were genuine, and the clouds had cleared from her eyes.

The last feelings of betrayal shattered, and I pulled her into a hug. "I forgive you. You were under a spell—"

"Keira, we must go. Now." There was urgency in Aether's voice.

I twirled round. The exit had burst into flames, consuming the ancient wood.

Aether grasped my hand and we raced across the room, my heart galloping in my chest. We reached the exit—

Something hard glanced off my temple. I fell to my knees cradling my head. The world spun.

Rila grasped my arm. "Get up!" Together, Aether and Rila hauled me to my feet, and we raced for the door.

Heat and flames roared toward us. We threw ourselves through the doorway, fire and flames snapping at us as we breached the barrier between the dream and reality.

We collapsed onto the ground and I lay on my back, my heart thumping wildly in my chest, my breaths coming in gasps.

The azure sky was so beautiful. I thought I'd never see it again.

Rila lay beside me, and our gazes locked. We broke into simultaneous grins. I reached for her hand and gave it a squeeze.

Heat lashed out. I released her hand, and we both scooted backward. The ancient oak was ablaze.

Lightning flashed, and the Sorcerer appeared in a cloud of smoke. "So, you managed to escape, but you still lost." He chortled, his voice dark and malevolent. The fire framed his body as he lifted his staff into the air. He began chanting.

Aether jumped to his feet. "I'm done being controlled by your mind games." He held the acorn before him. Stars rose from his hand, and the acorn transformed into a sword of polished silver. He stepped forward. "My mother knew someone would betray our kingdom. She didn't know who, but she prepared me."

The sorcerer raised his hands above his head as if to unleash his magic, but Aether was quicker, running toward him.

Valiha dodged and released a burst of dark matter toward Aether.

"Aether, watch out!" I struggled to my feet, knowing I was powerless to help.

Aether dropped to one knee, the magic passing over his head, then he barreled toward Valiha, ramming into him with his shoulder.

Valiha stumbled, but Aether wasn't letting up. "You killed my father. You imprisoned me, and my people. Now you'll get a taste of my magic."

Aether pointed his sword toward Valiha. A lightning bolt shot from the tip, straight into Valiha's chest.

Valiha dropped his staff and clutched the wound. His mouth dropped as if in disbelief. Then he toppled over.

Dead.

An intense trembling shook the ground. It cracked open, and a staircase appeared. At least two dozen elves spilled from the hole, looking ready to fight. When they saw the prince they knelt before him, bowing low.

Aether's sword shrank, until it was an acorn once more. He placed it in his pocket, then approached the elves.

"Each of you tried to save me, and for that I commend you. You are free."

The elves jumped to their feet, laughter filling the air as they crowded around their prince.

"Kiera?" Rila grasped my hand, and I turned to face my friend. "I know what I said to you, and I am ashamed. Even if I were under a spell, I should've been stronger than that.

I've always known your feelings for Aether. I've never cared for him as you have. If you want to pursue him, you have my blessing."

I threw my arms around my friend and hugged her close. "Our friendship is everything to me. Only if you're sure."

"I am. I love you, Kiera." She stepped away. "Now go, talk to him." Rila turned and headed for the group of celebrating elves.

Aether's gaze met mine, and my heart skipped a beat. He patted one elf on his shoulder and left the group, his long strides quickly closing the distance between us. When he reached me, his hands gently cupped my face.

"I see you, Titta Nénar. I remember you. Be mine, please."

I swallowed hard. "But I stole from you."

"The only thing you stole from me that day was my heart. I hoped then, somehow, I'd find you again. Even though you didn't know it at the time, I gave you the acorn, and you saved me. Just as my mother predicted." He raised my hands to his mouth and brushed his lips gently, reverently across the skin. "If it weren't for you, I'd be stuck in that dream until the end of time, not realizing the difference between illusion and reality. You cared enough to keep the acorn with you and return it when I needed it the most. When I needed you. I'm giving you my heart, and all that I am." His lips brushed the sensitive skin of my neck. "Say yes, please, my real, wonderful seductress."

I'd dreamt of this ever since we were elflings. I hadn't wanted to let him go then and wasn't going to now. My dream had come true.

"Yes."

He lifted me from the ground and twirled me round, our laughter ringing out over the land. We stopped; our bodies pressed as one. His lips nipped the sensitive, untouched lobe of my ear, and my toes curled at the exquisite sensation. Aether and I were thiramin – soul mates until the end of time. Joy burst from my heart.

Aether lifted my hand and kissed the sensitive palm. Stars ignited, dancing their way across my skin in celebration. Then our lips met, in a promise of forever.

The Star Tender

Hayden Lewis

The stars shrieked when they fell, burning iridescent trails across the abyssal sky. They bounced across the surface of the lake. Each impact rang like a thousand tiny bells, weaving an eerie and dissonant symphony that resonated through the jagged peaks.

The universe mourned.

Above the star-strewn lake, at the top of the world, a temple sat derelict. An ancient, twisted tree towered over it. Bleached white branches reached greedily upwards like skeletal hands, grasping for the falling stars, gesturing in the hot wind as if to say, "Come. Come to me."

When the stars fell, a heartbeat answered.

Ba-thump.

Ryn opened her eyes. The pale gold glow of her skin illuminated the inside of the cocoon. She blinked drowsily. Slender fingers feeling for the edges, she pulled back the flaps and sat up. Cool autumn air filled her lungs, chasing away the last dredges of a century-long dream. She could taste the decaying of leaves.

Silver moonlight streamed in through the temple's shattered windows. The cocoon hung fifty feet above the ground, nestled among the rafters of the vaulted ceiling. She swung her legs over the side and dropped. Weightless as a ghost, she landed lightly on bare feet. The stone tiles were cool and dusty.

Old, unlit candles had dripped wax down the sides of the altar. An offering that might once have been a bundle of wildflowers had crumbled into dust. It had been a long time since the people in the village had come to pay homage. It had been a long time since there were people in the village at all.

They'd considered her a god, though that was far from true. She'd been human once, long ago. Long, long ago. Every time she curled up in the cocoon to sleep, she emerged more changed. She ran a hand over her bare scalp. Her hair had long since fallen out. Her skin had lost its warm-blooded undertone and turned a pale metallic gold, luminescent in the darkness. Magic crackled in her desiccated veins. It kept her alive and unaging, even after all these centuries.

For now.

The tattered remains of another cocoon, paper-thin and dull, enveloped a skeleton like a shroud. The gilded bones were dry and clean of flesh. Ryn knelt and touched two fingers to the skull.

"So I am the last," she murmured. Gently, she cradled the skeleton and carried it to the large stone door at the back of the temple. She placed her palm on the door. Recognizing her touch, it opened, allowing her into the garden.

The tree overshadowed the temple. Once, its branches were lush with waxy, dark gold foliage, heavily laden with glowing fruits. Now it was dark. A brittle gray leaf fell from above and landed at her feet.

Beyond the tree sat row upon row of graves. Ninety-eight headstones in total, soon to be ninety-nine. Ninety-nine it would remain. There would be no one to bury her.

Ryn laid the skeleton down among the tangled roots. Tentatively, she touched the knotted wood and closed her eyes. Her chest tightened at the absence of its pulse – but she found it, deep inside and very faint. She concentrated, willing some of her own power into its ancient core. Her strength left her and she dropped to her knees, but the tree's heart beat steadily again, at least for now.

Dizzy, she rested her forehead against the trunk. "I can't keep this up, old friend," Ryn whispered. "I don't know how to help you."

The stars had been falling less and less often, and she'd been sleeping longer and longer. Every time she woke, the tree was worse. Every time she went to sleep, she feared she might not wake up.

And now she was the last. It was all up to her.

When her strength returned, she crossed back through the temple, grabbing a rough fabric sack along the way. She slung it over her shoulder and stepped outside. She still had a job to do.

The last stars fell, shrieking and glittering, ringing with each impact. She walked across bare rock where grass once grew to the edge of the cliff. Not much of anything grew anymore. She stepped off the cliff.

Light as the wind, she dropped, landing on the cool surface of the water as easily as if it were solid ground. A trail of glowing footprints followed in her wake.

The stars twinkled atop the midnight water as if they'd moved from one sky to another. She collected them one by one. By the time she finished, the sack was scarcely half filled. Ryn sighed. What used to take a hundred trips would now take only one.

Suddenly a shrieking rent the air, louder than she'd ever heard. Her head jerked up. An enormous star hurtled down, trailing astral fire. Ryn dove out of the way. It slammed into the water and skipped right over her head. Flame skimmed her scalp. The sack was knocked from her hand. Stars flew in every direction, ringing in a dissonant cacophony. Face down on the water, trembling arms covering her head, she squeezed her eyes shut and prayed this was not how it ended – please, no, not after everything she'd sacrificed!

Silence. She looked up.

All the stars she'd collected were once more strewn across the surface of the lake, still tinkling quietly from the impact. Her tunic was soaked. She stood, wringing water from the fabric. The large star had bounced almost halfway back to shore.

Her scalp burned. She probed the blistered skin with her fingertips. A hiss escaped her lips. It had been centuries since she'd felt pain.

Nothing like this had ever happened before. She snatched up her waterlogged sack and regathered the stars. Warily, she approached the large one. It flared and split open. Ryn shielded her eyes, squinting. A glowing figure rose from the broken star. The light faded, and the figure dropped.

Ryn yelped and lurched forward. She toppled into the remains of the star, but the stranger was safely in her arms. Ryn's eyes widened as she gazed at the one she'd caught.

Ah.

Surely this was what divinity looked like.

Her skin was warm, unlike Ryn's, the dazzling picture of a star-studded sky. Golden freckles dusted her cheeks and her bare shoulders, glowing like chips of sunshine. Tiny beads of light spun around her wrists and ankles. She had no hair, but a cloud of luminescent pink-gold dust drifted in ringlets and spirals around her face.

She was sunlight incarnate. She was a supernova. She was the halo of a singularity, the last echo of a light long lost.

Ryn lifted her with ease, the sack of stars over one shoulder, and carried her up to the temple. All the while the stranger never stirred, but Ryn could feel her pulse, strong and steady.

Questions burned in her mind as she set the stranger down gently on the temple floor. Who was she? *What* was she? Why was she here? She would get no answers until the stranger woke, but if time had taught her anything, it was patience.

Anyway, she had a grave to dig.

It was a weary sort of grief, to be the last of your kind. When the first of them had died, she'd sobbed until daybreak. She'd cried, too, for the second, and the third. But somewhere along the line, her tears had dried up. Now she had none left to give.

The sun was rising when Ryn returned from the garden, dirt staining her hands and her tunic. She closed the stone door behind her, then stopped in her tracks. The stranger was not on the floor where she'd left her.

She was awake, levitating by a shattered window, gazing out. She turned, and met Ryn's eyes. Her irises were dark. Ryn had expected them to be white, like her own. They stared at each other.

"I'm Ryn," she said finally. "What's your name?"

"My name," she said, speaking slowly as if for the first time. "I…don't think I was ever given a name."

"Oh. Should I give you one?" Ryn took her silence as permission. "How about Astra?" She couldn't imagine a name more perfect for a creature so divine.

"Astra," she repeated, as if trying it out. She beamed. "I like it. Astra, Astra, As-tra—" Her stomach rumbled loudly and she touched her belly with a bemused tilt of her head.

"Are you hungry?" Ryn dug through the sack of stars and pulled out one of the smaller, duller ones, no good for planting anyway. She held it out.

Astra looked at it, then back at Ryn questioningly.

"Like this." Ryn cracked its glossy shell, exposing the glowing jelly inside. She scooped an iridescent globule out with her fingers and popped it into her mouth. It fizzed sweetly on her tongue.

Astra took the star and sucked at it quietly. While she ate, Ryn got to work. She sat on the floor, sorting the stars into two piles. The brightest ones with the purest sounds would be planted in the garden. The rest would be eaten. Astra watched everything with curious eyes.

"Where did you come from, Astra?" Ryn asked when she'd finished.

"I don't know. I don't remember." Astra closed her eyes. "I think...It was very dark. It was very dark for a long time." She moved in a blink, suddenly floating over Ryn, hands hovering over her blistered scalp. "You're hurt. Did I do this?"

Ryn held her breath as the burns cooled and vanished under Astra's fingers. She sighed blissfully.

A miracle.

Astra retreated, hands curled close to her chest, brow furrowed and dark eyes directed at the floor. A shy smile graced her lips.

"Do you have somewhere to go?" Ryn asked.

Astra shook her head.

"Then you can stay with me, if you like. Though I have work to do."

With the night's return came another celestial chorus, sparser than the previous. The stars used to rain nightly all through the autumn, every year, then every decade, now less than once a century. Ryn doubted this starfall would last even a month.

Astra accompanied her out onto the water. She ran like a bird, high up on her toes, delighted by the ringing of the stars. "It's beautiful." She twirled, arms held aloft.

Ryn watched her dance. "Yes. It is."

While Ryn collected the rest in her sack, Astra skipped a star across the surface of the water, just to hear it echo.

Back at the temple, Ryn showed Astra how to sort the stars. They worked together every night after that. Astra was pleasant company, enraptured as she was by the world, with none of the dutiful sorrow once carried by those now buried in the garden.

"What does a star grow into?" Astra asked one day.

"A tree." Ryn caressed the surface of the brightest star she'd collected so far. "If it sprouts."

Bright as it was, it was nothing compared to the radiance of that first star to fall, oh so long ago. It was nothing compared to the radiance of Astra.

Ryn stole a glance at her. The shameful feelings forming in her heart confused and disgraced her. She was a star tender; she had a duty, first and foremost. But Astra was the most beautiful star of all.

"Does it grow more stars?"

"No. It used to grow fruit, but it hasn't had any for a long time. That's why we eat the stars now."

The starfall finished three days short of a month after Astra's arrival. They waited on the cliff all night, but no more came.

"What now?" Astra asked.

"Now we plant them," Ryn said, "and hope for the best. Then I go to sleep again, until the next starfall."

For once, Astra said nothing, only staring out over the lake.

Ryn didn't dare try to guess her thoughts. Her own thoughts were simple, yet utterly overwhelming.

I wish I could stay with her.

No wish of hers had ever been granted.

Dead gray leaves carpeted the garden. Ryn found the tree's pulse deep within, so faint and weak she could barely feel it. Once more she willed her power into it. Her own pulse skipped a beat and she crumpled to her knees.

"Ryn!" Astra banged on the stone door. "Ryn!"

By the time Ryn opened the door, her pulse had steadied.

Astra threw her arms around Ryn's neck, clutching her tightly as if afraid she might vanish. "I felt you fade."

Ryn cradled her awkwardly. "I'm sorry. I didn't mean to frighten you."

"What did you do?" Astra pulled back, dark eyes distraught and searching.

Ryn hesitated, then let her into the garden. She showed her the tree. Astra placed a hand on the bone-white bark.

"It's dying." Astra turned slowly to face Ryn, brow furrowed and mouth open in horror. "You've been keeping it alive with your own energy."

Ryn crushed a dead leaf in her fist. "It's the only thing I can do."

"It will kill you."

"I don't have a choice." She turned away. "Come on, we have work to do."

It took days to clear the dead leaves from the ground. Days more to dig up the cold, dark remains of the previously planted stars. None had sprouted.

"Why don't they grow?" Astra held a dead star in forlorn hands.

"I don't know," answered Ryn. "Nothing grows anymore."

The soil was dry and dusty, leached of magic. They crushed up some of the stars, mixing the star-sugar with water to reinvigorate the soil. It was an arduous, repetitive process, and even with two of them took weeks to complete.

It had never worked before. It *had* to work this time. Because without a miracle, this time would be the last.

All the while, Ryn continued to keep the tree alive. The burden had once been shared among all those who now slept beneath the garden, and one by one, they had succumbed to it. She would not give up. She wouldn't let that sacrifice be in vain.

After a particularly draining effort, Ryn slumped against the tree. She'd almost lost it. Opalescent light pulsed frantically in her irises, sputtering like a candle soon to be blown out.

Astra brought her a star and a bowl of water. "Why do you keep doing this to yourself? You're going to die, and it won't make a difference. That tree's time is up."

Ryn exhaled shakily. "You don't understand. I must do this."

"Why? Why is that plant's life more important than your own?"

"Magic comes from the stars, but it is not self-replenishing. It must be grown. It must be cared for. They—" She stopped, corrected herself. "We used too much, too greedily. I am as responsible for this sin as anyone. This tree is humanity's last hope. The garden used to be full of them, and it was my job to keep them. But one by one, they all died off. None of the starseeds I've planted have taken root. That tree is the last of its kind," she finished, "and if it dies, the world's magic dies with it."

"But who are you keeping that magic alive for, Ryn? The village is in ruins, there's no one there, I checked. There's no one for miles. No other heartbeats in my range but yours." She hesitated. "Are you sure there's anyone left in the world at all?"

She shook her head adamantly. "I can't stop now. This is my life. My purpose. If I give up, I'm nothing."

Ninety-nine of them had died for this dream. For this duty. To her last breath, to the last beat of her desiccated heart, she would see this through.

"You can't leave me," Astra whispered. "You can't leave me alone. Please."

Ryn took her hand silently. Any promises made would only be lies.

With the garden as ready as it could be, the soil rich with star-sugar, the planting began. Though the tree's condition continued to worsen, Ryn was hopeful. Maybe one of the stars would sprout, and magic could begin anew.

After all, Astra was here. That had to mean something.

By the time they buried the last star, Ryn could feel the long sleep calling her. She resisted its pull, wanting to say goodbye to Astra, but not sure how.

As she delayed the inevitable, dark clouds built up in the sky. The air smelled damp. Ryn's heart soared high with hope. Another miracle: it hadn't rained in centuries.

"What is rain like?" Astra asked.

"You'll see. I think you'll like it." Ryn decided to wait one more night. She could hold out that long, and she wanted to see Astra's reaction to the storm.

The rain started not long after sunset. Black clouds veiled the stars. Ryn stepped outside. Cool drops splattered against her bare scalp, running in rivulets down her face. She licked the water from her lips. It roused her, though the cocoon still called.

"Come on!" Ryn beckoned.

Astra followed. The rain sizzled on her skin, enveloping her in steam. Her light refracted off the water in an ethereal cloud of twinkling sparkles. She laughed and threw her head back. Each raindrop transformed into a dazzling prism in her presence.

"It feels strange!"

"You like it?" The corners of her mouth pulled upwards, muscles weak from disuse nonetheless impelled into action. For the first time in many centuries, Ryn smiled.

"Is it magic?" Astra spun in a circle, her feet hovering a few inches off the ground.

"No. The sky does this all on its own."

Lightning flashed on the horizon, followed by a boom of thunder. Astra's eyes grew wide.

"Are you sure it's not magic?" she pressed. "It has so much energy."

Ryn could feel it too, crackling in the air above them. It didn't have a pulse like magic did, though.

"I'm sure."

Astra skipped through the air and stopped just beyond the cliff, mesmerized by the lightning. Ryn stood at the edge and watched her. She didn't want to say goodbye. Rainwater surged across the rock and dry earth, flowing around her ankles in a gray torrent that plunged over the precipice to the lake far below.

Her thoughts distracted her, and though she felt the incoming energy, she didn't realize what it meant until it was too late.

Lightning struck the temple roof. Ryn's gut lurched as her connection to the cocoon was severed. No longer was she pulled towards sleep.

"No!" she screamed.

Fire roared hungrily through the temple. The dry branches of the tree crackled and popped. What little magic it had left exploded in kaleidoscopic bursts.

Ryn darted forward. Astra grabbed her arm.

"Let me go!" Ryn yelled, twisting. "I can still save it!"

"No, Ryn!" Astra said sharply. "Its time is up! Yours doesn't have to be!"

"But magic will die!"

"So be it! Let it go, Ryn! Let it go."

The temple was engulfed. Flames licked ravenously at every surface. Smoke billowed from the shattered windows in acrid clouds.

Ryn stopped struggling. She closed her eyes. The tree's pulse flickered brightly.

Ba-thump.

Then it was gone.

Ryn slid to the ground. "It was all for nothing. Everything I did, everything I sacrificed, so many lives lost and for what?" She clenched her fists.

"It wasn't for nothing." Astra knelt in the mud and took her hand. "I got to meet you, after all." She cupped her face. "I was in the dark for so long, Ryn. Nothing around me but black, empty space. I never want to go back to that. I would gladly give all the magic I have inside just to stay here instead. With you."

"Without magic, the world will be lost. It was my duty to protect it, and I failed." Ryn sobbed. She threw her head back and wailed at the uncaring sky. All the unshed tears flooded out, lost among the raindrops that washed clean her anguished face.

"This world was lost long ago." Astra rested their foreheads together. "You did not fail. You were failed by all those long ago who averted their eyes and sought to take more than could be given."

Her sobs quieted into shuddering breaths. A hollow ache filled her chest. "You know I won't long survive without magic." It crackled in her veins, animated her. Without it she would die, she knew that, had long accepted it – but Astra would be left alone.

"You won't die." Astra stared at her.

Ryn was lost in the depths of her dark eyes, mesmerized by the pink-gold reflection of the dust that drifted around her face. Astra was the last star. And Ryn? Ryn would do her duty as a star tender, until her final breath. She opened her mouth to say so.

Then Astra leaned forward and kissed her. It startled her, and for a moment she froze, but warmth surged through her and she pulled Astra closer, kissing her back. They embraced in the mud. Ryn never wanted to let her go. She felt the heat spread through her veins, and her heartbeat synced with Astra's. She knew what she'd done.

"Leave this place," Astra said breathlessly, when at last they broke apart. "Come with me. Let's see the world together."

"Okay," Ryn agreed.

The temple burned until nothing more could fuel the fire. The flames flickered lower and lower and died. The clouds rolled away, and the sky cleared. Already the world felt colder and less bright. But Astra was warm, and Ryn allowed herself to be drawn close as the sun rose on a world without magic.

* * *

Wind whistled through a burned and blackened ruin at the top of a long-dead world. It had been nearly a millennium since anyone had set foot there. No one mourned. No one was left.

Amid ninety-nine crumbled gravestones, in a soot-stained garden long untended, a sprout pushed through the ash and spread its dark gold leaves beneath a starry sky.

An Affair of the Heart

Trixie Nisbet

I looked around, curious to know where I was. Bright sunshine glowed through the diamond-leaded bay windows throwing crisscross shadows over the blue and white gingham tablecloths. White china gleamed; silver cutlery glinted. I wasn't surprised to find myself seated in what looked like a cosy café. A teapot sat on the table before me and beside it steamed a perfect cup of milky tea.

Typical, I thought. This place was just what I would expect of Conrad. Whenever we went out for the day, he'd usually contrive a visit to a teashop. To rest his old legs, he'd say. But I knew that he would arrange these stops for my benefit. I couldn't walk too far, or too fast back then. Darling Conrad, always thinking of my health, but self-conscious enough to hide it behind a smile and his own apparent need for coffee and cake.

I let myself be taken in by his gentle deception. I was always thankful for a rest and sharing a cream tea or a sticky bun with my husband became a pleasure. It seemed, looking around, that Conrad thought the same.

Details were vague. The room could be an amalgam of every tearoom we had visited. Outside the window was, perhaps, a sunny garden, or a country lane with wildflowers and flint walls velveted with moss. It was a scene distilled from many happy memories.

A tiny bell jangled as the door was opened. Blinking over his specs, Conrad peered in. He frowned, confused.

My heart might have missed a beat. It was so good to see him after all this time. I felt like running at him, folding him into a massive bearhug, never letting him go. But I forced myself to sit still.

I didn't draw his attention, though I couldn't help but smile. Dear Conrad. He appeared frail, but that was to be expected. Otherwise, he was much as I remembered him. His beard was a little whiter, and, without me around to nag him, it needed a bit of a trim, but in general he seemed to have kept himself in good shape, considering. He had his cane in his right hand. He always claimed he didn't need a walking stick, just something to lean on. He flicked it forward, gripping the silver-ball handle, and headed towards the counter. As usual, he tried to appear confident, but I noticed the shuffle of his step and the uncertainty in the flitting of his eyes.

Behind the counter a woman had appeared. In appearance, she was as vague as the café around her, but she had a curious domination of her surroundings. Knives, cake slices and other diamond-sharp utensils were arranged within her reach. Glass domes glittered over the sterile surfaces, covering, presumably, cakes or pastries. Their contents, though, defied scrutiny. I thought I detected some movement or pulse beneath some of the domes, and deliberately pushed that from my mind. The important thing, to me, was that Conrad was here: the details were window dressing.

I noticed the concern in the woman's eyes. "How are you feeling, Conrad?" she asked.

"To be honest," he said, "I feel a bit woozy." He gripped his cane for support. "I'm not even sure where I am."

"Try not to worry about that." The woman turned to glance over at an elaborate coffee machine behind her. It was black and chrome, covered in dials. A nozzle emitted a hiss of steam and from somewhere in its workings came a regular beeping sound. "Take a seat, Conrad," she said. "I'll bring over your coffee and a slab of our cherry Bakewell."

Conrad accepted this without question and shuffled towards the nearest table.

"Not that one," called the woman. She waved towards the table where I sat illuminated in the bay window. "She's been waiting for you for some time."

I tensed, suddenly nervous. I didn't want to be a shock to him, but I needn't have worried. Conrad's eyes locked with mine. For a moment, he froze with confusion, then his straggle of a beard split with the widest smile. Oh, how I had missed that smile.

"Mary?"

I stood and held out my hands. We held each other in a tight embrace. I savoured the warmth of his cheek against mine and the whisper of his voice close to my ear.

"Mary. Oh, how I've missed you."

I squeezed him to me, wanting to stay like this forever with my arms around his shoulders. Then, with a resolve that surprised even me, I eased him away to arm's length. "Sit down, Conrad." I managed to control my smile. We stared at each other for a moment across the table. He blinked slowly, his eyes heavy and obviously tired.

"I knew this day would come, Mary," he said. "It's the one thing no one can avoid. It's wrong of me, I know, but in a way, I've been looking forward to it."

That was precisely what I *didn't* want to hear. His voice was resigned and melancholy. I had to change that. I didn't want him to give up. I wanted him to fight.

"How is Lucy?" I asked.

Conrad's eyes brightened a little. I could see him working out what I would know and what he would have to tell me. "She married last year," he told me with a twinkle. "Oh, Mary, I was so proud to walk her down the aisle." Then his eyes clouded. "I would have given anything for you to have been there, too."

I felt a spasm of loss. There was so much I had missed out on already. "Life goes on," I said, and I meant it.

"But it's so hard without you, Mary."

I could feel the choke in Conrad's voice. I wanted so much to comfort him, but I had to force myself to stay calm.

The coffee machine behind the counter emitted a squealing jet of steam and the beeping became more rapid.

"My heart is broken." Conrad placed a hand to his chest. "I can feel it, an ache, a physical strangling pain. Every time I think of you. Every time something happens and you're not there to share it with me."

I glanced at the counter. The woman made some adjustment to the coffee machine, and the hiss of steam subsided. She gave me a nod to indicate that everything was under control.

"Tell me what I've missed." I kept my voice gentle. "Tell me about Lucy."

The frantic beeping from the counter became more regular as Conrad paused to take a breath.

"Her husband is a good chap," he said. "His name's Graham. They met at work. I know you'd approve of him." Conrad's eyes brightened. "And Lucy's pregnant. Mary, we're going to be grandparents in the spring."

A grandchild! This was wonderful news. I reached out to touch Conrad's hand. "Something to look forward to," I said. I needed him to look to the future.

He felt the significance in my words, took another deep inhalation and looked around again at the tearoom.

The woman from the counter had appeared at our table with a tray. She placed what appeared to be a mug of coffee in front of Conrad. "Drink this," she said. "It will do you good." Then she slid a slab of cake between us with two forks resting on the plate. "You have got to keep your strength up,

Conrad," she said. "How are you feeling, now?" I saw her turn to the coffee machine, assessing its dials and listening to the steady rhythmic beeping.

"I'm still very weary," Conrad admitted. He glanced down to where I still gripped his hand, resting on the gingham cloth next to our drinks and shared slice of cake. He looked up to the woman. "This isn't really a tearoom, is it?"

"Clever of you to work it out." She, too, assessed the cosy café: the neat tables; the sunny view beyond the bay windows; the array of machines and glassware stowed behind the counter. "Think of it as a dream," she said. "It's surprising what the mind can conjure when it's under sedation. You are worried about the procedure – that's completely understandable. But it's all mixed up with memories and..." she beamed in my direction, "just a little bit of wonder."

I squeezed Conrad's hand again. "You are having heart surgery," I told him. "This lady is the surgeon."

Conrad slumped back in his chair and nodded slightly as if this was what he had suspected. "My heartache..."

The woman gave Conrad a reassuring smile. "There's a whole team working on you," she waved vaguely behind the counter. "It's very busy back there in the kitchens."

Conrad looked to me as if for confirmation.

I felt his anxiety. This ordinary tearoom was suddenly fantastical and unreal. It was somewhere between his normal life with Lucy and our future grandchild and his expected reunion with me.

"It *is* a dream," he realised. "You've pumped me full of sedatives. I'm hallucinating."

I knew there was more substance to this situation than he might suspect. He was dreaming, yes, but with a blurring of reality that allowed me to be there with him. I wouldn't allow him to give up. *I love you, Conrad.* I hoped that he could see this in my eyes. I pulled my hand away from his, sat back in my chair and forced myself to say what I had to.

"It is good to see you, Conrad, really it is. And I'm sorry if I seem a bit distant. You see, the thing is, I don't want you here with me."

Conrad looked bemused, then hurt. "Are you rejecting me, Mary?" He placed a hand to his chest.

The coffee machine beeped wildly, its rhythm suddenly racing again.

The woman slid swiftly back behind the counter, lifting one of the glass cake domes. Beneath it, something pulsed and squirmed.

Conrad seemed lost for words. He gaped at me, eyes pleading. "I'm heartbroken," he said.

I hadn't intended to upset him. Only to nudge him in the right direction.

I was vaguely aware of some commotion in the kitchen, but Conrad held my attention. Poor, dear Conrad. I couldn't hurt him anymore.

"Your heart isn't broken," I insisted. "You have the most loving heart, the *strongest* heart I have ever known." I took his hand again across the table. "I love you, Conrad. And that's why I don't want you here with me. I want you to live."

A tear trickled from Conrad's eye. "I miss you so much, Mary."

"So I should hope." I managed a sad smile. "We'll be together soon enough. But this is not your time. Until then, be there for Lucy and her family. You'll make a fantastic granddad."

He produced a twitch of a smile himself. "I think I will," he agreed.

We sat, simply holding each other's hands for a while. Behind the counter, the coffee machine had calmed down and the woman was stacking an array of utensils in what appeared to be an elaborate dishwasher.

"Help me with this cake, would you?" Conrad handed me one of the forks. "Apparently I have to keep my strength up."

We finished the cake and our drinks while Conrad told me a little more of his recent day-to-day activities. Nothing sensational. He was worried about his health, of course. But he made time for family and friends. I was glad that he was keeping himself busy.

The woman appeared at our table with Conrad's cane in her hand. "You'll probably need this," she said, "while you recover." She eased Conrad up onto his feet. "And don't worry," she added. "This is your dream. A bit of a jumble – but you'll remember it when you come round."

I stood, too. Conrad and I had one more hug. His cheek was still warm against mine. Still very much alive. "I still love you, Mary," he said.

I felt a glow in my own heart. Those words would sustain me for a while.

The woman led Conrad to the café door. The silver bell jangled as she opened it for him.

"Remember," I called, "I don't want you here with me – not yet."

I saw him smile as the door closed behind him. I sat back down at the table in the bright bay window. I felt exhausted, happy and sad at the same time. One day Conrad and I would be together again. Until then I needed another pot of tea, and perhaps a sticky bun. I intended to be waiting for some time.

Dreams of Her

Anna Rose

John had lived all his thirty-four years in the same sleepy seaside town on the coast. It was the kind of place that resisted change, clinging to its rhythms the way barnacles clung to stone. The tide came and went, fishing boats nosed in and out of the harbour, and the gulls screamed their endless chorus over rooftops scoured by salt winds. The town's narrow streets curved like ribbons along the cliff, lined with pastel houses whose paint was always just beginning to peel. Tourists came in the summer and disappeared by autumn, leaving behind shuttered cafés and footprints in the sand. For those who stayed all year, life moved at the pace of the tide: predictable, slow, and sometimes unbearably small.

Most people in town knew John by sight, if not by name. He was the tall, quiet man with dark hair going thin at the crown, who walked the same route each morning past the bakery, who stopped at Mrs. Henshaw's corner shop for milk and bread, who came back each evening with the faintly stooped posture of a man who spent his days bent over screens. He had a kind face, though reserved, as if he kept his thoughts hidden under lock and key.

John was not unfriendly. He greeted neighbours politely, sometimes lingered a moment to hold a door, or stooped to pick up something someone had dropped on the cobbles. But no one knew him well. He had never married, never courted anyone seriously, never drawn attention to himself. His colleagues in Exeter, where he worked in IT support for a regional company, sometimes teased him with the good-natured cruelty of people who could not imagine living as he did.

How can a man your age be content with nothing but computers and sandwiches? they would laugh. John only smiled, his mouth tight.

Content, that was the word he told himself, repeatedly. He liked order. He liked quiet. He liked the way his small flat above the harbour remained exactly as he left it each morning. He liked the way the sea outside his window kept its rhythms without complaint, as faithful as any companion.

Sometimes, though, when the evening tide drew out and left the shore bare and glistening, when the wind rattled the windowpanes and the gulls fell silent, a different feeling stirred in him. Hollow. Restless. He told himself it was nothing, a trick of the mind, the vague ache everyone felt from time to time. What was there to miss, really? A man could not yearn for something he had never known. He had never held a woman close, never woken to the warmth of someone sleeping beside him, never confessed his secrets into another person's listening silence. These were not things to be missed, not for him.

His days unfolded like a neat row of dominoes, each one falling into the next. He rose at seven sharp. He shaved with practised efficiency. He brewed his single cup of coffee, strong and unsweetened, and caught the early train to Exeter on the days he worked in the office. At lunch, he ate a ham-and-cheese sandwich, unwrapped from foil with almost ceremonial precision. In the evenings he walked along the sea wall if the weather was good or read old paperbacks in his flat if it was not. Fridays meant a takeaway curry. Saturdays meant laundry. Sundays meant the quiet dread of Monday, soothed only by long walks along the cliffs.

It was not a bad life. But it was a life without surprise, without colour. A life that felt, though John would never admit it aloud, like waiting.

Now and then, others tried to breach his solitude. A colleague in Exeter once convinced him to join a pub quiz; he sat quietly through it, nursing a pint, answering a single question about computers before slipping away at the end. A neighbour had once suggested he come for dinner, but he made an excuse. Friends urged him to try dating apps, and for a short while he did. He matched with a few women, even met one for coffee. She was lovely, articulate, fond of hiking. He listened politely, but his heart did not stir. Afterward, he deleted the app from his phone.

What none of them understood was that John did not mind his own company. The silence suited him. The quiet routines of his life felt like a shield against the messiness of the world.

At least, that is what he believed.

Because beneath the stillness, beneath the calm predictability, something in him was waiting. He did not know it, not then, not until the first dream came.

* * *

John started to have unwelcome dreams. It began quietly, the way rain sometimes starts with a single drop. At first, there was only a flicker, a face glimpsed through fog. A woman's face. Dark hair spilling past her shoulders, eyes alive with some intensity he could not name. Not pretty in the soft, forgettable way some faces are pretty, but striking, like a sudden storm across a summer sky. He woke startled, his heart tapping against his ribs, the impression of her still sharp even as the morning sun lit the sea beyond his window. He wondered who she was and why was he dreaming about her.

Dreams were nothing unusual for John, but they usually consisted of nonsense. But this dream felt different; it felt real. He could recall the exact shade of her eyes, the faint curve of her smile. All day, he carried her face with him like a secret he did not understand.

The next night, she came again. And the night after.

Each time, she was clearer. Her lips moved, though he could not catch the words. Her hand lifted once, as if she meant to touch his arm, but the dream dissolved before she reached him. He began going to bed earlier, almost eager, like a child waiting for Christmas morning.

Then one night the dream expanded, no longer a flicker but an entire scene.

He was standing in a piazza beneath a blazing sun. The air shimmered with heat, filled with the chatter of Italian voices and the scent of oranges from a nearby stall. She was there, tugging at his hand. A sketchbook was tucked under her arm.

"You must try pistachio," she said in accented English, pulling him toward a gelato stand. Her laughter was quick and light, spilling into the square as though it belonged there as much as the bells and the pigeons.

They sat together on a low stone wall, sharing a spoonful of melting gelato, her laughter bubbling every time he made a face at the unexpected sweetness. He remembered the smear of green on her lip, the way she wiped it off with the back of her hand. Such a small, ordinary thing and yet when he woke the next morning, the taste of pistachio still seemed to linger on his tongue.

Another night, the dream carried him to the countryside. They were riding bicycles along a dusty track lined with olive trees, cicadas thrumming in the warm air.

They stopped by a stone wall overlooking the valley, where she unpacked a basket: bread, cheese, a handful of figs. She broke the bread with her hands, pressed a piece into his palm. He had never tasted anything so simple, or so alive.

On another night, they wandered through an art gallery. He did not know the paintings, but she did, pointing with the end of her pencil, her eyes bright as she spoke of colour and line and form. Before Botticelli's *Primavera*, she fell into silence, tilting her head.

"I dreamed of this once," she said softly. "Only…you were here beside me."

He looked at her in astonishment. "You dream too?"

Her smile was quick, secretive. "Perhaps."

The dreams began to feel less like dreams and more like a second life. A hidden one. They walked streets and fields, shared food, teased each other, fell into silences that were as intimate as any embrace. She was not a phantom, not some perfect fantasy conjured from loneliness. She was real – with moods and laughter and quiet moments when her eyes went far away, as though remembering something she could not say.

By day, John changed. He caught himself humming as he made his tea, staring at the sea as if it hid messages only he could read. He smiled more, though he told no one why. At work, colleagues noticed.

"You've been away with the fairies lately," one said, nudging him. "Something on your mind?"

"Just tired," John replied, though his heart raced. He could not speak of her. How could he explain that the best part of his life happened after he closed his eyes each night?

Sometimes he thought he was losing his grip on reality. No one had dreams like these – not so vivid, not so constant. Yet each time he tried to dismiss them, she returned, and the pull of her was undeniable.

Then, one night, she gave him her name.

They were standing in a courtyard drenched in moonlight, jasmine spilling over pale stone. She came close, her fingers brushing his cheek, her eyes heavy with longing.

"John," she whispered. "My name is Elizabetta."

The sound of it rolled through him like a bell. He woke with tears on his face; his hand pressed to his chest as though to hold the echo there.

From that moment, she was no longer a dream. She was someone.

* * *

The dreams brought John alive – but they also pulled him apart.

At work in Exeter, he began making mistakes. He mistyped code, left servers in loops that should never have happened. Once, he shut down a whole network by pressing the wrong command. His colleagues laughed it off at first, but the glances they exchanged grew less amused.

"You all right, mate?" David, who sat opposite him, asked one afternoon. "You have been miles away. Not like you."

"Fine," John muttered, but the word sounded hollow.

He was not fine. He was haunted.

The days became unbearable compared to the nights. Each morning, the world of wires and keyboards seemed lifeless, a poor imitation of the golden light in Elizabetta's eyes. Each evening, the sea outside his window looked vast and empty instead of soothing.

He tried to fight it. He joined colleagues at the pub one Friday evening, letting them fill his glass again. They joked, they shouted answers at a quiz, they told stories of disastrous dates. John smiled and nodded, but he felt like a ghost sitting among them. None of it touched him. His thoughts were already sliding toward the night ahead, toward the woman who waited in his dreams.

Even the dating apps made a brief return. One Sunday afternoon he matched with a woman named Claire, who suggested coffee. She was lovely, bright, articulate, her eyes kind. She spoke of hikes across Dartmoor, of her work in teaching. For a moment, John thought he might anchor himself in reality again. But then, as she stirred her cappuccino, his heart betrayed him. He was not looking at Claire across the table. He was seeing dark eyes framed by tumbling hair, a sketchbook resting on slender fingers.

When Claire texted the next day, he let the message go unanswered. He could not lie to himself any longer: no one in waking life could compare to Elizabetta.

Desperation began to gnaw at him. He opened his laptop late at night, searching for clues. He typed her name, *Elizabetta*, into search engines, scrolling through endless pages of Italian genealogies, portraits of noblewomen long dead, forgotten Facebook profiles. He devoured articles on reincarnation, dream synchronicity, twin flames bound across lifetimes. Most of it sounded absurd. Yet none of it felt as absurd as the truth he was living.

The dreams themselves grew heavier. Shadows crept into them. Where once she laughed easily, Elizabetta sometimes looked at him with sorrow in her eyes. Where once the dreams lingered in ordinary joys, gelato, bicycles, paintings, they began to veer toward urgency. A storm breaking over tiled rooftops. A crowd pulling them apart in the rain.

One night, they stood together on a hill overlooking Florence, the city blazing with lights below. The air was warm, cicadas droning, jasmine thick around them. He reached for her hand, and she let him take it, though her fingers trembled.

"John," she said softly.

The way she spoke his name sent a chill through him.

"What is it?" he whispered.

Her eyes lifted to his, storm dark. "I am not of your world. Not of your time."

He stared at her, uncomprehending.

"I live far from here," she went on, voice low. "Centuries ahead. The only reason we meet is because our lives… overlap, like threads woven in a pattern. But we were never meant to find each other."

The words felt like a blade sliding into him. "But this is real. You are real. Look at us – look at what we have."

She pressed her forehead to his, tears burning against his skin. "It is real. But not enough. Unless you leave your world – your present, your life – and step into mine, we cannot be together."

His breath caught. He had thought the dreams impossible enough, but this was madness. Leave his life? Step into a future that might not even exist?

But when he looked into her eyes, the madness seemed the only truth.

Before he could answer, thunder split the sky. Rain lashed the hilltop. She clung to him once more, her lips shaping words he could not hear before lightning tore the dream apart and hurled him back into his bed in Devon.

He woke gasping, his pillow damp, his chest aching as if it had been struck. For a long time, he sat in the dark, listening to the sea pound against the harbour wall, trying to steady his breath.

It was no longer enough to wait for dreams. If she was real, truly real, then he had to find her.

* * *

For days after the storm-drenched dream, John walked through his routines like a man split in two. On the surface, he was the same – catching the train to Exeter, answering emails, buying groceries. But beneath it, a current pulled at him, stronger each day.

He could not forget her words: *Unless you leave your world…*

At first, he resisted. It was madness. A fantasy spun by a lonely mind. And yet every glance at the sea outside his window, every walk along the cliffs, felt empty now, hollowed out by longing.

One evening, unable to bear it, he opened his laptop and typed two words: *Florence Italy.*

The images that filled his screen stunned him. The red dome of the Duomo against a sapphire sky. The sweep of the Arno beneath its bridges. Narrow lanes with ochre walls, sun-dappled and alive with shadow. He knew these places. He had walked them in dreams.

His pulse hammered. Florence was real.

It took him less than an hour to book the flight. A work conference in Milan offered a convenient excuse, but in truth, the reason pressed against his ribs until he could hardly breathe. He was going to find her.

* * *

The flight itself felt endless. Wedged into the narrow seat, the drone of engines filling his ears, John closed his eyes and tried to sleep, but dreams did not come. His body ached with exhaustion, but his mind churned with images: Elizabetta's eyes, the sound of her voice, the courtyard heavy with jasmine. He imagined stepping off the plane and finding her there, waiting. Then he imagined arriving and finding nothing, no one, only a city of strangers.

By the time the plane descended into Italy, his nerves were strung tight.

Florence in August shimmered with heat. The air was thick with scents, espresso, leather, roasting chestnuts from street vendors. The cobblestones burned beneath his shoes as he walked. Every corner jolted him with déjà vu. The narrow lanes spilling into bright piazzas. The green-and-white marble of the Duomo towering over the city. Shopfronts spilling with silk scarves, the air thrumming with scooters and voices.

He wandered half-dazed, his heart racing. It was like walking inside his own dream.

By late afternoon, he reached the Piazza della Signoria. Tourists thronged the square, cameras clicking, guides waving flags. Statues gleamed pale in the relentless sun, Neptune rising from his fountain, David's replica standing proud.

John paused at the edge, breathless. The noise swelled around him, a tide of voices in a dozen languages. And then, amid it all, he saw her.

Not in silks, not bathed in dream light, but in a simple summer dress the colour of cream. A sketchbook was cradled in her arm. Her dark hair tumbled loose across her shoulders.

She lifted her head. Their eyes met.

The world fell silent.

"Elizabetta," he breathed, though his throat was dry.

Her lips curved into the smile he had seen a hundred times in dreams. "John," she said softly, in accented English, as though she had always known his name.

For a moment he nearly stumbled. Then she laughed, a sound like water over stones, and reached for his hand. "I wondered how long it would take you."

The bells of the Palazzo Vecchio tolled the hour, the square roared back into sound – but around them, time seemed to fold inward, leaving only the two of them standing face to face at last.

* * *

They moved through Florence together as if continuing a story already begun. There was no awkwardness, no fumbling introductions. It felt like stepping back into a conversation paused only hours before.

They wandered museums, their footsteps echoing in cool halls. In the Uffizi, she guided him with the same brightness she had in his dreams, her pencil tapping the frames as she spoke of colour and form. Before Botticelli's *Primavera*, she turned to him with a half-smile. "I told you once I dreamed of this, with you beside me."

"And here we are," he whispered.

They shared meals at trattorias tucked down narrow lanes. He watched her tear bread with her fingers, her laughter bubbling as the waiter corrected his clumsy

Italian. One evening, rain swept suddenly over the city, and they dashed under an awning, dripping and breathless, laughing as thunder rolled across the Arno. She reached up to push wet hair from his face, and for a moment they stood suspended, as if the storm outside existed only to seal them together.

Another day, she took him across the river to quieter streets. They climbed into the hills, where olive groves spread silver-green beneath the sun. Cicadas sang, rosemary scented the air, and Elizabetta sketched the view while he sat beside her. He thought, with a sudden ache, that he could sit there forever, just watching her pencil move, her brow furrowed in concentration, her lips pressed together in thought.

At night, they walked the embankments of the Arno, golden lamps painting the water in rippling fire. Sometimes they spoke about art, about music, about their lives. Other times, silence was enough. He had never known silence could feel so complete, so full.

For John, those days were more real than anything that had come before. His flat in Devon, his desk in Exeter, his routines – they seemed like faint shadows, while this city, this woman, blazed with impossible clarity.

And yet, even in the brightest moments, he felt a shadow. A hesitation in her gaze. A softness in her laughter, edged with sorrow.

It was on their last night, as the bells tolled midnight, that she told him the truth.

They stood on the Ponte Vecchio, the water rushing black and gold beneath them. Around them, the city was alive with footsteps and voices, but the world seemed to fall away.

"John," she said softly, her hand warm in his.

He turned to her, his chest tight. "What is it?"

Her eyes glistened. "I cannot stay."

He shook his head, gripped her hand tighter. "Don't say that."

"My world is not yours," she whispered. "I live ahead, far ahead. These days we shared were borrowed. A gift. But now I must return."

He felt the words like a blow. "No. We have found each other. That cannot be for nothing."

Her fingers touched his cheek, tender, trembling. "It is not nothing. You have been asleep, John. Before me, you lived half a life. Now you are awake. You know what it is to love. Do not close your heart again."

Tears blurred his vision. "I don't want to wake without you."

"You will," she said, her voice breaking. "And when you do, you must live. Promise me."

The bells struck the hour, each toll heavy as a heartbeat. He clung to her hand, but the crowd surged around them, and when the last chime faded, she was gone.

John stood alone on the bridge, the city roaring back into sound. The water rushed beneath him, indifferent. His chest ached with loss, but beneath the ache burned something fierce and undeniable.

Back in Devon, the sea rolled on as it always had, grey in the mornings, silver under the moon, restless against the harbour wall. The gulls screamed. The cobbled streets still carried their peeling paint and familiar rhythms. Nothing in the town had changed.

But John had.

At first, the absence of Elizabetta hollowed him. He woke reaching for her, half expecting to hear her laughter in the street below, to find her sketchbook left on his table. When he walked the cliffs, he caught himself turning at the sound of a woman's voice, his heart stuttering before he realised it was not hers. For weeks, grief pressed heavy on him.

Yet slowly, something else began to stir. He noticed the light differently – the way dawn gilded the sea in pale gold, the way shadows deepened the harbour at dusk. He lingered longer in conversation with neighbours. He smiled at strangers. When he spoke, his voice carried a warmth he had not known was there.

One morning, he stepped into the café near the station, the one he usually hurried past. A woman ahead of him dropped her scarf, and without thinking, he bent to retrieve it. She turned with a grateful smile, a kind smile, open and genuine.

"Thank you," she said.

He found himself smiling back, steady, and sure. "You're welcome."

It was nothing, a moment easily forgotten. Yet as they stood together waiting for their orders, they began to talk. Not small talk, but easy conversation that flowed as naturally as the tide.

Later, walking home with coffee warming his hand, John realised something astonishing: he felt ready. Ready to let someone in. Ready to risk his heart.

Elizabetta was gone, but she had given him the greatest gift of all – the knowledge that he was capable of love.

And for the first time in his life, John felt the tide was carrying him not toward loneliness, but toward a beginning.

The Witchdoctor's Daughter

Peter K. Rothe

1 – Sacred Beauty

My Lord, I confess that I have sinned. I have yielded to my carnal desires and have strayed from your way.

I see her still, resplendent, beautiful, lying at the foot of the great iroko tree in that land of mist and water. Though she visits me only in my slumber, her soft skin, warm and sweet as chocolate, and her kisses, lingering upon my neck, feel more real than the clothes I wear as I write this account.

Her song threatens to break my resolve, tempting me to renounce my calling and to drink the nectar of her tongue, sweeter than honey and milk beneath my lips. Even if it carries me to the gates of hell.

How much longer must I endure?

– 25 March 1725 – Kingdom of Dahomey

* * *

The drums were beating during the Festival of Dangbe. When the Egungun, masked dancers in furtive robes, spun, and Yetunde sang to her ancestors, losing her place in the music when she saw him for the first time.

This stranger – yovo – from a faraway land, where great houses of stones sought to pierce the sky. She wouldn't have believed it, had she not witnessed these wonders herself, manifest in their dreams.

That evening, as on most nights, she set the talisman – a bronze trinket with a boat-shaped veve carved upon it – beside her cushion with a gris-gris satchel holding ground bones and a feather to ask Agbé for protection from the night people.

Yetunde sang her evening prayers and closed her eyes in Aiye and opened them in Orun, the realm of spirits.

All around her rose vast columns, so high up she was certain they touched the stars. Above it all, painted in dazzling colours, were figures in flowing robes of blue and red. Their faces were pale as yam paste, and each pointed towards a man with long flowing hair and a blinding sun radiating behind him. His eyes seemed to follow her, blinking.

This was the yovo's God.

Gustave's God.

She tore her eyes away from the ceiling and stepped between the rows of wooden pews. Beneath her feet, the waters of Agbé rippled, lapping against the stone pillar's base. High upon a dais, beyond the reach of the flooding, stood the marble statue of a woman with a crown holding a baby.

Marie, Mother of God.

Like Mawu-Lisa.

Marie studied Yetunde with her marble eyes and smiled.

The vision overwhelmed her. The sheer scale of the edifice, and the bizarre depictions of a world that didn't match her own. And yet, despite the majesty on display, Yetunde felt trapped. Like those mighty walls were designed to keep people out, rather than within. Was this what the *yovo* would bring to the Kingdom of Dahomey?

"*Pater noster, qui es in cælis, sanctificetur nomen tuum.*" On the front pew sat Gustave, arms clasped, eyes closed, praying in his strange tongue. Her heart fluttered when she saw him, his messy curls, his rough beard and eyes the colours of the sky. Had she not seen him during the Festival, she would have thought him another spirit.

He looked up and smiled. "Praise God, you're here."

Yetunde sat beside him, wrapped her arm through his. "I missed you."

"Tunde, I think we should stop seeing each other. I—" He had such a strange accent, each word bleeding into a tangled melody. She found it oh so wonderful, but almost impossible to understand.

"You bring praise to your God, here?" asked Yetunde.

Gustave blinked, as if noticing his surroundings for the first time. His eyes darkened. "Notre Dame."

"It's beautiful."

He turned to her, taking her hands. His eyes shone as they met hers, though some hidden burden lingered in them. "I…"

Yetunde swooped in and kissed him before he could finish. He hesitated, then surrendered to the rising swell. When they parted, his cheeks glowed pink. Adorable.

"We can't do this here," he said.

"You stubborn man."

"This place is sacred, Tunde."

"Let your spirits witness," said Yetunde.

Ever since that first meeting on the night of the Festival, when she found him in Orun, at the foot of her ancestral tree, Yetunde wondered. Why was he there? What strange powers did he hold? The women of the village spoke of spirit-wives and husbands. But Gustave was not a spirit; he was flesh and blood.

There were times Yetunde wanted more, but their relationship would not survive in Aiye. He was a priest for a foreign land. She was the daughter of the Mundungu, their village's chief and shaman. If Tā ever found out about them, he would send more than night people to tear them apart.

Yetunde clung to Gustave. She could not let him go. Not only because of her feelings for him, but also because Gustave's strange faith terrified her father. And she could use that to escape the burden that awaited her.

Only then would she feel safe.

Only then would she feel free.

2 – The Spirit of Africa

She sets my world in turmoil. My heart is torn, being pulled by opposing forces: devotion to my Lord, and passion for my African queen.

The truths hidden in her lineage reveal themselves in the visions we share at night, where I taste of her forbidden fruit as she unveils the tapestry of her ancestry.

Agbé, *the ruler of the oceans, his waters of such crystal purity that they mirror the splendour of heaven.* Sakpata, *who rises from the clay and shapes this vast and wild land of unimaginable bounty and beauty.* Ogoun, *who forges from iron and fire.* Dangbe, *the rainbow serpent who coils around the world.*

These visions come in song, as the smell of damp earth, as the whisper of crickets, the low hoot of owls, to a chorus of tam-tams pounding through the night. They come tall, terrible and terrifying, wearing masks in clay and bronze, whirling in their technicolour guises. Turning and turning, as the taste of palm-wine lingers thick in my mouth.

These spirits feel so much more tangible than the distant, ethereal God of the scriptures. What terrible fate awaits me, a sinner who lies with the daughter of the serpent? Who shall save my soul?

My love enchants me with her dance, swaying her hips by the moonlight on Agbé's *waters, breaking my resolve.*

– 4 April 1725

* * *

The foot of the iroko tree became their special place. Yetunde ran her fingers across his chest, fascinated by the skin that seemed to change colour as she pressed down on it.

"What will you show me tonight, yovo?"

A great city rose before them, unlike anything she'd ever imagined. The streets and the buildings were made of stone, and they rose so high that even the sacred tree felt small. Bells tolled faintly in the distance.

"This is Paris," said Gustave.

"It's marvellous!" said Yetunde, beaming. "Can you take me there?"

Shadowy figures crowded the street, more than she could count. Hard to believe that so many people existed anywhere in Aiye. Or that this place could lie far beyond the horizon, beyond the great desert, far from Agbé's blessing.

"One day, perhaps. We shall go to the Palais de Versailles," he said, eyes darkening.

"We can walk through the city," said Yetunde. "Go to the boulangeries, and eat fresh baguette in the morning."

Gustave laughed. "Yes, a vision of progress."

Yetunde paused. "Are they happy?"

He considered her question for a long while. "Some are happy. Some are not."

"Is that why you came to Dahomey?"

"I came to save people."

"My people do not need saving."

"We all need saving," he said, bitterly. "This is not progress. This is a cage."

The city shattered, cracked and fell into a cloud of dust. Through the drifting haze flared a crimson light. A powerful wind swept the remnants of the city, revealing wild grasses bursting out of red soil, with mighty baobabs far in the distance.

The land of her ancestors stretched out before them. The horizon curved beneath a rising sun. With it came the dawn chorus – birds calling, crickets chirping, a lion's roar followed by the screeches of baboons and the trumpet of an elephant. Their voices swelled, a cacophony of life until the land itself was singing.

She saw wonder blossom in his eyes. No, Gustave could not return to his palaces of dead stone. The spirit of the land had taken root within him.

"Is this progress?" asked Yetunde. "The Bush was here long before we were born and will remain long after we return to the spirits. Never changing, always the same."

"Why strive for paradise when it's right here?" he countered. "Look, Tunde. It's right there. True beauty. Look." And for the first time in a long time, she did.

3 – A Message

Could it be my calling to embrace this strange land and this woman who moves upon its waters? Was it the Lord's will that I should meet her? Might she be my salvation? Or my undoing?

– 16 April 1725

* * *

One morning, Yetunde was pounding yam paste behind her adobe hut. It was women's work to pound yams with the great wooden mortar and pestle, matching the rhythm of the earth. The men meanwhile, fetched water and tended to the crops. She laboured with three others, though they kept their distance. None would risk a curse from the Mundungu.

Yetunde's thoughts drifted as she yearned for the night, smiling despite herself, humming to the beat of her pounding.

A horn sounded from the hilltop.

A warning.

Danger.

She dropped her pestle and ran for the rallying point at the village centre, gathering her dress as she moved. But when she arrived, there was no one there.

"Habiba! Tā! Father!"

No reply.

Trees cracked to her right, then another. Splintering. Snapping. Where was everyone? Had she come to the wrong place?

She heard a rumble like great drums beneath the earth. She turned just as a wall of mud and churning waters tore through a row of huts.

She ran, but too late.

The flood took her, lifting her like another branch, dragging her into its vicious belly.

She fought, trying to find a way out, but the current turned her over and over. Her lungs gave, and she drank the black water.

Choking, her lungs burning, Yetunde surrendered to the swell.

4 – The Witchdoctor

I waited at our secret place, and she never came. Bewildered, I searched for her in the palaces of my slumber, scoured through the endless wilds and even dared to climb the great palm to the realm I was forbidden to enter.

When the fires arrived, their heat so fierce it turned the earth into a furnace, melting stone into rivers of magma, I thought it a vision of hell. That I had perished and found myself in perdition. I hid, closing my eyes upon that terror, taking refuge in a memory of my youth: my mother at the piano on our sunlit patio.

But even there, terror followed.

Figures of purest black – the night people – manifested from the shadows like living ink, ripping through my cherished recollection, twisting it, corrupting it. I fled, afraid, helpless, lost, praying for deliverance. But no salvation came.

Then the serpent appeared, vast and black, with eyes like burning coals. It struck at my heel, my side, my hands. Poison coursed through me, burning me from the inside until I was mercifully rescued, screaming back into the waking world.

Every night, I continue my search.

Every night the terror returns, but I will not yield.

Where is my beloved?

What have you done to her?

– 6 May 1725

* * *

The incessant crowing of the cockerel awoke Yetunde, was soaked. Her mattress was drenched, a puddle squelching beneath her. She drew long breaths to steady herself, grasping the talisman, brushing her thumb over the carved veve of Agbé.

She pinched herself to check she was truly in Aiye.

The flood. It felt so real. Her lungs still burned from inhaling the waters. The flood was a message. If she ignored it, more terrible visions would come, louder than the last.

The consequences would bleed out of Orun into the waking world.

What could it mean?

Was Agbé angry with her?

Only the village's Mundungu would know.

She washed with what little drinking water she had, cleansing her body and braiding her hair. She lit incense, even burned an effigy. Her father would know if she hadn't.

Clad in ritual robes, a necklace of cowrie shells, bracelets and gris-gris, she walked through the village to the hut on the hill. The people stared as she passed. Whether at her attire or because the ancestors had spoken to them, she didn't know.

She reached her father's hut. At the entrance stood a statue of Legba smirking, horned and erect.

The curtain parted. A man with a long, tangled grey beard studied her, wrinkling his nose. "At least you followed tradition this time. Come."

Inside, the air was heavy, oppressive like the heat of a kiln. Talismans hung from the rafters. Banners made from colourful fabric depicting the various kingdoms and spirits lined the wall. On her left, a shrine smouldered, shrouded in incense smoke. To her right, wooden masks leered at her. At the far end, her father sat upon his throne.

Yetunde knelt, making the proper signs.

Her father hacked a shuddering cough.

"Tā!" said Yetunde, reaching up to him.

"Speak!" he commanded, wiping his mouth with the sleeve of his bobo.

Yetunde nodded. "I have come to ask for your help."

"Why should I help you?"

"I had a vision…from Agbé."

Her father reclined on his throne, resting his fist beneath his chin. "Go on."

"I saw the village destroyed by a flood. What does it mean? Please, Tā."

His face twisted with rage. "I told you this would happen if you kept seeing that yovo."

He knew. Of course, he knew.

"Gustave has…"

"Do not say his name before the ancestors, Shla-nɔ"

"But…"

"I warned you his religion would destroy us. Told you it would anger the spirits. Those *yovos* come and take what they want. They steal our statues and taint our sacred rituals."

Yetunde could listen to no more. "You are wrong. Water does not only mean destruction. It means change. Progress."

"You use yovo words. I forbid you from seeing him again."

Yetunde seethed with fury. Her eyes welled up. Gustave would never force his faith upon her. Perhaps, in time, he might even accept her way of life.

"You are wrong. He respects me. He listens. He learns."

"Iyatunde, enough!"

"While you send curses my way and your night people to haunt us."

He said nothing.

"He is more powerful than you are. You will see."

Before he could reply with more lies, Yetunde left.

* * *

She wants me to confront her father. Only then will the nightmares cease. I'm relieved she is safe, yet how does she expect me to fight in a realm I cannot comprehend?

I must take up the only weapons I have at my disposal: the shield of faith and the sword of the Spirit.

Glorious Saint Michael, Prince of the heavenly host, who stands ready to give assistance to your humble servant, who fought with the dragon, the serpent, and cast him out of heaven into hell. I earnestly entreat you to assist me against this formidable foe.

Please...help me.

With Scriptures in one hand and rosary in the other, I go to battle.

– 7 April 1725

* * *

Yetunde chanted through the night, deep in a trance, until the first light of dawn poured through her open window.

"Tunde, Tunde!" Habiba burst inside, her eyes bloodshot. "It's your father."

Yetunde blinked, dazed, returning from the spirits. "What happened to Tā?"

Habiba stammered, "Your father has gone to join the ancestors."

5- The Virgin and the Serpent

What would happen to the village now that their Mundungu was gone? They spent the next week grieving and celebrating. To weep and to feast was the African way. Death was not the end, but the beginning of another journey.

Her father's warning sat heavily on Yetunde. She couldn't stop blaming herself for his passing, despite what the big city doctor had said. Though she was free now, she couldn't find the strength to face Gustave. She didn't blame him for what happened.

She missed him.

As was the way, after the week-long festival, Yetunde journeyed into the bush with nothing but her ceremonial staff, a calabash of water and some scant robes made of rough leather. The dry season made the trek hard, the sun often beating mercilessly on her back, her lips blistering. She would either find her way home…or she would not.

When the sun was high, she came upon a crossroads.

"You seem to have lost your way, nyonu."

A masked man sat cross-legged on the dirt track. Yetunde had not seen him at first. His voice was familiar – tender with a hint of mocking.

Yetunde collapsed to her knees, her throat raw, her voice barely a whisper. "Please…show me."

Legba tilted his head. "Why should I help you?"

"I must save my people," she croaked. "Lead them to a better future."

"And what do you know of the future, nyonu?"

The memory of the flood returned: huts swallowed by a wall of churning water, her lungs filling as the black pulled her down.

Now she would trade anything for a sip.

"Change is coming," she said.

"And this change, do you see it as good, or wicked?"

She thought of Gustave, and her heart quickened. Could she hope for a way forward, together? Yetunde could never abandon her roots. They were a part of her identity. What if Gustave could not leave his God behind?

"It could be good."

"Then you are a fool." Legba's voice rang with her father's tone.

"There must be a way."

"This is where your path shall lead."

The scene around smeared, swept aside like paint dragged hastily across wood.

A woman wearing the most vivid blue Yetunde had ever seen sat on a chair, a child nursing at her breast. A veil framed her face, and behind her shone beams of gold.

Marie – the mother of Gustave's God.

At Yetunde's feet, a serpent slid from the dust. Its scales shimmered with more colours than she could imagine, each like a living gem glistening with an inner light.

The snake coiled at the mother's feet, lifted its head towards the child and bowed in reverence.

Dangbe, god of fertility and protection, was blessing the child.

Could this be the way forward? A balance between her faith and Gustave's?

Marie's eyes narrowed in disgust. She covered her child and stomped on Dangbe's head.

"NO!"

Again and again, she crushed his skull. Dangbe remained unmoving, its scales dulled. Dead.

"Why?" wept Yetunde.

Marie's gaze fell upon her. For an instant, Yetunde thought she saw compassion there.

The vision's message could not be mistaken: even if her faith surrendered to Gustave's, it would in the end be destroyed. Her father had been right.

Yetunde rose to her feet. "You will not claim this land!" she cried in defiance.

Marie raised her hand, and with a flick, Yetunde was swept away.

The ground fell from her feet, and she was hurled into the abyss, tumbling. Above her, Marie, Dangbe's broken body and Legba receded as she fell, and fell.

* * *

Merciful Father, forgive me. How can I ever find the strength to put myself together?

I found my beloved at the foot of her tree, once proud, now shrivelled and rotten. There she lay, serene, beautiful...but gone. Where once was music, there's only silence. Where once the fragrance of incense burned, now there's only staleness. Where her caress had warmed me, I find only coldness. Where once a rich world churned with life and hope, now only emptiness remains.

I don't seek to question Your will, yet why? Why did You take her away? Whatever hell may await my condemned soul, it could never measure the grief I now endure. How can I live without her smile, her wisdom, her tenderness?

How can such beauty, such rich heritage, be the work of the devil?

I cannot believe it. I will not.

Please, Father, bring her back to me.

– 15 May 1725

* * *

Yetunde gasped.

She looked up and beheld a tapestry of stars. The waters of Orun lapped around her. Shimmering blue and green lights curled like curtains above, reflected perfectly in the still ocean below.

The light seemed to coalesce into various forms. A woman with a head wrapping and full cheeks smiled at her. Beside her stood a man who had once terrified her. His beard was short, his face was carved with wrinkles from many days of joy, when he would throw her high in the air and catch her.

Others appeared, countless people, both great and small. All gathered to witness.

"I know the way forward," Yetunde declared to them, but she looked straight at her father. He seemed to consider her, the way he did with those stern, knowing eyes.

At last, he nodded and turned to join the rest as they faded back into the light.

One figure remained, crowned, holding a trident.

Agbé, whose waters would always guard her. No matter what happened next, he would never abandon her, but would offer his wisdom and guidance.

"Thank you," she said, bowing.

When Agbé departed, Yetunde turned and saw Gustave weeping at the foot of her ancestral tree. She walked past him, resisting the ache to kneel and embrace him. Instead, she placed her hand upon the trunk. At her touch, the tree surged with life. New leaves sprouted from the branches, thickening until the tree was full and lush once more.

It was her place to lead her people now.

"Tunde! Praise God!" Tears cascaded down his face.

She closed her eyes and remained strong. "Gustave, I think we should stop seeing each other."

He looked as if she had struck him.

"My place is with my people. Your place is with your God."

"Tunde…"

She couldn't look at him.

"I love you."

"Gustave, please."

"Tunde—"

Before he could finish and change her mind, she threw him out of Orun. Alone once more at the foot of the great iroko tree, Yetunde wept.

* * *

My beloved Tunde,

I hope this letter finds you well. After months of reflection and prayer, I have come to the conviction that I cannot let you go. It has taken a long time to accept your decision, but I will not abandon us. Not now that I understand your way of life.

I know you see my faith as a threat, but I believe we have more in common than what divides us. You have the spirits to guide you, I have the saints. We both live by symbols and ritual. Only together can we stand our ground and find a better way forward.

I will never stop loving you and this mysterious land you revealed to me with its immutable beauty.

We must preserve it from those who would seek to exploit it. I won't force you to change your mind, only that you recall our bond and hear my plea.

If you should find that a better way exists, one shaped by love, hope and peace, let us walk it together.

I will wait for you, always, at our special place....

at the foot of the sacred tree.

Threads of Us

M.L. Smythe

Nights at Pine Ridge Memorial could be eerily quiet. Ella rarely had more than three patients on any given shift, save for the rare case of a mass casualty event.

This evening, she had only two.

Old Mister Dale in room three was recovering from a coronary artery bypass graft. Caring for him wasn't difficult; he was stable and independent, and only called approximately every six hours for his pain pill.

Then there was Jaden Pearce. He was young, no older than thirty. She had been told that he'd once been a boxer, and he certainly had the build to match. Now, however, he was in a liminal state between life and death following a stroke.

Ella often found her gaze lingering on him longer than necessary. Sadness filled her heart as she looked at him. He was around the same age as her and considerably handsome. His body had betrayed him, as bodies so often do. Now, this very well could be it for him.

The night shift was not something she was accustomed to yet, and the silent hours between midnight and dawn always threatened to draw her into sleep. She had taken to reading to fill the emptiness of her nights.

Tonight, as she looked on Jaden's dozing face, she was struck with an idea. Back in nursing school, she had been taught that when caring for the dead and dying, it was important to speak to them, because there was no way to know when brain activity ceased.

The armchair at Jaden's bedside was typical hospital furniture: pleather, for easy cleaning, uncomfortable, and in a color that no one would ever choose to have in their home. She settled into it, tucking her legs under herself and brushing aside a strand of hair. The steady beeping of the monitor was a comforting reminder that the man was still tethered to the world, despite looking like the peaceful dead.

"Jay?" she called out to him gently, almost conspiratorially, and placed a hand on his shoulder.

Jaden didn't stir.

"I hope you had a good day today," Ella went on. She tried to shake off the awkwardness. "At least I hope your day was better than mine."

A sad smile spread across her lips. Tears stung the back of her eyes, but she bit them back.

"My mother died a few days ago," she confessed. "It was time for her to go. She had been suffering…I know that, but it's still hard to imagine what life is going to be like without her."

Jaden's face remained expressionless.

She picked up the book of myths and legends and cracked it open.

"Lucky for us, I inherited her books, so we have plenty of stories."

Her voice filled the room as she began to read aloud. The words tasted like salt and heat on her tongue, an ancient tale of a wanderer crossing oceans and deserts in search of something he could not name. Each syllable that passed through her lips shimmered in the air like ripples in a pond.

As she watched over Jaden, she hoped that somewhere inside the silent fortress of his mind, he could hear her – that her words might find purchase in the barren soil of his consciousness.

* * *

The demon no longer looked as terrifying now that Jaden had laid it out on the butcher's block, its insides splayed in a sloppy, rotting mess.

Getting to its heart would be no easy task. He needed to carve through layers of calloused skin, thick rancid fat, and corded muscle before he could reach the cage of obsidian bone which housed it.

By now, the blood had been settling for a while and was beginning to coagulate into a semi-gelatinous sludge. The look of it alone was enough to turn a weaker man's stomach, but Jaden was on a mission. He couldn't afford to falter.

The reek of death and sulfur quickly filled the room as Jaden sliced and tore with his black dagger. Made from the bones of the creature's ilk, it was the only material strong enough to make short work of the corpse.

Once the connective tissue had been peeled away, he began to pound at the ribcage, being careful not to damage the delicate heart beneath. The ribs gave way with a sickening snap, and Jaden pried the fragments out of the chest cavity. He cut the crimson heart free and plucked it out, exposing it to the air.

Jaden took just a moment to admire its macabre beauty before unceremoniously shoving it into his mouth. It tasted bitter, like bile, and nearly gagged him, but he choked it down. As it slid down into his stomach, he finally began to feel human again.

The world shifted around him, like a curtain caught in the wind. The butcher's block dissolved – demon corpse and all – into the floor, now white marble slick with black water.

Shadows retreated to the edges of a vast chamber, and from them stepped a figure, cloaked in a pale light.

"Why would you consume the heart?" the figure asked in an all-too-familiar voice.

Jaden's hand flew to his chest, feeling for a pulse that wasn't there.

"You told me that I'd need it," he said, though try as he might, he couldn't recall when she had spoken the words.

She tilted her head, a glimmer of golden light catching beneath her hood, obscuring her features. "And did it make you feel stronger…or more like them?"

As he opened his mouth to answer, the ground lurched and he fell through the floor. Blinding lights and rhythmic beeps surrounded him as he picked up speed. The air had a sterile, chemical smell. Something he knew but couldn't name.

Jaden was falling alarmingly fast now, but for some reason, he felt no fear.

A patch of grassy earth appeared, coming ever closer to him as he tumbled through the air. His feet touched down gently, as though set down by an unseen hand.

"Again," the woman's voice tore through the silence.

"Again? Again what?" he shouted.

A blood-curdling scream grabbed his attention. He whipped his head toward the sound, where another demon loomed over a man cradling a crying infant.

Jaden drew his dagger and charged at the beast.

The monster's eyes burned like molten brass as it turned toward him, its jagged maw twisting into a sinister grin. It reared its scythe-like claws back and lunged for Jaden. He ducked low, feeling the hot air of the swing rush past his ear.

"Go! Run!" Jaden shouted to the father, who clutched his son to his chest and ran in the other direction.

Jaden's muscles burned with an energy that wasn't entirely his own as he pounced on the creature. Black ichor sprayed over his face as he plunged the dagger into the demon's thick neck. The foul fluid burned his eyes and throat, but he pushed through the pain, stabbing downward at an alarming rate until the beast was finally felled.

Though there was no butcher's block this time, Jaden still carved into the monster to retrieve its heart and devour it.

"Good." The woman's voice blanketed him as the world around him shimmered away, dissolving into an unfocused white void.

She appeared before him again, both impossibly beautiful and nearly imperceptible. She spoke in echoes all around him.

"You didn't know them, and yet you helped them," she noted. "Why?"

"I helped them because they needed it," he replied. "You don't know me, but you help me."

"I do help you. More than you know."

"Why?" he asked.

"Because it's what I do," she said.

"Because it's the right thing to do," Jaden said.

Her laughter came out soft, like the rustling of pages in a silent library.

"Perhaps," she said.

Jaden took a step toward her, trying to pierce through the shadows obstructing her face. Each movement only served to push her farther away, as though the space between them could stretch indefinitely.

"You aren't real," he said, though even as he spoke, he hoped it wasn't the truth.

She tilted her head in such a way that Jaden could see her eyes for only a split second – warm, sad, and strangely familiar.

"None of this is real," she whispered.

The ground gave way beneath him once more, leaving him tumbling into a rich black nothingness.

* * *

Ella watched Jaden closely as she read to him. There were a few times when she could have sworn she saw a slight movement – the flutter of his eyelids, flaring of the nostrils, a slight grimace. All subtle signs that there was still brain activity occurring. That there was still Jaden, somewhere in there.

The more she looked at his face, the more she noticed just how attractive it was. Strong jaw, full lips, thick lashes. From the times that she had pried apart his eyelids to check his pupillary response, she had known his eyes to be a stunning stone grey in color. He was heart stoppingly beautiful.

She felt a sudden, overwhelming urge to just…touch him. She reached out and caressed his cheek. There was no reflexive movement in the muscles of his face.

Ella's relief arrived at seven sharp, ready to receive the night's report.

"Mister Dale is doing well. Cantankerous as always, but he got his pain pill and slept most of the night," Ella reported to the day nurse. "And then Jaden…Well, he's Jaden. No changes, for better or worse."

"What are they going to do about him?" the day nurse asked. "He isn't getting any better, and we're not exactly set up for extensive care here…"

Ella shook her head. "He never has any visitors. I don't think he has family. It's going to be up to social services."

The day nurse pursed her lips. "They're either going to have to pull his support or send him to a long-term facility…hospice might be the best option for him."

Ella bit her lip. None of those sounded like what she wanted for Jaden, but she had no say in the matter. She couldn't bring herself to accept that those were his only options.

She lingered in the doorway a moment longer than she needed to. Through the narrow slit between the curtain and the wall, she could see him lying there, his chest rising and falling in the steady rhythm that the machines dictated.

No, his story wasn't over. This wasn't the end for him. She couldn't let it be.

* * *

A deep, aching emptiness surrounded Jaden. With each forceful breath, the inky dark filled his lungs. Every beat of his heart pushed the nothingness through his bloodstream.

He tried to call out to the omnipresent woman, but the sound died in his throat, choked by the void around him.

The darkness pressed in on him from every direction, so complete it was almost like it was alive.

A flicker of panic stirred in his chest. Had he done something to drive her away? Had he brought this darkness on himself somehow?

He tried to move, to search for the woman, but there was no ground beneath his feet, no horizon, only the oppressive black that seemed to drink him in.

A single point of light appeared in the middle distance, faint and trembling. He felt hope shimmer in his chest. Then there was the faintest scent of clean skin, accompanied by the soft impression of fingers brushing against his cheek.

* * *

Sorting through her mother's effects was proving to be physically and emotionally taxing.

Ella's mother was what some might call a hoarder, but she had preferred to refer to herself as a collector. Either way, the result was the same: Ella sorting through mountains of garbage bags and plastic bins. Many of the items brought with them painful memories of her mother. She found that she could only manage to work on the task for an hour or so a day before the mental fatigue became unbearable.

This afternoon, she sat cross-legged on the floor of the cramped spare room. A single shaft of dusty light cut across the stacks of yellowed newspapers, chipped glass, and impossibly tangled costume jewelry.

Every so often, she would unearth something truly unexpected – a pressed flower between the pages of a romance novel, a handwritten note, a faded photograph of her parents in their younger, happier years.

Today, it was a small leather-bound book that caught her eye.

The cover was worn smooth and bore no title. A strange sense of nostalgia filled her as she brushed her fingers against the leather, though she couldn't recall ever having seen it before.

Ella opened the book to a random page and saw the words written in her mother's hand. She had never known her mother to have an inclination toward writing stories, but given her love of literature, it didn't come as much of a surprise.

Flipping through the pages, she found tales of swords and sorcery, rogues and romance, and a recurring character named Ella. That fact gave her pause. Had she been named for the character in her mother's stories, or had the character been named for her?

She clutched the newfound book to her chest as though she could push the words into her soul. Something about those pages felt alive, the ink thrumming with an unnamable energy. Ella imagined what it might have been like to hear her mother's voice, low and melodic, reading the words that she had written.

An idea bloomed in Ella's mind. She would bring the notebook to the hospital and read it to Jaden. Reading her mother's words instead of those written by others would make her feel closer to her, while also keeping Jaden company. It would be healing for both of them.

She tucked the book away into her bag carefully, as though it were a precious relic.

* * *

Jaden spent an eternity in that blackness. Nothing, nowhere, and no one.

He was ready to give up.

If he could end it all, he would.

"Hey, Jay..."

The woman's voice echoed through the emptiness, shattering the void like glass. Thin golden light bled through the fissures, illuminating swirls of sand beneath his feet – a vast expanse of desert that hadn't been there moments before.

The woman stepped through the break in the darkness, her face shrouded in white light and her cloak snapping in a wind that he couldn't feel. She placed her hand on his shoulder, firm and steady, grounding him. All at once, he knew her name: Ella.

Light spilled into the darkness, unveiling a desert at twilight, bathed in purples and silvers. Her cloak drifted around her like smoke, and the light hit her face in such a way that he could see her eyes, glowing white.

"You've been gone," he said, sadness dripping from his voice.

"I found something," she said as she pulled a book from her cloak.

"I thought I'd lost you," Jaden murmured, stepping closer to her, drawn by some unknown force.

"You couldn't lose me, even if you wanted to," she said, her voice laced with tenderness.

There was a flash of light, and he found himself standing on a ship afloat a green sea. Massive tentacles rose from the water, threatening to capsize him – yet another beast.

Jaden reached for his black dagger but came back with a handful of black sand that blew away with the wind. He cursed under his breath and ran to the helm. Desperately, he turned the wheel. With great difficulty, he managed to ram the prow into the monster.

The demon screamed and pulled away, but its heart remained skewered by the ship. Its body fell beneath the waves, producing a massive swell that shook the ground beneath him.

He took a moment to regain his footing as he stared out at the still-warm bestial heart.

Hesitantly, Jaden began to move toward it. What should he do? Should he devour it, like he had the others? What would happen if he did? What would happen if he didn't?

Jaden shouldn't have been able to step off the ship and onto the surface of the water, but he did. Part of him was afraid that he would fall beneath the waves and join the kraken in the briny deep, but the surface tension of the water was remarkably strong, holding him upright.

The crimson heart called out to him, and he retrieved it. For just a moment, he held it in his hands.

What did any of this even mean?

He pushed the heart past his lips and ate it, tasting brine and bile on his tongue.

The world around him changed, shifting to a new alien landscape. The sky was painted in a golden hue, and a black sun cast its shadow over the strange flora around him.

At the center of the feathery fronds, Ella stood, staring at him with her piercing white eyes. The shadows clung to her like a jealous lover, revealing only the subtle curves of her face.

The plants swayed to an unheard rhythm, their tendrils brushing against his hands and arms, leaving behind trails of warmth that faded all too quickly. The air between them felt charged as she stepped closer to him.

Beneath their feet, the ground pulsed softly, as if the entire world had a heart that beat in time with Jaden's own.

Ella took his hand, interlacing their fingers. Her touch sent a bolt of electricity through his body.

"It's time for you to make a choice," she said. "Your time here is coming to an end."

"But where is here?" he asked, his lips quivering slightly.

"Here is with me," she answered. "But you must move on."

He stared into the shadows that warped her face. "What are my options? What happens if I don't choose?"

"If you don't make a choice, the dream will vanish. You'll be stuck in that emptiness forevermore." Her voice was heavy with sadness.

He froze. Stuck in that nothingness. Forever.

No.

He couldn't go back.

"What can I do?" Jaden asked.

"You can wake up and come back to reality. With me." The sadness in her voice deepened. "It won't be easy. Your body, your mind, they're broken. The road to recovery will be long and painful. You may even be altered permanently. I make no promises regarding the quality of life that you will have."

Jaden's brow furrowed. He tried to recall what his life had been like before the dream, but there was nothing.

"If I go back...you'll be with me?" he asked, his voice tinged with hope.

She made a pained face. "You may very well be in terrible pain for the rest of your life, but I will be there until the end."

"What's my other option?" he asked, his lip quivering ever so slightly.

"End it," she said matter-of-factly. "Die."

Her words hung in the air like fog, each syllable glinting with cold finality.

His gaze lingered on the curve of her mouth, the way the hidden corners of her face softened when she looked at him.

"If I wake up…I may not remember who I am. I may not be able to live normally. But I will have you," Jaden confirmed.

Her grip on his hand tightened, and for the first time, he saw a tremor in her composure, as if the choice weighed heavily on her too.

"You would still have me," she said softly, almost pleading, "but more importantly, you'd also have the truth, and you deserve to know who you are."

A strange ache bloomed in his chest – not fear, not longing, but some bittersweet amalgamation of the two.

"And if I choose to die? What will happen? Will it be like the nothingness of the dream?"

"I don't know what lies beyond the veil, only that you will have no pain, no suffering, no hardship."

"And no you."

Ella shook her head. "No. I can't go with you. There are other people here that need me."

Her words stung him deeper than he had expected. For just a moment, the strange plants around them stilled, as though the world was holding its breath.

Jaden's throat tightened. "Then if I choose to live…will I see you again?"

Ella brushed her fingers against his cheek in a fragile caress. In her fleeting touch, he understood everything that she didn't say.

"Yes. I will be there with you."

* * *

The steady beeping of the monitors had become nearly imperceptible to her now that she had spent the entire night at Jaden's bedside.

Mister Dale's call light went off in the next room, pulling her from her musings. She didn't even need to go into his room to know he was looking for his pain pill.

Ella was gone for less than twenty minutes, but when she returned, everything had changed.

Jaden's fingers twitched against the sheets in a slow, deliberate manner that made her breath catch.

"Jay?" she spoke in a voice barely more than a whisper.

She ran to his side and took hold of his hand. Tears came to her eyes as he squeezed her hand back.

His eyelids fluttered, the faintest crease forming between his brows as though just the act of waking was an impossible weight to bear.

Jaden's lips parted, dry and cracked, and shaped a single syllable that made her knees weak:

"You."

Ella's heart hammered in her chest. For a moment, she thought she'd imagined it, that the lack of sleep was getting to her. But his lips parted again, and another strained sound came from them:

"Ella."

Her throat closed around the sob that rose in her chest.

"Jay? Can you hear me?"

His eyes flicked open, the perfect storm-grey irises locking onto her.

"Found you..." he whispered.

She pressed a trembling hand to her mouth. He knew her. Recognized her from the stories. Ella leaned closer, so close that her tears fell warm on his skin. For the first time, she realized that she hadn't simply been keeping vigil at the bedside of a stranger. She had been walking alongside him. Guiding him back.

"Welcome back, Jay."

A Song for Ever

Kathleen Stanley

The tower was a solace and a prison. Aria had stopped counting the brave men who had failed to breech its walls. She had stopped counting the days of her confinement. She had stopped counting the lives it had cost. After all, Aria was the reason they were all dead. Her prison was a stronghold, and all that came upon it were destined for darkness.

She always knew when they approached. Day or night, awake or sleeping, the curse would lure her to the window. The knights focused on the beast that lay below, a monstrosity of talons and teeth. They thought it was he that they must defeat, that he was the danger. Then she would start to sing. The song poured from the darkest part of her soul, a violent ballad of death that always claimed its victims. For she was the siren, and none were strong enough to endure her torment.

She had tried to fight it, to hold back her poisonous voice, to give them a chance. The bones of the men that littered the land at the base of the tower were testament to her failure.

The weight of their deaths sat deep within her heart, and Aria wasn't sure how to keep carrying the darkness within.

It was so cold. The tower was a drafty stone pillar that let little light in and held no warmth. She used the small window to see the stars and dream of worlds beyond her own. Lately those dreams had evaded her. Between the profound cold and the deep depression from so many deaths, Aria rarely found sleep anymore. She laid for hours in her bed, longing for the curse to be broken, no longer to find love and freedom but just for a peaceful night's rest. She watched the beast that prowled her prison curl up into itself, settling into sleep at the base of the tower. Its golden eyes swept the surrounding area before they met hers through the window. Her song never affected the monster, as if the curse that forced her to sing of death recognised an old friend and left him unharmed. As they stared at each other, she wondered how different from him she was now.

Her siren song was often called up out of her control, the verse was one that she had never been able to forget. The power was a part of her, as much a part of her as the beast's claws and fangs belonged to him. She often tried to deny that part of herself, but tonight she was so very tired. What if she could sing a new song? One to soothe, to call sleep up into the air itself. Her powers weren't designed to cause her harm, and sleep was what she might need to make the song work. Aria conjured a melody in her mind; the notes wrapped in a dark, glittering blanket of magic. They felt like a gentle caress, sweeping gently over her eyelids, down her cheek, across her forehead. Watching the beast below, she felt her eyelids grow heavier with every blink, and with the last note of her lullaby, she drifted off to sleep.

Aria knew she was dreaming. Nothing but a dream could take her out of the tower, and she was deep in an unknown forest, sitting by a warm fire. The stars in the sky were the same as the ones she knew when she was awake, but the grass was soft under her body, and the warmth of the fire a foreign but welcome feeling. The magic had worked. A tiny bubble of something dangerous tried to rise to the surface of her mind. A tiny piece of happiness that she tried not to focus too hard on, for fear recognition might blow it away. It was far too sad to think that just the ability to dream herself away was the greatest comfort she could ever be allowed to feel anymore.

As if drawn to this moment, a dark shadow moved in the corner of her eye. Aria expected fear to lurch in, but a hollow emptiness was there instead. Even her dreams weren't safe, not when the darkness lurked within her. Resentment and a melancholy acceptance hovered over her as she turned towards the shadow. Her back continued to feel the warmth of the fire as the shadow paused just out of the fires reach. It seemed unsure, as if it didn't want to get too close but also couldn't stay away. Just enough light reached where it stood. It had a form that could stand. Aria inched forward slightly, drawn to it now, as if it lured her in, wanting her to discover the shape it took. She realised it was a human shape, huge and broad, turned away from the light. The darkness was a man, and it had been so long since Aria had been close to anything even remotely like a person that she felt a jolt of anticipation.

A part of her brain recognised that this man couldn't be real. For one, he was made of shadows. She was also dreaming, and so whoever he was, he existed only in her mind, in her dreams. But loneliness has a way of making you believe in the craziest things. So even if this was just her own darkness come to talk to her, she couldn't just walk away. How did one walk away from their dreams anyway?

"Hello? Are you…is…do you…are you real?" she tentatively asked.

She held her breath for a few seconds, waiting for a reply. Foolish, she was so very foolish for trying to talk to a shadow. How desperate for company did you have to be when you talk to the shapes inside your mind?

"Real?" a smooth silken voice replied from where the shadows formed. "What would make something real, I wonder?"

Aria felt her heart begin to race. The shadows had talked back. Philosophical nonsense, sure, but that seemed about right for what her mind would conjure up. Surely this was a sign she had gone crazy, but if she was mad, it was too late to turn back to sanity now.

"I don't know, can anything be real in a dream?" she asked.

"Perhaps," he replied. "Maybe the realest of things only live in our dreams."

That was something her darkness would say. Light, hope, happiness, that belonged only to her dreams. The company of another person would live only here too.

"You are darkness and shadows," she said. "There seems to be nowhere you do not exist."

The shadowy voice gave something like a chuckle before he replied, "Yes, darkness and shadows are a part of life. Maybe I am just another part."

She pondered that for a moment. She wanted to believe that darkness was just one part of life. The thought that there were other parts, parts she was destined to discover and enjoy, was something only her dream self could hope for. The edges of the forest began to blur, and Aria suspected that this dream, whatever strange shape it had begun to take on, was about to end. She fired one final question at the shadows, feeling herself beginning to drift away from the warmth of the fire and the comfort of his voice.

"Are you *my* darkness?"

The last thing she heard, as if whispered on a breeze, as the world around her faded away was his reply.

"I am yours."

When Aria woke, dawn had broken, and a glimmer of the morning sun was shining in through the tower window. It had been a long time since she had slept through the night. Sometimes that was due to the curse, a saviour appearing in the middle of the night, waking her to sing them to their death. Most nights though it was just her insomnia, born from this torturous existence. Last night had been a miracle.

She felt lighter, and she wondered if it had been because she was well rested for once. The shadowy voice from her dream had confirmed it was just her own darkness, but it had still felt so good to talk to something.

As she left the bed and walked to the window, Aria laughed to herself. It was madness to find so much comfort in talking to herself. Perhaps it was a part of herself she had never wanted to admit existed. She lived in the darkness, became it on a regular basis, surviving in it. But had she ever really dealt with it? She hated and resented its existence; knew it was there but she always ran from it. The darkness was what killed, trapped her here, made her a monster. Yet last night, it had almost felt like a friend. It had been so very long since she'd had a friend.

The sound of hoof beats broke her out of her revery. She watched in horror as the monster appeared from a door at the bottom of the tower. Out of the forest burst a horse, upon its back a heavily armoured rider. Aria's head swivelled between the rider and the waiting beast, silently praying that the horse would ride on, past the tower, towards some other far-off place away from here. She could feel the song rising within her, ready to burst forth and challenge this brave knight to a duel she feared he could not beat. A snarl came from the beast's throat as the rider slowed, and she wondered if the monster too was trying to warn him off. *Run*, its eyes seemed to plead. The rider dismounted, pulling a sword to face the only monster he could see. No one had told him to look for monsters with pretty faces, hiding in the sky. So, as the man turned towards the beast, Aria's voice was forced from her throat, and she began to sing.

* * *

Her dream took her back to the forest, and the warm, crackling fire. The weight of the rider's death hung heavy on her shoulders, and she hadn't hesitated tonight to sing herself to sleep. The shadowy force was already here, this time sitting on the other side of the fire. It was more human now, a broadly muscled man, and the energy from the shadows that surrounded his skin screamed of violence. Aria could make out the rough shape of a face, a pale spot in the gloomy depths of darkness. His eyes were shadows, but she made out a strong jaw. He wasn't traditionally beautiful, but a dark masterpiece of fierce edges. Black leather clothing held his form, and he seemed more settled to be in her presence. This time he spoke first.

"In dreams we meet again, Queen of the Oscines."

She started. "Queen of what?"

She could have sworn his mouth twitched into a grin. "Songbirds," he replied. "Are you not the mistress of song?"

Anger crept under her skin. "I am no such thing," she spat. "Song is my curse. My darkness. It is you, the monster that crawls within me, that causes my song. Do you feel no pity? No shame for the lives you take?"

He tilted his head, considering her words. "I have never taken a life without it bearing deeply on my soul. If the song is not within your control, songbird, why do you feel such shame?"

Aria shook her head. "How could I not feel shame for losing my fight with you?"

"You are not fighting with me."

"I am ALWAYS fighting with you," Aria cried.

"I don't want to fight with you," he said quietly. "I have always been on your side."

Confusion washed away much of her anger as she considered the dark, shadowy man across from her.

"Then why do you kill?" she asked.

"I will do what I must to protect you," he replied.

She didn't know what to say to that. She had never considered that her song was protecting her. Could that be true? Why would she need protecting from heroes destined to set her free? Ridiculous. The thought niggled at her. Her song never caused her harm, it couldn't. Yet it also never slayed the monster who stalked the depths below her either. Protecting…

"Why do you bring me here?" he asked, interrupting her thoughts.

"I didn't know I was," she replied truthfully. "Aren't you always here, in my mind?"

"That's an interesting thought, songbird," he said, the ghost of that smile appearing once again.

It was distracting, almost seductive, the way he smiled. "My name is Aria, you know," she said. Songbird was no name for the likes of her.

He chuckled, a small alluring smoky noise. "I did not know, although it's alarmingly appropriate." He smiled, unmistakably this time. "Nice to formerly meet you, Aria."

Her eyebrows shot up. Was her darkness trying to make an introduction? This dream was even stranger than last night. The thought of her darkness trying to befriend her created a warmth inside her chest. Was this how tragic she had become? Was she befriending herself? Had she created some kind of alter ego to keep herself company in her sleep? That might be the most desperate dream in existence, even if the thought of a friend was too intoxicating to resist.

"Do you have a name?" she asked.

"Everett," he started to reply, when his head whipped to the side. Listening to something out of sight. He suddenly roared, "WAKE UP ARIA!"

The shadows swallowed him whole as he vanished.

Aria jerked awake. It was still dark outside, but dawn wasn't far away. Before she could catch her bearings, she felt the song, the curse, lurch into her throat. Powerless to stop it, the first few notes poured out of her, the melody dark and unforgiving. She lunged for the window, and looked out, scanning the grounds below. She saw him then, the monster, engaged in a ferocious battle with a man in a dark cloak, a sharp double-headed axe in his hands, slicing out at the beast. Aria's song surged forward, swallowing the man below, leaving behind only bones and the axe, shining with blood. Aria's eyes roamed over the beast, which still stood despite a nasty looking gash on its front leg. She thought about what the darkness, Everett, had said. Was this monster here for her? Not to cage her, but to protect her, as Everett claimed the song was protecting her. Its golden eyes lifted to hers, and it dipped its head, as if it could read the questions held within her own. Aria retreated into the safety of her tower, ignoring a tug deep within her heart, a glimmer of relief, that the monster below was okay.

* * *

Three men had come for her today. The beast had taken out the first. It was rare that it beat her song to the job but at least it was one less body on her count. The other two had succumbed to her song, the last taking the beast's previously injured leg out from under it before becoming nothing more than bones and dust. The monster's golden eyes had filled with pain, but it nodded up reassuringly at her as it limped off inside the base of the tower to rest. Aria had felt panicked when she had seen it go down, surprised to find she was almost considering trying to find its den below to check if it truly was okay. The fear of the monster had been what had kept her inside all these years and yet she wasn't so sure that it was what she had to fear anymore.

When she dreamed of the forest that night, Everett sat beside her by the fire. They had been meeting for weeks now, but he had never been this close before. She marvelled at how solid he had become. No longer was he a darkness born of shadow, but a complete human man. Dressed in his black leather outfit, she could make out his dark black hair, the strong shape of his jaw and the hard shape of his features. He had long lashes, but his eyes were hooded, avoiding her gaze, staring into the flames. She could also smell him, smoky, not like the fire, but like a forest, and a brittle sort of scent mixed in. It reminded her of hard stone, yet unlike the stone of the tower, on Everett it smelt like safety and comfort. She marvelled at how her darkness now sat beside her as a living entity. How could a piece of her smell different? How could it make her feel safe and secure, when it was the darkest parts of her being? Her soul recognised something about him, but she couldn't keep denying what was in front of her. Everett was not darkness, not a crazy product of madness. He was something else, something that didn't belong only to her.

"You're close tonight," she started, unsure how to approach the question rising in her mind.

He angled his head ever so slightly towards her. "I was hoping that might be okay, my songbird."

Aria felt herself blush at the nickname. Like him, it had grown on her. It gave her the confidence to ask the question burning her up inside. "Who are you, Everett? Who are you really?"

She kept her eyes on him as he took her hand, a solid warm weight she hadn't been expecting. Eyes locked on their hands, he finally replied.

"I am who I've always been. Darkness. Yours. Only, never how you assumed that meant. I've been waiting a long time for you to ask me that question, Aria. I've been waiting for you to really see me. I've been hoping...that even if it's only in our dreams, you might love me, the way that I love you."

Aria's heart felt like it had stopped beating. He loved her. Everett loved her. She knew that she loved him too, but she had been denying it for so long. Partly out of fear he really was just the darkness inside her, and she had fallen in love with herself. That was too narcissistic for her to indulge in. Now however, now she knew he was someone else, now she could admit that she loved him too. Before she could say as much, Everett lifted his gaze to hers and their eyes met.

Golden eyes.

Eyes she had seen before. Eyes she had stared at in fear. In loneliness. In concern. The golden eyes of the monster that kept her caged in her tower. What had he said all those dreams ago? Protector. The protector at the bottom of the tower. He believed she was protecting herself, and he was part of that. Of course, he would believe that. After all, he was the monster. He stared back at her, and she knew he could read the doubt on her face. He started to turn away, but she grabbed at his arm. A sharp hiss of pain escaped his lips, and she realised it would have been where he had been injured earlier, fighting the man at the base of the tower.

"You're hurt," she said.

"I heal fast, but I think the time in your dreams slows it down. I rarely have injuries thanks to you, but holding three of them off today, well...even monsters get tired."

Aria's head swam. So, that confirmed he was the monster below. "What do you mean, holding them off? Thanks to me? I've been killing those rescuers, how can..." she started to ask but Everett cut her off.

"Rescuers? All this time you thought those men were here to rescue you. From what? Me?" he asked, hurt in his eyes.

"I...I don't...maybe yes, once, I did think that, but I don't know anymore. I don't understand..."

His gaze softened, and awareness lit his eyes. "They do come for you, Aria. Just, not to rescue you."

"They know I'm the true monster," Aria finished for him. "They are trying to defeat me, I'm in this tower to keep them safe, from *me*."

"They are ignorant fools. You are not a monster, Aria. Look at me." Everett grabbed her chin, forcing their eyes to meet. "You have a power they do not understand. They would rather lock you away, try to kill you, than understand you. You are powerful and wonderful and you are not a monster."

His eyes flared with so much passion it was like she was staring into pools of molten gold. She suddenly wondered how she had missed it all this time. She had been so convinced he was a monster, that she too was cursed, that she hadn't really seen the reality in front of her. Everett was no monster. He was her saviour. Her true knight. And he was suddenly grimacing in pain. She clung to him, but he cried out.

"Wake up, songbird. Save me," he begged, and in a flash of shadow, he was gone.

Aria was up and running as soon as her eyes opened. She could hear the roars of pain below, from Everett's monstrous form. Someone must have snuck up on him in the night. Everett had been distracted, been with her in their dream world and missed the warning signs. Empowered with the truth, Aria was no longer afraid of what lay below her tower. Wrenching the door open, she flew down the stairs. She let her song fly downwards with her, ahead of her, hoping it made it in time. As she reached the bottom landing, almost breathless from her song and the descent, she saw the last of what had once been a man dissolve, his bones crashing over the prone body of the monster she loved. Tears poured down her face as she ran to him, blood pouring from a deep wound in his side.

"Everett, can you hear me? Keep breathing, Everett, please," she begged him. A giant golden eye turned to her, and hope blossomed in her chest.

"Yes, Everett, okay, keep breathing for me. I've got you. I love you, please hang on for me," Aria pleaded. She spied several more gashes in his chest and fear began to take hold. Even if he could heal fast, it would take some serious healing magic to get him through this. More than he had in him. But what of her magic? She was so used to it taking life, could it maybe give life too? It had been taking her to him in her sleep for weeks now. It was worth a shot.

Aria began to sing. She sang a song of love, of healing. A song from one monster to another. She put all the love he had slowly been breathing into her, whilst they had been dreaming, into her song. She thought of the way he had been smoke and shadows and how love had transformed him into a man, how love could do so again. She was his songbird, and she sang and sang for him, the only one who had truly seen her, watched over her, as she watched over him now. As her song ended, the wounds had healed over, and the body transformed. No longer lay a leathery beast of fangs and claws, but instead a man, the one she loved. Everett.

"You sang me back to life, songbird," he smiled, taking her into his arms. "I've been waiting a long time for you to come down from that tower."

"Sorry it took me so long," she replied, "I've been dreaming." Then she kissed him, her one true love, her monster, her forever.

Sea Glass

Rose Strickman

The first thing Adriana noticed when she entered Sea Glass was the window. Indeed, it was impossible not to.

She paused, blinking, suitcase handle dragging at her fingers. The light, airy parlor was graced with a bow window overlooking the beach. The two side panes were plain and transparent, but the largest, central pane was a gorgeous display of stained, sculpted and bubbled glass, glowing with all the colors of the sea. There were hundreds of little panes, some sculpted, some bubbled, some warped, twisting the gray morning light into a glorious spectacle of color and light-play. And there was stained glass indeed, and the picture it depicted…

"Beautiful, isn't it?" Her new landlady, Mrs. Legrim, beamed from the entryway behind her. "Rochelle Anglesea's finest work, if you ask me."

"It's certainly very striking," Adriana agreed, not taking her eyes off the window. The morning light illuminated the image of a merman rising from green, gray and blue waters, foam splashing white around him. He didn't resemble images of other mermen Adriana had seen, old, muscular men holding tridents, long white beards tangled with crabs and sea stars. This merman was young, clean-shaven, hair as pale as foam, face smiling and joyous. His tail scales made up of a thousand minute glass panes, glowing silver-green.

"Some of the panes are magnifying glasses." Mrs. Legrim bustled to the window, motioning Adriana over. "You can view the furthest sea stacks through them!"

Adriana went to peer through the pane indicated. She blinked with surprise. The bulbous glass did indeed act as a magnifier, so clear and precise that she could see individual seabirds wheeling around the furthest of the great white sea stacks, waves washing around its base.

"Amazing." Adriana stepped back and took her gaze away, not without some relief. The window was so fabulous, so unexpected, that it was nice to look at the real world again. The parlor was warm and cozy, with a welcoming fire crackling away. Various artworks hung on the walls, paintings from previous tenants, and rows of ceramic figurines on the mantelpiece. Old books and novels, brought and abandoned by tourists, filled the shelves. The furniture was fine but worn and cozy, welcoming. Adriana rested her rolling suitcase on its wheels and thought this would do very nicely. She said as much to Mrs. Legrim.

Her landlady beamed. "All our guests say so," she said proudly. "We've had artists from all over the world come to stay here – you can see their names in the guest book there – and they've produced some wonderful works. Or simply had a rest, if that's what they wanted. That was what Ms. Anglesea always wanted, before—" She broke off. "Well. Before she disappeared. Luckily, she had it all worked out legally, so the foundation took over Sea Glass Cottage."

"Does anyone know what happened to her?" Adriana couldn't help asking.

"Oh, no, my dear," said Mrs. Legrim, so easily Adriana was sure every tenant asked the same question. "She just up and vanished one night during a bad storm. Probably washed out to sea, poor woman. They never did find her body. Now, I'll be back to clean and I can bring you groceries as well…"

After a few more exchanges about meals and cleaning schedules and good places to eat in town, Mrs. Legrim bade Adriana a cheerful farewell and drove off, her car growling up the coastal road back to the little town.

Adriana was left alone with the silence, broken only by waves and seabirds. She supposed she should unpack. Put her clothes away in the back bedroom, at least make a token effort to get out her art supplies, as though she really was going to paint something.

Instead, she went to open the front door, admitting a rush of salt air. She stepped outside, into the brightening morning.

The cottage stood at the top of an ivory-white cliff, softened with grasses and succulents. Adriana made her way down the staircase to the broad white beach, the sound of waves growing louder with every step. The sun was fully risen now, burning off the fog, and it reflected metallic on the water. With every smash of the waves, spindrift blew, igniting gold and silver, brief rainbows flashing. Gulls flew and shouted among the sea stacks, great fragments of the eternal war between land and sea, waves washing against their twisted white bones.

Staring out at the beautiful scene, Adriana sensed a deep, primeval power. She could almost believe she was looking at these shores from before the coming of man. Taking off her shoes, she roamed the beach, sand giving way beneath her soles.

Her heel came down on something hard. She bent over to retrieve a large piece of sea glass, its edges smoothed by the action of waves and sand. It was a cloudy green, a green that reminded her of the sea itself. Of the merman's eyes in the window.

Movement caught her eye, and she jerked her head up, blinking at the sea. Just for a moment there, she could have sworn…no. No, there was only the eternally moving waves. Perhaps a large fish. Certainly not a smooth-scaled flank rising from the foam, nor a swirl of pale hair.

Pocketing the sea glass, Adriana turned to go back to the cottage, her footprints a line swiftly erased by the rising tide.

* * *

That evening, as the sun set behind the dark mass of land, Adriana rode her bicycle into town.

The village was as beautiful as the coast itself, though a good deal more human and hospitable. It faced the ocean, the neat houses and quaint shops all oriented toward the one harbor on this wild coast, a fleet of fishing boats nodding and swaying. Adriana locked up her bike and wandered the main street, through the settling blue dusk, until her eye was caught by a large, elaborately carved wooden sign hanging above the door to a restaurant. It depicted a mermaid, blue of eye and green of hair, laughing as the sea surged around her.

Adriana entered the establishment to find a large, convivial dining room, loud with voices, shiny with polished wood and brass fittings. The waitress seated her at a table and left her with the menu. Adriana's gaze wandered the crowd, wondering how many were tourists, how many locals.

Then she saw the merman approaching across the room and nearly fell out of her chair. "Oh! I'm sorry!" she gasped when the waiter balked in surprise.

"It's fine." The waiter smiled, and his resemblance to the merman grew even greater. "My name's Paul, and I'll be your server tonight. You must be the new tenant at Sea Glass."

"How did you know?" Adriana asked, even more astonished.

"Because the last two tenants both jumped when they saw me too," Paul said easily. "Apparently, I look just like the merman in the stained-glass window there. Nice to know I'm that handsome!" He grinned, like sun flashing off the sea. "Can I get you started with something to drink?"

Adriana placed her drink order, still marveling at the resemblance. Paul was the flesh-and-blood image of the stained-glass merman, from his sea-green eyes to his sea-foam hair. He only lacked a tail. "I'm Adriana," she said. "I've taken the cottage for a few weeks."

"Are you going to make some new art?" Paul sounded genuinely interested.

"Maybe," Adriana sighed, thinking of her canvases and easel, still packed away.

"Ah." Paul nodded in understanding. "Inspiration running thin? I know what that's like."

"Are you an artist?"

"I carve driftwood. I made the sign outside this place, actually. Perhaps I could show you more sometime," he added shyly. "If you'd like."

Adriana found herself smiling. "I'd like that."

* * *

Perhaps there had been some strange spice in her meal, to color her dreams that night in violent hues.

Adriana dreamed that she stood on the beach by Sea Glass Cottage. It was dawn, the sun just rising over the ocean, burning a path of light across dark waters. The sun flashed in the spume, bright enough to burn, and the ocean turned silver as the light grew stronger, a vast, burning plain. The wind whistled through the curves and arches of the sea stacks, waves charging the shore like angry bulls. Adriana stood on the sand and took it all in. If the beach had seemed a place free of mankind this morning, now it seemed still more primeval, from a time before life awakened to itself in the ocean's depths, when only the elements reigned.

Without warning, the merman emerged from the ocean.

He burst out in a spray of shining water, fighting free of the waves. Sea foam clung to his pale hair, shells and pearls adorned his muscular arms and torso. His eyes shone green as the sea, fastened on Adriana with an expression of such joy that she laughed in mirrored delight. He rode the combers toward shore, his great green tail beating the water, until the waves deposited him on the sand. She jerked toward him then, anxiety gripping her – for he was a creature of the sea, how could he survive the land? – but his tail separated into human legs and he stood, naked and perfect, on the shore.

Opening his arms to her, he spoke her name.

Adriana jerked awake, that name echoing in her ears, the merman's own name on her lips, both names fading away into the dark and the endless murmur of the waves.

* * *

The dream troubled Adriana the next morning, making her clumsy and distracted. Outside, it was a bright day, the sun rising off the sea, the waves calm and contemplative. Adriana poured herself a mug of coffee and carried it into the parlor.

The merman smiled at her from the window. Sunlight was already starting to stream in, turning the glass panes to bright jewels. Adriana sipped her coffee, watching the window light up.

There was something moving in one of the magnifying panes near the merman's head. Adriana drifted closer, squinting.

A scene played out, like a tiny movie. It was a cloudy day in the glass, the ocean a chalky gray-green. A tall woman walked the shore, wind tossing her dark hair. Her dark eyes scanned the water eagerly.

Her patience was rewarded. With a burst of spray, the merman surfaced, face lit with joy. The woman cried out, holding out her arms, and the merman coasted to the shore, rising from the sand as a naked human man. Just like Adriana's dream.

She clutched the mug and watched as the merman ran into his lover's arms, there on the cloudy beach, among the fragments of cliff.

Adriana closed her eyes and counted to ten, very slowly. When she opened them again, black spots crawled in her vision. After they faded away, the pane was blank again, the window free of memory.

She stood a long moment, staring at the window. Then she whispered the name the merman had called her in her dream:

"*Rochelle*."

* * *

After breakfast, Adriana put on a jacket and walked along the shore.

The sun was cresting high, turning the water deep blue. Sea spray flashed silver and gold, and birds wheeled around the sea stacks. Adriana scanned the water, but though she saw a pod of dolphins leaping parallel to the shore and the spotted head of a harbor seal lifted to snort at her, she saw no sign of a scaled flank or drifting, foam-white hair. In her pocket, the sea glass fragment lay heavy.

The cliffs declined as she headed north, and the path curved away from the beach. Adriana climbed the slope, the sea falling away beneath her, until she came to a ramshackle fisherman's cottage perched on the bluff. It looked like it had been there forever, its planks stained with salt and sea-tar, seashells embedded on the walls.

There were several carved logs of driftwood leaning against the wall, and Adriana was unsurprised to see Paul standing at a worktable in the yard, sawdust and wood shavings scattered around him, frowning as he worked on a pale log. His knife flashed, and a curl of wood fell away.

Adriana waited until he had put the knife down before calling out. "Hello, Paul."

Paul jumped, and she was glad she hadn't startled him with a blade in his hand. "Adriana?" He squinted at her in the bright morning light. "What're you doing here?"

"Taking a walk." Adriana moved a little closer. "What're you working on? If you don't mind me asking."

"Not at all." Paul held up the small, half-carved log, already showing vague flukes and scales. "I'm turning it into a mermaid. The tourists love mermaids."

Adriana couldn't help the sudden shiver. Paul noticed and frowned. "Everything okay?"

"Yeah, I just..." *Had a bizarre vision about a merman this morning.* "Got a little cold." Adriana shoved her hands into her pockets. "How long have you lived here, Paul?"

"All my life." Paul began carving the wood again, shavings falling from his knife. Adriana envied the movement and surety of his hands. She hadn't made any art in so, so long. "This was my grandfather's house." He jerked his head back at the shack. "He left it to me after he died."

"That was lucky. Oh!" Adriana turned red. "That sounded – I'm so sorry—"

Paul laughed, a pleasant sound. "It's okay! I know what you meant." He glanced fondly at the white shore, the vast ocean. "It *was* lucky. I never would've been able to stay here otherwise. And I love it here."

Adriana wondered if she could grow to love it here too. There was something deep and compelling about this wild shore, whatever strange visions haunted it. "That sounds nice," she said, perhaps a shade too bitterly.

Paul looked up at her. "Everything all right?"

"It's fine." Adriana forced a smile. "It's just...I guess I'm a little jealous. I...I've never felt like I belonged anywhere. No matter where I lived." Was that why she couldn't paint anymore?

"Oh." Paul looked sympathetic. "That's sad."

Adriana found she was grateful for his simple acceptance of her statement. "Paul," she said hesitantly, "did you know Rochelle Anglesea when she lived here?"

"I met her a few times when I was little," said Paul, sounding a bit puzzled at the change of topic. "Bit of a strange woman, but then I was just a kid. She disappeared when I was only six or so."

"Does anyone know what happened to her?" Adriana hoped she sounded casual. "I mean, I've heard the legend. Rochelle Anglesea just up and vanished one night after a winter storm. They reckon she got washed out to sea, right?"

"Yeah, and that's the funny part. Ms. Anglesea wasn't a local exactly – she moved here from the city – but she wasn't some foolish tourist either. No offense meant," he added hastily. "But the sea around here can be super tricky and dangerous, and tourists often don't realize. But Ms. Anglesea knew how to keep safe. She'd lived here for years. So when she vanished during that storm…it seemed weird. They searched a long time but never found her. No one knows what happened."

"Creepy," Adriana whispered. In her pocket, the sea glass, green as the merman's eyes, prodded her.

Paul looked at her again, and there was real warmth and concern in his eyes. "The weather forecast says there's going to be a storm in just a few days," he said. "So be careful, Adriana."

She found herself smiling back at him, warmth lifting her heart like a tiny tide. "Thanks, Paul. I will."

* * *

Adriana laid the sea glass on her bedside table that night. So it was no surprise when again she dreamed.

The dream started out ordinary enough. Adriana rose from her bed and made her way through the dark cottage, shadows broken only by shafts of brilliant moonlight slicing from the windows. She opened the door to the parlor and was overcome by a burst of silver light. The moonlight turned the merman window into a fabulous mosaic of pearl, silver and dark rainbows, the merman himself even more beautiful and fantastical than when sunlight brought him to life.

In the odd way of dreams, Adriana found herself before the window, peering through one of the magnifying lenses, this one near the bottom of the window, under the glass sea. She saw Rochelle and her lover swimming in the ocean. The merman was in his element, tail flashing as he swam effortlessly around the clumsy, slowly kicking Rochelle. But Rochelle didn't seem to mind, laboring after the merman with a will, her dark hair floating in the water. Together they explored one of the offshore reefs, shellfish and anemones and sponges clinging to one of the sea stacks. A flashing fish landed in Rochelle's hair and when she shook it off, laughing, Adriana caught a glimpse of gills, fluttering just below her ear.

Adriana came awake gasping, as though she'd just surfaced from the sea. It was still dark outside, the moon long since set. The wind was picking up, whistling around the cottage.

* * *

Mrs. Legrim came, her car rolling up under an ominous sky. Black clouds were already obscuring the horizon, the sea muttering sullenly around the stacks. "We need to pull the storm shutters over the windows," Mrs. Legrim said, indicating outside the cottage. The wind snatched at the women's hair, tearing and grumbling. "Especially the front window. We can't have that damaged."

"Of course," Adriana murmured. The stained-glass window looked very different from the outside, dull and patched and opaque, with no indication of its beauty or its power. It disappeared completely when Mrs. Legrim pulled and latched the shutters.

After she had shuttered all the windows, she drove off, car rumbling away in the strengthening wind. Adriana, quelling a twinge of guilt, opened the shutters of the front window, folding them back. Then she went inside, leaving the door open behind her, letting the wind bring in the first snatches of rain, salty with sea spray.

Adriana sat in the parlor under the gaze of the merman, the sea-glass pebble in her pocket, and waited while the storm gathered.

* * *

The song began slowly, subtly. Adriana had almost nodded off, sitting in her chair, but she jerked awake at the melodious notes floating in from the ocean. Outside, it was almost completely dark, the storm obscuring the sun. Rain lashed around the cottage, and the ocean growled like a beast. But even the boom and roar of the waves couldn't obscure the high-pitched eerie song swimming up from the depths.

Slowly, unsteadily, she stood and made her way to the window. No light was streaming through it now, but still the merman rose from the water, rain flowing behind him like tears.

Adriana peered into one of the magnifying lenses. In the glass was a different storm, rain coming down in sheets, the waves smashing the shore. The merman ran along the beach in human form, distraught. She saw his mouth move, forming his lover's name, again and again. He ran into the sea, his tail regenerating, frantically searching the foaming waves, but found no sign of Rochelle.

She tried to go to him, Adriana realized, tears burning. *She tried to use the storm to assume full mermaid form. But it didn't work, and he never found her—*

The song grew suddenly louder, invading the house, and Adriana turned to face the singer.

He stood in the entryway, sea-foam hair stuck to his neck and bare chest. He smelled of the furthest reaches of the sea. His only garments were ropes of seashells and pearl, nothing else to hide his nakedness or his beauty. His eyes were as green as the sea, as green as in her dreams, and desperate with pleading as he reached out a long webbed hand to her in supplication.

Adriana reached into her pocket and withdrew the chunk of sea glass. She placed it in the merman's wet hand. "I'm sorry," she said softly. "I'm not Rochelle. She's gone."

Understanding and pain flooded the merman's eyes. His fingers closed around the sea-glass pebble, and he nodded. Then the memory of the merman Rochelle Anglesea had loved faded from the world, washing away like a wave receding down the shore.

Adriana stood a long time, tears flowing, before she went to shutter the front window and close the door.

* * *

Hours later, there came a knocking at the door to Sea Glass Cottage.

Adriana stirred at the sound. She had fallen asleep in the chair and now her neck ached and her mouth was dry. She massaged her neck, wincing, and worked her mouth as she slowly, painfully, stood up.

The storm had passed. It was still a dark, cloudy day outside, but the wind had died down and the sea was muted. A burst of sunlight lit the stained-glass window, igniting its colors, but while Adriana blinked at the sudden brilliance, she didn't go to look into the magnifying lenses. The loop in time was closed, the last memory of Rochelle and the merman wiped from the window. It would never show their history again.

The knocking sounded once more, hard and urgent. Still blinking, hair stuck to the side of her head, Adriana shuffled over to open the door.

The day struck her fully awake, the scent of the sea wild and overpowering. In the doorway, his light hair tossed in the breeze, stood Paul. Behind him stretched the ocean, the sea stacks stained dark by the storm, the water churning green, but not as green as his anxious eyes. "Adriana?" he said. "Are you okay?"

"I'm fine," Adriana recollected herself enough to say. "Why wouldn't I be?"

"I…I just…" Paul flushed, shifting. "I just heard there was some damage along the coast and I…wondered how you were."

She found she was smiling up at him. "Thanks for checking on me, Paul. But I'm okay. I got through the storm just fine."

Paul smiled, and it was brighter than the sun lighting up the window. "I'm glad to hear that, Adriana."

For a moment, they stood and looked at one another, the sea wind swirling around them. Then Adriana felt something she hadn't felt in a long time: a tingling in her fingers. The creative urge, stirring to life once again after its long sleep.

"Paul," she said before she could think better of it, "would you mind if I painted you sometime?"

Paul's smile grew brighter still. "I'd like that," he said simply.

Behind him, beside the ivory shore, the sea murmured and swept on, washing all time and all memory into its depths.

Dream of You

E.W.H. Thornton

Don't stop reading this.

I know your first impulse upon reading that will be to stop reading this. All I can do is beg you to listen.

I know I'm the last person you want to hear from, but there's something you have to know.

I have no idea how closely you've been following news of the disaster or how much of the truth has managed to get out after the city was quarantined, so I'll try to tell you everything I can.

Please indulge me. Everything has changed since you left.

The first recording of it was captured by a group of internet personalities, five young men who'd dubbed their collective Night Science. They'd decided to make a video of each of them pepper spraying one another in turn, and to that end had sought out an isolated alley in a part of the city that, at the time, was still far removed from the crushing wave of gentrification sweeping down from the north side. It wasn't a good place or a terrible one, but it was several degrees removed from the where they usually performed their viral antics, and exactly why they chose it remains a mystery.

No one noticed the anomaly until the one calling himself Maxxxy, staggering around in blind agony with a face full of chemicals, fell down. At first it appeared he'd simply collapsed in pain, but a quick pan across the ground revealed he'd caught his foot in a hole in the pavement. The cameraman took a few seconds to zoom in on the hole in question, thus capturing what would become to be the most exhaustively analyzed footage since the Zapruder film.

The hole was just large enough to catch your toe in if you happened to be lurching around randomly, but unlike your average pothole, it had no visible bottom. In words that would prove immortal, the person manning the camera remarked, "How deep does that go?" before refocusing on his wailing comrades.

Though the video garnered a substantial amount of views, the hole initially escaped everyone's attention. That didn't change when a car speeding through the alley broke an axle in a hole the size of a basketball hoop. The driver lodged a complaint with the city, though it would take several more damaged cars before they finally broke down and resolved to fix the problem.

By the time a truck full of hot asphalt arrived in the alley the hole was the size of a hula hoop. After confirming they were in fact in the right place, the workers began attempting to fill it. They worked in three-hour shifts, pouring heaps of steaming black rock into the hole, to no effect. By the end of the day they'd emptied the entire truck and had yet to hear a single stone hit bottom. They reported the odd situation back to their superiors, who ordered them not to speak a word of what they'd seen. Within a day news of it had spread to every corner of the internet.

After that the hole became an unofficial destination for a certain type of individual visiting the city, the kind of thing sophisticated travelers intent on eschewing the conventional tourist crap flock to. It had a certain compelling attraction, there was no denying that. Visitors would sidle up to its edge, stepping closer and closer until the cries of friends urging them to back away became shrill with panic.

People would crack glow sticks and drop them in the hole to watch them vanish, a diminishing point of light forming a halo of green or blue that rapidly closed in on itself until it became a remote speck that faded into nothing. Some people would lay down on the edge of the hole and dip their phone into it, recording nothing but walls of perfectly smooth, perfectly solid asphalt and concrete.

One person who was livestreaming dropped their phone, provoking an outburst of obscenities that quickly faded as the device tumbled downwards. What followed was several minutes of continuous footage depicting brief flashes of stone illuminated by the phone's light, granite changing to basalt and limestone and shale until the video abruptly ended, the phone either losing its signal or colliding with a wall with enough force to break it.

Whatever happened to it after that, one thing was certain.

It didn't hit bottom.

According to the popular narrative it stopped being fun the first time someone jumped, a homeless man with schizophrenia who dived in headfirst while yelling something about beautiful music, but in truth the hole's transition in the public's imagination from amusing novelty to existential threat was a gradual one, with no decisive turning point.

For some reason, be it denial, blind optimism, or an unfounded belief that normalcy simply had to reassert itself, we all believed the hole was going to stop growing soon. When we slowly realized it wasn't going to wane in accordance with our interest in it, amusement segued into a kind of defensive indifference. All the roadside attraction names people had given it like The Urban Abyss, Hell's Peephole, and Maxxxy's Folly fell out of use.

Now it was just the hole.

By then it was a good ten meters across, its size recorded by government officials and amateur enthusiasts alike, both groups making daily pilgrimages to the hole and measuring it with advanced equipment that determined its breadth within a nanometer's accuracy.

Still, we all did our best to ignore the slow-motion catastrophe unfolding beneath our feet. A mix of factors

– the hole attracted tourists, the property it was damaging wasn't particularly valuable, the only people jumping in were homeless or insane – made it possible for us to focus our attention elsewhere, so knowledge of the hole existed as nothing more than a muffled, gnawing anxiety at the back of our minds. That only changed when a family of four visiting the city to see the hole discovered it in the worst possible way. Footage from a nearby security camera captured the incident in merciless detail, the car taking the corner too fast, its front end dipping as the driver attempted to brake when the beam cast by the headlights abruptly vanished into nothing, the car teetering on the edge for a moment, then slowly plunging over with sickening inevitability.

After that the city government made sad token gestures to ensure safety, erecting concrete barriers and chain-link fences topped with razor wire, only to stop when it became apparent that the hole expanded faster in order to swallow whatever obstacles blocked it off. After that armed guards were posted around the hole, a strategy that was in turn abandoned when they began to disappear.

Realty prices collapsed as the hole began to inch towards more prosperous neighborhoods. Buildings would fall in piecemeal, walls and floors tumbling in bit by bit until some tipping point was reached and the whole structure gave way, collapsing into the hole with a catastrophic roar of disintegrating brick and glass. The city begged the federal government to declare the region a disaster area and provide emergency relief, but it was decided the hole was advancing too slowly to merit intervention. The buck was passed down to ever more local government institutions until every authority figure had washed their hands of the matter, leaving us to fend for ourselves.

Before the quarantine scientists of every discipline made regular pilgrimages to the site, but their research came up with nothing except more questions. They couldn't tell us what the hole was, only what it was not. It was not a sinkhole. It was not the result of plate tectonics. It was not man-made, nor was it a result of any observable natural process. There were no strange readings of any kind, be they atmospheric, magnetic, or radioactive. The hole defied all efforts to quantify it, its very existence proving an affront to understanding.

Attempts at investigating its lower depths likewise failed. Probes suspended from cables couldn't go deep enough, the longest physical tethers topping out at around thirty kilometers. After that drones were flown down into the hole, but they encountered some kind of interference around fifty kilometers down and ceased broadcasting. None of the cameras lowered into the hole recorded anything beyond the usual deep geological details of layered peridotite and andesite, findings that only contributed to our collective anxiety.

The rate of the hole's expansion was slowly but steadily increasing. This didn't occur via rock falling away into the hole, rather it seemed to simply vanish. Certain things were conspicuously absent. Samples taken from the walls of the hole were devoid of any form of life, even though bacteria was normally present deep into the earth's crust. Sound in the hole produced no echo, though conditions were perfect for it. Attempts to map the hole with sonar and radar proved useless as the hole seemed to absorb the frequencies, giving nothing back. The walls were unnaturally smooth and perfectly uniform.

Confronted with such data, most scientists wandered away like intellectual refugees, dazed by events that defied the parameters of everything they knew to be true. Despite it all a few remained, abandoning other intellectual pursuits and sometimes even homes and families in favor of keeping vigil and watching with a kind of frigid rapture as the hole grew and grew, devouring everything it touched.

We all still managed to believe nothing had really changed until we woke up one morning to find the city surrounded by soldiers. Only then did we realize we'd been exiled to a new reality that looked exactly like the old one, yet had none of the rules we depended on to govern our lives.

When the national guard cut off every possible means of escape fear and despair gripped us all, but so did a kind of euphoria, a perverse glee that manifested itself in intoxicating levels of spontaneous passion and nihilistic joy. People held what were called Minimum Safe Distance Parties when it came time for another building to collapse into the expanding hole. The bigger the building, the bigger the celebration. We would gamble on the precise hour the building would fall and the intensity of the revelry would steadily grow, ultimately reaching a fever pitch as one more piece of the city plummeted down to a chorus of jubilant cheers.

The prospect of our imminent doom united us, made us special. We were rebels, outsiders, the custodians of a primal truth the rest of the world dared not face. There were evenings of exaltation where we counted ourselves lucky and embraced our fate. Let the rest of the world rot in stagnant normalcy, our proximity to oblivion meant we and we alone were truly alive.

Then tomorrow would come and stark light would reveal a new void in the disintegrating skyline and an ever-expanding wound in the earth, and all but the most deluded of us would see our rapture for the desperation it really was.

And with desperation came bargaining.

People began sacrificing to the hole. They threw money into it; cash, jewelry, treasured heirlooms. The art museum's collection steadily dwindled as they hurled masterpiece after masterpiece into the hole. The last northern white rhino was taken out of its zoo enclosure and an attempt was made to herd her into the hole. She broke free and wandered the city for several days until she ventured too close to a military barricade and was felled by a hail of bullets. Her body was eventually retrieved by someone with a tow truck who dragged it through the city and dumped what little remained in the hole.

Rumors of human sacrifice began to circulate as people struggled to distance themselves from the hole and the alien harmonies emanating from it with such intensifying volume even the most sane among us could hear remote hints of it. People crept as close to the national guard's siege lines as they dared, cramming themselves into increasingly overcrowded districts and creating a broad no-man's-land between themselves and the hole, which by now was over three kilometers wide and coming alarmingly close to the the ocean.

This was why they barricaded the city, why they made every effort to prevent news of the hole's progress from reaching the outside world; why, if the rumors were true, they'd been jamming and even shooting down surveillance satellites. If the hole threatened to drink the ocean dry, the rest of the world would turn on us. The army had already made multiple futile attempts to seal the hole with explosives. Now that it was nearing the ocean, the next logical step was to attempt to seal it with nuclear weapons. If that didn't work, the step after that was more nukes, then even more, emptying missile silos until the thing was buried under half the continent.

Then it stopped.

Needless to say, all this happened after you left, after you cut me out of your life with astonishing precision. I still remember the day you left, can see it with all the radiant clarity of a handful of broken glass.

I've dissected that memory so much it's no longer whole, instead existing as a thousand distinct irreconcilable parts, disconnected and isolated and impossible to reassemble.

The routine of getting up and performing our daily ablutions together. A breakfast consisting of a sesame seed bagel and coffee. Television news with the volume lowered to a dull background murmur. The weather outside partly cloudy, light shifting from radiant gold to pallid gray, nature unable to make up her mind. Brief professions of love as we both left for work, sentiments worn so thin as to be transparent.

No matter how much I think about it, I can't remember you betraying any hint that you would leave.

I keep obsessing over it anyway.

Sometimes the only reason you pick at a scab is so it won't heal.

When I returned home my mind immediately rejected the possibility that you'd left. When I saw all your stuff was gone I thought we'd been the victims of a highly discerning burglar. After that I considered the prospect that you'd been abducted by someone very considerate, a kidnapper who wanted to provide you with all the comforts of home, including our cat. A litany of scenarios flitted through my head that ranged from the merely improbable to the utterly ludicrous: an elaborate prank or an alien abduction or spontaneous human combustion.

I considered everything except the possibility that you'd chosen to leave me.

I must have overlooked the envelope you left on the coffee table a dozen times. More. When I finally noticed it I thought it was a ransom note and frantically ripped it open. I tore your letter to pieces after reading the first sentence, then tore the pieces into pieces. It took a long time to reassemble it. I still have it. I returned it to the envelope. It's still sitting on the coffee table, exactly where you left it.

I appreciate that you took the trouble to write it by hand. You always had excellent handwriting. Such an anachronistic extravagance these days, yet when you have to write something like that, there's nothing quite like it.

Accept no substitutes.

Everything you said in your letter is true. I took you for granted, didn't give your feelings weight, grew distant and ignored your attempts to draw me back, heard what I wanted to hear and saw what I wanted to see and withdrew at the first sign of difficulty. I understand completely – which isn't to say I made any effort to change after you left.

All of our friends expressed some degree of reserved sympathy for me, the kind of measured concern you give to someone who sees a disaster coming but does nothing to prepare, someone who's as much a victim of themselves as anything else. You would be proud of them. When I asked where you'd gone they all professed ignorance, some more convincingly than others. After I realized they had all known what was coming, that I was the only oblivious party in this scenario, I let them go. They let go in turn and we drifted apart, them towards shore, I out to sea.

Sleeping became difficult. The bed was too empty, the weight and warmth of your body painfully absent. I would reach out for you and experience a sense of falling. Imagine a trapeze artist who leaps out into thin air to find the person who's caught them hundreds of times before is suddenly absent. It's over in an instant, before you've even had time to comprehend what's happening. There's nothing, then there's...a different kind of nothing.

There's a good reason sleep deprivation is a popular form of torture. Insomnia traps you with yourself to the point where your own company becomes unbearable.

I began taking walks at night.

It helped, a little. The streets were inhabited by people like me whose circadian rhythm had turned feral. We openly stared at one another in a way that was anathema during daytime, a deep gaze confirming our mutual emptiness as we passed and left one another behind.

I was too tired to be afraid, and eventually wandered very close to some very alien neighborhoods. It was then, on a night I'd ventured further away from our apartment than ever before, that I saw you.

It wasn't really you of course, just a random individual in a passing car, but for the instant I thought it was you, I was terrified. I wasn't just afraid that you'd see me but that you'd see what I'd become. I imagined how your pity would be leavened by relief, by the certainty that you had made the right choice. The impact lingered even after I realized it wasn't you. Still reeling, I sought shelter in a nearby alleyway.

I thought the relative darkness would comfort me but instead I sensed eyes everywhere, that I was the subject of a grotesque exhibition for an invisible audience. In front of me I could just make out a dumpster overflowing with old steel pipes. I grabbed one, hefting its hollow weight, and without thinking brought it down on the pavement as hard as I could, the force resonating up through my arms to rattle my teeth.

I kept doing it, striking the ground again and again, channeling pain into brute, mindless force. I kept doing it until I was utterly drained, until the physical sensations were the only ones left, emotion pulverized by the clash of metal on stone. The pipe clattered angrily as I dropped it and mechanically took out my phone, using its light to reveal whatever damage I'd managed to inflict.

There was a puncture barely the size of a pinhole, but I didn't see how I could have possibly made it. My puerile attempt at vandalism had ended in failure. There was nothing to do but go home.

An immense relief settled over me as I walked back, a relaxation so profound it was all I could do to stagger back to the apartment, collapse into bed, and finally, truly, sleep for the first time since you'd left.

I dreamt of stairs, massive slabs of white marble inlaid with twisting black veins. I followed the windowless stairways up and down as linear paths contorted into helical spirals, the steepness of the steps gradually changing from nearly flat to nearly vertical and back again. At one point the stairway grew so wide the walls on both sides receded until they were no longer visible, the guttering light of the lamps mounted on them growing so dim every step became an act of faith. Later the stairway narrowed until the walls were so close I could barely wedge myself between them.

As the dream continued the hope of the stairs actually going somewhere dwindled to nothing, leading me to accept that this place of echoing footfalls and deep shadows was a world unto itself, growing so accustomed to it that when I finally awoke in our apartment its sane proportions seemed unreal.

It took me a long time to draw the connection between that night and the hole. You know how gifted I am at not seeing what I don't want to see.

I think I would feel more guilty if the relief I experienced that night had lasted.

True, I slept better, but now there were the dreams. Unending visions of wandering through barren spaces to nonexistent destinations. Caves with endlessly forking tunnels that all concluded in dead ends. Petrified forests of impossibly tall trees whose bare, spindly limbs merged to form a canopy dense enough to obscure the sky. Long-abandoned cities with ruins so weathered and indistinct they resembled their own shadows. Deserts of sand colored a violet so pale it was almost gray, the endless dunes lying comatose beneath the wan remnants of a shattered moon.

My attempts to move on from you floundered. I told myself to be more open, more giving, to make myself available. Some well-meaning people even fell for it at first, but one by one they eventually realized what they were getting into and escaped. I didn't try to make them stay. I would have done the same thing were I in their position, if I could go anywhere I wasn't.

I began to seek out people more like myself, fellow conscripts in the army of the broken. It worked until it didn't, our delicate relationships imploding under the weight of mutual damage. Crude attempts at comforting one another faded into resentment at neither of us getting what we really needed, though neither of us could define precisely what that was.

As the hole kept expanding and the quarantine sealed us in and dread suffused our lives I took advantage of the desperate, ephemeral intimacy just like everyone else did, doing a lot of different things with a lot of different people, attempting to drown out the memory of you with the most instant of gratification. Again, it worked, but only briefly, for a night at most. Despite my best efforts, tomorrow kept coming.

I've had a great deal of time to consider my actions on the night I thought I saw you. I doubt anything constructive would have come from turning myself in to whatever authorities still exist; I would either be ignored or lynched, depending on their mood. I've wondered if I should have thrown myself into the hole as soon as it was big enough to accommodate me, but I've grown convinced I'm not its target.

Not specifically.

You see, I know what it wants. We have a connection – a common understanding born of mutual appetites.

I can hear it. Not the uncanny music other people hear. Something more personal.

I was trudging home one cold gray morning and trying to shrug off a dream of wandering empty catacombs so forgotten even the dead had abandoned them. That was when I heard it, a sound so low it seemed to scuttle across the ground, grope its way up my body and crawl inside my ear. It was a broken, heaving sound, a series of disjointed auditory convulsions like the final syllables discernible through a haze of encroaching static.

It was laughter.

It wasn't at my expense but rather a form of commiseration, a crude expression of the hysteria born of futility, of knowing some vital part of you is gone forever, of the lifetime of missing it you have to look forward to.

I hear it now as I write this. It's only grown louder since the hole stopped growing.

This message is not some plea for reconciliation or even understanding, this message is a warning. Before you dismiss what I have to say, please take a moment to consider the profound lengths I've gone to in order to reach you. I've spent nearly everything I had to hire a courier, someone who assures me she can not only get this message out of the city but find you. If by some miracle you have actually received this message and deigned to read this far, maybe I can convince you to take one more step.

Run.

I've told everyone I can to get out of the city by any means possible. None of them believe me. They think they're safe now that the hole has stopped expanding. There are even rumors that the quarantine will be lifted. Hope has returned at the worst possible time.

I can feel them coming.

Somewhere at depths unimaginable a seal has broken. Even now I know them, can sense the elegant contortion as finely articulated limbs draped in scales and chitin and bone and setae surely grip perfectly smooth walls and pull inexorably upward.

You can't imagine how many there are. The only reason I can is because I've seen the worlds they've left behind, wasted husks devoid of all life where silence rules kingdoms of nothing.

So run. You've made astonishingly clean breaks before, now do it again. The hole stopped just before it reached the shore. Maybe they don't like water. Cross an ocean if you can.

I'm not going anywhere. I intend to be the most gracious host they have ever encountered, to be welcoming and giving and sincere as I have never been before, to open myself to them fully, to hold nothing back.

It's a little funny. I still love you. I always will. I'm sorry. Even if I knew how to stop, I wouldn't. The hole is a part of me now, I need it like I need the space between heartbeats.

You may want to know what will happen when our guests arrive. I used to wonder if they'd learned anything from what happened to the worlds they'd abandoned, or if they are gripped by a hunger that won't abide restraint of any kind, but now I know.

They are like us.

If you feel any concern for me – don't.

I have what I wanted.

I shudder to think of the nightmares my dreams would become if I reached a destination of any kind, the unfathomable despair I would be faced with if I achieved my goal and served my purpose.

We carry the dream of you with us, our standard and burden. We now understand that memories and dreams are one and the same, generating thoughts and sensations that are gone the instant they're born, only to endure by haunting our life; even as they can tell us nothing more than what we no longer are. We either leave others behind or are ourselves left behind, but either way we must feed an endlessly ravenous future. Our only sanctuary is in one another, in the lies we tacitly agree to live by.

We hope you're still alive, or that you at least lived long enough to read this. We are all so desperate to be missed, for our absence to be acutely felt.

We can only mourn who you once were, our dream of you, one more infinitesimal mote floating in the inconceivable vastness of everything we've lost.

Please don't think this means we will spare you.

We are your future.

We will make your dreams ours.

It will be a comfort like no other, loss as bliss in the dim beauty of an extinguished world.

You and I will dream again once more beneath vacant skies.

Awakening

Theresa Tyree

You follow her to our home, another Chad or Brad or Trenton, drunk off too many cocktails that didn't taste like liquor, sucked sweet from near enough to her lips that it felt like kissing her even if she kept dodging away at the very last second.

But she went out, hunting you, so we might have that chance. So that the men like you – rich, entitled men who think their money gives them the power to make people into things – won't have killed me.

Not for good, anyway.

Lucky for us, men like you are suckers for a pretty face.

But you should have thrown this one back, made off with a different set of curves, wished on a different star – one that didn't hide her power behind a lithe figure and thin wrists you could hold both of in a single hand, if you had a mind to do it.

Men like you are pretty stupid when it comes to assessing what real danger looks like.

Her name is Mal, and she looks like poison masquerading as candy; pointy and purple and full of thorns you want to prick your fingers on. What I wouldn't give to see her again instead of just seeing through her eyes.

She knows you're drooling over her as she leads you through the foyer. Her appearance is the first of her tests, and you passed with flying colors.

You've got an eye for beauty.

Though not an eye for anything else, by the looks of it.

I imagine it's difficult to look through the haze of booze and lust to focus on what your shoes are jamming against as you follow her through the foyer. Men like you think you're invincible. No one tells you not to follow women to second locations. To tell your friends where you're going, or schedule a check-in time that, if missed, means you should call the cops. Men don't wait up all night worried their friend is dead in a ditch or a bridal chamber somewhere, throat cut open by sharpened acrylic nails.

Mal eats in the foyer when she's hunting for herself. Petrified statuesque remains and loose bones decorate the entry way because those they came from were unworthy to enter a house dedicated to beauty. She enjoys having a reserved place for them, and they serve as a warning to those that might hunt us.

They also remind her what will happen to me if she doesn't bring her next catch further into the house.

But you exit her graveyard without a thought for your own safety, following her up the stairs as she dances up them, always just out of reach, like some kind of fairy – tempting and gorgeous.

So gorgeous.

You must think her that way too; so beautiful you'd do anything to have her.

It's what she's counting on.

That your eye for beauty will make you a slave to it.

The house becomes even more beautiful on the stairs. If downstairs was a graveyard, upstairs is a cathedral.

You probably majored in something like business or marketing or maybe graphic design, if you fancy yourself artistic but 'practical enough to know not to go into the arts.' Maybe you recognize and revel in the glorious details of the Victorian style interior. She points out the roses on the wallpaper to you, just like she did the last one, making you notice how the rose petals bleed onto the thorn of the next flower to create an unending, living pattern. She calls it romantic every time, and every time you men laugh, like you think it's stupid but won't say so until you've managed to be inside her two or three times.

"They're beautiful," you say, "but nowhere near as beautiful as you."

It's a smooth line, one that might work on someone who was interested in you for sex instead of your rich, blue, baby-billionaire blood.

But you'll mistake the look of hunger in her eyes for lust when she asks you, "Would you like to see something even more beautiful?"

She dressed to kill, and out of every beautiful woman you could have gone home with tonight, your traitorous eyes landed on her.

So when she asks you this question, she already knows your answer.

You'll say yes, like they all do, and then she'll smile – a smile more real than any she's given you all night – and take you by the hand, up the rest of the stairs, and through the giant pair of double doors at the end of the hall. You desperately hope the doors lead to her bedroom, but instead they lead to me.

The room beyond the threshold is a sanctuary; a fortress Mal built to keep me safe while she hunts and to worship me in when she's home. A river runs through the middle of the room, offering the serene sound of running water, and the comfort of buoyancy. Pink briar roses and purple plumes of Astilbe line the banks of the river, enchanted to protect me from invaders should any try to approach me without my consent.

Both blooms feature prominently in the poetry Mal composes for me. When she recites, the roses become the pink glow of my smile, the velvet of my thigh, the bright scent of my skin, warmed and sliding over hers. The thorns become my fortress, my dragon protector, my incisors, cutting into the flesh of my enemies or sweetly pulling at her lip.

She uses the Astilbe solely to symbolize herself. Her fingers, feathering over my skin. Her power, paralyzing any who might approach me the moment they inhale the pollen. Her vow of patience in waiting for me to open my eyes once more, her devotion to the future we'll have once I rise.

But of all the flowers in her words and garden, I'm her favorite Briar Rose.

You stand in the doorway, staring with your little business/marketing/graphic design shaped mind, trying to figure out why a woman as gorgeous as this would think something as useless as a river flowing through her own home is beautiful, until you see me floating serenely in the middle.

This is my cradle, my tomb, my bed of resurrection.

And like the men who used their power to make an object of me in the past, you think I'm the most beautiful fucking thing you've ever seen.

"Who is that?" you ask, your voice as full of desire as my would-be husband's so long ago. As my father's was when he heard the sum of money my suitor was willing to pay for me. As the Kingdom was when they heard their princess was blessed by faeries upon her birth.

Only Mal has ever loved me for me.

She's never been a slave to beauty, money, or power.

She's wise enough to know balance, restraint, and kindness are what cultivate growth.

She's magic, and through her eyes, I am too.

Seeing myself through her is what's kept me sane all these years. She saved me from death when my suitor found out about us, weathered the rumors my father spread about my disappearance being a curse she put on me, turned both murderer and father into the first sacrifices with which to rebuild me. The cleft that had nearly split me in two is little more than a shadow in the modest scooped neckline of my dress. Mal's eyes can't help but catch on the receding edges of the wound next to my left breast, and her heart flutters thinking that it shouldn't take much more, not long now, soon, *soon*.

When her love wells up, I yearn for her to touch me.

Men like you stole my waking body, but you didn't steal my hearing or my skin. Mal's clear voice still reaches me. I still feel her deft, clever fingers.

Under her steady hand, men like you – overzealous goats eating everything in sight, stripping the land of growth, ruining it for future generations – will be culled.

But I'll grow fat on your carcasses.

Roses thrive best on blood and bone, you see.

"Her name is Aurora," Mal tells you.

"She's beautiful." You sit at the edge of the river and extend a hand towards me – pawing, disgusting – but my Mal planned for you and your grasping hands and your fingers only hit water. You won't touch even a lock of my hair while my Mal and her magic protect me. The water shifts me away from anyone but Mal. The rose bushes and Astilbe prime themselves at the edges of the river, ready to lash out with thorned canes and paralyzing pollen if you come into the current.

More than a few of you drowned in the water beneath me, only the red gold of my hair left to pay for your passage through Death's halls to the afterlife.

You'll never know their stories, though. Not even their bones are left to warn you of the danger, dissolved by the magic in the water that feeds me new life, absorbed to speed me back to Mal's side.

We can't have that fate for you, though.

Large bursts of nourishment can keep me afloat, but without a steady stream of lifeblood, I wilt.

Mal is always against the clock when there's no sacrifice on my spinning wheel. It's why she keeps her graveyard, to remind herself of what will happen should she fail.

Nothing lasts if it can't be sustained.

"How beautiful?" Mal prompts, spinning up her magic, cueing her words to make you sign your life away. "The most beautiful thing you've ever seen?"

You laugh – still drunk, thinking this is a game. "Sure."

"So beautiful, you'd do anything for her?" Mal wraps herself around you, sitting in your lap right there on the edge of the river. You're eating the words right out of her mouth, the crumbs of her spell out of her palm.

"Anything you want, babe."

Mal grins, teeth sharp and beautiful.

The best thing your eyes ever did was reflect her smile.

Using you as an anchor, she leans back across the water – the roses let her; they love her as much as I do. Her warm brown hand closes in on me, and oh, there's nothing like her touch. My skin tingles as she caresses my cheek and strokes my lips. I long to wrap my tongue around her fingers, kiss every one of her defending knuckles. She uses one purple nail – so sharp it barely even hurts – to wick a bead of blood from my lips.

She brings it to yours, and you lick it without thinking.

Probably a prop, fruit juice or stage blood, or something, you think, idiot that you are. Think you're the star of the show that's wandered into some fairyland porno, and this fake blood drop is your key to the big time boner-town of an ebony and ivory heaven's threesome you've always deserved; when what you've really done is sealed yourself as my next donor.

"Now you'll live no matter how much you bleed for her," Mal says.

You laugh again and move to kiss her, only to be brought up short. Her smile goes even sharper in your eyes as my blood spreads through your system, rewriting everything you live for.

She chose you for your eyes, because she knew you would value beauty most. And now, with her own Beauty's blood inside you, you'll serve me until you're all spent out.

You rise like a robot and lay Mal aside almost like a sack of potatoes – that's how little you care now, after her spell, my kiss. You move like a shambling zombie, walking the path of flagstones through the wildflowers to the tall waterfall that feeds the river, There, hidden by the rainbows and the spray, is a spinning wheel, the pedals rotated by the falling water, keeping the wheel steady and always spinning spinning spinning.

The bones of the last man fell off the spindle a week ago.

He hadn't been enough to wake me.

But perhaps you will be.

Stepping behind the waterfall, you shed your clothes to keep them from soaking up blood. Then, spear yourself on the spindle without a thought. It's sharpened and long, so it pierces your chest with ease, goes right through your heart, even though it keeps beating.

Mal hums and kicks her feet in the water near me as your blood starts to thread through it.

"Soon, my love," she says, caressing my mouth with her fingers. "Soon."

The first thing I'll do when I wake is sweep my tongue across hers in a kiss I suck sweet from her lips.

And then, we'll eat our way to a better world.

The Dreaming Temple

Rod A. White

The first time Liora dreamed of him, she was standing on the edge of an endless ocean, its surface ink-dark under a lilac sky that rippled with its own inner light. Stars wheeled overhead in patterns she had never seen, spelling out words in languages older than memory. A temple floated far out on the water, its pale stone glowing like a moonlit pearl against the cosmic darkness, its spires reaching toward the stars as if in supplication.

On the temple's sweeping marble steps knelt a man she had never met yet recognized with devastating certainty. He wore silver armor etched with a thousand tiny constellations, each star blazing with its own miniature fire, creating a map of some celestial realm across his chest and shoulders. His face was hidden behind a mask of white crystal that illuminated, refracting the light from the strange sky into rainbow fragments. When he lifted his head to look at her, she felt the weight of recognition slam into her like a tidal wave, even though the mask concealed every feature.

She awoke with tears streaking her cheeks, her nightclothes tangled in sweat that smelled inexplicably of ocean spray. The dream was so vivid she touched her lips to be sure she hadn't spoken to him, hadn't whispered secrets into his crystal-hidden ear. Her breath stuttered as she stared into the darkness of her little scholar's cell. The ache in her chest didn't fade for days, a persistent hollow sensation, as if some vital organ had been removed.

Dreams were not trifles in Varelle. They were sacred, divine communications that shaped the very foundation of the city's culture. The ancient metropolis had grown in concentric circles around the Temple of Whispers and the Hall of Night-Born Prophecies, its white stone buildings rising from the fertile valley where the first dream-seers had received their visions. Every child born within the city walls learned to respect the language of the sleeping mind, and the interpretation of dreams was considered the highest of all scholarly pursuits. For generations, the people of Varelle had been blessed by the Veil-Thin – a thinning of the boundary between the waking world and the divine realms where gods walked and prophecy took shape.

Liora was an apprentice archivist for the High Dreaming Council, one of dozens of young scholars who spent their days bent over parchment and ink in the Grand Library's Archive Chamber. Her world consisted of cramped fingers and tired eyes, of careful handwriting that transformed the spoken visions of others into permanent records. She transcribed the testimonies of noblemen who claimed glimpses of future battles, of ageing widows haunted by spectral lovers, and of priests who dreamed of angelic fire. Each vision was catalogued, cross-referenced, and stored in the vast archives that stretched beneath Varelle's foundational stones.

In all her years of recording others' dreams, none had spoken of oceans under alien skies. None described floating temples or masked figures who radiated recognition like heat from a raging forge. And none carried the weight of personal destiny that had settled on her shoulders as if donned by a cloak woven from starlight. She tried to dismiss the dream as cross-contamination from the countless visions she transcribed daily.

However, the second time she dreamed of him, denial became impossible. He stood beside her on the temple steps, no longer kneeling but upright and waiting, as if her presence had freed him from some invisible burden. She turned to him instinctively, and her hand brushed his armored gauntlet. The touch sent electricity through her dream-flesh that felt more real than anything she had ever experienced in waking life.

"You've come back late," he said with a voice that carried the warmth of familiarity. It felt like they were resuming a conversation that had once been as daily as the sunrise.

"I didn't know the way," she answered. She felt distant, as if she was someone from a life long ago whose memories had been carefully locked away.

He reached up with ceremonial precision and removed his crystal mask. The face revealed beneath was sun-burnished and strong, with high cheekbones and a jaw shadowed with dark stubble. But it was his eyes that froze her breath – vast, bottomless pools of starlight that seemed to contain entire galaxies within their darkness. Staring into them made her heart fold in on itself, overwhelmed by beauty, recognition, and a love so profound it bordered on pain.

"I've waited lifetimes," he whispered. His words carried the weight of literal truth.

She woke with his name on her tongue like she was offering a prayer half-remembered: "Cael."

There were strict rules in Varelle governing significant dreams. Dreaming of a stranger once was ordinary. Dreaming of them twice, perhaps a message. But dreaming thrice – especially of the same soul in vivid succession – meant something altogether different. The Doctrine of Emergence held that when a dream repeated itself three times with increasing clarity, it was not symbolic but real. Divine. A direct communication that the gods had chosen one specific mortal to bear.

To declare such a dream and be found wanting was to risk being marked as a false vessel, or worse – a romantic. The Council had grown suspicious of visions that seemed to serve individual emotional needs rather than the greater good of society. Love was not considered divine unless it served a greater prophecy, and souls who dreamed of fated lovers were often dismissed as self-indulgent.

So, when Liora dreamed of Cael a third time, she told no one. The risk was too great. She was twenty-six, unmarried by choice, and dedicated to the scholarship in ways that had already earned whispered speculation. To come forward with claims of a thrice-dreamed lover would likely end her career and any hope of scholarly respect.

In that third vision, they sat together atop the temple's highest tower beneath a great tree whose leaves were blossoms made of translucent glass. Each petal caught the starlight and hummed with ethereal notes, creating a symphony that resonated in her bones. The ocean shimmered below them like a living canvas painted in midnight and silver.

Cael read from a scroll written in characters of light, his voice speaking words in a language she didn't recognize but somehow understood. He uttered verses about love that transcended death, about souls that found each other across lifetimes, about promises that bound hearts through endless cycles of existence.

"You remember now, don't you?" he asked.

"I was yours," she murmured, the words rising from some deep well of memory.

"And you still are," he whispered.

"And you were mine."

She reached for his hand, marveling at its reality, its warmth. Their joined grasp generated a spark of intense recognition that was stronger than anything she had felt while awake.

Her eyes fluttered open, and she found herself alone, his name burning her lips like a brand as she spoke it.

By day, Liora continued transcribing others' visions, but the change in her was unmistakable. Her fingers trembled, creating blots on previously pristine parchments. Her mind wandered, causing her to lose track of complex testimonies. Master Aldric began to notice her distraction and suggested she needed rest or a change of assignment.

In her rare free moments, she began searching the archives for any reference to Cael. Most dream testimonies were anonymized, but she had learned the archive's hidden systems, the forgotten corners where controversial materials were stored. She dug through restricted collections labeled 'Unverified: Subversive,' which were testimonies too strange or passionate for official approval.

After days of searching through crumbling volumes, she found what she was looking for in a half-charred page that read: *During the Era of the Sapphire Eclipse, the dream-warrior, Cael of Elarion, vanished into the Deep Realm, vowing not to return until his beloved, Liora the Far-Seer, remembered his name and called him back through the Veil.*

Liora sat back hard against the cold stone wall. Cael of Elarion. The Deep Realm. Her own name, written in centuries-old ink, identifying her by a title she had never heard uttered – the Far-Seer. It couldn't be coincidence, but what was the Deep Realm, and how could she cross into a place that existed only in dreams?

She spent her nights in secret study of oneiromancy – dream magic so advanced it was considered theoretical at best, heretical at worst. In a sealed scroll hidden behind false walls, she found mention of the Astral Wells, which was an ancient gateway beneath Varelle where the divine realm and dreaming realm touched. The scroll warned that the Wells were not meant for mortals, that stepping into them might strip the soul from the body, severing one's tether to life.

The risk was enormous, potentially fatal in ways that transcended physical death. To lose oneself in the Astral Wells might mean eternal wandering between dreams, never able to return to waking life, and never able to truly die. But beneath her scholar's caution, something deeper was stirring, a certainty that had nothing to do with logic and everything to do with the heart's realization of its missing piece.

She made her choice with quiet determination. She would walk between worlds and risk everything, not for glory or knowledge or proof – but for love.

The path to the Wells was hidden beneath the Ziggurat of Forgotten Names, one of Varelle's oldest structures. The descent required navigating passages guarded by celestial flame wards and living stone guardians. She spent weeks learning the proper invocations, practicing mental disciplines that would allow her to pass through ancient defenses. Her months of dream study had changed her in subtle ways. She could slip through the guardians' attention by focusing on her sleeping mind, thinking of herself as already partially in the dream realm.

At last, she stood before the Astral Wells – interconnected chambers filled with water that contained its own light, glowing with captured moonbeams. She knelt beside the central well and whispered Cael's name repeatedly, pouring her longing into each syllable. The water's surface began to churn, responding to the emotional resonance, creating patterns of light that looked like writing in an unknown script.

When the glow reached its peak, she took what might be her last breath and stepped into the well.

The dreaming realm shattered her consciousness into fragments, each piece experiencing reality in ways that had no correlation to physical existence. She fell through kaleidoscopic skies, swam through rivers of crystallized music, and danced on staircases that twisted into clouds. There was no time except the pull of longing, no direction except the navigation provided by love itself.

She followed the tether in her heart, that invisible cord connecting her to Cael across whatever distances separated them. Along the way, she saw echoes of herself in other lifetimes – other incarnations of the soul that currently bore the name Liora. In one life, she was a veiled prophetess with silver eyes, speaking riddles that reshaped kingdoms, while beside her stood a knight whose armor bore Cael's constellations. In another, she was a warrior, bloodied and laughing beside that same masked knight after a battle against shadow-creatures. In a third vision, she was a child calling his name from a lighthouse, her voice carrying across impossible distances to realms where the dead walked.

It was always Cael. In every life, they had found each other, had recognized the deep harmony that bound them through countless cycles of death and rebirth. The pattern was so consistent she finally understood her dreams weren't visions of possibility but memories of a love story playing out across centuries, across the very fabric of existence itself.

Finally, she came upon the floating temple. This time, the great crystal doors opened before she could knock, responding to her presence with the recognition of a place built specifically for her arrival.

He was waiting inside, standing beneath a dome that showed the night sky of a dozen different worlds. He was older than in her dreams, his armor dulled by time, his stance heavy with patient exhaustion. Yet, when he saw her, something in him unraveled – not in defeat but in relief so profound it transformed his entire being. He dropped to his knees and buried his face in her dress, shoulders shaking with emotions too deep for words.

"I dreamed you would come," he breathed with a muffled voice.

"I dreamed my way here," she replied, her fingers intertwining in his black hair.

They embraced like long-lost stars finally colliding, two halves of the same celestial being finally coming together.

For hours, they lay beneath the glass-blossom tree that grew in the temple's courtyard, their breathing synchronizing until it matched the rhythm of the world itself.

When words finally came, Cael told her the full story. When she had died in their previous lifetime – burned for abilities that threatened the established order – he begged the gods for reunion. They granted his request with conditions. He must wait in the dreaming realm until she found the strength to cross between worlds and call him back.

"You died remembering my name," he said, as his fingers traced over her jaw with reverent tenderness. "Even as flames took you from me, you spoke it like a prayer. That's how I knew you would return. Love leaves marks deeper than death."

She wept from the unbearable weight of being completely seen, completely known, completely accepted. It was recognition she had never experienced in waking life, where she was always performing some version of herself.

They spent what might have been weeks or possibly centuries in the temple. Cael taught her to shape dreams into reality, to sing mountains into melodies, to conjure light from longing. Their love was quiet in intensity, vast in scope, and transcendent in its implications.

But eventually, the dreaming began to change. Cold winds blew through cracks in the Temple's foundation, carrying the scent of the waking world. The lilac sky darkened to storm gray, and she felt the pull of her physical body as the High Dreaming Council used ancient rituals to track her consciousness and force her return.

"You can stay," Cael offered. "Sever the connection to your physical form. We can have eternity together in the dreaming world."

The temptation was enormous, but she felt the pull of something beyond personal happiness. "There are others like us," she said. "Other soul-pairs scattered through time. They're dreaming alone, calling out to loves they remember only in sleep. I can help them."

Cael gazed at her with infinite tenderness mixed with inevitable sorrow. "Then let me follow you."

What Liora attempted next had never been successfully completed in recorded history. The Reverse Rite – bringing a soul from the dreaming realm into physical existence – was considered theoretically impossible. Using a dreaming stylus crafted from crystallized starlight, she inscribed runes on her own spine, symbols that would serve as anchors for Cael's consciousness. The process was agonizing, each symbol burning into her flesh with fire that existed on levels deeper than physical sensation. She tattooed his true name into her blood, making herself into a doorway between worlds.

When she stepped back into her body in the chamber of Astral Wells, Cael followed. The transition was violent – reality tearing like fabric as his essence forced its way from dreaming into waking. His breath was ragged, his limbs weak, his soul newly forged into flesh that had never known mortality's limitations.

"Liora?" he whispered. His voice was hoarse, but unmistakably real.

She laughed and sobbed simultaneously, kissing him until the memory of the floating Temple faded, replaced by the immediate reality of his lips against hers.

The High Dreaming Council's reaction was swift and hostile. Master Aldric accused her of heresy and using divine gifts for personal gain rather than service to the city. The High Interpreter declared she had violated every sacred principle by acting on romantic visions rather than seeking proper verification.

But their greatest fear was what she and Cael represented – proof that the boundaries the Council had spent centuries defining were far more fluid than orthodox doctrine admitted. They were evidence that love could be divine communication as valid as any prophecy, that personal revelation could carry as much weight as civic visions.

They tried to cast them out, but Liora had studied power structures too long to be easily defeated. With Cael at her side – still learning physical existence, but bringing dream magic beyond the Council's knowledge – she walked away from their threats. They found shelter in a crumbling building in the Temple District's most rundown quarter, in what had once been a shrine to a forgotten goddess whose blessing still lingered in the stone walls.

The Temple of the Returning Star began as a single room where Liora helped others understand dreams the official interpreters dismissed. Word spread slowly at first – whispered conversations between lovers who had dreamed of each other before meeting, between children who remembered previous lives, and between the grieving who claimed visits from deceased spouses.

These were people the orthodox hierarchy ignored, their experiences deemed too personal, too emotional, too threatening to the established order. But Liora listened with the attention she had once reserved for nobles' testimonies, finding patterns that spoke to truths the Council refused to acknowledge.

Cael proved invaluable in his work. His knowledge of the dreaming realm's mysteries, combined with his ability to see connections between souls, allowed him to guide people through processes of recognition and reunion that bordered on miraculous. Under their guidance, separated lovers found each other across continents, families torn apart by war discovered bonds that death could not sever, and individuals who had felt incomplete their entire lives learned to recognize their soul's other half.

The Temple grew steadily, and its influence spread through networks of personal connection rather than institutional decree. People came not because they were commanded by religious authority, but because they had heard stories of healing, of reunion, of love triumphant over every obstacle that reality could present.

Years passed in a delicate dance between official disapproval and popular support. The Temple expanded, requiring larger quarters, then larger still, until it occupied an entire district transformed from urban decay into something approaching sacred ground. Gardens bloomed where none should have grown, their flowers opening only under starlight and releasing fragrances that induced prophetic dreams.

Liora aged gracefully, her dark hair developing threads of silver that held their own light, her face gaining lines that spoke of wisdom earned through joy and sorrow equally. But her connection to Cael never weakened. If anything, it deepened with each passing year, their bond becoming more than a personal relationship – a living example of what was possible when souls refused to accept imposed limitations.

Cael adapted to physical existence with the patience of someone who had spent lifetimes learning to wait. His body solidified and strengthened, losing its ethereal quality, but his eyes retained their starlit depths, and his presence continued to carry the subtle authority of someone who had walked between worlds. He became a teacher in his own right, helping others understand dream navigation and soul recognition that spanned multiple lifetimes.

The High Dreaming Council, threatened by the growing influence of 'unauthorized dream interpretations,' began active opposition. They sent investigators, spread rumors about dangerous experimentation, and pressured officials to revoke the Temple's permits. But their efforts only publicized Liora and Cael's work, drawing seekers from across the known world who had their own stories of impossible love and supernatural connection.

On the tenth anniversary of the Temple's founding, as they watched the sunset paint Varelle's walls in gold and rose, Liora reflected on the journey that had brought them to where they were She had risked everything for love and discovered that sometimes the greatest risks yielded the most transformative rewards.

A Dream of Summer

Nemma Wollenfang

'Do you want to become a fairytale princess? This is your chance!

Prince Luca of the Summer Court is hosting a ball to find his future bride. All are invited. Fae and mortal. He will be selecting from among those attending. It could be you!'

A public invitation so full of hope. So full of promise. The kind to risk everything for...

One glance and I know I have lost him. The battle is over before I even step foot on the field. Or, ballroom, as it were. The Fae Prince already has another girl in his arms, spinning her gracefully across the sun-gleam floor. And his eyes are full of a rapture-shine so strong it is enough to dispel even the most stubborn of doubts. He is besotted.

She is his chosen.

Every peril faced to get here, every sacrifice made…all for nothing.

They move like a dream, flowing along with the feathery notes of aureate harp-strings, trailing summer fragrance. The taste of defeat stings even sharper seeing how perfect they are together. Effervescent, lyrical. Like twin dew-dappled rosebuds preening under dawn's first rays. Him, immaculate in polished regalia that perfectly accentuates his broad frame. Her, delicate as a fresh-bloom petal with her smooth, alabaster skin. Not a gold-silk hair out of place.

Me…the shadowy presence sheathed in jet-black gossamer, haunting the sidelines like some hovering spectre. So glaringly out of place. An encroaching storm-cloud to their bright, sunny day. A spider in their floral bouquet. It's not like I can control how I appear. It doesn't work that way. Otherwise, I would have made different choices. Lavender, for a start.

"*When ye get there, the potion will manifest yer innermost self,*" the old crone had warned, the one from whom I had procured the dream draught which allowed me to attend this soirée in my sleep. "*Be prepared. It will show ye as ye truly are.*"

I should have guessed that my 'innermost self' would possess a corrupting darkness, one not fit to meld into the gentle pastels of the Summer Court. Had I arrived earlier, before he met that blossoming Venus, it still would not have mattered. Summer princes did not wed shadow waifs. They were meant for grander, brighter destinies than that.

The happy couple glide by, escorted by a flutter of butterflies. The abundant rainbow blossom arrangements emit glitter-pollen as they pass by and the flocks of will-o'-the-wisps under the cathedral-arch ceiling shine even brighter. It's all highly romantic. Swoon-worthy. A picturesque, fairytale union for the golden prince and his chosen bride. Fae, clearly. And a princess already, judging by the spark-limned tiara woven into her intricately styled hair. He's chosen one from among his own kind. One who has not gambled everything to be with him.

I knew the stakes. Knew the cost. But…I didn't even get the chance to *try*. That's what's most disappointing. I am far from alone in feeling that sentiment, though. A host of other young, dejected girls line the floor. All those who answered the glimmering announcements found scattered about the kingdoms, who were drawn in, moths to a flame.

"You would not have been happy with him, lady."

A deep voice, smooth as silk. I turn and…He is the most devastatingly handsome male I have ever seen. More so than the prince. Every aspect of this Fae emanates sensuality and grace. From the fine, ebony suit brocaded with threads of silver and the lustrous, onyx hair, to the artfully carved cheekbones and skin that shines like starlight. Smoky shadows wreath around him, sinuous as snakes. And those eyes…so deep they echo the midnight sky.

I noticed him before. How could I not? Looming in the far corner like some dark angel. More than a storm-cloud cast against such sweeping, sunlit beauty, he is the ever-presence of inescapable black night. The depths of oblivion. All others present give him a wide berth.

For a being of such magnificence to approach me...

My mouth goes dry. I look away, inhale subtly, keep my voice steady. "Oh? Is that so?" No point playing ignorance. Every maiden present came with but one goal.

To capture Prince Luca's heart.

"What's not to be happy about? He is a royal Fae of the Summer Court." An everlasting meadow of singing wildflowers and eternal sunlight. A land of happiness, of healing. "A third son may be no heir but other qualities recommend him. He is elegant, charming. A patron of the arts. Fluent in many languages. Titled, rich." The public invite had listed his accolades. As if any more enticements were necessary to lure in the populace. "Kind, so I hear."

Striving for a blasé façade, I sneak a peripheral peek. The dark Fae is so effortlessly casual as he leans against a pillar. Swirling his glass, he sips from its nectar. My own drink remains untouched. Care must be taken not to imbibe in the Fae Realms or one may fall prey to any number of devious schemes. Like a binding. Fae contracts are a nightmare to break and the last thing I need is further complications. I have enough deal with. The consequences of the dream draught chief among them. More than a lack of fashion choice, it exacts a hefty toll.

"If ye ain't secured a Fae marriage bond by the stroke of midnight," the toothless crone had said with a wheeze-dry chortle. *After* the potion's purchase. *"Yer sleep will be eternal!"*

I'm not the only mortal here who faces that fate. I see them, dotted about. Anxious hand-wringers, skin and hair duller than their immortal counterparts. Every one of them will have taken that draught to be here. Every one of them will never open her waking eyes again.

For most, that caveat would be seen as a curse. For me, it's an acceptable alternative.

Better to sleep forever, I'd reasoned, *than to face what awaits me at dawn...*

"He is," the Fae concedes. He clicks his tongue, surveying the prince as he dances – such a white-shining antithesis to his black smokiness. "All of that and more. A fine catch, admittedly." He leans towards me. His nearness prickles down my spine. A breath wafts against my ear in a warm, velvet shiver. "He would have bored you witless."

"Being bored is hardly the largest consideration. Or the defining mark of happiness."

"And what would such a fair maid consider to be the defining mark of happiness?" Arms cross. He seeps a heavy sense of arrogance that only immortals can achieve.

Annoyance sparks. "A roof over one's head, a warm hearth on cold nights, a full belly." *A safe place to rest one's head at night...* "A life lived in comfort. A life *lived*."

None of those simple things are guaranteed in the waking world to those of lesser means than wealthy Fae.

They must be fought for. Hard. As a scullion of a bordello, I knew that well. My existence was one of toil and misery, but any unwanted advances that fell my way were deterred by my elder sisters. They shielded me, valiantly sacrificing their own bodies until, bruised and bloodied, they could take no more. And I was left unprotected. At the mercy of the house mistress; a haggish, bitter matron who spared me only until she could drum up enough interest to make the price appealing. By that point, the ball announcements had been posted and it felt like fate. A way *out*. Only 'untouched' maids were eligible to court the prince. So, when the madam sent the first man to my bed, I turned feral. Snarling, biting. Tearing bloody rivulets down his face when he proved unrelenting. In the end, his eagerness (and a daggered hairpin) got him killed. And landed me in a rat-infested, icy cell awaiting my own execution. The only exit? The potion in my pocket. I suppose I could have yielded, surrendered my body and accepted my lot, but that was never my nature. I was not meek, not compliant. Now, all that awaits me upon waking is a short walk and a gallows' noose…

The dark Fae inclines his head slightly, not quite a bow. "I meant no offence, lady."

I huff and turn away. Heart seething. Seeing nothing of the opulence. Stuck in memory.

"A life lived," he muses. "You took the crone's potion." True enough. But I see no need to enlighten him to the heavier circumstances. "And what of vengeance satisfied?"

My attention sharpens on him. "You read thoughts, sir?"

How else could he glean such a detail?

That black gaze holds mine, a yawning abyss. "Sense desires is a closer approximation. And yours bleed across this court like screams. You want no flowered, pampered youth. You crave something more sinister. There is darkness in you, such darkness that would smother that poor princeling's light. You would chew him up and spit out his bones. You want—"

"*What* do I want?"

There's a warning in my voice. A simmering threat.

His smile dims but a wicked flare ignites. "Retribution. For beloved blood spilled. For innocence tainted, maimed."

Emotions roil inside like an angry tide. I want to bite at him, growl that he has no idea what I want. Snap that he… but the lie tangles on my tongue and falls silent. Because it's exactly that, a lie. I *do* want vengeance. Badly. On the coin-grabbing madam, on every patron who ever set foot through her perfume-soaked doors, on the father who sold his own children.

Rapid blinks. I shake off the rawness burning behind my eyes. It's unnerving, how astutely he cut to the core of my mind. I push that aside. *Focusing* on now. On how to salvage the night. Because I am not defeated. Not yet. The Summer Prince may be beyond reach but there are other Fae here. Nobles, gentry. Other possibilities for a marriage binding. In the – I glance at the humongous gold clock swinging its pendulum above – two hours before midnight.

My fate may not yet be sealed. Even this dark Fae beside me is showing interest…

He shifts closer, every movement laced with lethal, feral power. Tendrils of starless night trail in his wake, stretching out, as if seeking…I hold my ground. Stand rigid against his lazy smile. Even as his nearness makes my heart flutter in its cage.

"What is your name, *Ròs Sgàil*?"

Shadow Rose. I've studied the Fae dialects.

His low voice is lined with every sin imaginable. It touches without touch. Kissing air over skin. It's always wise to be wary of giving any real name to a Fae – there lay too much power in that – but what does it matter now? What more can I lose?

I tilt my chin up. "Asha."

A muscle feathers at the edge of his mouth, as if he's suppressing a smile. "You definitely do not fit into the Summer Court when named after the destructive consequence of flames."

"And your name is so much brighter, I assume? Perhaps Edur or Gaeaf?"

Meaning Snow and Frost Season. Wintry names. For all his dark murkiness, this lord must be of the Winter Court.

A twitch of lips. He's enjoying this. "It is Cyfnos."

Twilight. Named for the dark. The Fae are fastidious in their name selections. Choosing only those which relate to their own realms. To mark them as they are. Their true natures.

A deep unease ripples through me. "Are you not… from Winter?"

A laugh under his breath. Smooth as obsidian silk. "No. I am not of the seasonal courts. I am of somewhere much more extensive and eternal. I am Night. I come from dreams and nightmares and the infinite vastness of the universe beyond these small realms."

I am beginning to sense that. To sense I am in the presence of something primordially endless and far beyond my scope.

In my short time here, I've heard stories of the Night Court. Mysterious and perilous, even to their own kind. Feared. The other courts keep their distance. I should too.

Because he's certainly no prospect.

"Sir." A swift curtsy and I flit into the milling crowds, putting distance between us. Then I begin to prowl, searching for potential suitors. Any who may meet enough of the potion's needs to save me. The intuitive Fae feel it too, sense that hunting intent. And shy away. As if I'm Night Fae too. Any enthusiasm I managed to invoke for this plan soon evaporates. This isn't me. Desperation is clouding everything. I drift to a halt beside an overflowing bouquet.

Mortals fight death. It's instinct. Even if it's inevitable. But of the choices, mine isn't so bad. Sleeping forever over a grim execution? It's good, actually. This way is gentler *and* I can have one last night of lightness and frivolity. A final huzzah! Before the end. Few are granted the opportunity to farewell their life in so benign a way. I should be content…

The happy couple make another circuit of the floor, sweeping by. They're so lovely it's nauseating. Sugary sweet. I can't help but hate the princess. However undeserved, however unreasonable. It feels as if she has stolen everything from me. My last chance at a brighter future. Maybe it's the imbalance too. How pristine she is. Sheltered, pampered, untouched by evil. Floating along like a feather on a breeze, wafting fuchsia roses with every swirling glide. Whereas I bleed shadows across the white-shine marble with every step, spreading my darkness like a stain. If these Fae are meadow flowers in full bloom, I'm a decaying blossom, bruised and crushed into the dirt. Among so many delicate pastels, I stand out like an injury.

I do not want to be this, a villain of the story. I want a happy ending too. But that's no longer possible. I soon find myself, moping and alone, by a drinking fountain. Failing in my new resolution. The soft elegance, the bounteous feasts, the abundance of flowers, hold no appeal. The champagne-sparkling air is full only of false promises and broken dreams.

"Still hopeful of another prospect?"

That dark silk voice. Low, soft, intimate.

I don't turn his way. Not to that heartbreaking, perilous beauty.

Peripherally, I watch as he saunters closer, now-empty hands slipping into his pockets. He casually leans against a white-marble pillar. The epitome of lazy ease.

"Summer believes in peace, in harmony. In the neutral path. Those darker desires you harbour need to be forfeited if you wish to find a place here. From both heart and mind."

The life taken. Those more I crave to take. It stains my soul…

"We all must make sacrifices." And compromises. The Gods know my sisters did for me. They gave everything. So if that is what it takes to carve a place in this court, I will. I will forgo revenge, relinquish that driving negativity to banish my shadows. Swallowing that bitter disappointment will be easy in a place so sweet and honeyed. A small price to pay to secure peace. It's what my dear sisters would have wanted for me, what they gave their lives for.

The dark Fae steps into my sightline. There's no mockery in him, only seriousness. "Such a concession would consume you. Body and soul."

I sigh. "And are there other options which are so much more appealing? I'm sure you have sensed that there are few enough within my reach."

His night-dark eyes bore deep. "You toll at your eleventh hour. But your gong strikes loud, refuses to be silent."

Sometimes, the Fae speak in the strangest of ways. He slinks closer, lissom as a feline. The way he moves is captivating…but that underlying wariness remains, has me retreating again, hurrying away, whipping past a heavy white drape onto a sunlit balcony.

He follows. I feel his presence. A warning prickle along my spine. My pace quickens.

Ahead of me, Summer blackens, the balcony eclipsing into starlit midnight.

The fear ratchets up, breaths skittering in my throat. He's close. Too close. His "Please wait" barely registers as survival instincts flare and— Before I realise what I'm doing, I'm spinning around, shoving a torso, slamming it into a wall. Pressing a needle-blade to a breath-catching throat. His eyes are so wide I can see their whites. It takes a beat to register that the blade in my hand is a hairpin. *My* hairpin. Manifested by the dream yet still as sharp.

"Why are you following me?" I snarl. "Speak plainly, sir. State your intention."

Fae cannot lie. And dodging truth is harder with direct questions.

His throat bobs in a swallow and blood beads at the needle's point. I may not have meant to press so hard, but there's no use buckling now. Can't show fear.

Those midnight eyes gleam with a deadly edge, more pleased than afraid. It should make me want to back away. Instead, my body wavers closer.

"It is not the first time you have drawn this blade," he croons with a lover's purr. "Nor the first time that it has tasted blood. The metal sings with it. Sings of the life it drank." His gaze flicks to mine, deep and scorching. "And the fierce warrior who slaked its thirst. There is darkness in you. Such exquisite darkness. The kind that should be encouraged to shine. It calls out. Calls for its match. Calls for its equal."

His words are so vivid I can feel them, taste their headiness on my tongue, like the darkest of red wines. I wet my lips and the blackness in him sparks.

Being so near to him…My pulse drums, my belly clenches. His voice drops to a whisper, an erotic caress that heats the blood in my cheeks. "That young princeling out there is not the only one who came here in search of his future. And I think I have found mine too."

My heart flips. Does he mean…? "My waking self is on Death Row." I feel impelled to tell him. At this stage why keep it secret? "Even if I were to overcome the effects of the dream draught, I am due to meet the hangman at dawn."

Something flashes over him. The darkness around him ripples. "I can give my queen power. Such power that she will conquer death and bring her enemies to their knees."

"Are you…*what* are you proposing?" Is it possible? Is there still a way?

A blink. An indent on his perfect brow. "Is it not plain?"

"I – I…" My eyes flit between his, and despite every shield I've forged, all of the armour I have donned, when faced with a true chance of reprieve…the sense of injury reignites, the grief for my sisters, the exhaustion from fighting for so *so* long. I want to rest. Heal. His eyes narrow in a way I'm coming to realise means 'sensing desire'. Saltwater brims. I look down.

Strong, warm hands lift my chin. "The stars of Night are gentle, soothing. Their light can be greatly healing. Under it, you would not only recover, you would flourish."

His lips dip to mine in a warm, slow brush. A tease of possibility that—

The clock overhead tolls eleven, its booming chimes counting down to my doom.

I jolt back. "Midnight approaches."

Not long until the crone's potion exacts its toll. And I sleep forever...

An undertone of urgency creeps into Cyfnos's smooth demeanour. "The only counter to the draught's power is a binding. And your time grows short. You want sustenance, warmth. Safety, comfort. Vengeance. And more...You desire a title, to wield power, to *mean* something." The back of his hand skims over my cheek. "To be cherished." His gaze sheds its gravity, growing roguish as it dips to my chest, where my breaths hitch beneath the corset. "I can give you that. All of that and more. If you accept me, I can give you everything your heart desires—"

My mouth slams into his. Not gentle, not shy. A kiss possessed of something dark and conquering. The hairpin clatters to the floor as my hands find purchase, fisting in the opulent fabric of his suit. My lips slip lower, to his jaw, his neck. They lap up the coppery bead of liquid red. A low sound rumbles at the back of his throat. Wild, feral. Territorial. As his hands, and lips, join greedily into this all-consuming madness that is hurtling through my veins.

Some part of me knows he's not been specific in his offer. That Fae can lie by omission. But another part of me doesn't care anymore. Why not entertain myself? My new resolution had been to enjoy what remained of the night. If it may be my last, why not do so with him?

A sense of disorientation suddenly overtakes me. Everything is misting, spinning. Weightless. I clutch at him, feel the strength of his securing arms. Once the swirling subsides and the ground is once again solid beneath my feet, it is immediately apparent that, wherever we are, it is no longer the Summer Court. No more flowers. No more people. No more white. Diamond-flecked obsidian pillars abound and vast open-air balconies. Veils of breeze-swept, jet gossamer. There's a different *sense* here too; an ancientness that seeps from its very stones.

His enfolding arms did not let me stumble. As they loosen, I step back, looking up to his eyes. Twin shadows in the night. Dark flames, flickering. He's already moving, pulling at my laces, nimbly undoing them. One tug at a time. His dark ardour, fierce and blazing.

"We won't be disturbed here. In my own abode. In my own court."

So that's where we are. The infamous Night Court. A realm of star-filled midnight skies and— He recaptures my mouth in a heated kiss, one that banishes all other thoughts. Fingers move deftly between us, the corset falls away, then he's hitching the dress over my navel, my head, to toss aside. Cool air alights feverish skin. Fingers trail fire. Everything is fast, chaotic. My heart bangs so hard in my chest I can barely catch a breath. He steals what little air I manage to claim with his kisses. On my lips, the underside of my jaw, my collarbone, lower.

Languid, torturous, sensuously searing.

Some are soft and smooth. One nips at my neck hard enough to draw blood – he licks away its sting. Every one of them makes my body sing.

A hazy thought filters through. "Your…your *own* court?"

His grin is wicked. "Did I forget to mention that I am a king?"

The King of Night…

Somehow every scrap of clothing is gone. I'm stripped bare. He's lifting me, tumbling us onto softness and silk, a humongous bed of star-bright plushness, as expert lips trail across the exposed map of my skin, encouraging fizzling energy to erupt from the core of my being and blanket the entire length of my body. I feel swollen, throbbing. Frantic, pulsing. Sensitive to every ministration. A living spark. A bolt of lightning in the dark. My hips buck, wanting…I have no word for it other than *him*. My mind is a blurred flurry as he shirks his shirt and unbuttons his pants, as he shimmies them down and climbs up my body, nestling between—

I freeze. The memory hurtles in hard and fast. Of the man the madam sent to my bed. Of bruising grips and callous touches. Of a complete disregard for any objection.

He catches the change in body language immediately, and stills. He looks to my face. "Are you all right? Did I…" Those midnight eyes glaze and intuition tells me he is reading me, sensing the underlying reason. He softens. "There will be no pain, no injury. Not from me," he says gently. "And *only* what you permit. Sealing the contract can wait if you wish." His breath wisps against my neck, chased by a feather kiss as he backs away. "You will have my aid regardless, bride. If this is difficult for you, we need not—"

My kiss is a hard, determined collision.

Because I *do* want this. Now. If this final part of my life has taught me anything, it's that opportunities need to be grasped before they can slip through your fingers. Gone forever.

He needs no more enticement. I make a sound somewhere between a moan and a purr as his kisses intensify, as his touches grow bolder. Making me keen, arch closer, desperate for more but unsure how to… "You. Lead," I gasp between kisses. "Cyfnos, please."

And he does. He takes charge. Gripping, kissing, manoeuvring us to an angle that feels beyond good. Legs hooked over his waist. Shivers scuttling down my spine. Chest heaving, breaths ragged. Head spinning from the lack of oxygen. Magic dusts my blood, stokes its fire until it overcomes everything. Until I can't remember where I am. Who I am. Even my own name. The feeling is amplified by the way he looks down at me. With pure, uninhibited awe.

"You are *divine*, Asha." His dark eyes shine bright. "Tell me what you want."

My hands clutch at him, at the smooth runnels of muscle in his arms. Overcome by his sheer, shattering beauty. "This. I want this."

With a groan of relief, he rocks his hips forward, sheathing himself inside. The stretch makes me huff, grimace, but as he moves, the feeling turns sinful, euphoric. Every thrust makes me see the night-bright stars of the heavens, makes me whimper for more. Writhe in a puddle of molten, liquid want beneath him. Stomach clenching. Core aching. Pleading.

He promises many things, as his lips trail over my skin. As his body adores mine. Wealth, infamy. A crown. While in this dream, I choose to believe him. Indulging the fantasy.

He gives and gives. Magic coiling deep into flesh and bone, where it teases out threads of pleasure, feeds them as our bodies grind, rising to a crescendo, higher and higher and—

I'm catapulted into a white-blinding, toe-curling ecstasy unlike anything I've ever felt. The kind that sweeps me up and consumes me whole. That transcends the boundaries of the dream. Making us no longer mortal and immortal, but one unified, divine entity.

He's there with me, my collapsing dark star, loosing guttural groans as his hips snap until, suddenly, he stills, following me into oblivion with a final, strangled curse. Body crumpling into the cradle of mine. "Asha," he rasps, spent. And the way he says my name… Breathless, devastated, like some wicked prayer to an ancient, dark goddess.

It's disorienting, that *I* could be the reverential subject of such a glorious being. That *I* could reduce him to a prostrate penitent, worshipping at my altar.

He levers himself up. Dappled with sweat, still trying to catch his breath, his smile is blazing. "You'll make the perfect queen."

Somewhere distant, a clock strikes midnight.

* * *

A blink-snap. My eyes pop open onto unforgiving, bare, prison stone that seeps despair.

I'm...back in my cell. Back in the ice-chill, sewer-stench purgatory of waking.

No. No. *How*?

I had an agreement. A binding. With the King of Night, no less... Didn't I? The qualms I pushed aside come hurtling back to taunt me. The Fae are tricky. They twist words, and...I rack my brain...he never specifically stated, did he? Never made an actual vow.

The dream draught, though. My acceptable alternative. Even without a binding, I was never supposed to wake again. And I was content with that. I was settled. At peace.

I flop back, scrub my dirt-smeared face. Maybe I was strong enough to overcome the potion. Maybe my hour with Cyfnos was enough to satisfy its demands. Whatever the case, it's clear he's not here. That he did not keep me as his queen. A lie, then. Or as close to one as the Fae came. No specific promise. All edging words. For a gullible, desperate mortal who wished for too much.

A groan creeps up from deep in my chest. The dawn light filtering between the bars of my lone window is harsh. Too crisp, too bright. I crave the comfort of the dark. I want it back. I want the Night Court dream. Or to never wake, as I was meant to. How am I supposed to go back to this? To endure my own execution? Scale the steps against the raw screech of the crowd. Stand still as a frayed rope is placed about my neck. Wait for the lever to—

A shift in the room, a shape coalesces out of every crevice the morning sun has not yet reached. And there he is. All dark-lit shadows and unfurling twilight.

Cyfnos. The King of Night. Standing in my cell.

"You're here." A raw croak. Nothing like my dream-self's smooth voice.

I look nothing like that girl either. Ragged hessian and grease-heavy tangles of hair… How can he stand to share the same space now he sees me as I am? No dark goddess but a bedraggled, half-starved waif only fit to dine with rats. But he doesn't recoil, doesn't sneer. His gaze roves over the shit-stained floor and sore-inducing manacles and even though his face is a calm mask, those midnight eyes burn with undiluted rage at the conditions. Tendrils of darkness pulse from him as he stalks closer. "To take you to the Night Court, as I vowed."

"You came for me?" Tentative, unsure. And scared. Scared this will be snatched from me. That it's a trick. "I thought you were gone. I thought you'd…" *Abandoned me to this.*

"A body must be woken before it can fully transition to the Fae Realms. You had to be released from the dream. But know this." The timbre of his voice is diamond-hard vehemence. "I will never forsake you. I am yours now, as you are mine. Bound by the blood-bond we share."

The blood bead at his throat I licked. His nip at my neck.

Imbibing, even blood, can ignite Fae bindings…

So we are wed.

A hiccup. A sniffle. The beginnings of a sob rises up in my throat.

"*Mo Ròs Sgàil*." My Shadow Rose. He steps closer, bows low, offering a strong hand as those feline lips tilt in a smile. "I am still in need of my queen."

Biographies

Benjamin Adams – *The Dreaming of Dwynwen*
(First Publication)
Benjamin Adams was a 2002 Bram Stoker Award nominee for co-editing the anthology *The Children of Cthulhu* (Del Rey Books). He has also written professionally for *Doctor Who*, in a pair of Big Finish Productions' *Short Trips* anthologies. His stories generally deal with grief, love, pain, and trauma, although sometimes they're just about monsters. Alongside his wife Kim, he road-tripped through Wales and stood in the shadow of Yr Wyddfa in the summer of 2025.

Aishatu Ado – *The Sky Bride*
(First Publication)
Aishatu Ado is an Afro-German author, poet, and peace technologist dedicated to social justice. She is a winner of the 2025 CRAFT Literary First Chapters Contest and won the 2025 Fractured Lit Ghosts, Fables, and Fairy Tales Prize. A Clarion West graduate, she has received fellowships from Tin House, VONA, Voodoonauts, RWW, and others. Her work appears or is forthcoming in *Heartlines Spec*, *Obsidian*, and Flame Tree's *Afrofuturism* Short Stories. More at aishatu.carrd.co.

Dee Alberts – *The Veil Between*
(First Publication)
Dee Alberts is an author, devoted teacher, and mother of five whose greatest passion is writing. She draws inspiration from everyday experiences, turning real moments into meaningful stories that resonate with others. Whether in the classroom, at home, or in her notebook, Dee believes in the power of words to connect and uplift.

Her work reflects warmth, authenticity, and a deep love of storytelling, which continues to guide her creative journey.

Alexandra Beaumont – *Foreword*
Alexandra lives a double life of folklore fantasy and professional tree-hugging. When not haunting gothic moors, she can be found LARPing as a muddy ranger or a forge witch. Her debut, *Testament of the Stars*, is a gothic romantic fantasy of cults and prophecies. Her folklore fantasies, *Dissonance of Bird Song* (Indie Press Award Distinguished Favourite) and *Ballad of River Bones*, are lyrical tales of love, loss and sacrifice.

Danielle Marie Cahill – *The Witch of Ravendell*
(First Publication)
Danielle Marie Cahill writes from leafy North London. She studied English at the University of Cambridge, and she won The Caledonia Novel Award in 2024. Danielle's credits include (amongst others) *Witches*, *Suburban Witchcraft*, *Quarter Press*, and *Micromance* magazines, she contributed to *The Little Book of Positive Birth Stories* (Virago Press), her debut poetry collection, *Burnt Offerings,* was recently published (Alien Buddha Press), and her fiction has been shortlisted for The Bridport Prize and nominated for The Pushcart Prize.

Bella Chacha – *The Last Night Market*
(First Publication)
Bella Chacha is a Nigerian speculative fiction writer whose work explores folklore, surrealism, and the fragile borders between dream and reality. Her stories have appeared in *Cast of Wonders*, *Incensepunk* magazine, *Plott Hound* magazine, *Aurora: Winter* books and *Defenestrationism.net* as a runner-up for 2025's Short Story Contest and also as a Pushcart nominee for 2026. She writes to illuminate the quiet strangeness of ordinary life and the resilience of the human spirit.

Victor W. Clubb – *The Severance Pact*
(First Publication)
Victor W. Clubb is a writer whose work explores liminal spaces of belief, identity, grief, and moral fracture. His fiction often focuses on damaged characters navigating systems larger than themselves,

blending emotional realism with speculative and mythic elements. He is the creator of Bent But True, a literary project combining fiction, memoir, and social observation. Victor lives in the Pacific Northwest with his wife, Tracy, where he continues to write and collaborate on creative projects.

Irene W. Collins – *The Whisper Tree*
(First Publication)
Irene W. Collins is a Ghanaian-Nigerian writer living in Nigeria, crafting stories that blend folklore, memory, and the transformative power of imagination. Her work explores the quiet magic hidden in ordinary places and the emotional landscapes shaped by myth and mystery. She has appeared in various literary venues such as *IHRAM Publishes*, *Heartlines Spec* and forthcoming in *Cast of Wonders*, *FIYAH Lit Mag*, *If There's Anyone Left* publication. She continues to grow her craft through mentorship and community.

K.S. Dearsley – *The Silent War*
(Originally Published in *QWF* (*Quality Women's Fiction*), 1998)
K.S. Dearsley's fiction has appeared in numerous publications, including *Daily SF* and *Diabolical Plots*. She lives with her husband in the middle of England, and when she is not writing they borrow other people's dogs to take for walks. Her novel, *Discord's Shadow*, was nominated for Best Novel in the British Science Fiction Association Awards 2021. Find out more at ksdearsley.com.

H.L. Docherty – *The Glass Ghost*
(First Publication)
H.L. Docherty is a UK-based author with a master's degree in psychology, which fuels her love of character-driven storytelling and the complexities of human connection. She is currently working on a romantic fantasy series exploring class divides, forbidden love and fated mates, themes which resonate throughout her short fiction. When not writing, she can be found living in a fantasy book world, playing guitar, or immersed in a playlist that punches her in the feels – usually Taylor Swift.

Philip Brian Hall – *No Regrets*
(First Publication)
Philip Brian Hall is a graduate of Oxford. A former diplomat and teacher, he's stood for parliament, sung baritone solos, and ridden in many steeplechases. He lives in Scotland. Philip's stories have appeared in five previous Flame Tree anthologies, with others published in the UK, USA and Canada. He writes regularly on Substack. His novels *The Prophets of Baal* and *The Family Demon* are available in ebook, in paperback and one as an author-narrated audiobook.

Diyora Kabilova – *Where the Moths Burn Gold*
(First Publication)
Diyora Kabilova is a young writer whose work blends myth, memory, and the quiet strangeness of the everyday. Her fiction often explores the thresholds between dream and waking, guided by a deep interest in human interiority and the emotional histories objects carry. She is the winner of multiple youth literary prizes, and her writing has appeared in international competitions celebrating emerging voices. She lives in Uzbekistan and is currently developing a longer work of fiction.

Shona Kinsella – *When Love Lies Dreaming*
(First Publication)
Shona Kinsella is a Scottish author of mythic fantasy. Her works include *Daughters of Nicnevin, The Heart of Winter, Petra MacDonald and the Queen of the Fae, The Flame and the Flood*, and non-fiction *Outlander and the Real Jacobites: Scotland's Fight for the Stuarts.* Shona is the Chair of the British Fantasy Society. She has been shortlisted for four British Fantasy Awards. She lives near Loch Lomond with her husband and children.

Vanessa Ziff Lasdon – *The Dream-Eater's Kiss*
(First Publication)
Stories are spells that Vanessa Ziff Lasdon weaves with passion and pluck. An L.A.-based author, editor, educator, and founder of W.O.R.D. Ink Agency, Vanessa holds an MFA in Writing for Children & Young Adults and helps emergent writers discover their unique voice. Her short story 'Venus Descending' was recently featured in Flame

Tree's *Aphrodite* anthology. When not storycrafting, Vanessa's bingeing epic fantasy, dystopian sci-fi, gothic thrillers, and swoon-worthy romances alongside six fur babies and one very understanding husband. 'The Dream-Eater's Kiss' is her latest dark, sexy, high-stakes new adult romantasy, where terror and desire collide in a kiss that devours.

Corina Lee – *Seduction and Shadows*
(First Publication)
Corina Lee writes fantasy and paranormal romance, drawn to stories where love turns shadow into light and the supernatural brushes against the everyday. She holds a BA in English, and this story marks her debut with Flame Tree Publishing. When not writing, she wanders mountain landscapes, drifts through fantasy worlds, and moves through life guided by enduring love.

Hayden Lewis – *The Star Tender*
(First Publication)
Hayden Lewis lives in Colorado with their pet ball python. They love creating lush fantasy worlds to get lost and find love in, which is an excellent use of that BA in Ecology and Evolutionary Biology, if they do say so themself. When they're not pouring little pieces of their soul into their stories, they enjoy doodling starry dreamscapes, reading, and walking through the neighborhood wetlands.

Trixie Nisbet – *An Affair of the Heart*
(First Publication)
Trixie Nisbet has had over 200 stories printed. She has written extensively for women's magazines, with some of her romances leaning towards fantasy. Using her husband's name, she also writes science fiction and has had, to date, seven audio scripts produced by Big Finish / BBC for their *Doctor Who* range. She has won several international writing competitions including the 2022 Kepler Award for a fantasy short story.

Anna Rose – *Dreams of Her*
(First Publication)
Anna Rose is a London-based writer whose work explores inner worlds, memory, and emotional connection. She is currently completing an

MA in Contemporary Creative Writing and draws on a background in mediation and counselling, which informs her interest in character, relationships, and human experience. Alongside fiction, she has written travel articles and guides inspired by extensive personal travel. She is so excited that 'Dreams of Her' is being published.

Peter K. Rothe – *The Witchdoctor's Daughter*
(First Publication)
Peter K. Rothe is a German/Cameroonian writer based in the United Kingdom. He has a passion for crafting immersive worlds and vivid characters, inspired by his upbringing travelling the world and growing up in the Balkans and West Africa. He primarily writes fantasy and horror. His previous short fiction has been featured in Flame Tree Publishing's *African Ghost Short Stories*, *Myths, Gods and Immortals: Anansi*, and in various other anthologies. He is currently working on getting his novel published.

M.L. Smythe – *Threads of Us*
(First Publication)
M.L. Smythe is a writer and registered nurse rooted in the wild Florida swamplands. They care for patients in memory and stroke units, channeling the heartbreak and resilience of healthcare into darkly imaginative fiction. Fantasy and horror become a refuge, a place to alchemize trauma into story. Off-shift, they're reading, gaming, or wrangling their spouse, two kids, and four cats beneath the relentless sunshine, dreaming up new worlds to explore.

Kathleen Stanley – *A Song for Ever*
(First Publication)
Kathleen Stanley is a writer and academic who lives in Adelaide, South Australia, with her husband and children. She is currently in her final year of a PhD at Flinders University, where she studies small-town Christmas romance fiction. She loves to read and write all genres but holds a special place in her heart for romance. She also has a story published in Flame Tree's anthology *A Breath of Time*.

Rose Strickman – *Sea Glass*
(First Publication)
Rose Strickman is a speculative fiction writer living in Seattle, Washington. Her work has appeared over 70 times, in anthologies such as *Sword and Sorceress 32*, *Wild Hearts* and *Lurking in the Gene Pool*. Her novella *Island of the Drowned* was published by Graveside Press and she has self-published several novellas on Amazon. She loves the ocean but, alas, has never seen any mermen. Connect on BlueSky @rosestrickman.bsky.social.

E.W.H. Thornton – *Dream of You*
(First Publication)
E.W.H. Thornton's work has appeared on the *NoSleep* podcast, in the *BlazeVOX Journal*, *Horrific Scribblings*, *Unorthodox Fiction*, *After The Storm Magazine*, *Dark Dead Things*, *Liminal Tales*, *Reader Beware Magazine*, *This Exquisite Topology*, and the *meat4meat* anthology. They maintain a blog presenting magazine content from pre-, mid- and post-World War Two era America at thegildedcentury.tumblr.com.

Theresa Tyree – *Awakening*
(First Publication)
Theresa (they/she) grew up in the Oregon woods, dreaming of magic amongst the trees. She lives in Portland, with their platonic life partner and cat. As a nonbinary queer woman and abuse survivor, Theresa focuses on tales of queer healing to make their readers feel hope and a little less alone. You can read more of her work on her website, theresatyree.com. Follow them on BluSky at @theresatyree.

Rod A. White – *The Dreaming Temple*
(First Publication)
Rod A. White has operated a full-time writing/ghostwriting/editing business since 2010, providing articles, blog posts, ebooks, books, and other writing services to a global clientele. Rod also enjoys creating his own short stories, novels, screenplays, comic books, graphic novels, etc. He's had numerous short stories accepted for publication recently, including a tale for Flame Tree's *Odysseus* anthology.

Nemma Wollenfang – *A Dream of Summer*
(First Publication)
Nemma Wollenfang is a prize-winning writer who lives in Northern England. Over fifty of her short works have been published in various venues, including: Titan Books, Broken Eye Books and previously with Flame Tree Publishing. Some of her novelettes have featured in Amazon #1 bestselling anthologies, she is a Speculative Literature Foundation grant winner and a participant of Writers on the Moon. She can be found on Amazon and Facebook.

Illustrations

Key cover art: Xinyue Chen
Xinyue Chen is an illustrator and book artist based in New York, mostly working in traditional media. Since receiving their BFA from the Central Academy of Fine Arts in Beijing and their MFA from the School of Visual Arts in New York, they have provided editorial illustrations, book illustrations and designs for many renowned clients, including the *New York Times*, *Scientific American*, NBC News, NPR, Bloomberg and many more.

Illustration page 7: Shari Borba
Shari Borba is an illustrator and graphic designer based in Oakdale, California specializing in detailed, whimsical illustrations with a strong interest in fantasy and special edition book artwork and bookish merch for adult readers.

Illustration page 13: Rita Földessy
Rita 'Reetha' Földessy is a passionate hobbyist artist based in Austria. In her youth, she was inspired by anime/manga which has had an influence on her style and linework. She then spent time at the Visionary Art Academy in Vienna where she learned from artists such as Rebecca Yanovskaya and Olga Klimova. In her personal work, she uses traditional and digital ways of creating art.

Illustration page 404: Naomi Samarasekera

Naomi Samarasekera is a Sri Lankan-American illustrator and comic artist based in Cleveland, Ohio. She retells mythology, folklore, and original narratives through intricate inkwork and watercolor. Her instagram is @nelum_flower.

Illustration page 414: Paige Chapman

Paige Chapman is an avid reader and loves sketching and drawing as a hobby. She loves any and all things fantasy where gaming or reading is concerned. Her online persona is Oxyy95.

Romantic Fantasy

Flame Tree Romantic Fantasy is a captivating blend of our signature Gothic Fantasy collections with the passion and magic of Romantasy. This new series featuring stories selected from open submissions is an exciting addition to Flame Tree's Beyond & Within, Myths, Gods & Immortals, Gothic Fantasy, Classic Stories and Epic Tales Collections, all beautifully presented, perfect as a gift and offering a lifetime of reading pleasure.

FLAME TREE MYTH, FOLKLORE & FICTION

A wide range of new and classic fiction, from myth to modern stories, with tales from the distant past to the far future, including short story anthologies, Folk & Fairy Tales, Collector's Editions, Collectable Classics, Gothic Fantasy collections and Epic Tales of mythology and folklore.

•

Available at all good bookstores, and online at flametreepublishing.com